THE WATCHDOGS OF ABADDON

Novels by Ib Melchior

The Watchdogs of Abaddon

The Haigerloch Project

Sleeper Agent

Order of Battle

THE WATCHDOGS

OF **ABADDON**

A NOVEL BY

IB MELCHIOR

HARPER & ROW, PUBLISHERS

NEW YORK, HAGERSTOWN, SAN FRANCISCO, LONDON

FIRST EDITION

Designed by Sidney Feinberg

Library of Congress Cataloging in Publication Data
Melchior, Ib.
   The watchdogs of Abaddon.
   Bibliography: p.
   I. Title.
PZ4.M51457Wat 1979   [PS3563.E435]   813'.5'4   78-69507
ISBN 0-06-012967-0

79 80 81 82 83 10 9 8 7 6 5 4 3 2 1

To Cleo
whose patient support is
matched only by her talent

The headlines and news stories that appear at the end of chapters are taken from actual reports in the world press during the late 1970s.

I.M.

Acknowledgments

I would like to express my appreciation for the valuable assistance in my research given me by—

The Los Angeles Police Department
The Anti-Defamation League of B'nai B'rith
The Atlantic Richfield Company
The Modern Military Branch, Military Archives Division, National Archives and Records Service
The Jewish Defense League

I.M.

CONTENTS

And he opened the pit of the abyss, and smoke ascended out of the pit as the smoke of a great furnace, and the sun was darkened, also the air, by the smoke of the pit. And out of the smoke locusts came forth upon the earth. . . . They have over them a King, the angel of the abyss. In Hebrew his name is ABADDON.

Revelation IX: 2, 3 & 11

. . . out of the ruins of our cities and monuments there will burst forth anew the hatred for the people who alone are ultimately responsible—the Jews . . . there will rise in the history of Germany the seed of a glorious rebirth of the National Socialist movement.

Adolf Hitler's Political Testament
29 April 1945

PROLOGUE

Berlin

20 April 1945

Only hours before, the dog run had been destroyed by a direct hit. Luckily, Blondi and her pups had been in the bunker below. Now the enemy terror bombing had let up, but a distant rumble of Russian guns from the front remained as an ominous reminder of the destruction that at any moment could again come screaming down on the bomb-cratered garden of the Reich Chancellery.

Standartenführer Dr. Franz Schindler gazed soberly at the desolation around him as he and a group of officers and high officials strode into the garden through the heavy steel door from the blockhouse entrance to the Führerbunker. Blocks of jagged concrete and soot-blackened timbers lay strewn among stripped, uprooted trees in the once beautifully kept grounds. He glanced up at the sun, high in the sky, trying to penetrate the smoky haze that lay like a red shroud over the tortured city of Berlin. It was only a few minutes past noon, April 20, 1945. The birthday of Adolf Hitler.

He was in good company, he thought. Bormann, Himmler, Goebbels, Goering, Axmann, Naumann—and, of course, the Führer himself. They had all followed him as he laboriously climbed the fifty stone steps from the bunker to the garden above.

Lined up in front of a shrapnel-scarred wall, a row of boys barely in their teens stood rigidly at attention, awaiting the approaching group. They were the last heroes of the crumbling Third Reich, clad in oversized uniforms, their peaked caps perched jauntily on close-cropped heads: Hitler Youth soldiers.

With their leader, the one-armed Reichsjugendführer Artur Axmann, at his side, Hitler stopped in front of the first boy. Axmann presented the starry-eyed youth to him, and with a slightly trembling hand the Führer solemnly shook the boy's hand. The boy soldiers watched with awe as the prematurely old man, stoop-shouldered and sallow-faced, slowly shuffled from one to the other, patting their blond heads and their cheeks with a shaky hand, and pinning Iron Cross medals on their chests. He was still the Führer. He was still Adolf Hitler—and they carried his name proudly.

Standartenführer Schindler was watching. He was shocked at

the Führer's appearance—so markedly in contrast to the youngsters before him.

They are the ones, he thought. They—and others like them—who will lift the burden from the shoulders of their leader. In their hands lies the destiny of the fatherland.

Hitler stopped in front of one of the smallest boys in the group. He gazed into the cherubic face, meeting huge, round, awe-filled eyes.

"What is your name, my boy?" Hitler asked, his voice hoarse.

The child-soldier drew himself even more erect. "Czech, Alfred, *mein Führer!*" His young voice rang with pride.

"Gefreiter Czech displayed exceptional bravery under fire, *mein Führer,*" Axmann said. "And he discovered and arrested an enemy spy. He has been recommended for the Iron Cross, Second Class."

Hitler smiled at the boy. "How did you discover this spy?" he asked.

"He was wearing his corporal's stripe on the wrong arm, *mein Führer,*" the boy replied.

Hitler nodded. He pinned the medal on the boy's tunic. He touched his cheek.

"How old are you?" he asked.

"Twelve, *mein Führer!*"

Again Hitler nodded. He gazed at the boy. Suddenly his eyes, deep in his pallid face, clouded over. He turned away.

"Dr. Schindler!" he called.

Standartenführer Dr. Franz Schindler stepped forward. *"Zu Befehl, mein Führer!*—At your orders!"

Hitler looked into his face—eyes suddenly burning with intensity. *"Es ist soweit,"* he said, his voice low. "The time has come."

Schindler felt a surge of elation. He knew what those simple words meant. He knew they were to be the most important in his life.

"I will see you in my rooms at once," Hitler said. The harsh-voiced command still carried unchallenged authority. "At once!"

The Führer turned away. Away from the boys. Away from the waiting entourage. Away from Standartenführer Dr. Franz Schindler. Bent and limping slightly, the collar of his greatcoat turned up around his ears as if to ward off the disasters that crowded in on him, he strode purposefully toward the entrance to his bunker, his right hand firmly clasping his trembling left arm.

Schindler followed.

The three men were alone in the spartan conference and map room adjoining Hitler's quarters deep in the Führerbunker. They were seated at one end of a long table. The maps that covered it had been pushed aside to make room for a small pile of papers.

Schindler was listening intently to a squat, heavy-set man seated across from him. Reichsleiter Martin Bormann looked solemn and grim.

"Kulmbach has fallen," he said. "Already several days ago." His small eyes glinted. "We have only now had definite confirmation that the entire *Sondersicherheitzone*—the entire special-security area—is in enemy hands." He looked toward Hitler sitting stiffly at the end of the table.

"My generals have betrayed me," the Führer said, his voice hoarse. "But there is still time." He fixed Schindler with an intent gaze. His waxen face twitched. "The right man," he said. "The right man can still carry out the mission successfully. Do you have this man?"

"I do, *mein Führer.*" Schindler's steady voice did not betray the excitement that was building in him. "His name is Sepp Knauer. Sturmbannführer Sepp Knauer. Of the Leibstandarte Adolf Hitler."

Hitler nodded with satisfaction.

"He is young, *mein Führer.* His men are young. It will take the audacity of youth to carry out this mission as it must be carried out."

Again Hitler nodded. He turned to Bormann.

"Is Jenbach ready?" he asked.

"Yes." Bormann riffled through the papers in front of him. "Here is the latest dispatch, received two days ago." He found the document and held it out to the Führer.

Hitler ignored it. He stood up. He looked down on Schindler.

"You know the charge I have given you," he said weightily.

"You know its momentous importance. It will begin—now." He reached out his hand.

Schindler at once rose to his feet. He stood ramrod straight. He grasped the Führer's hand.

"It will be your life, Standartenführer Dr. Schindler," Hitler intoned. "From now on it will be your entire life. You cannot fail!" There was a strange imploring command in Hitler's voice. "You *must* not fail!"

Schindler's eyes met Hitler's and locked onto them.

"Mein Führer," he said, his voice raw with emotion, "I pledge to you—*I will not fail!"*

For a brief moment the two men stood immobile as if carved in rock. Then Hitler abruptly let go of Schindler's hand, turned on his heel and walked quickly from the room.

Schindler was conscious of letting out his breath. Had he held it that long? He turned toward Bormann.

The Reichsleiter pulled a map toward him. "Knauer and his *Sondereinsatzgruppe* will leave Berlin by way of Potsdam." With a stubby finger he traced the route on the map. Schindler bent over him to follow. "South to Torgau on the Elbe and on to Dresden. The route is clear. The American front is somewhere in the vicinity of Plauen. Here." He looked up gravely. "The last fifty kilometers will be in enemy-held territory."

Schindler nodded. "I shall leave for Mariendorf at once," he said. "Knauer is at a unit HQ there. Elements of the Hitlerjugend Division. He—"

"You will have to wait," Bormann interrupted. "There are final documents to be prepared. Papers to be assembled." He stood up, collecting the papers on the table. "You will personally carry a set to Jenbach. A special courier will carry a duplicate set to Switzerland. To Bern. All financial matters have been arranged through there."

Schindler frowned. "How long a delay?" he asked. Now that action was imminent, he felt impatient.

"You will leave here at 2100 hours."

"Knauer will want twenty-four hours to get his men and equipment together before jumping off."

Bormann slowly shook his head. "In twenty-four hours his mission will have been accomplished," he said quietly, "or it will have failed."

He fixed his pale, cold eyes on Schindler.

"Hals-und-Beinbruch!" He gave the traditional "good luck" wish impersonally. "May you break your neck and your leg!"

He turned away.

"You will not return here."

Emerging from the underground garages of the Chancellery, Standartenführer Dr. Franz Schindler turned south past the Tiergarten.

Only that morning the Zoo had been closed down when the electricity throughout the city failed and it became impossible to pump water and maintain the special environments needed for many of the animals. The Zoo director had made an impassioned plea to Bormann himself to save the popular hippo, Rosa, and her two-year-old baby, Knautsche. Of course the Reichsleiter had had to dismiss the man. The animals would have to be destroyed. Certainly the dangerous ones.

Schindler thread-needled his open Volkswagen through the rubble-strewn street toward Potsdamer Platz. He'd picked the sturdy little vehicle instead of a more comfortable staff car and driver. It was less apt to get bogged down in debris—and it was easy and fast to get out of, in case of trouble.

At Potsdamer Platz he cut across to Wilhelmstrasse, one of the few thoroughfares kept passable. His mind was still whirling with excitement. The city around him was dying. The people were dying. The Reich itself. But *he* felt like a Phoenix reborn from the ashes, preparing for glorious flight.

In the cause and in the name of the Führer, Adolf Hitler . . .

His thoughts flew briefly back. As an eighteen-year-old medical student he had been with the Führer at the first magnificent Party Rally at Nürnberg in 1933. He had devoted his life to the man and his ideals ever since, serving him faithfully. From his triumphs— to now. Five years ago he had been with Hitler in Paris, when the Führer visited Napoleon's tomb in the Invalides. They had stood gazing down upon the sarcophagus in the huge, round pit. And Schindler remembered his Führer's outrage.

"They put him in a hole!" Hitler had exclaimed. "Napoleon! People must look *down* on him! I shall never make such a mistake." His voice had been tense. "I know how to keep my hold on the world—even after I am gone. My life, my destiny shall not be denied, shall not end with my death." And his eyes had burned with a strange fire. "That—to the contrary—shall be the beginning!" And he had gripped the marble balustrade and stared down into the pit.

Now. Now he, Franz Schindler, knew what his Führer had meant. And now—from the ashes and destruction, from the suffering and defeat of war—Hitler's prophecy was about to be fulfilled. It is an omen, he thought, a providential omen, that the first step should be taken on the birthday of the Führer. . . .

He touched the black briefcase lying on the seat beside him, as if to reassure himself.

At the heavily damaged Reichsluftfahrtministerium, Goering's huge Air Ministry Building, he turned south on Wilhelmstrasse, the center of government offices. The destruction was abominable. Building walls had collapsed into the streets, adding obstacles of broken masonry to the burst water mains, the gaping bomb craters, the fallen lampposts. Shattered glass and rubble lay everywhere. Ashes from still blazing fires floated down like black snow.

He was profoundly shocked. He had not been outside the Führerbunker for over a week. He could well believe Speer's estimate that 600,000 buildings had been destroyed in the city.

He crossed the canal and jolted down Mehring Dam toward Tempelhof Airfield. A haze of reddish brick dust from the last air raid still hung in the air, creating a false overcast. The night streets, illuminated by the many fires still burning, were deserted. People were huddling in the cellars. Terror lay over the mortally wounded city like a blanket over a corpse.

He passed Tempelhof off to his left. He'd double back after briefing Knauer and catch his plane to the south.

Suddenly, ahead of him, loomed several huge black shadows.

Roadblocks.

He slowed down.

Placed across the street, interlocking like the massive teeth of gigantic combs, the jury-rigged defense barriers, hastily made from old tramcars and trucks filled with bricks and broken masonry, guarded the approaches to the airfield. One of them had crude lettering across its side: BERLIN BLEIBT DEUTSCH (Berlin Stays German).

He began to wind his way through.

The *witz*—the joke that had been whispered in the bunker—flitted through his mind:

It will take the Russians four hours and fifteen minutes to get through those barriers, they'd said. Four hours of laughing. Fifteen minutes of blasting!

He bit his lip. It might have been amusing—once. Gallows humor. But not now. Not with the Russians only thirty-five kilometers from the city. He guided his way through the obstacles and sped on.

He was approaching the suburb of Mariendorf, careening past the cemetery. Even the dead had not been spared the enemy's terror bombing. The once beautiful shade trees of their resting place had become charred stumps, or lay uprooted, still encased in their ornamental ironwork. Headless angels with shattered wings uselessly stood guard over open craters.

Suddenly he hit the brakes. Ahead of him, eerily illuminated by the flames of a burning building, a small group of soldiers was blocking the road, guns held ready. As he came to a stop, he saw they were boys. Fourteen? Fifteen? He knew at once what they were. He knew about the Hitler Youth patrols that were roaming the city streets in search of deserters and renegades. Ruthless packs of little savages, meting out quick justice. Or—injustice. In the name of the man whose name they bore. Despite his rank and his wholly legitimate mission, Schindler felt himself grow tense.

The leader of the patrol, a Hitlerjugend Gefolgschaftsführer, perhaps sixteen, an angular youth whose cheeks had never felt the steel of a razor, stepped up to him. His patrol of children flanked the Volkswagen—watching its occupant with eager, hungry eyes.

The Gefolgschaftsführer stuck his hand out. He did not salute.

"Papiere herzeigen!" His voice was young and arrogant. "Show your papers!"

Schindler felt a flush of anger hot on his neck. Nevertheless, he reached into his tunic for his ID.

"I am Standartenführer Dr. Franz Schindler," he said coldly. "Courier for the Führer."

"That's what they all say." The boy mocked him openly. He grabbed the papers from Schindler, glanced at them and returned them.

"Even a Standartenführer can be a deserter," he observed insolently. "You would not be the first."

"You have examined my papers," Schindler said curtly. "Now—get out of my way and let me through!"

"Not so fast, *Herr Standartenführer,*" the boy said, with obvious scorn. "You have only told us *who* you are. Not—*what* you are doing here." His voice grew ominous. "Alone. Driving your vehicle yourself. *Herr Standartenführer!*"

"I've told you I am a courier for the Führer," Schindler snapped. He felt a gathering clamminess in his armpits. Damn the young whelp!

"Prove it!" the boy challenged. "Prove it. Now! Or you may have to join your friend over there." He nodded toward the edge of the street.

Schindler looked. And blanched.

From an ornamented bronze lamppost turned gibbet dangled the limp body of a soldier. An Unteroffizier. The noose around his elongated, broken neck pushed his head awkwardly askew. On his chest hung a large cardboard placard. The flames from the fire gave a flickering life to the childish scrawl that proclaimed: ICH WOLLTE MIT DEN BOLSCHEWIKEN HERUMBUMMELN! (I Was Going to Bum Around with the Bolsheviks!).

"That one," the Hitler Youth scoffed. "*He* was also on a *special mission.*" He shrugged elaborately. "He could not prove it. Either. But he had a pocket full of gold watches."

He gave a brief, scornful laugh. "Perhaps you, too, *Herr Standartenführer,* are on your way to the Bolsheviks, huh? For a little *schwanzstreicheln*—a little cock-stroking!"

One of the boys giggled.

The Gefolgschaftsführer snickered.

Schindler felt cold. Bleak. Would a snot-nosed brat destroy the Führer's dream?

The Hitler Youth leader pointed to the briefcase on the seat beside Schindler. "What's in the case?" he demanded.

"State papers," Schindler answered.

"Open it."

"They are secret documents."

"Open it!"

"That is impossible."

"Is it?" the Hitler Youth said disdainfully. He pointed his gun at Schindler's forehead. "Either *you* open it—now. Or *I* will—after you are dead!"

Schindler felt suddenly calm. Icy. He knew what he had to do. He had no choice whatsoever.

He placed the briefcase on his lap. He opened it. He put his hand inside—

"Slowly," the Hitler Youth cautioned. "Nice and easy. And be sure that what you come up with is only paper!"

"Of course," Schindler said curtly.

The sudden crack of the shot splattered shock across the children's faces. The bullet from the Luger tore through the briefcase and caught the Hitler Youth leader squarely in the throat. He toppled back, astonished eyes glazed in instant death.

In the same split second Schindler stomped down on the accelerator. Firing gravel and dirt from its spinning tires, the Volkswagen shot forward. In the few seconds it took the boys to recover from their shock, the car was already disappearing into the gloom. Schindler hardly heard the bursts of gunfire behind him.

He drove at the greatest possible speed. Knauer's HQ was only a short distance farther. He had a brief moment of regret. The young Gefolgschaftsführer had merely done his duty. Only hours before, he, Schindler, had seen similar boys being honored by the Führer himself. What was their motto? Etched in steel on their little daggers? BLUT UND EHRE! (Blood and Honor!). So be it. . . .

He dismissed the feeling.

No choice.

No choice whatsoever . . .

The HQ of Kampfgruppe Knauer—Task Force Knauer—composed of elements of the 12th SS Panzer Division "Hitlerjugend" —was located in the basement storage rooms of a boys' school. It seemed appropriate. Division recruits were originally drawn from the Hitler Youth with experienced officers and noncoms from Hitler's former bodyguard, the Leibstandarte SS Adolf Hitler.

Sturmbannführer Sepp Knauer sprang to his feet when he saw Schindler enter. *"Heil Hitler!"* His arm shot up in a smart salute.

Schindler didn't break stride as he walked straight for a door on the far side of the room.

"Knauer," he barked, "I want to see you. Alone. Now."

The small, windowless cubicle that served as Knauer's private quarters had been a storage room for gym equipment. It was lit by a single glaring light bulb hanging naked from the ceiling. A pommeled horse, a balancing bench, a worn vaulting horse and box, a heavy, coiled climbing rope and a cardboard box with limply inflated volleyballs had been pushed against one wall. A few rings hung from a large rusty nail, and several soiled gym mats had been folded and placed on top of one another to form a makeshift bed. There was a faint odor of stale sweat in the air. Seating was provided by a couple of locker-room benches, and an old table served as a desk.

Schindler placed his briefcase on the cluttered table and sat down on a bench beside it. He motioned toward the stacked gym mats.

"Sit down," he ordered curtly.

He was surprised at the harshness in his voice. Perhaps it was the magnitude of the mission he was about to set in motion. He turned to Knauer.

"First—what is your present situation?"

"As expected, *Herr Standartenführer.*" Knauer exhibited an easy, aweless calm. With a mixture of approval and annoyance Schindler took note of it. The young officer continued, "This damned place is half a step from hell—and losing ground fast. We are opposite a crack outfit pushing hard, the Soviet 28th Guard Rifle Company, and I've got nothing but kids and old men to hold them with."

With a curt move of his hand Schindler dismissed it. "As of now, you are relieved of command," he stated flatly.

Knauer felt a surge of apprehension tinged with astonishment. Had he screwed up somewhere?

"As soon as I leave," Schindler went on, "you will turn your command over to your executive officer. *Verstanden?*"

"Understood, *Herr Standartenführer.*" What the hell was going on?

Solemnly Schindler pulled his briefcase to him. "You have known for some time, Knauer, that I have selected you for a special, top-secret mission—when time and the situation demanded it."

Knauer nodded. So that was it. He perked up. "Yes, *Herr Standartenführer.* I am honored."

Schindler fixed him with an intent gaze. "You have an admirable record, Knauer," he said. "Admirable."

"Thank you, *Herr Standartenführer.*"

"It remains to be seen if you are up to carrying out this present mission successfully."

"I shall do my best, *Herr Standartenführer.*"

"Will that be good enough?" Schindler shot at him, his voice suddenly piercing.

"Yes, *Herr Standartenführer.*"

"*Why?*"

"Why?" Knauer was momentarily flustered. "Because—I—"

"Why?" Schindler interrupted sharply. "What makes you think so? You don't even know *what* the mission is, do you?"

"No, *Herr Standartenführer,*" Knauer answered in a firm voice. He had regained complete control.

"Then *how* do you know you will succeed?" Schindler fired the question at him.

"Sir. The Fatherland has trained me. In the Hitler Youth. In the SS. In the Leibstandarte Adolf Hitler. The best training in the world, *Herr Standartenführer.* You and the Fatherland have selected me for the mission. The Fatherland is never wrong. I shall succeed."

Schindler contemplated the young officer, a hint of a cynical smile on his lips.

"It is a good answer, Knauer," he said. "It is *Kwatsch*, of course —a lot of bullshit—but it is a good answer to an unreasonable question by your superior! You think on your feet. I knew I was right in selecting you."

He unlocked and opened his briefcase, studiously ignoring the powder-burned bullet hole. He became coldly authoritative once more.

"You were ordered to have at hand at all times an up-to-date list of men. Hand-picked men. Young. Aggressive. You have such a list?"

"I do, *Herr Standartenführer.*"

Schindler nodded. He had expected nothing else. He took a sheaf of papers from his briefcase.

Knauer was watching him. Despite his outward calm, he did feel a certain awe. Standartenführer Dr. Franz Schindler was a man to be regarded with awe. At thirty he had already distinguished himself in his special work for the Party to become one of the Führer's most intimate and trusted confidants—the envy of many older, more important Party bigwigs. His enormously efficient work in supervising the Führer's program for elimination of the mentally retarded and defective had earned him a reputation of utmost competence.

Schindler looked up from his papers. "The time for your mission is *now,* Knauer. I am here to brief you personally. I want not even the possibility of a slip-up."

"*Jawohl, Herr Standartenführer.*"

Schindler handed Knauer the papers. "Read this," he said. "Commit it to memory. It is your mission."

Knauer took the papers. He began to read.

Schindler rose from the hard bench. He felt strangely keyed up. *It had begun.* He lit a cigarette. The smoke burned bitter in his mouth. The taste was awful. What the devil *did* they put in those things? Dried horseshit? But he smoked it, taking deep gulps. He glanced at Knauer, engrossed in reading the papers. He was conscious of the enormously important role the young SS officer would play. If Knauer failed, all would be lost. His, Schindler's, own future; the plans of the Führer himself. Everything. He looked closely at the young man. At twenty-six he seemed the personification of the mythical blond, clean-cut Aryan of Goebbels' propaganda posters. It was almost inconceivable that he could fail. . . .

Knauer looked up. His eyes were shining, excited.

"I am ready, *Herr Standartenführer,*" he said.

Schindler took back the papers. Carefully he placed them in his briefcase. He locked it. Then he turned to Knauer.

"How do you propose to mount the mission?" he asked, quiet tension in his voice.

"A small *Einsatzkommando, Herr Standartenführer*," Knauer said. "Sixteen men including myself."

"As you can see, Fichtendorf is the key."

"Yes."

"What do you need?"

"Twelve heavy motorcycles. BMW 750s. Eight with sidecars. Four without."

Schindler took notes. "Other vehicles?"

"None. The operation calls for special mobility, *Herr Standartenführer*. We must have as great a mobility as possible—in any kind of terrain." He grinned. "We'll have to make it a *Bubibummel*—a schoolboy fuck. In—and out!"

Schindler ignored his vulgarism. "Armament?"

"Light arms only, *Herr Standartenführer*. Schmeissers. Lugers."

"Agreed. You have, of course, top priority on any equipment, any manpower you want."

"I shall use it, *Herr Standartenführer*."

Schindler eyed him. "Your men?" he asked. "From where are you drawing them?"

"From my own unit, *Herr Standartenführer*. Men I know. Men I can trust. Young—but combat-seasoned. Courageous—but not reckless. Devils on motorcycles, all of them!" He looked at Schindler. "What can I tell them about the mission?"

"Nothing! Nothing—except that it is for the Führer."

"That is enough."

"You must mount your operation at once, Knauer. The enemy situation is such that the mission *must* be completed within twenty-four hours."

Knauer frowned in concentration. He walked to his cluttered table and rummaged until he found a map. He bent over it.

"I can be ready to take off in—four hours," he said. He looked at his watch. "At 0200 hours." He studied the map. "It's close to 450 kilometers to Plauen via Torgau-Dresden. Allow—twelve hours. Another couple of hours to get to Fichtendorf in the enemy-held special-security zone. That should place us at the Kugelberg target at about 1600 hours."

Schindler nodded. "Good. You are ordered to avoid direct confrontation with the enemy forces—if at all possible."

"Jawohl, Herr Standartenführer." Knauer frowned. "Sir. My plan of action must, of course, cover all contingencies. Of necessity this means also—a firefight. Perhaps—capture. Should, I repeat, *should* this occur, what are my orders?"

Schindler sighed. Gravely he looked at the young SS officer.

"You must do everything you can—take any evasive measures —make any sacrifices to avoid capture and to safeguard the secrecy of your mission." His eyes grew dark. "But—*should* you be in danger of being taken, you will destroy any survivors. You will destroy—the object of your mission. And yourself."

Knauer met his superior's gaze steadily. *"Jawohl, Herr Standartenführer,"* he said quietly.

"The destiny of everything we believe in, Knauer. Everything we have fought for—and died for—is now in your hands. All will depend on what you do in the next twenty-four hours."

He picked up his briefcase.

"For a long time now, you have been concerned with only two things. Every waking hour," he continued earnestly. "Killing the enemy—and staying alive yourself. Simple. Life—and death." He stepped closer to the young SS officer. He looked at him with penetrating eyes. "After Fichtendorf," he said quietly, "nothing is going to be quite that simple for either of us ever again!"

ONE

Los Angeles

6–17 March 1978

1

The rains had finally stopped. Los Angeles had begun the Herculean task of digging out after the series of devastating storms and the almost biblical downpour that had turned the county into a federal disaster area, converting the lowlands into rivers of mud, gouging out roadways and toppling houses from the hillsides. Angelenos would not soon forget the storms of early 1978.

Past midnight Jaymar Street was deserted. It usually was at that time. And dark. The neon lights from Lassen's Liquor Store on the corner of Franklin did not reach very far down Jaymar, and street-lamps were few and far between in the modest neighborhood.

His apartment hotel, incongruously named the King's Court, was on the east side of the street, and the outdoor spots that used to illuminate the shrubbery in front of the building with red and green lights had long since been turned off to save energy. And money.

He hurried along, the six-pack promisingly heavy in the brown bag. His mind was full. So much was happening. . . .

Suddenly an urgent whisper from behind him shocked him out of his reveries:

"Don't turn around, man, or you're dead! Keep walking. Drop your wallet. And your watch."

He whirled around, the heavy beer bag swinging from his arm. Before him loomed two men. Burly. Young. Teenagers. He saw the face of the nearest one, distorted with fear and hate. He saw the piece of iron pipe clutched in the boy's hand descend toward his head. He seemed frozen in the eternity of no time at all. In the split second before death he registered the vicious blow that crashed into his temple. . . .

Sprawled in an awkward heap on the sidewalk, he was unaware of the swift, callous hands that rifled his pockets and tore his watch from his wrist. He did not hear the hurried footsteps that disappeared into the night and the dark.

He was merely another mugging victim left in the shadows on the street—stripped of his valuables—and his life. . . .

2

He knocked over the open aspirin bottle on the night table next to his bed as he groped for the telephone. He heard the tablets roll across the tabletop and clatter on the bare floor where the imitation Persian rug didn't quite reach the wall. Damn! That meant rummaging around on hands and knees. He fumbled the receiver to his ear.

"Bendicks," he growled, his sleep-numbed voice a full octave lower than normal.

He listened for a short while.

"Thirty minutes," he said.

He worked the receiver back onto its cradle. The large luminous figures on his digital alarm clock glowed 1:27.

Investigator II Harry Bendicks lay back in his bed. Just one more minute. He hated these calls in the middle of the night. He stretched. His joints felt stiff. At least the aspirin had taken care of the dull ache in his arm.

He let his left arm fall to the other side of the bed. It had been ten years since he had felt Edith there—or the warmth her body had generated. But he still slept on his own side of the double bed. And his arm—knowing it would find nothing—still automatically sought her. Some habits are hard to break.

He yawned and swung his legs out from under the sheet that was his only cover. He was wide awake. That was the worst of it, he thought. No way could he do his job half asleep, like most other working stiffs.

Hurriedly he began to dress.

At fifty-seven he was in pretty good shape, although the spare tire around his middle *was* getting a little too inflated—a fact he noticed every time he buttoned the top button of his pants, like now—and despite the fact that he occasionally had to cheat a little on the tests for his physical-fitness reports. Still, standing six feet one, with his full head of graying hair and strong features, he cut an impressive figure. And he had no trouble putting a nice, tight pattern in the paper man on the range.

He had five days to go. Five days before "busting out"—after thirty-two years. He felt a twinge of annoyance. What the hell was this DB in the street going to do to his last few days? He'd been looking forward to turning them into one long retirement party. A Dead Body could too damned easily turn into a dead end. . . .

Harry had joined the Los Angeles Police Department in 1946, a few months after his honorable discharge from the Army. He was still in top shape and he'd hated standing in line every week with the other members of the "52–20 Club" to collect his Veteran's Readjustment Allowance of a lousy twenty bucks. It was no life for a man who had volunteered immediately after Pearl Harbor and had served better than four years in the ETO as an agent in the CIC—the Counter Intelligence Corps. Detachment 212, XII Corps, AUS. Through France, the Battle of the Bulge, across the Rhine, through all of Germany into Czechoslovakia, and nine months of occupation. The works. It had been an obvious assignment. Harald "Harry" Bendicks was a second-generation Dane and spoke both Danish and German fluently. Moreover, he'd been familiar with those countries and their people from several vacation trips to the old country as a teenager in the 1930s. If it were possible to "enjoy" a war, Harry had enjoyed his investigative work as a CIC agent, and he'd opted to continue that kind of work with the LAPD. He'd had no trouble at all making the grade.

With his junior teammate, Pete, Investigator II Peter Hastings, he formed SIT-7—Special Investigation Team #7, Homicide, working out of the Hollywood Division of the LAPD.

He glanced at the digital alarm clock as he shrugged into his shoulder holster. 1:44. Pete would beat him to the scene. . . .

Harry turned the corner from Franklin into Jaymar. Ahead of him down the street he could see the flashing red lights of the ambulance and the patrol cars. A patch of sidewalk was illuminated by the headlights. The proverbial "scene of the crime."

Looks something like a theater stage, he thought as he brought his car to a stop behind the Division Commander's vehicle, or a movie. . . . There's the set. The big star is the DB, the victim, his co-star the murderer. Offstage—for the moment. And the supporting players and bits, each acting out his role: the investigators, the uniformed cops, the Division officers, the deputy coroner, the

ambulance attendants, the photo-and-print Man. Cast of thousands! And, of course, the curious. The extras. Just like shooting
some two-bit movie. Only—this one's real. . . .

Would anyone but a *Hollywood* cop think crazy like that? He
grinned to himself.

As he got out of his car he saw Pete talking to one of the IHD
investigators.

He took in the scene quickly. He *was* the last one to arrive. As
if he'd missed his cue. He walked over to his partner.

"Car trouble?" Pete asked sweetly.

"Very funny," Harry growled. "What've we got?"

"Mugging," Pete answered matter-of-factly. "Murder. Male
Caucasian. Late fifties. Got himself his head bashed in."

"ID?"

Pete shook his head. "Negative. He was completely cleaned.
Except for this." He handed Harry a small slip of paper.

Harry looked at it. It was a cash-register receipt. Lassen's Liquor
Store. $1.75. 6 March 1978. He nodded toward the corner.

"That's the joint up there," he said. "Today's date."

"Yeah." Pete nodded. "I figure he was on his way back home
with a six-pack." He gestured toward the gutter. "It's lying out
there. Budweiser. The guy probably lived around here."

"Okay," Harry said. "First stop, Lassen's Liquor." He turned to
the IHD investigator. "Who found him?"

The man from Investigative Headquarters Division at Parker
Center, downtown LA, shrugged. "Who knows? A conscientious
citizen who'd rather not get involved."

"So what's new?" Pete observed.

"A 187 was routed to IHD about an hour ago," the investigator
went on. He glanced at the dead man. "And we rolled on it. It's
a who-done-it. Have fun."

"Thanks a heap," Harry said sourly. Some fun for his last five
days . . .

The deputy coroner came up to them. "You boys going to handle this one?" he asked.

Harry nodded. "What's the story?"

"Well, unless we find a dose of arsenic or some exotic South
American poison in his belly," the deputy said cheerfully, "I'd say

he died of a crushed skull. Left temple caved in. Dead about two hours.

Harry looked at Pete. "Any weapon?"

Pete shook his head. "None found."

"Iron pipe," Harry mused grimly. "Vicelords?"

"Could be," Pete agreed. "Likely as not. It's their MO."

"Well, back to bed," the deputy coroner said. "Unless there are more fun and games waiting somewhere." He walked off.

Harry turned to Pete. "Get Photo and Prints to give you a Polaroid mug shot of the stiff," he said. "We might need it."

Pete nodded. "Done." He walked away.

A police lieutenant started toward Harry. Harry watched him approach. He knew what was coming. Lieutenant Jack L. Stein was in charge of SIT at the Division.

"Bendicks," Stein said crisply, "this looks like just the case for SIT-7. Routine." He grinned at Harry. "Something to while away the long hours before your retirement."

"Don't expect me to break into a song-and-dance routine for joy," Harry said sourly.

"Harry, don't beef too much." Stein looked toward the dead man. The coroner was placing him on a litter. "It's a Meter Maid case. No reason to run your ass off on this one. You should already have a good idea who the bastards are."

"Yeah. We do. The Vicelords."

Stein nodded. "Our ruling resident gang shows surprisingly little imagination. Only this time they were a little too enthusiastic."

"The victim had no ID," Harry said. He showed Stein the liquor-store receipt. "We have a good lead, though."

"Okay, don't let me keep you." Stein turned to go. "I'll look for the papers on my desk tomorrow morning." He walked away.

"Sure. Look," Harry grumbled.

Pete joined him. "Got it."

Harry nodded. "Light's still on," he said. "Let's go see what they know at the booze bazaar."

Lassen's Liquor Store was blazing with light, but the door was locked and a cardboard sign with a corner missing hung inside it,

CLOSED

Harry and Pete could see a scrawny, elderly man working inside. They banged on the door.

Without turning toward them, the man called, "We're closed!"

Harry took out his badge and clanged it sharply on the glass. "Police!" he called. "We want to talk to you!"

The man looked up. Slowly, warily, he came to the door. He did not open it. He shouted through the glass. "What do you want?"

Harry held up his badge. "I'm Investigator Bendicks," he called. He nodded toward Pete. "That's Investigator Hastings. We'd like to talk to you."

The man peered nearsightedly at Harry's badge. He looked at the two men without the slightest expression of friendliness. Slowly he opened the door.

"What's going on down on Jaymar?" he grumbled. "Another break-in? It's getting so you can't—"

"Are you Mr. Lassen?" Harry interrupted.

"Yeah. I'm Lassen."

"We'd like to ask you a few questions."

"What about?"

"May we come in?"

"Sure. Come in." The man stood aside.

Harry and Pete entered the store. They looked around. Several empty and half-empty boxes and crates neatly divided into twelve bottle-sized spaces stood near a door to a back room.

"Have you been here for the last few hours, Mr. Lassen?" Pete asked.

"Yeah. I've been working on the inventory."

"You're working late," Harry observed.

"What the hell else is there to do?"

Harry fished the Polaroid snapshot of the mugging victim from his pocket. "Do you know this man, Mr. Lassen?" He showed him the photo.

Lassen looked uneasy as he inspected it. "Yeah. I know him."

"Who is he?"

"Name's Muller. Ernest Muller." He averted his eyes from the snapshot. "Lives down the street. At the King's Court."

"When did you see him last, Mr. Lassen?" Pete asked.

Lassen shifted uneasily on his feet. "Look," he said, "I don't want to get involved."

"Just answer the question!" Harry snapped. He bristled. Damn them! Nobody ever wanted to get involved. . . .

"Okay, okay." Lassen peered sullenly at Harry. "But I don't know anything."

"When did you see Muller last?" Harry repeated the question.

"This evening," Lassen said. He seemed apprehensive. "Just —just before I closed. Couple of hours ago." He licked his lips nervously. "He's a—customer. Regular. Bought a six-pack of beer."

"Budweiser," Pete commented.

Lassen looked at him, startled. "Yeah. Budweiser." He looked suspiciously from one to the other.

Harry again showed him the snapshot. "And this is Ernest Muller?"

Lassen nodded affirmation. "Yeah." He swallowed. "Is he—has anything happened to him?"

"He was mugged," Harry said. "He's dead."

Lassen grew pale. "I—I know nothing about it," he mumbled.

"Nobody said you did," Harry snapped. He glowered at the storekeeper. "Anybody else? Who's been here since Muller left?"

Lassen shook his head. "Look—eh, officer, I don't know anything. Really. I don't want to get involved. I don't want to answer any more questions." He found sudden courage. "I—I don't have to! I'm not under arrest or anything. It's none of my affair."

Harry contemplated the man for a moment. Slowly he walked a little farther into the store. He looked around. He turned to Lassen, who was watching him apprehensively.

"That's right, Mr. Lassen," he said, his voice like poisoned honey. "You don't have to answer any questions. Now . . ." He looked around appraisingly. "You have a nice store here, Mr. Lassen. Very nice. Business is probably good, right? As long as nobody cuts a hole in your pocket, right?" He looked straight into the man's face. His voice grew dangerously low. "Someone—like me . . ."

He let the implication hang in the air.

Lassen stared at him.

"Now, as I was asking you, Mr. Lassen, has anyone else been here after Muller left?"

Lassen nodded. He looked frightened. "Yes. One. Just one. A young man. Just to use the phone. He didn't buy anything." He licked his suddenly dry lips. "He said it was an emergency."

"Did you know him?"

Lassen shook his head.

"Think, Mr. Lassen," Harry said silkily. "Think. Try to remember. Did you know the young man?"

"No."

"Can you describe him?" Pete asked.

Lassen shrugged. "I don't know. I didn't really look at him good."

"How old was he?"

"Maybe twenty. Or—thirty. I don't know."

"Can you be a little more specific?"

"I'm not good on ages."

"How tall was he? How was he built?"

"Sort of—medium, I guess."

"Color of hair?"

"Brown—sort of."

"Was it long? How did he comb it?"

"Comb it?" Lassen shook his head. "I didn't notice. It wasn't too long, though—I don't think."

"Eyes?"

"I don't know."

"What was his ethnic background?"

"His what?"

"Was he white? Black? Chicano? Oriental?"

"Oh. White."

"How was he dressed?"

"I don't remember. A jacket. Yeah—some kind of dark jacket."

"Leather?"

Lassen shrugged. "I couldn't say."

"Anything unusual about him? A limp? Tattoo?"

"No. Nothing. He was just—average, I'd say."

Harry listened with growing annoyance. The description could fit half the guys walking the streets of Los Angeles. Medium. Average. Shit! One of his pet peeves was the worthless descriptions the uniformed cops so often handed in. Not worth a damn to anyone —except the perpetrator. But when he ran into someone like Lassen, he realized what the men were up against. Dammit, there were so many things the store owner could have noticed. How did the guy speak when he asked about telephoning? Did he have an accent? A high voice? Low? Did he wear a beard? A mustache? Glasses? Christ, there were hundreds of details anyone with two eyes could see.

He was about to break in when Pete gave him a glance of exasperation. He clammed up. It would be a waste of time. Lassen wasn't going to give them anything concrete. And, anyway, the subject was only marginally involved. Not worth the time and temper it would take. He let it go.

"Is there anything else you can tell us about the man, Mr. Lassen?" Pete finally asked. "Anything at all that you remember?"

"No," Lassen said. "Nothing. Except—"

He stopped.

"Except?"

"Well . . . There was a girl with him. She waited outside. I—I seen her."

"Do you know her?"

"Yeah. But only by name. She's a—a prostitute." He looked away. "They call her—Titi."

"Did you hear what the young man said on the phone?" Pete asked.

"No. No—he spoke very softly. And he—he covered his mouth with his hand."

"All right, Mr. Lassen," Pete said. "Thank you for your cooperation." He handed the man a card. "If you should remember anything else, please call us at this number."

Lassen took the card. He didn't glance at it. "Sure," he said quickly. "Sure thing."

Outside the store Harry turned to Pete.

"Okay, so what've we got?" he asked. He answered his own

question. "Some hooker named Titi picks up a John. Probably down on Hollywood. She's taking him to her trick pad somewhere on Jaymar when they stumble over Muller. The 'Honest Citizen' John calls the police, but doesn't want to get further involved—having both a dead body and a live whore to explain. . . ."

"Would you?"

"What?"

"Get involved?"

"Drop dead!"

Pete grinned.

"No use to go looking for Titi tonight," Harry continued. "She's probably holed up with another John. Tomorrow." He looked down the street toward the King's Court. "But I'd like to take a look at Muller's place. See what we can find out about him."

He started down the street. "That's the part I hate," he said.

"What?"

"The relatives. Having to tell the relatives. . . ."

"Mr. Muller lives alone." The manager at the King's Court apartments, an elderly, gray-haired man with a sallow skin and unfashionable steel-rimmed glasses fixed his water-blue eyes on Harry and Pete. "Are you looking for Mr. Muller for—eh, professional reasons?" he asked suspiciously. "Mr. Muller is not at home."

"We know," Harry said.

The manager eyed him. "Is he—is he in any trouble?"

"No. No more." Harry looked straight into the man's pale eyes. "He's dead."

The manager's eyes widened for an instant. His knuckles showed white where he gripped the counter. Then his eyes narrowed as they flitted quickly from one to the other.

"How?" he breathed.

Harry ignored the question. "What do you know about Muller?" he asked.

"I? Nothing. Except that he is a good tenant. No trouble. Pays his rent on time." His lips grew thin. "I'm not in the habit of prying into the private affairs of the tenants."

"Do you know where he worked?"

"As I told you, I'm not here to pry into the private lives of the tenants."

"I take it that means you don't know?" Pete said.

"You are correct."

"How long did Muller live here? I presume you do know that?" Harry continued his questioning.

"About two years."

"You have a key to his rooms?"

"I do. The master key."

"Okay. You can let me in."

The manager hesitated. "Well," he said, "I don't know if I should. Aren't you supposed to have a—a search warrant?"

Harry looked at the man for a moment. Then he smiled benevolently.

"Yes," he said pleasantly. "A search warrant. Of course." He leaned closer to the man. "I'll tell you what. We'll get a search warrant. It's simply a matter of routine in a case like this. And when we get it—I promise you we'll use it to take this place apart inch by inch and make damned sure every one of your guests is made abundantly aware of the thorough investigation we will be conducting."

He straightened up.

"On the other hand," he continued. "If we can make our routine search now with your permission, it shouldn't be any big deal."

"It's on the second floor," the manager said sourly. "Apartment 207."

Harry turned to his partner. "Pete," he said, "why don't you go ring some doorbells? Get a few good citizens outta bed. Some neighbor with insomnia may have heard or seen something." He glanced back at the sullen manager. "I'll take a look at the guy's place. Meet you here later."

Ernest Muller had lived in a small, one-bedroom apartment. One room with a countered-off kitchenette, a tiny bedroom and a bathroom with an old, free-standing, lion-legged bathtub.

Harry stood inside the door for a long moment—looking around, absorbing the place.

It would be the last time anyone would see it like that, he

thought. It, too—like its owner—would be changed by death.

An indefinable feeling of uneasiness crept over him. Why? He tried to analyze it.

The place was neat and orderly; it looked almost as if nobody lived there. The furniture was sparse and cheap; obviously it belonged to the King's Court. On a sidetable stood a vase with a variety of colorful blooms cradled in green. All plastic. And dusty. Waxen and unsmellable, they gave off a sterile sense of artificial life. On the walls hung a few cheap prints cheaply framed. But there were no personal items. Nothing with the stamp of the occupant—of one Ernest Muller—on it. Perhaps that was what disturbed him. It was unnatural.

He sighed—and went to work. . . .

An hour later he closed the last drawer in the paint-chipped dresser in the little bedroom. He straightened up—and let his hands fall to his side in an unconscious gesture of puzzled futility.

He never searched a room without experiencing a feeling of discomfort. It somehow got to him—poking around in some stranger's pad, breathing the private smells of the guy's bedroom, learning things about him he'd never told anyone. Or ever would.

Only—in the case of Ernest Muller, there was nothing to be learned.

Absolutely nothing.

No personal mementoes. No letters or snapshots. No papers or records or documents of any kind. Not a checkbook stub nor a laundry list. Nothing. Nothing that showed *who* Ernest Muller really was. Nothing to tell what kind of man . . .

He'd looked behind every picture on the walls, and searched under every drawer. He'd peered into the toilet tank and the heater vent. Nothing. He'd felt through pillows and upholstery, looked under rugs and behind draperies and curtains. Everywhere.

Nothing.

Yet someone had lived there.

The food in the old refrigerator and the squeeze-wrinkled toothpaste tube in the wall cabinet above the sink in the bathroom

attested to that, as did several other impersonal personal posses-
sions that could be anyone's.

But *nothing* that spelled Ernest Muller.

Again he stood at the door and looked around the room.

He frowned.

There *had* to be something. It was almost as if Muller had
deliberately tried to keep his existence a secret.

There had to be—something. . . .

He searched the room with new eyes. *If* something *was* hidden
in the damned place, where would it be? In the most obvious spot.
The one place no one would think to look. The blotter on the
scarred desk? He'd had it apart. Mixed in with the half-dozen
semi-pornographic magazines on the chipped coffee table? He'd
looked through them.

His eyes fell on the sidetable. He walked over to it. Perhaps it
was the kind of table that extended to a larger size. Often there
was a hollow space in the center where the leaves met. He'd often
thought that would make a good hiding place. Right out in the
open—yet unseen.

He examined the table. It was narrow, scratched, with sturdy
round legs. But it did not extend.

He banged it against the wall in angry frustration and nearly
overturned the vase. He glared at it, as if holding it personally
responsible for his failure.

And the thought came to him.

The legs.

It was a small table. A light table. Why the unnecessarily heavy
legs?

Quickly he removed the vase with the lifeless flowers. He
turned the table on its side.

The third leg he tried turned in his hands.

He unscrewed it.

From the hollow top he pulled out a rolled-up packet wrapped
in plastic.

He stared at it.

He'd found Ernest Muller.

Hurriedly he unwrapped the packet. There was just one document. With mounting astonishment he examined it. And then he saw the snapshot, creased and dog-eared.

He stared at it. The blood drained from his face—leaving him chilled.

Slowly he turned the little photograph over and over in his hands.

It was a snapshot of a picturesque, Germanic-looking, rustic cabin nestled among evergreens. A short distance from it stood a well pump, distinctively carved, with a wrought-iron pump handle. A painted sign hung over the cabin door, flanked by a pair of stag antlers. The ornate inscription on the sign could barely be made out: GRÜSS GOTT, TRITT EIN, BRING GLÜCK HEREIN! In the distance, seen through a little clearing, a large rock formation bare of vegetation protruded from the ground. Shaped like half a gigantic ball embedded in the earth, it looked massive and unassailable.

Harry stared fixedly at the faded photograph. It set off an avalanche of memories. He *knew* that place. He *knew* that hut.

He shivered.

He felt the long shadows of the past reaching for him.

Pete was in the lobby talking to the manager when Harry came down from Muller's apartment.

"I told you all I know," the manager was saying, exasperation in his voice. "All I know is that he was connected in some way with the motion-picture industry."

"Isn't everybody?" Pete commented sourly.

"Well, that's all I know." The manager's voice had a tone of finality. "I *don't* know where Mr. Muller worked."

Harry walked up to Pete.

"Find out anything?" his partner asked.

Harry handed him the document. "Take a look at this," he said soberly, "and you tell me."

Pete took the paper. He looked at it. The style and writing were unfamiliar to him—but there was no mistaking the embossed eagle holding a swastika in its claws!

Orders. Official Nazi orders. Dated *"Führerhauptquartier,* 20.4.1945."

He knew enough of the foreign language to make out the gist of the document:

SS Oberstumführer Ernst Helmut Müller . . . on special duty for the Reich . . . top secret . . . by order of the Führer Adolf Hitler . . .

Incredulously he gaped at the document. He looked up at Harry, who was watching him grim-faced. His eyes went from his partner to the manager of the King's Court and back.

"Holy shit!" he exclaimed. "Muller was a Nazi SS officer!"

U.S. TO BEGIN DEPORTATION PROCEEDINGS AGAINST 7 ALLEGED NAZI WAR CRIMINALS

WASHINGTON—The Department of Justice said Monday it planned to begin proceedings against seven men alleged to have committed Nazi crimes in Europe before and during World War II. Four of the seven are U.S. citizens and will first have to be stripped of their citizenship.

3

Harry was getting his second wind. In recent years he'd noticed it always happened about an hour after he'd eaten dinner. He'd run himself ragged all day, have a good dinner—and feel like flaking out. Then an hour later he'd be good for a few more turns. It didn't used to be like that, he thought, it wasn't too long since he could go twenty-four hours and not know the difference.

They drove their unmarked car down Hollywood Boulevard toward Western, Pete at the wheel. The late-evening traffic was heavy and slow. As usual. Harry often wondered where the hell all those cars came from. And where they were going. Just—cruising. It was getting worse all the time. Real honky-tonk town.

He had a pang of regret. And anger. Helluva way to let a community go to pot. Hell—if it weren't for old Hollywood, where'd LA be? The City of the Angels owed her very existence to this place —the former glamour capital of the world. Where dreams were made true. More like nightmares now. An eyesore—acting like a magnet for perverts and criminals . . .

His eyes roamed the boulevard—and the side streets protruding from it like garish appendages. Gaudy neon signs blinking temptations, impervious to any energy shortage. It was a display he'd seen often enough. But it never failed to disgust him.

The efforts to clean up the place by the city fathers—and whatever other relatives had thought it expedient to get involved—had had little effect. Trashy bars lined the streets; pool halls and lice-ridden massage parlors; adult bookstores and movie arcades extolled their kinky wares. *Adult.* Crazy how the English language had been turned upside down, he thought. *Adult*—when it should read *puerile.* His thoughts wandered. . . .

There was a whole flock of words nowadays that were used to convey their exact opposite. *Love children*—for selfish kids filled with anger and hate; *gays*—for the saddest creatures on the street; *mothers*—for real lowdown slobs. The language was being butchered and served up as a grotesque facsimile of the real thing. Real words, good words were being used in ways that destroyed them forever. People's Rights slogans graffitied on other people's properties in direct violation of *their* rights . . . Peace and Freedom for political extremists committed to violence and repression . . . People's Democratic this-and-that where dictatorial oppression reigned. The double-speak of Orwell's 1984—come a few years early . . .

He looked ahead. They were all there, roaming the streets, a miserable bunch of "free spirits" enslaved by drugs, who'd liberated themselves into a stinking mess of hang-ups. The street people . . ."Johns" from all over Southern California looking for an easy lay . . . Hookers, drag queens, pimps and pushers . . . Boy hustlers and chickenhawks. The works. No wonder his division was the busiest in the city.

He grinned wryly to himself. He was getting to be an opin-

ionated, intolerant old fart. Guess he'd been seeing too much of
the seamy side of civilization. Civilization? More like a goddamned jungle! But that was unfair. In this specimen of civilization you double-lock every window and door at night. In the jungle they sleep in open huts. . . .

They cruised slowly down the boulevard, caught in the stream
of traffic, eyed by the girls strolling on the sidewalk and lounging
in doorways.

Harry'd spent the morning making out his reports on the mugging and he'd brought the paperwork to Stein himself. The lieutenant had given him a dirty look. "I suppose you did remember
to notify IHD and have them put this on the Chief's log," he'd
growled, dripping sarcasm. "Or were you too eager to hit the
sack?" "Listen," Harry'd answered, "with five days to go, I need
my beauty sleep more than an at-a-boy!"

He'd turned the investigation of the mugging itself over to Pete.
He himself was much more interested in the victim, Muller, than
in the punks who wasted him.

He turned to his partner.

"How'd you make out with PATRIC?" he asked.

Pete had spent a good deal of the day with the Pattern Recognition & Information Correlation computer checking out the crime
MO, refining and re-submitting until he'd nailed down the exact
information he wanted.

"Okay," he said. "Super sleuth kicked out a bull's-eye hit. I've
got enough print-outs to wipe my ass for a year."

"And?"

"If it wasn't the Vicelords—it's gotta be Billy Graham."

"That's what I figured."

"Bigfoot says they're laying low."

"That your snitch with the limp?"

"Yeah. He says the Vicelords are keeping a real low profile. A
sure sign the word is out to be invisible. He says there's talk that
two of the lords are in the fire for bringing down the heat on the
gang."

"Okay." Harry sighed. "So it'll only be a matter of time before
they have names."

"Yeah." Pete glanced at his partner. "How'd you make out with Muller?"

Harry shrugged.

"Negative," he said. "The guy doesn't exist. Weird. It doesn't make sense." He pulled out a small notebook. He opened it. "Records and Identification—negative," he said. "Department of Motor Vehicles—negative. Movie-industry union locals and guilds —negative. Utilities—negative. Telecredit—negative. Hell, nobody's heard of an Ernest Muller residing at the King's Court in Hollywood." He sounded exasperated. Frustrated. Angrily he flipped the page in his notebook.

"Immigration and Naturalization—negative," he continued, disgust in his voice. "Criminal Intelligence and Investigation in Sacramento—negative, dammit!" He looked up at Pete. "Hell, if CII never heard of the guy, he's not *in* California!" He tightened his lips in annoyance. "I even jumped the gun and sent a query to the FBI. Figured the guy might be a war criminal or something, and the mugging could be considered federal."

"Reaching, aren't you?"

"Gave them Ernest Muller AKA Ernst Helmut Müller. No dice so far."

"Whoever he was, he's dead," Pete said unconcernedly. "So who cares? As long as we get the punks who did it."

I care, Harry thought. I want to find out who—or what—Muller was. *I* do. He touched his jacket pocket. In it rested a creased and dog-eared snaphot. A picture of a German forest cabin.

Perhaps it wasn't kosher to keep it. But what the hell—it wasn't actual evidence in the mugging case. And he *had* to know.

"Crazy," Pete mused. "What made Muller keep that old Nazi document? Hiding it in a hollow table leg, for crissake!"

"Who the hell knows?" Harry shrugged. He himself would give a year of retirement benefits to know. And what about the snapshot?

"Have you asked Leif?"

"My son the shrink?"

"He might have some good ideas, Harry. What kind of guy would do a thing like that?"

"Yeah. I know."

"He's done pretty good for the department in a lot of cases."

Harry nodded. "I tried to get him on the phone. He was with a patient."

"Why don't you get him called in? As a referral? We can make a pretty good case for it being a special."

"Yeah. We'll see." Harry sounded reluctant.

Pete gave him a sidelong glance. He said nothing.

Harry frowned in thought. His son, Leif, who held a doctorate in psychology, had quite often been used by the department as a referral psychologist on special cases. He was a regular. But never on one of Harry's own. He wondered if he'd consciously steered away from working with his son. Having him act in an advisory capacity. Or if it had just—happened. Harry had wanted Leif to join the department. He'd had visions of the two of them working together as an investigation team. The department's crack team. That had been a long time ago. Before Edith passed on. But Leif had been interested in psychology, clinical psychology, and at thirty-one already had a nice practice going. At least he worked for the department in some capacity. And perhaps he, Harry, had not worked with his son because he'd felt reluctant to accept anything but a full commitment to the job. Perhaps . . . Then—maybe this would be a good case to work on together. It would be the last chance. He'd see. . . .

They were getting closer to Western, headed for a couple of two-bit bars just around the corner from Hollywood.

They'd lucked out. Williams in Vice had recognized the name of the hustler outside Lassen's. Titi. She was a chicano. Titi. From Tijuana? Probably illegal. Worked out of a couple of shabby bars on Western. Early twenties. Dark complexion. Shouldn't be too difficult to spot. Most of the whores on Western were black. Few chicano hookers ventured outside the barrio. Harry looked at his watch. Should be about time for the street hustlers to come out. Hopefully, Titi hadn't picked up her first trick yet.

Pete turned from Hollywood onto Western. Here the street joints were even more raunchy and crude. Tawdry hole-in-the-wall dumps advertising "Girls! Girls! Girls!" or "Dirty Dolly's— Nude Wrestling." Sex shops, peepshows and sex parlors—"Adult

Pleasures—Sexy Young Girls in Bed!" Sex, sex, sex. "Open All Night." Here the bars were real "toilets." Prostitutes—male and female—hustling their bodies bold as bluejays, carnivorously watching every potential trick. Lost souls strung out on drugs . . .

"Oral Love," promised a paint-chipped sign over a curtained storefront. A promise that could not possibly be fulfilled. *Love?*

Outside, two specimens of the S-M crowd loitered, lovingly admiring a pair of slave bracelets. Harry particularly detested the sado-masochists who'd made Hollywood their special stomping ground. He loathed busting some creep who'd deliberately invite manhandling, writhe in ecstasy and groan—"Oooh! Do it to me! I love it! Do it to me!"—as he was being handcuffed. It made Harry feel as if he were part of some obscene, kinky sex act.

Pete pulled the car over to the curb and stopped. Ahead, across the street, a broken neon sign sputtered: AL'S POT UCK. The missing letter would be an L, Harry thought. Although in this neighborhood you never knew. . . .

"That's it." Pete nodded toward the bar.

"I'll check it out," Harry said.

"Be my guest." Pete sounded bored.

Harry crossed the street in the middle of the block. At the corner to an alley a black hooker was having a loud and profane argument with her pimp. A length of heavy steel chain dangled from her hand as the man pushed her repeatedly in the chest.

Welcome to Western, Harry thought, as he ducked into AL'S POT UCK.

The dimly lit place was pretty empty. A dank stink of beer and stale tobacco smoke assailed his nostrils. At one of two tables in the rear a couple of young men were shooting pool. Another couple of men were watching, looking bored. In a booth sat two more men, one mature, heavy-set, one in his early teens, with eyes obviously for nobody but themselves. A buxom black girl was worrying a pinball machine near the door, and two more girls sat at the bar—at opposite ends.

One black. One chicano.

Harry went up to the bar. The bartender, a thin, pimply-faced young man with scrawny hair, dirty fingernails and a personality like a sweaty palm, looked at him from hooded eyes.

"Hey, buddy," Harry said, "You gotta girl in here named Titi?"

The bartender's eyes made an almost imperceptible flitting motion toward the chicano girl at the far end before he caught himself.

Good, Harry thought. But not good enough . . .

"Who wants to know?" the bartender asked, his high-pitched voice hostile.

"I do," Harry said pleasantly. "Investigator Harry Bendicks, Hollywood Division." He leaned toward the bartender, his voice conspiratorial. "I'll show you my pretty badge—if you want me to empty your fucking joint!"

"Okay, okay," the bartender said hastily. "I'll take your word for it. But I don't know no Titi."

He turned toward the cash register on the back counter and picked up a handleless cup with a few coins in it.

"Anyway—she ain't here," he finished.

"How do you know that—if you don't know her?" Harry asked.

The bartender shrugged. He opened the cash register and dumped the coins into the drawer, ringing up NO SALE.

Harry grinned to himself. Subtle he ain't! he thought wryly.

"I know most all of the girls that come in here," the bartender stated flatly. "There ain't no Titi."

Harry said nothing. He let his awareness take stock of his surroundings. The NO SALE sign had had its effect. The two men in the booth had stopped their intimate whispering. They were watching Harry uneasily. He could feel the hard eyes of the three hookers fixed on him. The bartender was studiously avoiding him. One of the men moved from the pool-table area and took up a watchful position at a darkened jukebox. A pimp looking out for one of his chicks? He was nattily dressed. There's a lot of money in pussy. . . .

Harry got up. He walked to the far end of the bar and sat down next to the chicano girl.

"Hi, Titi," he said pleasantly.

The girl looked at him, her huge, dark eyes filled with antagonism and apprehension.

"How you know me?" she said, her soft Mexican accent both

appealing and exciting despite her unfriendly tone of voice. "I don't know you."

"That's right, doll baby," Harry said. "You don't."

Pretty little thing, he thought—almost regretfully. How the hell did she end up in a dump like this? He stopped himself. He'd seen too damned much to ask a moronic question like that. But— every time he ran into one of those young, vulnerable-looking types . . .

"But I know you," he finished.

"You the vice?"

"Right again."

"Why you hassle me?" Quick anger flared in the girl's dark eyes, quickly suppressed. "I done nothing. I was not—soliciting—you!"

Even that word sounded pleasant in the girl's euphonious accent, Harry thought. He smiled. Put her at ease. The only way to make her open up.

"But I'm buying, honey," he said with a broad grin. "I want to buy you a drink—and ask you a few questions." He motioned to the bartender.

"Yeah?" Titi sounded puzzled, suspicious. "What questions? What about?"

The bartender came over. "Yeah?" he inquired sullenly.

"What's your name?" Harry asked pleasantly.

"Eh—Bill," the man answered, startled.

"Bill—I want you to meet a friend of mine. Titi." Harry grinned. "Titi, this is Bill."

The bartender and the girl stared at him as if his ears were on backward.

"How about a drink here, Bill?"

The bartender cleared his throat. He rubbed his sweaty palms on his dirty apron. What the hell was coming down?

"What d'you want?"

"Nothing for me, Bill," Harry confided. "I *never* drink on duty!" He was dying for a beer, but he had long since learned that a cop can't focus on his target through the bottom of an empty glass. A little booze in the blood could easily blur that one tiny clue that might break a case . . . a fleeting change of expression or tone of voice, a look in the eyes or an involuntary gesture, the little artery in the temple that would beat with sudden guilt—that one little telltale indication so easily missed. "Bring Titi here whatever she wants," he ordered.

"Gin and tonic," Titi said firmly.

Harry grinned to himself. Spunky damned kid. He knew she was taking him. And he was sure she was quite aware that he knew. He kind of admired her for it. Gin and tonic. The classic sucker drink. You can't tell if there's any booze in the damned thing. You can't see it—and you can hardly taste it. The bartender would pour her straight tonic and charge him for a full drink. A buck fifty. And Titi would collect an extra half a buck later.

Bill, the bartender, brought the drink.

"Buck fifty," he said to Harry, a challenge in his squeaky voice as if he anticipated an argument.

Harry paid. The girl was watching him. When they were alone she asked:

"What you want?"

"Last night," Harry said, "you picked up a John—"

"Says who?" Titi flared.

"—and took him over on Jaymar," Harry finished.

The girl suddenly looked frightened.

"Why you ask me a question like that?" she said. "Is no big deal." She was trying to sound unconcerned, pass over the question, make it seem of less importance than it was. "You can't prove nothing!"

"Get it on, Titi. I'm not trying to," Harry said quietly. "I'm only interested in information. Not in anything *you* may or may not have done." He looked closely at her. "I don't give a shit about your hustling, Titi. I want information about a stiff!"

Titi's warm brown color suddenly turned dead gray. She licked her lips with a quick dart of a pink tongue.

"I—I don't know nothing," she whispered.

Harry's face hardened. His voice grew cold. "Maybe. Maybe not. But you'd better start answering some questions—or I might begin to think you *are* involved."

"I am not!"

"How about it, then? The John?"

"I . . . He was just a date. I don't know him. Honest."

"Where'd you pick him up?"

"On—on Hollywood."

"Where were you taking him?"

"To—the Adams."

Harry knew the joint. A flea-bag hotel with 400-percent occupancy.

"On Jaymar?"

Titi nodded.

"Was he your first trick that night?"

Titi shook her head.

"Then—someone else had paid for the trick pad?"

The girl nodded.

"Tell me about it."

"About—what?"

"Cut it, Titi! You know damned well about what."

The girl cringed. "We—we found him." Her voice was low. "Lying in—in the street."

"Dead?"

She nodded, her eyes wide and frightened.

"What did you do then?"

"My date—the John—he, he knew the guy."

"Did he say from where?"

"Yeah. He said the guy lived in the same place he did."

"Did he say where?"

Titi shook her head. "No."

The King's Court, Harry thought. Back to square one. The King's Court.

"Did your date touch the body?" he asked.

"No."

"Did you?"

Titi looked at him in horror. "No! He was—dead."

"How do you know?"

"He—he didn't move. And—and his head was all bloody. And his eyes were open. There was—dirt on them. Right on—on the eyes. And they were looking—looking right at you. But—dead . . ." She lowered her head. She was shivering.

Harry snapped his fingers at the bartender. "Bill," he called, his voice suddenly authoritative. "Get her another drink. A real one!"

The bartender quickly brought a shot of cognac. Titi downed it, using the tonic as a chaser.

"Okay, Titi," Harry said, not unkindly. "You're doing good."

She looked up at him. Her color was coming back. The shot worked fast.

Harry watched her. Christ—just a kid. He couldn't control himself, however corny it would sound.

"What the hell are you doing here, Titi?" he asked quietly. "What the hell are you *doing?*"

The girl shrugged. She suddenly looked even younger. Forlorn.

"It ain't so bad," she said. "There's worse things can happen to you than flatbacking it." She looked at him, a small, bitter smile on her lips. "My life may be a pile of crap—but it is the only pile of crap I got. The Johns—they do not buy *me*. Not me inside. They rent my body for a few minutes. That is all they get. Is no big deal." Her look grew defiant. "Listen. It's lucky I got a piece of equipment that can bring in the bread!" It was obvious that she was deliberately trying to be hard-bitten and crass. Harry chose to ignore it.

"One more thing, Titi," he said. "Your—date. Did he call the police to inform them of the stiff?"

Titi nodded. "From the liquor store."

"What did you do then?"

"Nothing." The girl shrugged. She gave him a crooked smile. "He said he wasn't in the mood no more."

"Where'd you go?"

"Back. Here."

"And he?"

"Beats me."

"Last question. Can you describe this date—this John you were with?"

"Sure." She bit her lip in concentration. "He was about this much taller than me." She held her fingers four inches apart. "I am five feet four. He had short, straight hair. Dark brown. No beard or nothing." She pursed her lips and looked into space as if seeing her date hovering out there somewhere "He was not fat, not thin, but—how you say?—slender. He wore tan pants, a blue shirt with stripes and a dark-brown coat. Some kind of rough material. His shoes were—eh—*sucio*—dirty. No shine. He was not chicano. White boy—maybe twenty-three. Twenty-four. No much more. He speak as if he had good education. Maybe high school, even. And—and he had been hurt. Once. Long ago. He had scar on his eye. His right eye." She looked at Harry. "That is all I remember."

Harry gaped at her. He'd give his eye teeth anytime for a description as complete and detailed as that from one of the patrol officers. The manager of the King's Court should have no difficulty in recognizing his tenant.

He rose. He looked at the girl at the bar. Perhaps . . .

"Hey," Titi said, giving him a cynical smile. "How about a tip? For a drink?"

Harry threw a buck on the counter.

"Give her a shot," he said to the bartender.

Without looking back, he left.

59 KNOWN NAZI CRIMINALS IN THE U.S.

WASHINGTON—An ex-Immigration Service investigator named Anthony De Vito, who wants to see justice done before it is too late, has supplied the Immigration and Naturalization Service with a list of 59 high-ranking Nazis and Nazi war criminals from the Hitler era still at large in the United States.

4

Harry was tooling down Santa Monica Boulevard toward the Alpha Beta Market on the corner of Elwood.

First thing that morning he and Pete had called on the manager of the King's Court. The man had been less than overjoyed at seeing them, but from Harry's detailed description it had been impossible for him not to give them the identity of the tenant they were looking for.

John Ellison was the name of the young man. He worked at a supermarket. He'd already left for work.

John, Harry'd thought. How appropriate . . .

Pete had taken off to light a fire under his snitch and get the latest street talk about the Vicelords. Harry would tackle Titi's date. It was the way he wanted it. The man had known Muller. Perhaps he'd finally get some straight dope on the ex-SS man. And the snapshot . . .

The supermarket was part of a shopping center, and the parking lot was full when Harry pulled in. He circled it once. Then he saw a woman, her arms full of packages, making for her car, and he pulled up, positioning himself so that he could swing into the space when she left. He stopped and waited.

The woman took her sweet time. The packages had to be stowed in the back seat. And then there was a touch-up of lipstick and a comb-out of the hair without which some women drivers can't seem to start a car. Finally she backed out and drove away.

Harry was starting to turn into the empty spot when a small sports car sped up on the inside, neatly cut him off and swung into the space.

Harry came to an abrupt stop. He got out of his car and met the driver of the sports car as he was leaving.

"Excuse me," Harry said. "Didn't you see me waiting for this space?"

The driver, still in his teens, looked Harry up and down, an insolent smirk on his face.

"So?"

"You cut me off."

"So?"

"Would you please move your car so I can have the space I was waiting for?"

The young man gave a short laugh. "Go fuck yourself, you old cocksucker!" He was enjoying himself.

Harry's mien didn't change. "I beg your pardon?" he said.

"You heard me."

"I'm afraid I didn't. Would you mind repeating it?"

"Sure. I said, go fuck yourself, you old cocksucker!"

Harry brought the badge out of his pocket and shoved it in the young man's face.

"That's what I thought I heard," he said, his voice suddenly harsh with authority. "You're under arrest!"

The young man's eyes grew wide in alarm.

"Hey!" he exclaimed, suddenly high-voiced with fear. "I didn't do anything. You can't arrest me! I have my rights! What for?"

"Section 27–44. Using obscene language in public."

"But—"

"Hands on the car!" Harry ordered brusquely. "Legs apart!"

"But—"

"*Move!*"

The young man started as if he'd received a physical blow. He leaned against his car. Harry kicked his legs apart. Quickly he patted him down. He could feel the boy trembling under his touch.

"Okay. Turn around. Let me see your driver's license."

The young man started to fumble his wallet from his back pocket.

"Look, officer," he pleaded, his voice shaky. "I—I'm sorry. I—I didn't know you were a cop."

"Or you would have called me a pig instead of a cocksucker, is that it?"

"No. No, sir! I—"

"You wouldn't have called me anything, right?"

"Yes, I—"

"You only call other citizens dirty names, right?"

"Right. No. I mean—"

"Let me see your license," Harry said with disgust.

The young man opened his wallet and held it out to him.

"Take it out of your wallet."

The young man obeyed. His fingers were awkward. He handed Harry the license. Harry inspected it.

"You still live at this address, Mr. Latimer?"

"Yes." The young man looked at Harry, eyes moist and imploring. His lips trembled. "Please," he said. "I'm sorry. I didn't mean anything. I live at home. My father—" His voice broke.

"I'm sure he'll be proud of you," Harry said, flat-voiced.

"Please, officer. Please don't arrest me. Please let me go!" He sobbed. One convulsive sob.

Harry glared at him, hard-eyed. He took out his notebook. He began scribbling in it. The boy watched him fearfully.

"I'm making a note of your name, Mr. Latimer," Harry said. "It will be circulated in the department." He looked up at the trembling young man. "If you ever get in trouble again—if you get any kind of citation, even a parking ticket, we'll throw the book at you!" He gave the young man back his license. "Now—get out of here!"

He turned and walked back to his car.

By the time he started up, the parking space was free and clear.

He grinned to himself. It had been a lot of bull he'd handed that young punk. But at least there'd be one careful and courteous driver on the road.

For a while . . .

The manager of the supermarket looked at Harry's ID.

"Yes, officer. John—Mr. Ellison—works here. In produce. He's probably in the back." He frowned. "Is he—is there any trouble?"

"Thank you," Harry said. "No trouble. Just a few routine questions." He put his ID away. "I'll find him."

"I can show you the way," the manager said, a shade too eagerly. "Be glad to."

"That won't be necessary," Harry said firmly. The last thing he needed was an audience.

Titi's description of her date had been perfect. Even from the back there was no mistaking the young man busy stacking empty tomato crates in the rear produce-storage room of the market. Harry walked up to him.

"Mr. Ellison?" he said. "John Ellison?"

The young man turned. "Yes?"

Harry started. Titi had been generous in her description of the scar. It ran angrily from the young man's temple across his right eye, pulling it down toward his cheek, giving him a disturbing, slightly grotesque look. A mental picture of Charles Laughton as Quasimodo flashed through Harry's mind. How the hell could that old asshole Lassen have missed that? But he knew he was being unfair. It was only the startling effect of seeing it close up and unexpectedly that gave the scar its prominence. It could have been missed at a distance if the head had been slightly turned. Anyway, what the hell difference did it make? He was talking to the guy right now, scar and all. He had an extraneous thought. That scar probably accounted for a young man like Ellison picking up a hooker. . . .

He showed his badge.

"Mr. Ellison, my name is Bendicks. Investigator Harry Bendicks. Hollywood Division. I'd like to ask you a few questions."

"Yeah. Eh—okay." Ellison suddenly looked apprehensive. It wasn't lost on Harry. "What about?"

"Two nights ago, Mr. Ellison, while in the company of a—a girl named Titi," Harry said, "on Jaymar Street north of Franklin, you came upon the body of a man lying in the street, is that correct?"

Ellison looked at him, wide-eyed. "How do you . . . I mean— yeah." His face was working nervously. "I was—you know—"

"Please tell me what happened."

"Yeah. Sure. We—we were coming down the street, you know, and we—eh—well, it was dark, you know, and we saw this man lying on the sidewalk."

"You knew the man? You could identify him?"

"Yes. It was Mr. Muller. His name is—eh, was—Ernest Muller, I think. He lives—eh, I mean, lived at the same place as me. The King's Court."

"What did you do?"

"Do?"

"Yes. What did you do when you discovered the body? Did you touch it?"

"Hey, no, man. He was dead!"

"You subsequently made a report by telephone to the police. Why did you not identify yourself?"

Ellison shuffled uneasily. "Well, you know, I didn't want to get, you know, involved and all that. I figured, as long as they knew . . ."

Harry was watching the young man thoughtfully. He acted nervous and fidgety.

"Is there anything else you can tell me about Mr. Muller?" he asked.

"No. I don't, you know, I don't *know* the guy. Only to say hello and that sort of thing. That's all. I—I can't tell you anything else."

"Tell me exactly what happened, Mr. Ellison," Harry insisted.

"Well, I—eh, we saw Mr. Muller lying in the, you know, the street. We—looked at him. Just looked, you know. He was obviously—eh, he was dead. And then I—I made the call to the, you know, the police. From Lassen's Liquor Store on the corner. And then Titi left—and I went home, you know, to the Court. And that's all. That's—eh, everything. . . ."

"Did you see anyone in the vicinity?"

"No. Nobody at all. The street was, you know, empty."

"Where did the girl go?"

"I don't—I mean, I don't know."

"You knew she was a prostitute, did you not?"

"Yeah . . . Well, you know, I'm not really into the, I mean, the —eh—prostitute scene. Really. It was just, you know, eh—"

He stammered himself into an embarrassed silence. He was beginning to perspire.

"And that's the full story?" Harry asked.

Ellison nodded earnestly. "Yeah. Like I told you."

Harry contemplated the sweat-nervous young man. It was the usual reaction. Nervousness. Even perfectly innocent citizens got uneasy when they were questioned by an investigator. He guessed everyone had something to hide. Their guilty consciences made them sweat. Leif had once said something like that, he remembered.

But there was something else too. The hunch. That indefinable something which every investigator developed after questioning hundreds of suspects. The kind of hunch that was impossible to explain—but was seldom wrong.

He'd known it—along with all his buddies—in the CIC during the war. He'd known it as an investigator with the LAPD. He knew it now.

Ellison was not telling all he knew. Why?

And how to crack him?

Right now?

He suddenly grinned to himself. The incident in the parking lot gave him an idea. Time for a little innocent bluff . . .

He looked at Ellison, his expression that of a bereaved bloodhound. He slowly shook his head.

"I'm sorry, Mr. Ellison," he said, his voice sepulchral, "but I'm afraid I'll have to take you in."

"Ta-take me in!" Ellison flushed.

"For questioning in depth, Mr. Ellison. Perhaps—arrest."

Ellison looked stricken.

"You have the right to remain silent," Harry intoned with solemn monotony, finishing the "rights" as Ellison looked more and more terrified. He reached back to his belt under his jacket and brought out his handcuffs.

Ellison stared at them, horror on his flushed face. The scar across his eye burned bright red.

"What—what for?" he stammered. "I—I had nothing to do with —with Mr. Muller's death. I swear it!"

"Perhaps, Mr. Ellison, perhaps." Harry shook his head regretfully. "Unfortunately, your story differs from that of—eh, your companion."

Ellison stared at him. "The girl? But—that's impossible. I'm telling you the truth!"

"Well, Mr. Ellison, if you *are* telling the truth—*all* of the truth —you have nothing to worry about. It will all be established in the interrogation—after you have been booked."

"Please. Don't—arrest me! I'll—I'll lose my job. I *am* telling you the truth. I had nothing to do with it. Believe me. That—girl *couldn't* have said anything else. Please believe me!"

Harry contemplated the frightened young man, a deep frown on his face. He was interested in observing that under real stress Ellison dropped his annoying "you know's". . . .

"Well," he said slowly. "You and she were not together all the time, were you? You said you didn't know *where* she went."

Ellison blanched. "No. Not—all the time. I—I told you. She left after I'd made the call."

"I—see," Harry said significantly. "Turn around, please. Put your hands behind your back."

"Wait! Please!" Ellison sounded frantic. "There is—one thing. . . ."

"Yes?"

"You—you won't have to arrest me if I tell you *everything* now, will you? If I *swear* it's the truth? Will you?"

Harry looked properly hesitant. "Well. If there is no reason for a thorough interrogation . . ." He let the sentence hang.

Ellison licked his lips. "Okay. There is one more thing. That's—that's probably what Titi told you. She—must have seen me."

He took a deep breath. He was trembling slightly.

"I—I didn't mean to do anything wrong. But—when I walked back to my place, I—I knew I'd have to pass by where Mr. Muller was. So—I went across to the other side of the street. You understand. And—and that's where I—I found it."

"Found what?" Harry was at once fully alert.

"The wallet. Mr. Muller's wallet."

"How do you know it was *his* wallet?" Harry shot the question at him.

"Well, I—I picked it up. I was, you know, curious. It wasn't that I thought there'd be, you know, any money in it or anything like that. There wasn't." He blinked his eyes rapidly. "I—I know I should have turned it in. But—I didn't want to get involved. I was afraid that—that I'd be suspected. Of killing him, I mean. If I had his wallet. And I thought if I threw it back you could perhaps trace it to me. I've—I've seen all that stuff, you know, on TV. And I—"

"What *did* you do with it?"

"I—I wanted to get rid of it, you know, so no one would find out I'd had it. Because—I'd done, I mean, nothing wrong. . . ."

"Mr. Ellison!" Harry said sharply. "What did you do with Muller's wallet?"

"Nothing. I mean, I got it right here. In my locker."

"Get it!"

Ellison hurried to a row of old, banged-up metal lockers in the back of the area. Harry followed him. Ellison unlocked one of the spaces, reached in and brought out a wallet. He handed it to Harry.

Quickly Harry opened it.

The money compartment was empty. He had expected it to be. But a few cards and papers had been slipped into the side compartments. He took them out. One was a blue card. He stared at it.

How—stupid!

How goddamned *stupid*, he thought with deep disgust. What the hell was the matter with him? Making a rookie mistake! He must be getting old.

He turned the card over in his hand.

Muller was suddenly no longer a mystery.

Dammit—he should have known!

AFFILIATED   PROPERTY   CRAFTSMEN
LOCAL 44   I.A.T.S.E., A.F. OF L.

read the printed legend on the blue card. Above it had been typed: PROPERTY.

Muller had been a studio property man. The manager had said he worked in the movie industry.

There was a damned good reason why Harry had been unable to find any trace of Ernest Muller. Anywhere.

The card said, *Issued to: Ernest Helmut.*

Muller was using his middle name as his professional name. Why? That was something Harry still had to find out.

But he *should* have thought to run the name Helmut through all the damned ID traces as well as Muller. And what the hell was wrong with Pete?

He cursed himself.

Finding that damned snapshot must really have shaken him.

He had a creepy feeling in his guts that it was the key to some-thing.

Something big . . .

3 FACE EXPULSION AS NAZI
WAR CRIMINALS

WASHINGTON (AP)—U.S. immigration authorities began deportation proceed-ings Wednesday against three aliens charged with persecuting and killing hundreds of Jews in Latvia and Lithuania during World War II.

5

Harry felt irritable with dissatisfaction and a growing sense of "missing out." With the exception of the union membership card, the items in Muller's wallet were in the same impersonal personal category as the man's belongings in his home—totally unimportant and uninformative: a Los Angeles Public Library card; a 1977–78 pocket calendar; a slip of paper with a tele-phone number that turned out to be a soundstage at MGM; a business card from a prop-rental place (STAGE ONE—*Props for All Occasions*); a page from a current bus schedule between Hollywood and Burbank; and a form-printed rent receipt from the King's Court for the month of March, made out to Ernest Muller.

After his talk with Ellison, Harry had returned to the King's Court and confronted the manager with his Muller/Helmut dis-covery. It had been a frustrating if not downright humiliating experience. The manager had shown no surprise whatsoever. Of course he knew that Muller used his middle name in his profession. Lots of studio people in all areas of endeavor used separate private and professional names. Why hadn't he mentioned it? Because nobody asked him. And he had not been aware that it was up to *him* to instruct the police investigators in the correct procedures to follow. Harry had seethed—but he'd held his peace.

Dammit! He'd asked for it. . . .

But the upshot was, he knew damned little more about the ex-Nazi than he had before.

Ex? Maybe not. Just because they lost the war, that didn't necessarily mean the bastards had changed their views.

Muller? Or Helmut? From what crimes was he running away? Seeking sanctuary in the States? Who—and what—was he?

The union official at Local 44 on Sunset had been unimpressed and efficiently cooperative. He had at once been able to put his finger on the information Harry requested.

Ernest Helmut had been a union member for two years and seven months. He held a property man's card. His evaluation report from the Qualification Committee when he joined had been good. The official had taken Harry to the Call Board in a downstairs office. Helmut had been working for an independent company, Handel Productions, shooting at Valley Studio. The property master on the job was one Victor Strand. Helmut had failed to report on the job the day before, and the union had sent a replacement. They'd had no word from Helmut.

Harry didn't tell them they never would. . . .

The security guard at the Valley Studio main gate on Olive Avenue bent down and peered at Harry, not recognizing him.

"Handel Productions," Harry said. "They're shooting a picture on this lot. Where can I find them?"

"Do you have an appointment?" the guard asked.

Harry showed him his ID. "No," he said. "But I want to talk to someone in the company. Who's the head man?"

"Mr. Handel, of course. He's the executive producer," the guard said. "But you'll want to see the director, Mr. Buter. Irwin Buter. Very talented young man. I'm sure you know his work."

Harry shrugged. "Never heard of him."

The guard looked personally affronted. "He's one of the best action directors in the business today," he said. "In fact, one of the best I can remember. And I've been with the studio a long time. Ever since the Warners . . ."

"Can you direct me to where the company is shooting?"

The guard turned and entered his cubicle. He consulted a mimeographed list hanging on the wall and returned to Harry.

"They're not working on this lot," he said. "They're over at the Spread."

"The Spread?"

"It's one of the studio back lots," the guard explained. "It's not far. A few minutes. The main entrance is on Elm Street and Hollywood Way."

"Thanks." Harry wheeled his car around the guardhouse and drove off down Olive toward Hollywood Way.

It was going to be one of those days. . . .

The guard at the gate of the Spread directed him to the far area of the back lot. Park in the Western set, he told him, nobody's shooting there today.

Harry drove onto the lot. He crossed what appeared to be the quiet town square of a little Midwestern town, except for a row of vehicles pulled up along the Main Street: portable dressing rooms, wardrobe and make-up vans, generator trucks and vans marked ELECTRICAL and GRIPS, a big portable toilet trailer poetically named the HONEYWAGON in the industry, a couple of big gray buses and several smaller cars. Harry surmised it was a location caravan. Parked on the molded cobblestones, it effectively gave the lie to the reality of the grassy commons.

The Western street with its saloon, sheriff's office, wooden walkways and balconied hotel was filled with current-model automobiles—an incongruous sight, Harry thought, but certainly in keeping with the make-believe atmosphere of the place. He found a parking space next to an old open smithy strewn with rusty iron tools and old wagon wheels, left the car and walked toward the studio area next to the Western set. Rounding the corner of a clapboard building with a faded sign over the door reading LIVERY STABLE, he stopped dead in his tracks.

He was facing a group of men bristling with grenades and small arms. In their soiled gray uniforms and their squat, swastika-adorned steel helmets, they were a familiar, never-to-be-forgotten specter. *Nazis.*

Nazi Waffen SS soldiers!

Grimy faces turned toward him—and dismissed him without interest.

He felt himself go tense, aware of the adrenalin shooting through his system. He knew at once that the Nazi soldiers were movie extras, but so real did they look, so strong and deep were his own memories, that he reacted to the visual shock as though they were real.

He turned to one of them. "You," he said, startling himself with the unintended harshness in his voice. The guy was an actor, for crissake!, not the enemy. "Where can I find the director? Irwin Buter?"

The young man looked at him with surprise. He pointed. "Over there, I guess," he said. "Other side of the church. They're shooting in front of the jail."

"Thanks." Harry knew he sounded abrupt. He didn't care. It was partly embarrassment, partly remembered uneasiness. The hell with it. He started to walk briskly into the back-lot area used by Handel Productions and found himself in a German town heavily scarred by war. Buildings collapsed in heaps of rubble or fire-gutted into squat, skeletal emptiness. Brick-and-mortar ruins pockmarked by bullets and shrapnel, soot-blackened timbers pointing crazily skyward. Piles of household debris. Shell craters and the twisted, tortured, abandoned machinery of war.

It was a town Harry had been through. Countless times. Thirty-three years ago . . .

He walked past the church, a typical Bavarian village church, but badly shot up. The stained-glass windows were broken; half the onion-shaped cupola had been blasted away, the top of the steeple blown jaggedly open. The building fronted on a small square bustling with activity. In the center stood a 1914–18 War Memorial partly demolished.

An avalanche of cruel memories struck his mind. The war-ravaged German village, its half-timbered houses in ruins, was a grim replica of hundreds he'd seen in the war. The savage, indiscriminate devastation, the rubble, the dirt, the scorched tree stumps and the mangled military equipment deserted in the streets. The pitiful messages chalked on doors and boarded up windows . . . *Clara Singer hier i. d. Trümmer* (Clara Singer is here in the rubble), and the pathetic pleas . . . *Franz, lebst du? Erna* (Franz, are you alive? Erna) . . . A torn and grimy poster tacked on a splintered fence, HAMSTERIN—SCHÄME DICH! (Hoarder—Shame on You!) . . . and the crude propaganda battle-cries painted in white on still standing walls . . . HARTE ZEITEN, HARTE PFLICHTEN, HARTE HERZEN (Hard Times, Hard Duties, Hard Hearts). The ever-present drum-beat slogan, EIN VOLK, EIN REICH, EIN FÜHRER (One People, One State, One Leader) . . . It was all there before him, battering his memory. But so was a mass of unfamiliar equipment and a host of people busying themselves with it. Several tall steel-frame towers on wheels, crowned with huge spotlights; reflectors on spindly iron stands; floodlights and black flats mounted on metal poles—and, dominating it all, looking like a behemoth, a mammoth crane on the boom of which a camera was mounted. The place echoed with the din of many voices and sounds.

All the equipment and people formed a jumbled semicircle in front of a small section of the ruins. In the midst of a pile of rubble stood a young girl looking lovely and vulnerable, wearing an appealing short-sleeved blouse and a dirndl skirt.

Harry started toward the camera crane, carefully stepping across the thick electric cables that patterned the ground like dusty snakes. He was annoyed with himself for feeling a little awed at being on the set.

Suddenly a bell rang shrilly. At the same time a revolving red light on a stand close to Harry began to blink. A man's voice rang out: "Quiet on the set!"

At once all sounds stopped. Harry froze in his tracks. He stood stock still, utterly intimidated, hardly daring to breathe.

"Roll 'em!" a voice called out.

From the camera crane someone said, "Rolling," and a short

distance away, where a man wearing earphones was sitting before a sound console, a voice called, "Speed!"

A young man standing by the girl in the rubble held a slate up in front of her face, the diagonally striped clapstick spread open. "281 Apple Take 3!" he shouted. He slammed the clapstick shut with a definite clack and scrambled out of the way.

"Action!"

The girl threw up a hand in obvious alarm and shouted something. Harry couldn't make it out.

"Cut!"

The bell rang; the red light stopped flashing—and the general hubbub started up at once. Harry breathed again and walked over to the group of people gathered around the camera. He was aware of many voices all talking at once. "Is it a print?"—the voice of a girl holding a script and a stopwatch. "N.G. We'll do it again." The answer came from a handsome young man talking to an elderly one with a sort of smoky looking-glass hanging around his neck. "Aren't we still getting a reflection off that window?" the young man complained. "Check it." The elderly man called to someone off somewhere: "Barndoor the senior on two tower—just a hair!" The handsome young man turned to another man. "Les, give me a cookie on that wall behind her. Break it up." "Okay." The man hurried off.

Harry stepped up to the young man, who was obviously in charge. "Mr. Buter?" he asked.

The man turned to him. "Who are you?"

"Investigator Harry Bendicks," Harry answered. He held out his ID. "Hollywood Division."

The young man didn't look at Harry's ID. "Oh, Christ!" he exclaimed. He turned to the operator sitting on a small seat behind the camera on the crane boom. "Wally. Raise it just a hair. I think the angle is a little too low." "You got it," the operator said. Buter turned to Harry. "What do you want?"

"I'd like to ask you a few questions," Harry said. "About a man who worked as a property man for your company. A Mr.—"

Buter interrupted him. "Are you kidding? I'm right in the middle of a shot!" He turned and strode briskly toward the girl standing patiently in the rubble. "Shirley, honey," he called. "Just one more thing . . ."

Harry glared after him. So that was the oh-so-talented Irwin Buter. A still-wet-behind-the-ears, hot-shit director who'd never heard a shot fired in anger—directing a war picture, for crissake!

A bearded young man came up to Harry. "Investigator Bendicks?" he asked.

Harry nodded curtly. He was not ready yet to be friendly.

"I'm Mike," the young man continued. "Second AD. Assistant Director. I heard you introduce yourself to Buter." He smiled. "Can I be of help?"

"I'd appreciate being able to talk to someone," Harry growled. "I've been snubbed by the best"—he nodded toward the rubble pile, where Buter stood talking to the girl, his arm possessively around her shoulder, his mouth close to her ear—"but that guy is a master!"

Mike laughed. "Irwin's okay," he said. "Right now he's uptight. He's riding high. Had two big hits. But in this crazy business you're only as good as your last picture. It's pretty tough to stay on top."

"Is that where he is?"

"Sure. And going strong." Mike grinned. "He's got the busiest casting couch in town. They say he's never had any complaints. How else do you measure success?"

Harry was beginning to like the young AD. "I want a few words with him," he said. "Is he always that difficult to buttonhole?"

"As I said, he's a little edgy right now," Mike explained. "We're behind schedule. We're supposed to be taking off right now for some night location shooting at the beach. If we run late out there, it means golden time. Bad for the budget—and the director's reputation."

Harry contemplated the young man. "Did you know a man called Ernest Helmut?" he asked. "Worked for this company as a property man."

"Ernie? Sure," Mike said. "But he's not here. He was replaced."

"I know."

Something in Harry's voice made Mike look up quickly. "Anything happen to him?"

Harry nodded. "He was mugged," he said. "Killed."

"Jesus!" Mike was shocked. "That's what you want to talk to Buter about?"

Harry nodded. "That's it."

"Save your breath," Mike said. "Buter won't be able to tell you anything. You want to talk to Vic. Victor Strand. The Property Master on the show."

"He's second on my list."

"Promote him to first. But you won't get to see him today."

"Why not?"

"He's already taken off for the location. He finished loading his prop boxes half an hour ago—as soon as we started to shoot this last close-up insert."

"Prop boxes?" Harry asked.

"He's got five of them. It's where all the hand props are kept. Any item that's to be handled by the actors. Weapons. Personal things. Anything that's called for in the script—and what the Property Master anticipates might be called for."

"Where are these prop boxes kept when you're not filming?"

"On the set."

"With the weapons?"

"Sure. They're locked. They'd be damned hard to break into. Besides—the lot is guarded."

Harry looked pensive. He knew he was grasping at straws, but enough of them might make a worthwhile stack.

"Who has the keys to these prop boxes?" he asked.

"Vic," said the young AD. "They're his personal property. And his assistants on the show. He's got two property men."

"Helmut?"

Mike nodded. "Helmut."

"I'd like to see those boxes."

"Should be no trouble," Mike said. "Tomorrow. We'll be back shooting here in the afternoon. Got some pretty exciting action stuff scheduled. A stunt shot. From the church tower. And some great combat scenes. Why don't you come back then? You can talk to Vic then, too."

Harry thought it over. It might be better to do just that rather than try to force the issue now.

"Deal," he said.

"You might be interested anyway," Mike said. "As you can see, we're shooting a World War II epic. Good strong cast. Good script. *Hitler's Werewolves.* Not like in vampires or that kind of crap. These guys actually existed. They were Nazis. They—"

Harry suddenly felt cold. He let the young man talk on. He didn't listen. He knew about the Nazi werewolves. Only too damned well. A bunch of fanatics. Hitler Youth, SS men— even civilians, men and women, sworn to kill and destroy for Adolf—and to assassinate Ike. Assassination was their specialty. The werewolves had boasted on their radio station that they'd knock off the Lord Mayor of the city of Aachen, who'd been installed by the U.S. Military Government when it'd kicked the Nazi mayor out on his ass . . . and they had. And they'd also killed Smitty, one of Harry's CIC teammates, and a helluva nice guy.

They'd ambushed him. Killed his driver and left Smitty tied, sitting in his jeep. Alive. They'd gouged out his eyes, sliced off his ears and stuffed them in his mouth. They'd left a crudely lettered handbill protruding from his bloody mouth like a big, white, maggoty cigar:

BEWARE AMERICANS! THE WEREWOLVES ARE
STALKING YOU. THEY SEE ALL! THEY
HEAR ALL! THEY—KILL!

Hitler's Werewolves were not strangers to Harry. . . .

". . . we've shot most of the sequence already," Mike was saying. "This American Counter Intelligence agent and a German Fräulein are coming out of the building the CIC has taken over. The local jail. A couple of werewolves are laying for him." He handed Harry a script and pointed to a page. "Here. That's the scene. Take a look. Sorry about the coffee ring. We're just shooting the close-up dialogue insert—281A—of the girl, then we're through."

Harry took the script. . . .

277   T-2

EXT.   STREET IN FRONT OF JAIL.   DAY   Pan p.l

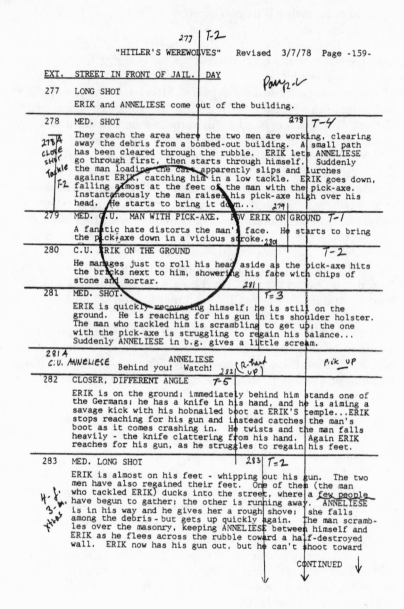

277   LONG SHOT

ERIK and ANNELIESE come out of the building.

278   MED. SHOT   278 T-4

278A
CLOSE
SHOT
Tackle   They reach the area where the two men are working, clearing
            away the debris from a bombed-out building. A small path
            has been cleared through the rubble. ERIK lets ANNELIESE
            go through first, then starts through himself. Suddenly
F-2   the man loading the cart apparently slips and lurches
            against ERIK, catching him in a low tackle. ERIK goes down,
            falling almost at the feet of the man with the pick-axe.
            Instantaneously the man raises his pick-axe high over his
            head. He starts to bring it down...   279

279   MED. C.U. MAN WITH PICK-AXE. POV ERIK ON GROUND T-1

A fanatic hate distorts the man's face. He starts to bring
the pick-axe down in a vicious stroke. 280

280   C.U. ERIK ON THE GROUND   T-2

He manages just to roll his head aside as the pick-axe hits
the bricks next to him, showering his face with chips of
stone and mortar. 281

281   MED. SHOT.   T=3

ERIK is quickly recovering himself; he is still on the
ground. He is reaching for his gun in its shoulder holster.
The man who tackled him is scrambling to get up; the one
with the pick-axe is struggling to regain his balance...
Suddenly ANNELIESE in b.g. gives a little scream.

281A
C.U. ANNELIESE   ANNELIESE   (R-hand   Pick up
            Behind you! Watch! 282   up)

282   CLOSER, DIFFERENT ANGLE   T-5

ERIK is on the ground; immediately behind him stands one of
the Germans; he has a knife in his hand, and he is aiming a
savage kick with his hobnailed boot at ERIK'S temple...ERIK
stops reaching for his gun and instead catches the man's
boot as it comes crashing in. He twists and the man falls
heavily - the knife clattering from his hand. Again ERIK
reaches for his gun, as he struggles to regain his feet.

283   MED. LONG SHOT   283 T-2

ERIK is almost on his feet - whipping out his gun. The two
men have also regained their feet. One of them (the man
4-f.   who tackled ERIK) ducks into the street, where a few people
3-in.   have begun to gather; the other is running away. ANNELIESE
Xtras   is in his way and he gives her a rough shove; she falls
            among the debris - but gets up quickly again. The man scramb-
            les over the masonry, keeping ANNELIESE between himself and
            ERIK as he flees across the rubble toward a half-destroyed
            wall. ERIK now has his gun out, but he can't shoot toward

CONTINUED

They'd been laying for Smitty, too.

Harry closed the script.

Hitler's Werewolves.

He'd hunted them once. Would he be doing it again? Or— someone like them?

The bell rang. The red light flashed.

"Action!" Buter called.

Action! Harry thought. That's what he needed. Action. He felt as if tracking down the dope on ex-SS man Muller was like trying to sprint in a sea of molasses wearing GI boots.

But he was too damned ornery to let it lie. Too damned stubborn. He'd find out about that bastard Ernest Helmut Muller. It would be his last act as a member of the LAPD . . . and some deep, reawakened CIC hunch told him it would be worth it.

EX-NAZI FACES DEPORTATION

Has Staved Off Order For 25 Years

WASHINGTON—Andrija Artukovic of Seal Beach, Calif., a former Nazi wanted in Yugoslavia on charges of murdering thousands of Serbs, Jews and gypsies, has been notified that he faces deportation proceedings, the *Times* learned Wednesday.

6

"I can think of two fairly obvious reasons," he said. "First—a basic insecurity. A reluctance to sever the final link to the past. A past where he might have felt taken care of. Secure." He smiled at his father. "How many of us hold on to our teddy bears well into adulthood?"

Leif Bendicks felt good. He freely admitted it to himself—and he knew why. It was the first time in—in as long as he had worked with the LAPD organic psychological personnel on an advisory referral basis—the first time his father had come to him and asked his advice. He felt as if they had reached a milestone. A milestone too long in showing up. And—being a psychologist—he wondered what could be so important to his father that it had brought them to this milestone now, on the eve of his retirement.

"Secondly," he said, "there could be a more practical reason for the man—Muller?—to hold on to a seemingly meaningless piece of paper."

"What do you mean?" Harry gave Leif full attention. He still felt vaguely uncomfortable soliciting advice from his son, and a little surprised at how knowledgeable and reasonable the boy sounded. But he was glad he'd taken Pete's suggestion and gone to see him. Professionally, as it were. And perhaps get a clue to what kind of nut would keep a thirty-three-year-old Nazi document hidden in a hollow table leg. . . .

Before leaving the studio earlier in the day, he'd called in from the back-lot security office. Pete was out, but had left word he'd meet Harry at the station later in the afternoon. It had given him a few hours' time—and Leif had been free.

He'd told his son all about the Muller case—but hadn't mentioned the dog-eared snapshot. Not yet. Leif had listened attentively and obviously understood. But Harry had an uneasy suspicion that he himself had sounded too damned—intense—about the whole thing. Perhaps he was.

He fidgeted with his cufflinks. It was a habit he had when he felt, well, a little unsure of himself. He was aware of it. He'd had those cufflinks forever. He'd had them made from the two brass emblems he'd worn on his collar tabs as a CIC agent during the war. Now he always wore them when he had on a shirt that didn't have buttons on the cuffs. Like now. Two little U.S. officer's emblems —a kind of symbol of the old days. His—teddy bear? The thought made him glance quickly at Leif—and take his fingers away.

"I mean, there's also the possibility that Muller kept the document," Leif was saying, "as a very practical hedge against the future." He looked at his father earnestly. "It may not sound rational. But one cannot expect rational thinking or rational behavior from someone who is irrational. Which Muller may well have been." He frowned lightly in concentration. "It's possible that Muller, in his own mind, foresaw a day in the future when he'd have to prove his *real* identity. His *real* allegiance." He stopped. He looked at his father, wondering.

Clearly, his father was extremely anxious to learn everything he could about Muller. Almost too anxious. Leif wondered why. It seemed not all that important. The man was dead. And apparently catching his killers was merely a matter of time. Why, then, was his father so obsessed with finding out about that particular mugging victim? The ex-Nazi angle? It was a dead-horse issue, really. He found himself much more interested in his father's obsession than in the ex-Nazi's possible motive for not "letting go." Was his father also loath to let go of the past? He looked at him. He wondered what Harry was really like. *Can* a child ever know about his parent?

He felt the familiar pang of regret that he and his father were not closer. Of course, they loved one another. They were—father and son. But a real closeness, the closeness that makes one human being part of another, was lacking. Had it ever been there?

His father had always been dedicated totally to his work, and there had been little time for father-son activities when Leif was a child. Or when he was growing up . . . and apart.

Leif remembered the first real clash between them. How painful it had been to him. It was in the middle '60s—he'd been barely twenty. The papers were full of the phrases of political extremism —police brutality and student radicalism and activism. He'd been fired by the excitement of a turbulent time. He had steered clear of the drug scene, realizing the dangers, and had not succumbed to peer pressure, unlike so many of his brilliant friends who, in their hunger for independence and identity, enslaved and destroyed themselves. But—he had joined in protests and demonstrations for causes in which he believed.

His father had been deeply angry and deeply hurt when his son —the son of a police officer—was arrested during a campus demonstration against some real or imagined racial discrimination. There had been a bitter argument between father and son. His mother had wept bitterly. And Leif had felt that his father had never really forgiven him.

Had he himself—believing this—kept aloof? Not wanting to run the risk of getting hurt? Perhaps . . .

"What kind of a man would he be?" Harry pressed. "Judging from the document, he couldn't have been much of a big shot. SS lieutenant is all." He frowned in thought. "On some sort of special duty—for the Führer, it said. But that was a long generation ago." He looked at Leif. "What was he? A war criminal? A political fugitive? Some sort of—agent?"

"He could have been any or all of those," Leif said. "I just don't know, Dad." How he wished he could come up with some magic-formula answer. "I'd need a lot more background information about the man to develop even a half-valid personality profile."

"Yeah, I know." Harry sounded disappointed.

"I'm sorry, Dad. But behavioral science isn't fortune-telling." He was sorry the instant he said it.

Harry stood up. "I'll have to come up with some more facts for you," he said unenthusiastically. He walked over to the window and looked out. The window opened onto a small inside courtyard planted with ferns and succulents.

Leif's office was located in a modest medical building on San Vicente near Wilshire. He hadn't made it big enough yet to have plush quarters in Beverly Hills and the rich, self-indulgent clients that went with them. He preferred it that way.

Harry stood staring out into space. Maybe he shouldn't have come. What had he expected anyway? That his son could somehow present the solution of the Muller mystery to him on a silver couch? Now there was that damned barrier between them again. That curtain of wary reserve which had first been drawn between them after that stupid incident in the '60s and had never completely disappeared since. He sighed. It had been the time Edith had taken ill. He knew she had been—concerned. When she died in '68 he had felt as if his world had come to an end, and in his grief —seeking something, someone, to lash out against—he'd even in his own bleak mind blamed his son, although he knew that was pure nonsense. Had his son felt the same way about him? Had each in turn "blamed" the other? He didn't know. He only knew that even when Leif lost his wife, Ellen, after less than a year of marriage, in a freak skiing accident in Colorado, he'd not been close enough to his son to offer any real, meaningful succor. That had been four years ago, and Leif had not remarried.

He thought back on how happy he and Edith had been when Leif was born. In a moment of Old World nostalgia they'd named the boy after the Viking explorer who discovered America, Leif Erikson. Leif—pronounced the Scandinavian way, *life,* and not the American way, *leaf* . . .

Leif had always loved his name—especially when he found out as a young boy that Leif Erikson's nickname was Leif the Lucky, and despite the unending puns, one worse than the other, that he and his parents had had to put up with. By now they'd heard them all . . . Living *Leif* to the fullest, his son had been called the *Leif* of the party countless times. He had experienced *Leif* in the raw as well as the thrill of a *Leif*time. One friend after another had bet his *Leif* that he, Leif, would succeed in his pursuit of the good *Leif* —although, unlike his father's, his *Leif* would not be at stake doing it. It had literally been worth his *Leif* to fend off puns in graduate school; he was forever being offered *Leif*savers—and of course he used to have his own weekly magazine. . . .

Once, when he was a teenager, Leif had made a list of all the outrageous puns on his name he could possibly think of. He'd reached 217. And then someone had casually dropped number 218—and he'd given up. Laughing at that had been one of the times Harry and his son had felt the closest.

"There is one more thing, Dad." Leif sounded reluctant. "Remote, perhaps. But it should be considered."

"What?" Harry asked.

Leif genuinely wanted to be of help to his father, and he resented that this first time it couldn't be with something concrete, rather than with a strange, nebulous obsession he didn't want to encourage. Yet he felt obliged to share everything he thought on the subject.

"Muller," he said slowly. "What you have told me about him— his almost antiseptic quarters as far as personal things were concerned, his use of at least two different names, the lack of bureaucratic information about him—it all could indicate a—a disturbed, a paranoid personality. A personality with an overwhelming need to remain—anonymous." He looked at his father. "Dad," he said gravely, "how do you know that the victim, Muller, is in fact the same man mentioned in the document?"

Harry started. He stared at his son. *The same man?* Ridiculous! Of course he was the same man. . . . Or—was he?

"As I said," Leif continued, "it is remote. But there *is* a possibility that the document you found didn't in fact refer to the Muller who was killed. He could have obtained it somehow. That's not difficult. Autograph dealers and military-souvenir shops often have such memorabilia for sale. There are many collectors interested in things of that sort. Muller could have gotten hold of the document. Perhaps it did bear his own name. Perhaps he began to identify with the Muller who originally owned it. He was obviously a loner. Perhaps he retreated into some mysterious mental world of his own. It is not unusual." He tried a little laugh and smiled at his father, who looked suddenly stricken. "After all," he said, "we still have several Napoleons in our mental institutions."

"It's got to be the same man," Harry said. He did not sound convincing. He felt cold.

"It's only a possibility, Dad. An alternate explanation. But—I don't think you can afford to ignore it."

Dammit, Muller is Muller! Harry thought. He felt angry. What kind of idiocy was his son handing him? . . . But he knew Leif was right. It *was* a possibility—however remote. And he *had* to check it out. He could do no less. Dammit!

"I'll look into it," he said. "Thanks." He looked at his watch. "I've got to run. Pete's waiting for me at the station." He looked sideways at his son. "Eh—if I can talk Stein into it, would you be interested in doing some—eh, consulting on this case?"

"Of course, Dad," Leif said. "Of course . . ."

Pete threw a couple of record folders onto the desk in front of Harry.

"There they are, Harry, old cock. Our Vicelord muggers. Picked them up this afternoon. Already booked. Murder One."

"Great," Harry said. Preoccupied, he fingered the reports. "Great . . ."

The case was closed.

The two punks had been caught—and were ready to receive their slaps on the wrist. Muller had been identified. . . . Dammit, he *had!* . . . He was probably a war criminal in hiding. According to the papers, there were still a lot of the bastards around. And not doddering old fools. Hell, he himself was of their time. And he still had a lot of damned good years left. Or the man—just possibly—was deranged, a nut. In any case, he was dead. So what difference did it really make? No one would be remotely interested in any further investigation; there were enough unsolved cases on the book.

The Muller case was a closed issue for everyone.

Except Harry.

And Harry had only three days left on the force.

He'd drop the whole damned mess—except for two things.

A faded, dog-eared snapshot.

And a hunch that refused to lie down and die . . .

TASK FORCE FORMED TO HUNT NAZI WAR CRIMINALS IN U.S.

WASHINGTON—The Immigration and Naturalization Service Wednesday announced the organization of a special unit to track accused Nazi war criminals who have taken refuge in the United States.

7

The afternoon was overcast when Harry arrived at the Valley Studio back lot. He wondered if the company would be shooting, but the set was teeming with activity.

Once again he felt an uneasy excitement—a heightened awareness—as he walked through the war-torn German village, all his senses unnaturally alert. Even the fake-front buildings with their plaster bricks and the grotesquely twisted street signs looked too damned real; they awakened long-dormant memories. He felt vaguely disturbed at seeing a group of Kraut soldiers and GIs sitting around together. Automatically he touched his gun in its shoulder holster—and felt sheepish doing it. But he couldn't help it.

The lighting and camera equipment had been set up in a different part of the back-lot set, this time in front of a large, official-looking building, gutted and badly damaged. And this time there was also a fire truck. A slogan had been painted on the scarred wall: UNSERE MAUERN BRACHEN—UNSERE HERZEN NICHT! (Our Walls May Be Broken—But Not Our Hearts!). Harry guessed the building represented the ruins of the Town Hall. The street before it was littered with rubble, and piles of debris had been pushed together to make a crude path.

Mike spotted him and came over. "See you made it," the AD said. "You're just in time for the big bang." He motioned toward the camera crane. "Buter is rehearsing the principals—then we'll shoot it."

"Find out anything about Helmut?" Harry asked.

"Not a thing. Buter'll talk to you after we wrap the set-up. But he doesn't know anything. And I've alerted Vic—that's the Property Master, Victor Strand—and he's all set to tell you anything he knows."

"Fine."

"Stick around. It won't be long. I'll have to leave you on your own."

"No sweat."

Harry walked over toward the camera crane.

Buter was sitting on the crane boom in the director's seat next to the camera. The boom had been raised a few feet in the air so that he had an overall view of the area.

Below stood two actors dressed as GIs. Harry recognized them. "Special Effects ready?" Buter called.

"All set," a voice boomed. "You've got two rows of squibs on the path. The first at the oil drum. The second six feet farther into the set."

"Okay . . . Bob! Take your own cue," Buter called. "Let 'em get close. Make it look real . . . but don't kill 'em! We need 'em for tomorrow!" He laughed at his own joke. "Okay. Stand by! We'll run it once more. Dry. No effects." He leaned down toward the two actors below. "Steve. Charlie. Give me a little more of a broken run. Make it look harder. More dangerous. Remember, you've got no real cover until you reach that pile of rubble. And the bastards are shooting at you! Let's do it once more."

The two actors walked off to their opening positions. Harry listened to the unfamiliar proceedings. Buter seemed to have everything well under control, he had to admit. Pretty big operation at that.

"Ready?" Buter called.

There was a muffled answer from the distance.

"Okay . . . Action!"

The two GIs began a fast, crouched, broken-field run down the rubble-strewn street, holding their carbines in both hands before them. They neared the oil drum off the path. "Squibs!" a voice rang out. The two men veered and sped on. And again: "Squibs!" The men jumped. They reached the pile of rubble and dove for cover.

"Hold it!" Buter called. "Hold it!" He leaned down toward the actors. "Steve! Don't buckle that helmet strap under your chin," he called. "Let it hang loose. The concussion from the explosion would take your bloody head off!"

Harry looked with grudging respect at the young director. He knew his business. Not only motion-picture making, but the realities of war. No damned-fool infantryman ever wore his helmet strapped down in combat. Buter was okay.

"Let's try it again," Buter called. "Dry run."

Mike came up to Harry accompanied by an older, sour-looking man.

"Officer Bendicks," Mike said, "this is Vic Strand, our Property Master. I've told him the kind of information you're after."

Harry nodded pleasantly to the older man. "Mr. Strand," he said.

The Property Master nodded back. He looked slightly put-upon.

"Let me know if there's anything I can do," Mike said. He left.

"Mr. Strand," Harry said, "what do you know about Ernest Muller—I mean Ernest Helmut?"

The man shrugged. "Nothing."

"But—you hired him."

"My regulars were busy. I needed a property man. Got him through the union."

"Helmut lives in Hollywood. Why would he live so far from the studio?"

"What's far? It depends on what studio you work at. He made the rounds. MGM is in Culver City. We're here in Burbank. Hollywood is in between." He seemed to imply that any idiot could see that.

"What did Helmut do for you?"

"Props," the Property Master answered laconically.

Harry was getting a little annoyed. The man was not being helpful. Barely civil.

"Could you be a little more specific?"

"He worked the bible," Strand said.

"The bible?"

The Property Master looked at Harry as he would at a moron. "The yellow pages," he explained with exaggerated patience. "The telephone book. Lining up prop sources. Organizations. World War II information."

"I understand you are also in charge of weapons," Harry said. "Guns. That sort of thing."

"That's right."

"But only harmless fakes, I suppose," Harry said. He allowed a hint of condescension to color his voice. Two can play your game, he thought wryly.

Strand bristled. "We handle live weapons," he said curtly.

"Kept in your prop boxes," Harry said. "Along with the ammunition."

"That's right."

"And the boxes are locked."

"Yeah."

"And you and your property men all have keys."

"Yeah."

"I'd like to see those boxes," Harry said.

Without a word Strand turned on his heel and walked toward one of the damaged buildings of the set. Harry followed.

The prop boxes behind the false-front house were more like wheeled cabinets containing several large drawers. A wealth of assorted items was neatly stored away in them. There were five boxes.

"Did Helmut work with any one of these boxes in particular?"

Strand shook his head.

"With all of them?"

Strand nodded. "Sure."

Harry rummaged through a few of the drawers. He quickly realized that there'd be no way of knowing it even if he did run across a clue.

Half the items were Nazi-related. Armbands, medals, documents and daggers . . . Flags, shoulder straps, emblems and field equipment . . . Grenades, ammo boxes, guns and belts . . .

All of them the real article.

If any of them had meant something special to Muller, it was impossible to tell. . . .

Harry had a sudden sinking feeling. Was the Muller document just a "prop" after all?

He turned to the man watching him in silence. "Thank you, Mr. Strand," he said politely. "You've been most helpful."

And fuck you, too . . . !

He walked back toward the camera crane. A studio worker came up to him.

"Mr. Bendicks?" he asked.

"I'm Bendicks."

"They're about ready to shoot," the man said. "Mike thought you'd like to watch from a good vantage point. It's kind of hard to see from back here without getting in the way."

"Sure," Harry said. It was a diplomatic ploy to get him out of the way, he thought. He didn't mind. He was acutely aware of being on unfamiliar ground.

"I'll take you," the man said.

Harry followed him toward the damaged church on the village square. They entered.

Harry was fascinated. The inside of the whole church was one big open space, supported by struts, steel rods and wooden beams. In the middle stood several portable dressing rooms, with doors marked MALE STUNTS, FEMALE STUNTS, XTRA GIRLS and XTRA MEN. A stack of old broken pews was piled in one corner, and in another a ladder led up to a narrow catwalk encircling the room just below the roofline. Another almost vertical ladder led onto a platform high overhead in the church tower and on up into the top steeple, laid open by an artillery round. The dirt floor was strewn with equipment and rubble. Lights, paint cans, cables and boxes. Dismantled parallels. Several light-stands stood bunched together against one wall.

They walked through the cluttered building and out on the other side. They crossed a narrow street; went through a doorway, across which a plank had been placed with a sign, KEEP OUT; into a false-front building only a few feet deep; out onto another street and past a few bomb-damaged houses to a spot near a massive-looking ruin.

Harry looked around. He had a fine view of the big, gutted Town Hall structure about fifteen feet on his left, and of the area of action directly in front of him. On the right he could barely see the camera crane around the wall.

"You'll have a good view from here," the man said. He grinned. "Fifty-yard-line spot. Just don't move forward or you'll get in the shot. As a matter of fact, if you stay back so you can't see the camera, it can't see you."

"Okay," Harry said.

"Mike'll get you when the shooting is done," the man said.

"Thanks."

Harry found it all vastly interesting. It was a new world to him. And anything new always fascinated him.

He heard Buter's voice call, "Okay! Stand by! . . . Bob! When they throw the grenades—give it a count of two; then let 'er blow!" And the answer, "Got you!"

He knew the routine by now. The bell. The light. The cues. He was fast becoming an expert.

A voice boomed out: "Fire in the hole!"

"Action!"

In the distance the two actors began their broken-field run down the ravaged street, their movement followed by the camera on the boom. Weaving, bobbing, turning, they ran among the broken masonry and piles of rubble.

Harry watched with fascination. He was completely absorbed. It was easy to imagine he was watching the real thing. Instinctively he ducked down closer behind the demolished wall, watching intently.

The two GIs were within a few feet of the bullet-riddled oil drum lying at the edge of the path. Their sweat-grimed faces showed the strain. Suddenly a row of little dirt geysers spewed from the ground and stitched its way directly across their path— and almost immediately a second row of exploding dust puffs erupted, running back. Desperately the two men leaped to avoid them. They were being raked by machine-gun fire.

With a last-sprint effort they reached the heap of debris—and dove for cover.

Almost at once each man reached for a hand grenade, ripped the pin from it with his teeth—and in unison the two brought their arms back and lobbed the grenades in a high arc into the air.

Harry was completely caught up in the scene. He saw the two grenades soar into the air—and in the same instant realization froze his mind. The grenades were arching through the air in his general direction. They would strike the gutted Town Hall ruins only several feet away from him. With the speed of the thought itself he acted. He catapulted himself across the massive wall stump and pressed himself against its base, shielding the back of his head with his arms. Even as he did, he knew it was ridiculous. They're dummies! his mind shrieked. It's only a movie! . . . And he was ruining the shot—diving right into it!

In the very instant he hit the ground a tremendous explosion rent his senses. Stones, bricks, masonry, splintered timbers from the ruins shot through the air in an ear-shattering eruption. A massive, scorched beam that had rested solidly on the ravaged ruins dropped down at one end with a jarring thud and began to topple. It crashed to the ground at the exact spot where Harry had stood only seconds before, sending clouds of choking dust into the air and shaking the ground with a tremendous impact that toppled part of the ruined wall down over Harry. . . .

He was aware of many voices, many hands tearing broken bricks and chunks of mortar away from him. Others helped him to his feet. Mike . . .

"Jesus," the AD said. "Are you okay?"

The standard question, Harry thought irrelevantly. I could have been cut in half and he'd still have asked it.

"I'm okay," he said.

He saw Buter come running up. The man looked ashen-faced.

"He's okay, Irwin," Mike called to him.

Buter stopped in front of Harry. He glared at him. He was shaking.

"What the *hell* are you doing here?" he exploded. "Didn't you see the damned signs? We've got the whole bloody area roped off! We've got a million signs! We've got a guard! And you manage to—"

"Hold it!" Harry snapped. The authority in his voice froze Buter in mid-sentence. "Just—hold it." He looked angrily at the young director. "One of your men took me here. Told me to watch from here."

Buter gaped at him "One of *my* men? You're out of your bloody mind!"

Harry turned to Mike. "Did you ask someone to take me to a good spot to watch the action?"

Mike shook his head. "No," he said, frowning. "I didn't."

Grimly Harry turned back to Buter. "*Someone* did," he said. "And I saw no signs. No roped-off area. No damned guard. What is that—area, anyway?"

"How *did* you get there?" Buter asked.

"Someone in your crew took me through the church and a couple of streets," Harry said impatiently.

"If he went that way, Irwin," Mike said, "he wouldn't have run into the guard."

"You just bumbled your damned way into the blast-and-crash-path area," Buter said coldly. "You managed to pick the exact spot to stand and gawk—the exact spot where a two-ton beam had been rigged to fall!" He turned to Mike. "Get him off the lot!" he barked. "That's it for today. I'll have to take a look at the rushes to see what damage that idiot did, before I decide if I have to do the whole bloody thing over again!"

Without so much as a glance at Harry, he turned on his heel and stalked off.

Harry glowered. He was painfully conscious of the fact that he didn't present a helluva dignified picture. He was disheveled, dusty, and had just made a colossal fool of himself. It intimidated him.

"He's shook," Mike said, looking after Buter. "Real shook." He glanced toward the massive beam lying on the ground. "Usually we use a hollow or special light-weight beam in a crash like this. But—when there's no one in the shot, a real, heavy one gives a helluva better effect. And when Buter wants a crash, he wants a *crash!*"

"The—grenades?" Harry asked.

"Dummies," Mike said. "Special Effects has planted a controlled explosive charge exactly where they want it to occur. When the dummy grenades hit, the operator sets it off by remote control. The set is rigged to come apart exactly as they want. That beam —it was calculated to fall exactly as it did." Soberly he looked at Harry. "You could have been killed."

"I told you, I didn't choose the damned spot myself," Harry growled. "Some sonovabitch took me there."

Mike looked embarrassed. "Who?" he asked. He couldn't quite keep his skepticism out of his voice.

"I don't know the bastard's name, for crissake," Harry shot at him. "But I can describe him to you."

He did.

Mike stared at him, a strange look in his eyes.

"We have nobody in this company who fits that description," he said quietly.

Slowly Harry turned to look at the massive, soot-blackened beam resting solidly on the ground. He felt his hackles rise. . . .

FBI PROBES NAZI HIT LIST
FOR MURDER

CHICAGO—The *Journal* has learned that FBI agents in Chicago, Cleveland and other cities have investigations under way to determine whether some fringe elements of the Nazi party have "hit" lists to eliminate prominent people, and to determine if Raymond Lee Schultz, who poisoned Sydney Cohen, 63, with cyanide fumes, was part of a conspiracy. . . .

8

"Okay, okay . . ." Harry waved his hands resignedly. "So you think I'm off my rocker." He looked earnestly at the lieutenant sitting at his desk in his office. "I don't buy the story that the guy was mixed up. That he'd misunderstood and didn't know what he was doing. I'm telling you, Jack, that bastard deliberately planted me right in the bull's-eye."

"And you think he was out to get you?"

Lieutenant Jack Stein contemplated Harry. Stein was a deceptively easy-going fellow. It was an impression which, to the uninitiated, was strengthened when they found out what he did to relax. Needlepoint. He made the finest, most colorful and intricate cushion designs for the wives of his fellow officers and friends. Like everything else he did, he did it extremely well—with meticulous precision. But anyone who made the mistake of thinking that Stein was as soft as one of his pillows was in for quite an education. Stein was as cool and sharp a police officer as could be found anywhere in the department; a hard, unyielding man to deal with, if you were on the wrong side.

Harry walked over to the window overlooking the parking lot in back of the Hollywood station. It was beginning to grow dark. The distinctively marked black-and-whites parked on the lot were beginning to merge in appearance with the more mundane private cars. In the dark all cars are gray, Harry thought. . . .

"All right," he said. "Maybe it does sound paranoid. But the truth is—I do. It *was* a deliberate attempt to get me!"

"Because of Muller . . ."

Harry nodded gravely. "Because of Muller."

"Why? What the hell could he possibly have to do with it?"

"I don't know, Jack. Dammit, I don't *know*. That's just it. I—don't—know! That's why I want you to keep the case open."

"On what grounds, Harry? Be reasonable. Because you nearly got yourself killed on a movie set? Being in the wrong spot at the right time?" Stein shook his head. "Come on, Harry. What do you think the Chief would do with that?"

Harry turned to Stein. "Jack. Dammit! I *know* there's something going on. I just don't know what." He scowled. "I have a—a feeling it's got something to do with Muller."

Stein sighed. There it was again—that damned hunch of Harry's. He'd come to trust it, however grudgingly, from past experience.

"Okay, Harry. One week. I'll put somebody on the Muller case for one week. Get everything we can on Muller. But that's it."

"Good! Who?"

"The only investigator I can spare."

"*Who?*"

"Pollard."

Harry gaped incredulously at his superior. "Supercop?" he exclaimed. "You gotta be kidding!"

He struck a theatrical pose; his voice grew exaggeratedly dramatic. "Master of expedient bullshit! Sucker for a *loco* motive! Able to leap a pet rock in a single bound! . . . Come on, Jack . . ."

Stein shook his head slowly. "Har-ry!" he said reprovingly. "Watch those low blows."

"Why?" Harry grinned sourly. "A pun is *supposed* to be the lowest form of humor." He grew sober. "Seriously, Jack. You *know* Pollard. Nice guy. Good to his mother. But he can't even catch his breath, let alone catch hold of a clue. He's the kind of guy who's got his hands full even when he's not carrying anything. All he does is run around like a wind-up duck out of whack. You might as well put Little Bo-Peep on the damned case!"

Stein leaned back in his chair. "Finished?" he inquired pleasantly. "Any more witty sayings? It's Pollard or nothing."

"That's a choice?" Harry shrugged. "What about Pete? SIT-7 will be split up when I blow. What about him?"

"He's already got his new assignment."

"Shit, Jack! What's the use of putting someone on the case who can't even find a turd in a cow pasture?"

Stein said nothing. He just shook his head slowly.

Harry looked at him soberly. "You don't believe me, do you, Jack?" he said gravely. "You don't believe there's something to it?"

"Let's put it this way, Harry," Stein mused. "It's not easy. You've got to admit there's damned little evidence to go on. How the hell would I justify keeping the investigation open when the killers have been apprehended? Because of a—hunch? Dammit, I'm sticking my neck out just putting Pollard on it—as a sort of clean-up operation—and I'll probably end up with my ass in a sling, too!"

Harry sighed. He knew Stein was right. He'd tried. . . .

"Thanks," he said. "I want to keep myself informed. Even after I'm out. No objections?"

"No objections."

Harry turned to leave.

"Harry," Stein said.

Harry stopped and turned back to him.

"I want your Follow-Up Report on the Muller case tomorrow before you go on the sign-off circuit."

"You'll have it." Harry felt a sudden pang. It would be the last one he'd ever fill out. He'd bitched over each one of them. But— the last one . . .

301		Deformed	
Susp.		No.	
1	2	3	
1	1	1	Leg
2	2	2	Arm
3	3	3	Hand
4	4	4	Limp
5	5	5	Fingers
6	6	6	Bowlegged

Harry left the category blank. Sitting at his desk in the little SIT-7 office at the station, he was wading through the suspect's PERSONAL ODDITIES section of the FOLLOW-UP REPORT. It was already late. His mind wasn't on his work. The incident at the studio *couldn't* have been an accident. *He* knew it. But how the hell could he convince anyone else?

305 Facial Oddities . . .

Birthmarks . . . Pockmarks . . . Moles . . . Freckles . . . Pimples . . . Lips—thick . . . Lips—thin . . . Chin—protrudes . . . Chin—recedes . . . Hollow cheek . . . That guy at the studio had had a kind of jowly look. The hell with it. He pushed the report aside. He couldn't keep his mind on it.

He glanced at the pile of sign-off reports he still had to fill out —in triplicate—before he went on the circuit.

Retirement.

New ID: *Retired* Police Officer.

He got up.

Tomorrow. He'd face all that crap tomorrow.

He buttoned the top button of his trousers that he'd unbuttoned to ease the pressure on his stomach as he sat at the desk. He suddenly remembered a remark the captain had made a couple of days ago as he, Harry, had been standing in the squad room trying to look efficient. "Pull it in, Bendicks!" he'd said, and given him a little slap on the belly. He sighed. He might be getting a little out of shape if somebody could tell him to pull in his stomach when he already had.

He walked from the office.

Stomach pulled in.

He strode across the darkened parking lot toward his car. His mind was worrying the puzzle of the studio incident—or he might have become aware of it sooner.

As it was, he didn't hear the car behind him until it was almost on him.

Startled, he whirled around.

The instant he did, the bright headlights of the car blazed on and imprisoned him in two stabbing beams, blinding him, and the car came roaring directly down on him. There was no possible chance of getting out of the way. In less than a second he would be struck.

Images flashed through his mind . . . The victims of collisions he'd seen in the past . . . The man with his whole face bashed in, his shattered jaw hanging loose in bloody flesh . . . The young woman slashed open from shoulder to hip . . . The boy crushed under the wheels of a truck, his pelvis flattened like a squashed cockroach . . .

The wheels!

In the last instant he leaped straight up into the air. Oh, God! Let me not be caught under the wheels! . . . Instantly he was aware of the numbing force of the impact—and the awareness shattered like a fishbowl, each separate shard with an awareness of its own. . . . He felt the bruising blow as he was catapulted across the hood of the car. . . . He felt the bone-jarring thud as he was deflected by the windshield. . . . With flash-card recognition he saw the pale blur that was the face of the driver, and a glint of—glasses? . . . He felt himself hurled from the speeding car and slammed into a parked black-and-white. . . .

He crashed to the hard pavement.

NAZI BUFF SLAYS 5
PERSONS, WOUNDS 5,
THEN KILLS SELF

NEW ROCHELLE, N.Y.—An army-trained sharpshooter, Freddie Cowan, 35, who admired Adolf Hitler, killed five persons Monday. . . .

9

The iron fist of a giant clutched his chest, squeezing relentlessly. It hurt. It was pushing him down into a white, misty mass. He had an icy dread of being submerged. He struggled to keep his head high. It hurt like hell. Slowly he forced his leaden eyes open.

Light swam before him. Above him a darker shape hovered in the white mist. Gradually it became the face of his son.

"Hi, Dad," it said; a cottony sound coming from far away. "Welcome back."

Harry strained to concentrate. *Back?* Back from where?

It suddenly flooded into his mind. The parking lot. The blinding car lights bearing down on him. The impact . . .

"What—happened?" he whispered. It was a great effort. He felt as if his tongue had turned to jelly.

"You were run down, Dad," Leif answered. "Hit and run."

Harry tried to shake his head. It hurt too much. Not that . . . He knew that . . .

"To—me," he whispered. "What's—the damage?"

"You'll be all right."

"Don't give me that," Harry said. His voice was gaining strength. "I want it—straight."

Leif nodded. He should have known.

"Two broken ribs," he said calmly. "They've taped you up.

Concussion. Lacerations and contusions. No internal injuries." He smiled at his father. "You were lucky. You were thrown clear. The car did not run over you."

I know, Harry thought, I know. . . .

"Did they—get him?" he asked.

"No," Leif said. "Lieutenant Stein was in his office. He heard the thud. He saw the car speed off, but it was too dark to see anything but the taillights. By the time they got to you, it was long gone."

Harry felt the mist engulfing him. He fought it. There was— something else—something important. . . .

"The accident is under investigation," Leif finished.

"It was—no accident," Harry whispered. He felt himself sinking down into the misty mass. "It was—deliberate. . . . Muller *is*— Muller. They—they—"

"Take it easy, Dad." Leif sounded concerned. "The doctor has given you a shot. Get some rest."

"They—they tried . . . again . . ." Harry closed his eyes. It was getting too difficult.

Leif stood looking down at his father, his face serious. He was suddenly aware of a feeling of great affection. It made his chest tight, his eyes smart. He was enormously happy that his father was alive. . . . It was strange. During all the years his father had been exposed to danger, he, Leif, had never really given it much thought. This was the first time his father had been seriously injured. And apparently by accident.

He frowned. Accident? His father had again insisted it was deliberate. It was an understandable reaction, perhaps. His whole system had been dealt a severe shock. He'd suffered a concussion. And there was the sedation. It would not be surprising if he felt himself intentionally attacked. Anyway—why would anyone try to run his father down? In the police parking lot? Assassins in a movie studio and in a parking lot? More probably the accident had been due to Harry's own preoccupation—okay, carelessness—perhaps induced by the prospect of having to change an entire life-style. Lieutenant Stein had voiced two opinions: hopped-up kids cutting across the lot—or, remotely possible, revenge for the on-going crackdown on crime in the Hollywood area, spearheaded by the Hollywood

Division. Realistically—there was little chance of ever finding out. . . .

The house was a comfortable single-family home somewhere in the greater Los Angeles area. The room was comfortable, but with no distinctive features.

An elderly, gray-haired man sat in a comfortable easy chair reading, engrossed in his book.

The phone rang shrilly.

The man looked up quickly. He let it ring four times—as usual —then quickly picked up the receiver.

"Yes?" His voice was clipped.

The voice on the phone sounded tinny.

"He is still alive, *Herr Doktor*," it said. A man's voice.

There was a long silence. The listener frowned slightly. He had to evaluate the information. Decide on an immediate course of action. Or—equally important—lack of action. Finally he spoke.

"All right, Berger, do nothing," he said curtly. "Wait for new orders."

He replaced the receiver.

For a moment he sat staring into space.

A minor nuisance was turning into an irritating problem.

At the worst possible time . . .

When Harry opened his eyes, he saw Leif sitting next to his bed. How long had his son been there? He moved tentatively. He felt stiff—and he ached all over. But his head was clear.

Leif stood up and walked over to the bed. "How do you feel?" he asked.

"Okay." Harry moved his shoulder. "A little stiff." He looked at his son with an oddly perplexed expression. "Have you been here since . . . Have you been here all the time?"

Leif gave a little laugh. He sat down on the edge of his father's bed.

"You've been out like the proverbial light for twenty-one hours, Dad. I came back an hour ago. They told me you'd be coming out of it by now."

"Twenty-one hours!" Harry started. He tried to sit up. He winced. "Give me a hand."

"I'll raise the head of the bed," Leif said. "You take it easy." He found the controls, and with a muffled hum the upper section of the hospital bed rose slowly until Harry was sitting almost upright. "Better?"

"Yeah." Harry looked closely at his son. "I—I told you already, didn't I?" he said. "I remember telling you—I think?"

"Telling me what, Dad?"

"That someone was trying to kill me. Deliberately."

Leif grew sober. He frowned slightly.

"Yes," he said. "You did say—something like that. You were still pretty groggy."

"No," Harry said grimly. "It is true. I'm not delirious. Nor paranoid. Never have been." He looked solemnly at his son. "There was that—incident. At the studio . . . Leif—I *know* it was no accident. Don't ask me how. I just know. And that hit-and-run bastard. He was coming straight for me. For *me*—do you hear? No way could he not have seen me, or not recognized me. He did his damnedest to run me down!"

"But—who'd want to do that?" Leif was getting concerned. His father had never talked like this before. Apparently he was not as rational as he appeared. "Why?" he asked.

Harry looked grim. "I know what you're thinking, Leif," he said soberly. "Don't. Don't try to—analyze me. I'm not nuts."

"Dad, I never—"

Harry stopped him. "Hear me out," he said. "Then decide." He looked closely at his son. "It may sound crazy to you—but, dammit, I'm sure. . . . I *know* why someone's out to get me."

"Why?"

"Because of Muller."

"Muller?" Despite his good intentions, Leif sounded incredulous. "The man who was mugged? What on earth does he have to do with it?"

"He was an SS officer. I'm certain the papers *were* his."

"But—he's dead."

"*He* is. There may be others."

"You think—you think there are other SS men here? And that they're out to—to kill *you?* What on earth for?"

"Dammit, don't make it sound so—so idiotic!"

"But—Dad—"

"The Nazis *were* the enemy, Leif."

"A long time ago, Dad. We're not at war now."

"Aren't we? There's always a war on. The only difference is that sometimes the guns are firing—sometimes not." His eyes searched Leif's intently. "Don't sell me short, son," he said. He gave a little crooked smile. "Investigators—whatever side they're on—have a lot in common. The Gestapo officers had an expression—*Fingerspitzengefühl.* It meant knowing with absolute certainty but without concrete proof about something or somebody in the tips of your fingers. I *know* what they meant. I can feel it now."

Leif gazed at Harry. He was genuinely concerned by the persistence of his father's obsession—but he was too good a psychologist just to dismiss it.

"Granted, you had two close calls, Dad," he said. "Right on top of each other." He looked steadily at his father. "But—it could be —a coincidence, couldn't it?"

Coincidence? Harry felt a twinge of doubt. He remembered Walter. . . .

Walter was a GI, an infantry man "liberated" by Harry's CIC team. He was a German Jew from Leipzig near the Czech border. In 1939 his parents had managed to get him out of Germany to England a heartbeat ahead of the Gestapo. He'd been fifteen. But his father and mother had been unable to follow him. Eventually Walter had ended up in Detroit with some distant relatives, and immediately following Pearl Harbor he'd enlisted in the U.S. Army to help destroy the regime that had destroyed his family.

Although he spoke German fluently, Walter had been assigned to the infantry, and since the Army in that unfathomable wisdom which made mechanics into cooks and cooks into mechanics had staffed its intelligence-gathering services designed to work in Germany—including the CIC—with a lot of non-German-speaking personnel, the various CIC detachments raided available infantry units for GIs of German descent who could speak the language. It was certainly not efficient—but since when was war efficient?

In most of the CIC teams only one member spoke German, and the "liberated" GIs were very useful in translating and carrying out certain routine duties.

One such was locating a suitable building to serve as HQ for the CIC when they entered a newly taken town.

Harry's team had gone into Mainz on the Rhine just after a massive air raid had left the inner city in ruins, and Walter had taken off to find a house still standing for them to occupy. It was 22 March 45. Harry'd never forget the date.

Walter finally found a large, forbidding-looking villa, virtually undamaged, on the outskirts of town. It was obviously occupied. A thin plume of smoke was rising from the chimney.

He banged on the massive front door. It was locked, and for a while there was no answer. He banged louder and more insistently. Finally the door was opened. In the doorway stood a woman.

It was his mother!

And here, in this devastated city more than two hundred miles from his birthplace, Walter found not only his mother but his father too—neither of whom he'd seen in six years, and whom he had thought long dead in the horror of some concentration camp! With them were over thirty other Jews who for years had been hidden and kept alive in the large cellar of the house by two Gestapo majors who through the years had collected condemned Jews there. Having found it impossible to accept the mass slaughter decreed by their Führer, these two had adopted a chilling MO in their work—a desperate method of carrying out their assigned Gestapo duties while saving as many lives as they could.

To protect themselves, whenever they were ordered to arrest a Jewish family they would do so—sending them off to certain death. But whenever they learned of a family about to be arrested by *other* Gestapo agents, they would warn the victims—and, if possible, spirit them away into hiding. Walter's parents among them . . .

Harry had never told Walter's story to anyone. No one could possibly believe it. It was impossible. But it *had* happened. It made him uneasy. How long *is* the arm of coincidence? Since then he had never been able to disbelieve in coincidences. It was, perhaps, one of the idiosyncrasies that had made him such a painstaking investigator.

"It could," he said slowly. "It *could* be a coincidence." His voice grew firm. "But—and here's that damned *Fingerspitzengefühl* again—*it is not!*"

He looked around the room. "Where are my clothes?" he asked. Leif nodded toward a closet. "In there, I suppose."

"Get my jacket."

Puzzled, Leif obeyed.

"In the inside pocket there's a little photograph. Take it out." Leif found the photograph. He took it out. It was creased and faded.

"I found that," Harry said, "in the same hiding place where Muller had stashed his SS document. It is my final proof."

Leif stared at the snapshot. He suddenly felt uneasy. What did this faded picture have to do with a hit-and-run accident?

"You see that cabin?" Harry asked. "In the picture?"

Leif studied the photograph. "Looks like an alpine hut," he observed. "A hunting cabin? Switzerland?"

"Close. It's in Upper Bavaria," Harry said. "Near a town called Kulmbach." He held out his hand. "Give it to me."

Leif handed him the photograph. Harry looked at it, then showed it to Leif.

"See that big rock sticking up out of the ground back there?" His finger indicated the spot. "Looks just like a big ball half out of the dirt. That's Kugelberg. *Kugel* in German means ball. Ball Mountain." He looked soberly at Leif. "I was there," he said quietly. "During the war. I know that cabin. The pump. That sign over the door. The deer antlers." He paused. His jaws corded. "That's where my buddy . . . that's where Andy bought it."

His thoughts winged back. He and Andy Dexter had been CIC teammates. Worked together on a file drawer full of cases. Pulled each other out of dozens of tight spots. Staring at the photograph, he could suddenly hear the staccato gunfire. He could smell the acrid dust puffed into the air when the bullets hit. He could feel the warmth of blood running over his hands. Andy's blood . . .

Leif remained silent. His eyes rested gravely on his father.

"It was in April," Harry went on, his voice curiously flat. "1945. Toward the end of the war. We'd just entered Kulmbach. Set up shop in the best house we could find."

A mental picture of Walter flitted through his mind. He dismissed it. He looked up at his son.

"You know how we always did that," he said. "I must have told you. We always picked a house that was still occupied by the Krauts—and kicked them out. Gave them fifteen minutes to split." He gave a short, strained laugh. "Hell, if we didn't—if we moved into an empty house, we'd get our asses blown off! I must have told you. . . ."

Leif nodded. He understood what his father was doing. Putting it off. Putting off telling about something he'd rather forget.

"Anyway," Harry continued, "the Krauts had the damned nasty habit of booby-trapping the empty houses. All the comfort-of-home spots. You'd squat on the john—and get your balls blown off. You'd flop on a bed—and find yourself smeared all over the ceiling. Shit! Kicking out a Kraut family was a hell of a lot safer. They could always come back when we moved on again. A hell of a lot easier than trying to glue your damned balls back on."

Leif glanced away. He'd never served in the Army and he always felt vaguely ill at ease with barracks humor.

Harry looked again at the photograph in his hand. "Kulmbach was a burg of about twenty thousand," he said. "And, like usual, it seemed that one half of the sterling burgers was eager to denounce the other half. Anyway—they made a great beer there. Black beer. Andy was crazy about it."

He stopped for a moment, gazing at the photograph in silence. Then—

"We were ready to move on—leap-frog another detachment team—when some guy told us about a place up in the mountains near a little village called Fichtendorf—that means Pine Village—a place called Kugelberg. There was supposed to be a hunting cabin up there with some mysterious, secretive people holed up in it, strangers to the area. We figured it might be some Nazi bigwigs—some mandatory arrestees—hiding out, and we figured we'd pick them up before we moved on. Leave the place nice and clean, you know.

"The snitch told us there were three or four warm bodies up there, so Andy and I took along a sergeant as a driver, just in case, and I picked up a Thompson—more for show than for firepower.

The place was by then well inside our lines, and we didn't figure on any trouble. No problem."

He paused. Strange how some incidents in your life remain so vivid in your mind that they seem to have happened yesterday, he thought, while yesterday's events are already fading away.

"Only—there *was* a problem," he continued soberly. "A damned big one . . ."

. . . They had seen the distinctive form of Kugelberg before the cabin itself came into view, cozily nestled in a clearing hedged by evergreens. The road to the hut was narrow and rutted—with deep tracks that didn't fit the jeep wheelbase. They were constantly sliding and jolting in and out of them. Harry, sitting next to the driver, put his hand on the rim of the windshield to steady himself. The sergeant shifted into four-wheel drive and the jeep labored on with a deep power grind. He had no reason to know that this action would cost him his life. . . .

The rustic cabin stood in the little clearing closer to the far edge. When they spotted it, there was no one to be seen. A short distance away stood a well pump, distinctively carved, with a wrought-iron pump handle. A sign painted with an ornate inscription hung over the cabin door, flanked by a pair of stag antlers. They started to drive down toward the cabin—big as life.

The enemy fire caught them completely off guard. Several things seared themselves simultaneously on Harry's mind: the ear-shattering din of rapid submachine-gun fire; the fire flashpoints that seemed to spit from every opening in the cabin; the lurch of the jeep as the windshield shattered into a thousand pieces; the dull thuds—louder in his ears than anything else—as several bullets slammed into the driver. . . .

The man was dead the instant he was hit. He collapsed across the wheel with unmistakable finality, and, urged on by his lifeless, booted foot, the jeep leaped forward. It careened a short distance down the path, joggling between the deep ruts. Harry tried desperately to dislodge the driver's body from its death grip on the wheel. The jeep left the path and rammed into a stack of logs piled at the road shoulder. It began to climb the pile of wood, and the timbers went spinning under the wheels—overturning it.

It saved their lives.

The savage fire from the cabin found them again at the instant the jeep rolled over, and the bullets slammed into the heavy steel bottom.

Harry and Andy spilled out. Somehow they managed to take cover behind the overturned jeep—the body of the dead sergeant pinned to the thirsty, slowly reddening ground between them. Somehow—and he didn't know how, with some instinctive muscle memory perhaps—Harry had held on to his Thompson, and he and Andy began returning the murderous fire from the cabin.

The noise was terrible. And terrifying.

But through it Harry thought he could hear the sound of motors revving up. Suddenly three or four motorcycles with sidecars attached came tearing out from behind the hut and raced off toward the woods at the far side of the clearing. From his one glimpse of the figures hunched over the motorcycle handlebars Harry recognized them as SS.

The fire from the cabin intensified. The bullets stitched patterns in the mangled jeep. Suddenly Andy slumped against Harry. Automatically Harry put his hand up to shove him off. And felt it.

Andy was bleeding.

Badly.

Harry took his friend by the shoulders, horror welling up in his craw. Andy had been hit in the neck. His lifeblood was spilling out of him. He was already dead. . . .

With the unreasoning fury born of imminent doom Harry turned toward the cabin. He knew he'd had it. He was alone—outnumbered ten to one.

But all at once the firing stopped—and suddenly a second string of motorcycles shot out from behind the hut and roared for the far woods.

Rage boiled in Harry. He didn't know what he was doing. He leaped to his feet and ran after the motorcycles careening down the path, firing his Thompson crazily. Long, wild bursts . . .

One of the cycles was hit. It exploded into a fireball, hurling the driver to the ground. He was still alive. He crawled away from the searing heat, screaming. One of the motorcycles slewed around and came to a dirt-spurting stop. The rider raised his Schmeisser submachine gun—and emptied it into the crawling man, slicing him nearly in two. He died while his shriek still echoed through the forest.

Harry was too blinded by rage to focus on the bizarre action. Firing wildly, he raced in a broken-field run toward the motorcycle that had stopped.

The rider gunned it and roared off, spewing gravel. Suddenly he lost control. The cycle crashed into a tree. The others didn't stop. They just careened off.

Harry ran to the SS driver sprawled on the ground beside the tree. He was ready to pump the bastard full of .45 slugs. But the man was dying.

Harry stood staring down at him, his Thompson slack in his hands. The German looked up at him, eyes terrible. With pain-racked effort he turned to gaze after the other cycles disappearing into the forest. Then he fixed his burning eyes on Harry and, with a thin smile stretching his bloodless lips, he died.

Harry's left arm suddenly burned. He touched it. His hand came away red and moist with blood. Astonished, he stared at it. He must have been grazed. When? He had not been aware of it. . . .

. . . Sitting up in bed, Harry absentmindedly touched his arm. "I'll never forget that goddamned cabin," he growled deep in his throat. "That fucking sign . . ." He looked up at his son, savagely. "Know what it means? *God Greet You. Step In—and Bring Happiness with You!*" he said bitterly. "Happiness!"

He looked away.

"All we got was one lousy SS bastard. One. It was a *Sturmbannführer*—an SS Major. I grabbed his ID disc. I'll never forget the bastard's name. Knauer. *Sepp Knauer.* An officer of the Leibstandarte Adolf Hitler. . . .

"The cabin was empty. No trace of the so-called mysterious strangers that had supposedly shacked out there. I turned the case over to AIC."

He slapped the photograph in his hand angrily.

"I was the only one who . . . The sergeant . . . Andy—" He stopped.

"You never told me before how—how you got that scar, Dad," Leif said quietly. "How—Andy died."

Harry looked up at his son. "You never asked," he said.

He contemplated the photograph.

"I'd give my right nut to know what this photo was doing in Muller's possession," he said. "An ex-SS officer. Why the hell would he keep it? Hide it away? It—it isn't like with the document. . . ."

He turned the snapshot over.

"There's something written on the back of it," he pointed out. "A name. Scribbled in Gothic script. Jenbach. It doesn't mean a damn thing to me. It's got nothing to do with the area around Kugelberg."

"Could it be the name of a person, perhaps? The photographer?"

Harry shrugged. "Could be. I'd sure as hell like to know."

He handed the photograph to Leif, and his son put it back in the inside pocket of the jacket.

Harry looked up at Leif. "I want to get out of here," he said. "I want you to give me a hand."

"Dad." Leif was suddenly alarmed. "You can't do that."

"Watch me!" Harry countered. He swung his legs over the edge of the bed. And winced.

Leif put his hand on his shoulder. "No, Dad. You need time to mend." He grinned. "It's not going to kill you!" His voice was calm. "Give those ribs a chance to heal. Why don't you just lie back . . . ?"

"Why?" Harry growled. "I'll tell you why. Because I feel like a sitting duck. Worse. A prostrate duck—all trussed up and laid out on a platter."

He looked closely at Leif.

"Look, son," he said, calming down. "I'm not stupid. I've always felt that incident at the cabin was a hell of a lot more important that just saving the necks of a couple of Nazi big shots. I *wanted* to follow through. Then. But that was the damned frustrating thing. I couldn't. I never could. I had to go on to new cases. I had to turn the cabin thing over to Army Investigation. They did the follow-up." He studied his son for a brief moment. "It wasn't just some mandatory arrestee trying to hide out," he said quietly. "There was something else. Something big. Then. Don't ask me the hell what, for I don't know. Something. The whole affair didn't make sense. It was too—too well organized. The SS were there in force. So why the hell did they take off, instead of finishing the job on us? Why?"

"Maybe they thought you were just the advance party of a bigger unit," Leif interrupted.

Harry shrugged. "Possible. I don't know. All I do know is that some bastard SS officer thought it important enough to keep an old photo of the fucking hut around. . . . That photo, it *does* mean something, Leif. I've got that old hunch about it, dammit! Since I found it, and since I started asking questions about Muller, there have been two attempts on my life—whatever you may think. Too uncomfortable to be coincidences. I'm obviously stepping on some toes. Some damned sore toes at that. Getting close to something. And don't ask me what. I haven't got a hint of an idea. All I know is, it is connected with Muller. The late SS Obersturmführer Ernst Helmut Müller—and that damned photograph he kept hidden away. With that word scribbled on the back."

Leif contemplated his father. He knew the set look on his face. He'd seen it before. His father's mind was made up. It would take some major argument to make him change it. He was concerned about his father's adamant stand. But he thought he understood. The fact of his father's rapidly approaching retirement. The specter of impending inactivity. Being out of it. Perhaps he simply didn't want to let go of those days filled with excitement and action.

Sure there were still Nazi war criminals around. Hiding. But they were harmless. Old men. Occasionally one was ferreted out. Deported. To face long-overdue retribution for his crimes. The newspapers often carried some brief item of the sort. But—who really cared?

Apparently his father did.

"Look, Dad," he said, "I'll make a deal with you. You do need to stay here—at least for a few days. You won't be much good if you insist on running around in your present condition. Later— okay. So. If you'll stay put—I'll do some unofficial investigating of my own. After all—" he grinned—"I've been around you long enough for some of the know-how to rub off—and I've worked with the department often enough before. How about it?"

Harry slowly nodded. He seriously doubted that his son could do much good. He sighed. He hated to admit it—but his damned ribs hurt like hell.

"Deal," he said.

He frowned. Perhaps Leif was right. Perhaps the whole thing didn't mean a damn. But he felt uneasy. The old CIC juices stirred in his veins.

"Deal," Leif said.

Harry looked closely at his son. "You don't think there's anything to it, do you, Leif?"

"No, Dad. I don't."

Harry nodded. "Just—look over your shoulder," he said softly.

NAZIS IN AMERICA

LORRAIN, OHIO—
Editor's Note: J. Ross Baughman of the *Journal* staff infiltrated the American Nazi movement in October.... He had an inside look at the people and plans of this frightening group. . . . "I found a world that extended far beyond the common public notion of American Nazis as splintered, extreme right-wing fanatics...."

10

Leif's first inquiry early the next morning, Saturday the eleventh, had produced a negative result. But then—as his father often said—a negative result is better than no result at all.

Harry thought he'd seen the split-second glint of a reflection on the face of the man driving the hit-and-run car. The man could have been wearing glasses. As far as he knew, the only one who was aware of his interest in Muller and who wore glasses was the manager of the King's Court. He'd suggested that Leif start his questioning with him.

It had been an uncomfortable confrontation. The manager had

been acrimonious and Leif had been reluctant. Still—he *had* promised his father.

The manager had an alibi for the time the hit-and-run "accident" took place. He'd been on duty. He could produce nearly as many witnesses as there were tenants in the building. And he almost did. Leif had been deeply embarrassed. . . .

He felt it would be a waste of time to duplicate the work done by his father and Pete in Muller's own neighborhood, but he was curious about what had actually happened at the studio. If—and that was the biggest little word in the English language—*if* the accident at the studio had in fact *not* been an accident, then someone who knew that Harry would return after his first visit would have had to "arrange" for it to happen.

The guard at the back-lot studio gate shook his head regretfully.

"Sorry, Mr. Bendicks," he said. *"Hitler's Werewolves* is a closed set."

"Closed set?"

"Absolutely no visitors," the guard explained. "Even a pass from the head office won't get you in. Director's orders!"

Leif frowned.

"As a matter of fact," the guard confided, "normally they wouldn't be shooting at all today. Saturday. But some dumb tourist ruined a big scene the other day. Walked right into the shot. Disregarding warning signs and all." He shook his head. "We get all kinds. Believe me. Anyway, the director has to work today to get back on schedule."

Leif thought for a moment. He didn't think he needed to explain that he was personally acquainted with the dumb tourist. "Would it be possible for me to talk to someone in the company?" he asked. "Here? Off the set? Just for a few minutes?"

The guard looked dubious. "Who would that be?"

"The Assistant Director. Mike. I'm afraid I don't know his last name."

"Sure. Mike. I'll see."

He entered the little guard station and picked up the phone. A moment later he reappeared.

"If you'll wait a few minutes," he said, "Mike will meet you here. They're about to take a break."

Mike and Leif walked a short distance onto the back lot and sat down on a green-painted wooden bench overlooking the Midwestern town square.

"I'm sorry about what happened to your father the other day," Mike said. "Perhaps I should have kept more of an eye on him." He looked at Leif. "But a shooting set is a pretty hectic place." He grinned disarmingly. "Especially for a Second Assistant Director!"

"What really did happen?" Leif asked. "I don't mean the accident itself. Before. How *did* my father get to that particular spot?" He looked at the young man earnestly. "What is your honest opinion?"

Mike grew sober. "My—honest opinion?"

Leif nodded.

"You may not like it."

"I'd like to hear it."

"Okay." Mike gathered his thoughts. "Your father described to me the man he said conducted him to the spot. A lean, long-faced, clean-shaven man in his sixties, with bad teeth and graying hair." He looked at Leif. "We don't have anyone who even remotely answers that description. Outside of a few key people, this is a much younger crowd. And with the exception of Vic Strand, who may look sixty although he's only in his early fifties, you'd hardly call any of them lean. What's more, I haven't seen one bad tooth among them. All the extras are young men. Soldier types." He frowned slightly. "My honest opinion? Perhaps—perhaps your father was—eh, too embarrassed. Embarrassed at having wandered into the wrong spot and—eh, emerged with egg on his face. An—eh, explanation of having been taken there by someone would—eh, take some of the edge off the situation." Mike was obviously ill at ease. "I can't believe that *anyone* took him there deliberately. And I can't figure *who* it could possibly have been that your father—eh, talked to." He looked at Leif. "Sorry . . ."

For a moment Leif was silent. How little he knew his own father —if Mike's analysis was correct. But he dismissed the idea at once.

His father had never been afraid of taking responsibility. It seemed far more likely to Leif that the man who'd showed his father to the fateful spot was the one who was "covering up." Out of—embarrassment? But why should Mike deny that the man existed? And why would the man tell his father that Mike had said to look after him, when Mike obviously had not? He believed the young AD. Who *was* that mysterious guide? Did he really exist? He suddenly wished he had his father's deductive reasoning. And he was afraid his visit to the studio would yield not even a negative result.

He looked at Mike. "Thank you," he said. "I appreciate your being honest with me."

Mike looked at his watch. "Got to get back," he said. He stood up and offered Leif his hand. "Hope you get it all unraveled."

Leif took his hand. "Thanks for your help."

Mike started away. He suddenly stopped and walked back to Leif.

"I almost forgot," he said. He fished a piece of folded paper from his pocket. "Vic Strand, the Property Master, gave me this." He handed the paper to Leif. "He said it might have belonged to Helmut. The man your father was asking questions about. It was found in the phone book. The yellow pages that he used. None of the other prop men put it there. It could, of course, have been left there from a previous production—but it does have to do with Nazis and the war; with the subject of our film. I thought you'd like to give it to your father."

"Thanks. I will."

Mike left.

Leif unfolded the paper. It was a printed list headed:

T H E   M I L I T A R I A
Military Miniatures & Model Kits
War Memorabilia

N. Zuckermann   11279 Ranchero Street
North Hollywood, Ca. 91903

Authentic Nazi Armbands Available

Below, several Nazi armbands were listed and described, with astoundingly high prices indicated for each:

Im Dienste der Sicherheitspolizei
(In the Service of Security Police)
Black lettering on green armband. . . .$27.00

Deutsche Volkssturm, Wehrmacht
(German People's Forces, Army)
White lettering, black band with
eagle on red armband. . . . $15.00

Verkehrs-Aufsicht
(Army Traffic Control)
Black lettering on pink armband. . . . $12.00

Described in detail were the golden sword-swastika-wreath emblem of SA sports leaders and the oakleaf-bordered armbands of political officials—including a special, a Reichsleiter armband, at a whopping $500 . . . The yellow armbands of civilian Wehrmacht workers and the General Airforce Ordnance . . . The green armbands of the various auxiliary police organizations—*Im Dienste der Deutschen Polizei, Hilfsgendarmerie, Sicherheits-u-Hilfsdienst* . . . Regulation Nazi Party armbands with the official black label on the inside bearing the legend *Vom Reichsführer SS befohlene Auführung, RZM, 61/35,* embroidered on it with silver thread . . . Hitler Youth and Veterans' Associations; the *Afrikakorps*—and even the big "L" on the blue-green armband of the official real-estate assessors at $17.50 . . .

Obviously, the Militaria was well stocked with Nazi memorabilia. Would it have old Nazi documents as well? Had it had one with the name Muller on it?

The Militaria would be Leif's next stop.

NAZI CAMP IN VALLEY

FBI Investigates "Commando Base" in Panorama City, California

VAN NUYS—The FBI has been investigating a report that Panorama City was

picked by leaders of the American Nazi
movement as a base for a so-called "com-
mando training" camp, an FBI official
disclosed yesterday.

II

On the middle shelf Hannibal was crossing the Alps; on the shelf
below, a brown-shirted Nazi band and torch parade goose-stepped
to the edge of the glass.

Leif looked at the array of military miniatures with fascination.
The dusty display cases held literally thousands ranging from delicate, cardboard-thin figures in bas-relief barely an inch tall, many
depicting famous historical scenes, to solid three-dimensional
figures more than three inches high. Some were made of metal,
some of plastic; some were unpainted, the color of the raw metal
or plastic, others were intricately and colorfully painted, turned
into minor works of art.

The Militaria, on Ranchero Street just off Lankershim Boulevard in North Hollywood in the Valley, only a few minutes drive
from the Valley Studio back lot, housed a cluttered conglomera-
tion of military memorabilia, miniatures and model kits. Plastic
tank models shared space with authentic badges of British, American and Russian armored troops; World War II Japanese and
French helmets stood incongruously side by side with the ornate
headgear of a German Uhlan and an 1891 Prussian Pickelhaube;
a collection of Nazi daggers hung on the wall next to U.S. bayonets
and paratrooper knives in uneasy cameraderie; a large black bookcase held military books and pamphlets in several languages, and
on a high shelf above the door presumably leading to the back of
the house, several ornately painted antique German military
steins haughtily surveyed the jumbled scene below, where war
posters and handbills, uniform items and caps, guns, rifles and
empty grenades—an accumulation of gear and equipment—were
crammed into every available space.

"The most sought-after Nazi document is, of course, one signed
by Adolf Hitler, you should be so lucky to find one," the elderly

man behind the counter said, peering at Leif. "You can expect to have to pay two hundred and fifty to three hundred dollars for just a routine document." He sighed. "It used to be Napoleon. Now it is Hitler."

Leif nodded. He contemplated the proprietor of the Militaria, facing him across a glass counter which was lined with trays of medals, badges and emblems from every army in the world.

N. Zuckermann. N for Nathan—according to the legend painted on the window. A man in his early sixties—it was difficult to tell —gray-haired, lean, with a clean-shaven face. His voice was strangely toneless. Tired. But he obviously knew his business. War mementoes. Especially Nazi.

"There are, however, many Nazi papers and documents that are signed by lesser personages," Zuckermann continued, "at a considerably lower price. Military orders. Discharges. Transfers. That sort of thing." He peered expectantly at Leif. "I do have a few myself. Are you interested in anything particular?"

"Actually not," Leif said. He felt ill at ease. He really didn't want Zuckermann to get the impression that he was a potential customer. "I'm—I'm just trying to get an idea of what's available." He looked around the shop. "In—general," he finished lamely.

"I see." Zuckermann sounded disappointed. "Please. Look around. I hope you should find what you're looking for." He busied himself with some papers on the counter next to an old cash register.

Leif let his eyes wander around the store. But he stole occasional glances at the proprietor at the counter. The man was almost certainly Jewish. His English was faultless. Only occasionally did his consonants slur and his vowels slip. German? Or simply Yiddish? The lines in his face etched a haunting hieroglyphic biography. There were wit and wisdom. Intelligence. Suffering and bitterness. Resignation. Struggle—without fulfillment. His eyes were a thousand years old. Leif felt uneasy. There was something about the man. Something indefinable. Something—disturbing . . .

Perhaps it was the garish Nazi flag that hung on the wall directly behind the elderly Jew, framing him.

He decided to use the approach he thought his father would have used. To be blunt. Brutally blunt.

"Mr. Zuckermann," he said, "don't you feel strange? Resentful? Handling all these Nazi memorabilia? Being—Jewish?"

Unhurriedly Zuckermann looked up from his papers. His haunted, thousand-year-old eyes gazed somberly at Leif. No flicker of animation reached them. Almost imperceptibly he raised his shoulders and spread his hands.

"Does a mortician resent the dead?" he asked tonelessly. "I am —a mortician. Handling the inanimate mementoes of a time long dead."

Almost lovingly, like the caress of death, he ran his fingertips over the embossed SS emblem on the black hilt of a Nazi ceremonial dagger. "History," he said. "Dead history. Buried in the ruins of the Third Reich."

"Memories live," Leif said quietly.

Zuckermann sighed. "And—bitterness," he whispered. His face looked gray.

Leif glanced at the blood-red Nazi flag behind the old man. Perhaps—ideals, too, he thought. He looked back at Zuckermann. Defeat, he thought. That's what it is. That was the something about the man that made him uncomfortable. The vibes of a lifetime of adversity. Grief. And—defeat . . .

Zuckermann turned to a small glass case standing on the counter. He opened it and brought out a colorfully painted, metal figure five inches tall. A French grenadier. Late eighteenth century? He held it up for Leif to see.

"Not all, God forbid, is Nazi," he said. "This little fellow—he is a movie extra. From the fil-lums." He pronounced the word in two syllables. "A distant extra, they called him." There was near reverence in his soft voice. "Forty years old, he is. He comes from a motion picture made in 1938. By MGM. *Marie Antoinette*. With Norma Shearer and Tyrone Power. And John Barrymore, of course. And directed by the great W. S. Van Dyke. A beautiful picture. Not like the trash they make today. They should stop already with their naked ladies for all to see." He sighed—perhaps in memory of the golden days of Hollywood. He looked at the little soldier. "With his comrades he stood at attention. Row after row," he continued, "in forced perspective. Drawn up in parade formation—not far in the distance, but only twenty feet away; with the actors working in front his regiment would give the illusion of a great many real soldiers in three dimension, instead of the unreality of a two-dimensional painted flat." He ran a finger tenderly over the little figure. "He's heavy," he said. "Made from lead. He was reliable. He was easy to care for and he demanded no big salary—bigger every day." He peered at Leif. He held the little soldier up for inspection. "I want you should look at him," he said. "How fine he is painted. But—to make even greater savings, and since he always stood facing the same way—" He turned the little soldier around. "They only painted him on one side."

Despite himself, Leif laughed. The back of the figure was simply left a dull metal gray.

Zuckermann moved to put the little movie extra aside. Behind him the bright Nazi flag once again demanded attention. Leif grew sober. He had one more question for Nathan Zuckermann.

"Mr. Zuckermann," he said, "how well did you know Ernest Muller?"

He thought the man stiffened imperceptibly. He could have been mistaken.

"Muller?" Zuckermann said without turning around. "I—I don't understand."

Leif felt a surge of excitement. Was Zuckermann going to deny knowing Muller? "Ernest Helmut Muller," he said firmly. "The motion-picture property man."

Zuckermann turned to him. "Of course," he said. "Mr. *Helmut*. Ernest *Helmut*. Of course." He nodded as if he'd made a great discovery.

Leif felt the warm flush on his cheeks. He could have kicked himself. Some investigator he turned out to be. Couldn't even get the name of his subject right. Helmut. Of course. That was the name Muller used at the studio.

He cleared his throat.

"Mr. Helmut did come here, did he not?" he asked.

Solemnly Zuckermann nodded. "Now and again," he acknowledged. "Whenever he was looking for authentic props. Military props. For his fil-lums." He looked at Leif with his joyless old eyes.

"Quite a few property men come here. I have one of the finest collections in town. Of World War II items. From the movie studios they come. And television. NBC—and CBS . . ."

"Did you know Mr. Helmut well?" Leif asked.

"He was interested in my things," Zuckermann said. He shrugged. "We talked." He seemed reluctant to elaborate.

"Did you ever sell him one of your Nazi documents?"

Zuckermann shook his head. "That was not the kind of thing he was interested in," he said.

"Not professionally, Mr. Zuckermann. For his own use."

Zuckermann shook his head.

"Are you certain?"

Zuckermann looked puzzled. "I am certain," he said.

Leif felt let down and relieved at the same time. He didn't really know if it was the answer he had expected. Or wanted. If Zuckermann was telling the truth—and there was no reason he should not—then the document his father found in Muller's apartment was the real thing. . . . Of course he could have obtained the document elsewhere—but it looked more and more as if Muller *was* Ernst Helmut Müller, SS Obersturmführer.

He looked at the older man. "Was Helmut a friend of yours, Mr. Zuckermann?"

Zuckermann fixed his rueful eyes on him. "What's friend?" He shrugged. "We talked."

Leif deliberated with himself whether he should tell the old man about Muller's—about Helmut's Nazi past. He decided against it. His father always said—never volunteer any information if you don't absolutely have to.

"Can you tell me anything about him?" Leif asked.

For a moment Zuckermann stared into space. He was frowning slightly, obviously uncomfortable at the trend the conversation had taken.

"He—is not a happy man," he said finally.

"Helmut is dead, Mr. Zuckermann," Leif said quietly. "He was killed in a street mugging."

Slowly Zuckermann lowered his head. Gently he began to rock to and fro.

"Such is life," he whispered.

Driving across Laurel Canyon from the Valley toward Hollywood, Leif was far from pleased with the results of his interrogation. What had he learned? Nothing . . .

He took stock. That wasn't quite correct. He knew that
Muller had not picked up his document at the Militaria. At
least, Zuckermann had said so. He knew that Muller—*Helmut*
—had frequented the Zuckermann shop. Was it simply in his
capacity of studio property man? Or had the ex-SS man perhaps been engaged in a perverse search for "security" by making friends with a Jew? Or—atonement? And Zuckermann? He
knew the man was Jewish, but was he what he seemed to be?
A harmless old man running a—a curio shop crammed with
Nazi memorabilia? Was this obvious interest in things Nazi
strictly professional—or was there something else? A different
kind of connection between Zuckermann and Muller-Helmut?
On the surface it seemed preposterous. Obviously the two
were poles apart. . . .

But before he returned to his father with his report, he'd better
do a little more digging. Check out old Nathan Zuckermann. It did
seem obvious what he was, but his father said—never accept the
obvious. Plain as the nose on your face? he'd ask. Maybe. But how
often do you see your own damned nose?

Harry had mentioned an organization with which he'd had contact in the past. The Jewish Defense League. A Mr. Rubin. Irv
Rubin. When Leif had seemed dubious—after all, the JDL was a
pretty controversial group—his father had snorted. Controversial?
he'd said. Sure they're controversial. And militant. A pain in the
ass sometimes. That's their bag. They thrive on it. But they're the
only damned organization in this area that doesn't just sit on its
collective butt. They're doers. Go see them.

Okay. He would.

They might have some information about Nathan Zuckermann.
And his relationship with an ex-SS officer . . .

TENSION MOUNTS OVER
SAN FRANCISCO NAZIS

Nazi Shop Jolts a
Neighborhood

SAN FRANCISCO—The Nazis opened a
bookstore here—the Rudolf Hess Book
Store. The landlord, an Auschwitz survivor, learned the identity of his new tenant as the local branch of the American
Nazi Party, he said, when a party trooper
appeared in uniform complete with armband swastika and jack boots. A big black-
on-white swastika sign advertising the
Rudolf Hess Book Store came next, and
then, early this week, there was a formal
opening with Nazi flags, men in uniform
and all the regalia of the Nazi era . . . and
current T-shirts with a photo of Hitler
emblazoned with the words HE LIVES!

12

The stern face of Nazi-hunter Simon Wiesenthal stared at him
from the wall, sharing space with a bulletin board covered with
clippings reporting neo-Nazi activities throughout the world. A
detailed map of Israel dominated the area above a massive, beat-
up desk. Beside it—prominently displayed—was a large collage of
harrowing photographs from Bergen-Belsen and Buchenwald,
from Auschwitz and Dachau, Mauthausen and Ravensbrück. And
below, the words: NEVER AGAIN!

The offices of the Jewish Defense League were across a courtyard on the second floor of a small office building on La Brea.
Three pairs of hard, dark eyes gazed steadily at Leif as he sat
facing the desk and the three young men grouped around it: the

oldest, Irv Rubin, and the brothers Barry and Earl Krugel. Their eyes were neither friendly nor hostile. Only wary. Wary and alert.

"We are not in the habit of giving out information about our fellow Jews," Rubin said. "We have a law in Judaism: A Jew cannot give information about another Jew to anyone." His hooded eyes never left Leif. "Especially not to a non-Jew." The statement was delivered completely matter-of-factly. No trace of animosity. "Even if we did know Nathan Zuckermann—which we don't—we would not give out information about him. And we do not keep records or dossiers on our people." He eyed Leif. "Our first reaction to your request regarding information about this man must be—*Who* are you? *What?* And *why* are you looking for the information?" He paused. His expression did not change. "Your father is a police officer. Why not ask him?"

Leif was taken aback. He had told Rubin nothing about himself when he made the appointment earlier to meet this Monday morning. He had told them nothing in the few minutes they had talked. He stared at the three intense young men facing him. An uncomfortable feeling of being under cold scrutiny crawled over him.

"We checked you out, Dr. Bendicks," Barry said, "or you would not have stepped through that door. A preliminary check only, of course."

"Then you will also know that my father is in the hospital," Leif said. He was not able quite to keep his irritation out of his voice.

Barry shrugged. "We know."

"We are suspicious," Earl added. "We have to be."

"I'm glad I passed muster," Leif said with a nervous little smile.

The three men watched him, their expressions unchanged. They said nothing.

Leif shifted on his hard, straight-backed chair. "I—I really only thought you could tell me a little about him," he said. "About Mr. Zuckermann. This is not a police investigation. I—"

"But you do work with the LAPD," Irv Rubin said. It was a statement, not a question.

Leif looked at the man. Checked out? They'd learned quite a lot about him in a very short time.

"On a referral basis," he said. "But you undoubtedly already know that."

The three young men did not react.

"Why are you interested in Nathan Zuckermann?" Barry asked.

Leif turned to him. "Only because his shop was frequented by the former SS officer I told you about."

"Who is now dead." It was Earl.

Leif turned to him. "Yes. As I—"

"There are over seven million original Third Reich Nazis still alive today," Rubin stated, his voice flat. "Many of them are right here in the United States. They trade with everyone. Even Jews."

"Of course. I didn't—"

"One large group," Rubin overrode him, "which includes the notorious Angel of Death, Dr. Josef Mengele, has found a safe haven in South America. Another group has taken refuge in the Middle East. Egypt. Syria. *Mein Kampf* has even been translated into Arabic now."

"Neo-Nazi organizations and movements are gathering strength every day," Earl added. "Throughout the world. One neo-Nazi group right here—the National States Rights Party—has well over twenty-five thousand members in more than one hundred chapters."

"They publish a hate sheet called *Thunderbolt* in more than fifteen thousand copies every month," Barry said. *"Thunderbolt* recently wrote that all Jews in America should be removed from positions of power and authority. And if that couldn't be done— then the *final solution* should be brought back!"

"Did you see the headline in this morning's *LA Times?"* Rubin asked, his face grim. "It said: *Neo-Nazis Unite in National Coalition."*

"No," Leif said, "I didn't."

Rubin pulled over a newspaper folded to an inside page. He pushed it over to Leif.

"Take a look," he said. "What just happened down in St. Louis, the demonstrations and everything, is exactly the kind of thing that happened in Germany back in the early twenties when Hitler's Storm Troopers first started to march."

Leif looked at the newspaper report. Page 4. An AP dispatch.

Dateline, March 13, 1978. Today. The various groups of American Nazis, during their national convention, had formed *one* national organization under the banner of the National Socialist Party of America, thereby considerably strengthening their influence. Their leader, Frank Collin of Chicago, had stated that the street demonstration against their march in St. Louis had been organized by "a few New York Jewish agitators and open communists who'd traveled all the way down there to incite people," and he had predicted: "Once we can clear these agitators out—we are on our way!" Leif felt chilled as he read the story. It *was* as if he were reading a news story from Germany—decades old. . . .

"It's quite possible that attacks like the bloody raid on the Israeli buses two days ago won't be isolated incidents anymore," Barry said. "Nor confined to Israel. It could happen here. The organization for it exists. It numbers both old Nazis and neo-Nazis. And it is growing stronger."

"You think Nathan Zuckermann is connected with any such group?" Rubin asked.

"No. I don't." Leif was acutely aware of somehow having been put on the defensive. He was annoyed with himself. "But the fact is," he said firmly, "that he did know *one* ex-Nazi—or old Nazi, if you will. And he—"

"Did Zuckermann know the man was an ex-Nazi?" Rubin interrupted.

Leif stopped.

"No," he said. "That is—I don't know." Right then and there he resolved that that was something he'd find out—with or without the help of the JDL. "To be honest with you, I don't know if the ex-Nazi, Ernst Helmut Müller, was anything more sinister than just that," he said. "That's what I'm attempting to find out. The man *may* have been a war criminal. He *may* have been in touch with others. He—"

"You are using a misnomer, Dr. Bendicks," Barry interrupted. "The Nazis began committing their crimes against humanity long before the war. Their atrocities have only a little to do with the war itself. They should be called Nazi criminals. Not war criminals."

Leif stared at him.

"If you *are* on the trail of a Nazi criminal," Earl said, "we'd be very interested."

"We are here to help the Jewish people in any way we can," Rubin stated. "We act as—catalysts—bringing matters of injustice, of danger, to the attention of the public. Whenever necessary we use direct confrontation to bring such matters into the open where they can be dealt with."

"We *act*," Earl said grimly. "In small groups. Within or without the law. We will stop at nothing to save a Jew."

Leif looked from one to the other of the three intense young men. He realized he'd get no information from them. Certainly not about Nathan Zuckermann. It seemed his father had sent him on a fool's errand. His eyes fell upon the gruesome concentration-camp collage.

"The holocaust," Rubin said, bitterness in his voice. "That is what we live with every day. . . ."

He stood up. Leif followed suit.

The interview was at an end.

As the door closed behind Leif, Irv Rubin looked soberly at the two brothers.

"Who *is* this Nathan Zuckermann?" he asked quietly.

The brothers glanced at one another.

"I think we should find out," Barry said. . . .

Leif was thoroughly disappointed. The JDL meeting had been a dismal flop, and following it he had spent the greater part of the day in Zuckermann's neighborhood, discreetly asking questions. He'd come up with a big, fat zero. Apparently Zuckermann was a quiet man who kept to himself. He lived in the back of the house on Ranchero Street where he had his shop. He did not belong to any temple or *shul* in the neighborhood. And he had never been in any kind of trouble.

Leif was back in his office. He tried to analyze what he knew so far. It added up to pathetically little. More like nothing . . .

He suddenly sat up. *Nothing.* As with Muller! He, too, had no past. He, too, was virtually non-existent—except for his work. Muller. And Zuckermann. Was there a connection, after all? He suddenly felt excited. Despite his failure as an investigator, Zuckermann was taking shape. In a negative way. But, as his father said, negative information is also information.

Perhaps he *had* come up with a concrete lead after all.

He checked his telephone service. There were two calls. A cancellation of an appointment for the next day because of a cold, and a terse message: *Call me. Rubin.*

Irv Rubin's voice on the telephone was impersonal and businesslike. "Dr. Bendicks," he said crisply. "You came to us seeking information about Nathan Zuckermann. You seemed to suspect him. . . ."

"Mr. Rubin," Leif said. "I didn't—"

"Hear me out," Rubin interrupted. "We have conducted a brief investigation of Zuckermann. Out of courtesy to you—and primarily for the sake of Nathan Zuckermann—we have decided to advise you of the results."

He paused. Leif remained silent. Now was not the time to interrupt.

"Nathan Zuckermann is a survivor of the holocaust," Rubin went on, his voice curiously flat, as if any emotion it might betray was being consciously controlled. "A survivor of Dachau and the dual labor-extermination camp Auschwitz-Birkenau. A sole survivor. His entire family was exterminated. . . . Before his arrest early in 1940 he managed to get his wife, Sarah, out of Germany. She went first to Holland. Then to England. Literally only hours before the Gestapo came for them. She was twenty-one. She and Nathan had been married seven months when he was picked up."

Again he paused. And again Leif remained silent.

"Nathan Zuckermann spent five years in the camps. Five years in those places hell itself has tried vainly to duplicate. . . . But he was strong. Resourceful. His spirit indomitable. He survived."

Despite his attempts to sound utterly unemotional, a ring of pride crept into Rubin's voice. It was quickly subdued.

"After the war," he continued, "after liberation from the camp, Nathan Zuckermann obtained permission from the Allied forces to join his wife. She had by then moved to Los Angeles. Here she found a small apartment where she waited for the day her husband would join her. She never doubted it would come. . . . Two days before Nathan Zuckermann arrived, Sarah fell to her death from her sixth-floor apartment. They said she had been trying to fix a window box. To make it look nice for Nathan—the place where they would start their new life. . . ."

Despite himself, Rubin's voice lost its impersonal tone.

"Nathan Zuckermann is a survivor," he said. "A survivor of the holocaust. Of the camps. Of his own tragedy . . . Survivors are precious to us. We treasure them. We want to protect them. From others. And from themselves. Some have never left the camps and the dehumanizing brutalities. These things exist in their minds. They live in constant fear. They may have been liberated. But no one liberated them from their memories. Often the slightest incident will turn this anxiety into panic. A police siren in the street. A stranger approaching them. An unexpected knock at the door. And terror will knife through their minds . . . *They're coming for me! Again.* . . . This you must try to understand."

Leif did. It would have to be thus. Only—he'd never thought about it. How many had?

Once again Rubin's voice became businesslike. "The JDL believes Nathan Zuckermann to be exactly what he appears to be, Dr. Bendicks. We have told you of our investigation so that you may conduct yourself accordingly. Your further actions will have to be decided by you. That is all we can say to you."

He hung up.

For a moment Leif sat in silent thought. Then he reached for the telephone. He dialed. He waited.

"Investigator Pete Hastings," he said.

Pete turned from the microfilm viewer.

"Parker Center comes through again," he said. "Here it is. 17 October 1946. Take a look."

He moved aside and Leif took his place. He studied the police form projected on the viewer.

Los Angeles Police Department
DEATH REPORT

DATE AND TIME REPORTED
TO PD:
    17 Oct. 1946

TYPE (Traffic, natural, suicide, accidental, homicide, etc.):
    Accidental

DATE AND TIME DEATH
OCCURRED:
    17 Oct. 1946

LOCATION OF OCCURRENCE:
    1167 Fairway, LA

DESCRIPTION OF DECEASED
Sex: F   Descent: Jewish   Age: 27   Height: 5'6"
Weight: 119   Hair: Black   Eyes: Brown
Build: Medium/full   Complexion: Dark

. . . and the name:

Sarah Zuckermann

Leif's eyes skipped down the form to the space headed: (1) RECONSTRUCT THE CIRCUMSTANCES SURROUNDING THE DEATH (2) DESCRIBE PHYSICAL EVIDENCE, LOCATION FOUND, AND GIVE DISPOSITION. He read. . . .

1. Victim lived in 6th floor walk-up apartment. Two windows facing back alley had attached flower boxes. Window at right box was open. A creeping vine grew in box. On outside wall around window wires had been affixed to wall for said vine to climb on. Victim was trying to fix broken wire. Reaching out she leaned on box which gave way, and she fell to her death in the alley below.
2. Broken wire outside window. Wooden window box partially ripped off sill. Roll of wire, clippers and cut wire pieces found on floor in room. Dirt and plant material from window box had fallen with victim and was found on and around body. Wire and clippers in police property. Other evidence left on scene.

One more item to check. Leif searched the form. There . . .

NEAREST RELATIVE
    Nathan Zuckermann

RELATIONSHIP
    Husband

NAZI CAMP SURVIVORS
FEAR A SECOND HORROR

CHICAGO—A Chicago Nazi leader has been promising to march his followers in full uniform. . . . A survivor of Auschwitz and Dachau said: "Do not tell me it cannot happen here. Do not tell me it cannot happen again. . . ."

13

Hannibal had progressed not one inch in his march across the Alps, his elephants still plodded the dusty shelf. The Nazis' goose steps had brought them nowhere, and the movie-extra soldier stiffly presented only his good side to the world. The Militaria was exactly as Leif had seen it before.

Only Nathan Zuckermann had changed.

Although his shoulders were still stooped, his face solemn and his eyes lackluster, to Leif, looking at him with newly gained knowledge, the lean, gray-haired Zuckermann seemed more dignified, commanding greater respect. Or was this only in the eye of the beholder?

Zuckermann had recognized him, but phlegmatic recognition had been his only reaction to seeing Leif again.

He refused to discuss Muller-Helmut by simply ignoring any reference to the man and changing the subject when Leif tried to bring it up. It was quite obvious he was not pleased at Leif's visit.

"Mr. Zuckermann," Leif said earnestly, "I don't want to badger you. But getting any information I can about Mr. Helmut is of great importance to me. Please try to remember. Anything at all you can tell me about him."

Zuckermann looked steadily at Leif, his age-old eyes dark. "You want I should tell you about things I don't know about?" He sounded testy.

"Of course not, Mr. Zuckermann. But you said yourself that you often talked with Mr. Helmut. What about? What kind of man was he? Who were his friends? You must have learned something about the man you can tell me."

Zuckermann looked away. "Ernest Helmut is dead, he should rest in peace."

For a moment Leif was silent. He realized that if he wanted to break through Zuckermann's reticence and get him to talk he'd have to shake him up. It was not an approach he relished, but of his twin roles of psychologist and investigator he chose the latter.

When he spoke, his voice was low. "Mr. Zuckermann," he said, "I cannot understand your reluctance to talk about Mr. Helmut."

Zuckermann squinted at him, his face cloudy. He said nothing.

"And I certainly don't understand that you so willingly associated with an ex-SS officer," he finished.

Zuckermann's eyes widened. He stared at Leif.

"SS—officer?" he rasped. *What—SS?*"

"I thought you knew, Mr. Zuckermann." Leif looked directly at him. "Ernest Helmut Muller was an ex-SS officer."

For the first time Leif saw raw emotion in the old man's eyes. His face had gone ashen and he gripped the counter edge, slender fingers straining on the glass.

"No!" he whispered, his voice hoarse. "Ernest?" He shook his head. "That is not possible."

"It is true, Mr. Zuckermann. We have proof. Documentary proof," Leif asserted quietly. "A document—just like the ones you have. Found in Helmut's possession. Naming *him.*" He paused. Zuckermann sank down on a stool behind the counter, his horrified eyes never leaving Leif. "Helmut is—was—SS Obersturmführer Ernst Helmut Müller."

Zuckermann's eyes glazed over.

"SS." He breathed the dreaded letters. "SS . . . SS . . ." With a conscious effort he returned his attention to Leif. Slowly he pushed up his sleeve. Tattooed on the pale skin of his forearm was a line of blue-black numbers. A22839.

"Auschwitz," he whispered. "Auschwitz-Birkenau . . . *Arbeit Macht Frei. . . .*" Dreaded words. The motto over the gate of the camp—*Work Makes You Free.* "I—worked," he said, barely audible. "I, too, worked. Baling hair. Human hair. Cut from the heads of the dead. The finest from the young girls. The children . . . Every day—every day they—*the SS*—burned twelve thousand people in their ovens. Men. Women. Children."

He reached for a magazine lying on the counter. The front cover showed a Napoleonic cap on a bright red background. With trembling fingers he tore a small piece of red paper from the cover. He held it up, his hand shaking uncontrollably.

"It was a game," he breathed. "Just a game. To them. The SS." He stared at the piece of blood-red paper. "But to us—to me—my very life became a little slip of red paper." He looked at Leif, his eyes burning. "They gave it to us," he said huskily. "To each one of us. One small piece of red paper. Red—because it was easy to see. One hundred of us they would select. Fifty would live. Fifty would die."

His eyes were drawn back to the slip of red paper. "They stood us, our faces against the wall, our toes touching and our hands behind our backs. Naked we were. Our hungry skin stretched over our bones. And they gave us the little piece of red paper. With our noses we should hold it. Against the wall. It was not difficult. Not for the first hours. Not . . ." He stopped. A sob escaped him, unnoticed. "But then—then the cramps began. In the shoulders. In the arms. In the legs . . . Ooh," he moaned softly, "so bad in the legs. And all the time you must not move—or the red paper will fall. Fifty will die. The first fifty who let their little piece of red paper fall . . ."

He crumpled the slip of paper in his hand and let it fall on the counter. "Your life," he whispered. "A slip of red paper. You could see it flutter to the ground to lie at your naked feet—and you knew the shot would come—in the back of your neck. You knew. . . . And you would count . . . thirty . . . forty . . . fifty . . . and you would live. Until next time . . ."

He looked down. "Perhaps—perhaps it was an easier death than dying in the experiments their doctors performed. But it is never easy to wait for death—when he stands right behind you. . . . And still—we had hope. Perhaps that is why so many died. Hope kills. You only fight back when all hope is gone. . . ."

"Mr. Zuckermann," Leif began. He had to stop to clear his throat. "Mr. Zuckermann, I—"

"That was the SS," Zuckermann said, oblivious to Leif's interruption. *"The SS.* For them it was *spass*—just fun. And they could bet: *'I bet the old Jew-swine with the missing teeth will be among the first ten!' "*

He suddenly glared at Leif. "I was there. I survived. My Sarah. She was safe. And I *had* to come back to her. Only—she . . ."

"I know about your wife, Mr. Zuckermann," Leif said softly. "I —am truly sorry."

Zuckermann nodded. Leif's knowledge did not seem to surprise him. Clearly he had gone back in time.

"Four days," he whispered, "and the endless nights between we were wedged into the dark boxcar. So many we could not sit. We had no food. No water. No way to empty our bladders and our bowels—except where we stood. My nostrils shall never be clean again. Even the ones who died—would remain standing up. . . ." His story came out in brief staccato sentences. "Their jackboots crunched on the gravel when we stopped. The SS . . . And loud blows broke the seals on the boxcar doors. They slid them open— and we spilled out. The ones of us who were still alive.

"It was—*Auschwitz.* We were—split up. One group, right. One group, left. While a prisoner orchestra played tangoes and waltzes —the latest *schlager* . . . Music played by the dead—for the dead . . ." He sighed. A sigh that was more a moan. "And in the air, heavy and sickly sweet, the smell of burning flesh . . . And we would march. Run. We, the slaughterhouse breed—the race of the dead . . ."

He closed his eyes. "Oh, Israel, deliver us. . . ."

He looked at Leif, his eyes terrible. "Why have you brought this back to me?"

Leif wanted to talk to the old man. To comfort him. To— But he dared not trust his own voice.

He started to speak, but stopped himself, chagrined at the extent of his emotional involvement. It was never easy for him not to become involved with a patient. But this did not interfere with his effectiveness as a psychologist. Patient? Zuckermann was not a patient. He was a—a subject to be interrogated. Leif found the distinction difficult to make. And the horror of the old man's story was beyond anything he'd heard before. Still—it disturbed him that he should have come so close to losing his professional composure. Of course, Zuckermann was not a patient. It *was* different. The rationalization made him feel better. Anyway, there was nothing he could possibly say that could take away the remembered horror and pain. Nothing that could make it better . . . or worse. There is a limit to how much pain, be it of the flesh or of the soul, the body and the brain can feel. Beyond that—nothing makes a difference.

Zuckermann slowly rose and drew himself erect. He fixed his dark eyes on Leif. He seemed lost in thought—struggling with himself. Then he made up his mind.

"I know little about Ernest Helmut," he said. Somehow he spoke the name differently now. With revulsion. Hatred. "But one thing I can tell you. A man. The name of a man. Helmut knew him. He came with him to my shop one day. A German, I am sure. I heard them talk. . . ."

"Who is this man, Mr. Zuckermann?" Leif asked.

Zuckermann didn't seem to hear him. "This man," he said. "He looked at me. Me—a Jew. A look I have seen so many times . . . The guards. The SS. The—Aryans . . . That *Aryan* look, cast upon the *Untermensch*—the less-than-human creature . . ."

"Who, Mr. Zuckermann? Who?"

Zuckermann gazed at Leif. "He called him—Konrad."

"Was that his first name? His last?"

Zuckermann slowly shook his head. "I do not know. He only called him Konrad."

"Is that all you know about him, Mr. Zuckermann? You don't know his full name? What he does? Where he lives?"

Slowly Zuckermann nodded his head. "I know where he lives," he said.

"Where?"

"I heard them talk. I heard Ernest Helmut say he would see this man later. At the hotel. Where they both lived."

Leif drew a deep breath. The King's Court.

Once again—the King's Court.

NAZIS PLAN MARCH

SKOKIE, Ill.—For weeks Nazi leader Frank Collin has promised to march his band of storm troopers through a predominantly Jewish community of Skokie. . . . "There are some Jewish leaders," Rabbi Meir Kahane said, "who sincerely believe that it would be better to let the Nazis march . . . that the numbers are so small that they don't matter, and therefore are not a danger. . . . But 50 years ago a comical man with a comical mustache and 11 followers began a small movement in a beer hall in Munich. From that beginning of the Third Reich came thousands, and from the thousands millions, and from that came 6 million dead. . . ."

14

"The word from here is I'm getting out first thing tomorrow morning, good as new," Harry said with evident satisfaction. He wrinkled his nose. "Foul-smelling place, Leif. Carbolic acid or something all over the damned place. Even the nurses don't smell like women." He looked at his son, obviously cheered at the prospect of getting into action again. "I feel good. They stopped the damned medication and my teeth no longer wear socks." He slapped Leif on the knee. "Tomorrow you and I'll call on our bespectacled friend at the King's Court."

Leif looked sober. "Dad," he said, "why don't we wait for a while? Why don't you give yourself a break? Anyway, Lieutenant Stein has put that investigator, Pollard, on the case. As he promised. I could give him the information. Let him follow through. He'll be on the case another couple of days."

"Has he come up with anything yet?"

Leif shook his head. "No. Not that I know of."

Harry snorted disdainfully. "Exactly. Dammit, Leif, Pollard hasn't got it. He won't find anything. His damned brain is about as big as an electric-light switch—and as intelligent."

"I didn't get much of anything either."

"You got a helluva lot more than Pollard ever will," Harry said. He grinned. "I knew that if you wheted the curiosity of the boys in the JDL they'd dig something up for you. And you got the Konrad lead out of Zuckermann." He snorted again. "That's more than Pollard could have done in a month of paydays. He's got his little pea mind set on one thing and one thing only. Broads. Every time he unzips his pants, his brains fall out. Forget about Pollard. You and I will follow through at the King's Court."

Leif looked uneasy. "Dad, I—"

Harry suddenly looked closely at his son. His eyes narrowed in sudden understanding.

"You—still don't think it's worth looking into," he said, incredulity coloring his voice, "do you?"

Leif did not answer.

"Well, do you?" Harry's voice betrayed his disappointment and annoyance.

Leif slowly shook his head. "No, Dad, I don't," he said quietly. "Mr. Zuckermann checked out as a harmless, a tragic old man. The fact that I thought him—well, strange—was probably just that he felt threatened by me. That is certainly understandable. Your accidents? That's just what they were. Accidents. Coincidental, perhaps, but still just accidents."

"And Muller?" Harry snapped pointedly. "He sure was real enough. Yeah. But was he just a war criminal who'd holed up in the States? Or was there another purpose to his being here? He —and his friend?"

"Listen, Dad—"

"No, *you* listen." Harry was getting worked up. He sat stiffly erect in his bed. "I don't care if *you* think the Nazi war criminals are a bunch of doddering old fools, broken-down medal-wearers and generals who lost a war. They're still criminals. And I happen to think they're still dangerous—if you get too close to them. Too old? They're *my* age, dammit. And I've still got plenty of clout!"

"Oh, come on, Dad." Leif sounded exasperated. "That's not the point and you know it. The old Nazis are really nothing but curiosities now. Fillers on a slow news day. They're dying out. Soon they'll all be gone. Why get yourself involved in kicking a dead horse?"

"How about justice?" his father snapped. "For a starter? Most of the Nazi criminals survived the war. Ninety percent or more. Should a criminal be immune just because he's been able to hide from justice long enough? I think not!" Harry spoke heatedly. "The Nazis were the only winners through the years and years of the Cold War. They were left alone. We were too damned busy looking for reds under every rock to bother with the Hitler gang. Why do I get involved? I'll tell you, dammit. I go after a murderer who kills an old man on the street with a piece of pipe. Shouldn't I go after a murderer who sat behind a desk and killed thousands with one phone call? A dead horse, you call it. Well—I still believe that dead horse of yours can kick!"

"But why should it? How?"

"How the hell should I know *why* and *how?*" Harry growled. "I've been a cop a lot of years. I can't stop being a cop just because I turned in my badge and signed a bunch of papers. I—I just *feel* it. . . ."

Leif started to talk. Harry silenced him.

"Save it! I know you don't believe in my so-called hunches. Your scientific know-how tells you there's no such animal." He glared at his son. "What do you know? Your knowledge all comes out of books. You know nothing. Nothing of the stink of rotting corpses in a concentration camp. Nothing of the sight of a mutilated child. Nothing of the savagery of the street people. And *nothing* of the feeling that chills you when you *know* you're on to something! How the hell . . . How the hell can you be my son and I be your father—and we be so damned different?"

"Maybe we aren't, Dad," Leif said quietly. "Maybe we're expressing the same things—in different ways. . . ."

For a moment Leif looked at his father in silence. They hadn't quarreled like this since back in the '60s. His father was just as adamant then as now. He thought he understood. There were pressures. Then—and now.

"All right, Dad," he said. "I'll pick you up tomorrow morning and we'll go to see the manager of the King's Court. Together."

He picked up the phone. He dialed. He knew the number by heart, and he kept no record of it anywhere in the house. While he listened to the evenly spaced rings he looked around the room. It was comfortable. Pleasant. And he hated it. It would be only a matter of weeks now, and he'd never have to look at it again.

On the fourth ring he hung up. At once he re-dialed. The phone was answered on the first ring.

"Yes?"

"New orders on the Muller case," he said crisply. "To be carried out at once . . . Eliminate."

"Yes, *Herr Doktor.*"

"Without fail. The day is too close to tolerate *any* interference."

"Of course, *Herr Doktor.*"

"You realize the importance of your mission," the elderly, gray-haired man said. "We have waited thirty-three years. We have suffered postponements. Setbacks. Disasters . . ."

His mind touched fleetingly on some of them. The tragedy in Brazil . . . The capture of Eichmann by Israeli agents. He recalled with satisfaction the wave of violent anti-Semitism that had spontaneously broken out in cities throughout South America following the outrage. The swastikas that appeared all over; the desecration of the eyesores that were the Jewish cemeteries; the destructive protests against Jewish merchants. It had been gratifying, but the loss was nonetheless great. . . . There had been Stangl's capture and extradition in '67 . . . Time's inexorable erosion of the *Treuege-folgschaft*— the loyal old guard . . . The attempt on Mengele's life ten years before . . . Bormann's recent death . . . All had necessitated reorganization and contributed to the delay. . . .

"But," he continued strongly, "conditions have never been more favorable for total success. We cannot afford to wait. The plan *must* go forward *now!* You will take the necessary steps. Understood?"

"Understood, *Herr Doktor.* Eliminate." The voice on the phone was crisp and impersonal. *"The order shall be carried out at once."*

EXTREME RIGHT IN WEST GERMANY

BONN, West Germany—In his annual assessment of the political situation within the Federal Republic of Germany, the Minister of the Interior noted last spring that: "At no time since the collapse of 1945 has National Socialism been glorified so openly in speeches, pamphlets and activities. . . ."

15

The nurse pushed a gleaming chrome wheelchair ahead of her into the room. She smiled at Harry and Leif. "Well-well-well," she said with exaggerated cheerfulness. "Are we all ready to go home?"

Harry eyed her. "Don't know about you," he growled. "*I* am." He stood up from his chair and grabbed his overnight bag. He'd been waiting. Impatiently.

"That's just fine," the nurse said. She maneuvered the wheelchair closer.

Harry gave it a suspicious look. "What's that for?" he asked.

"Why, Mr. Bendicks," the nurse said. She sounded as though she were speaking to a retarded kindergarten child. "That's for you."

Harry gave her a stare that would have quick-frozen hell itself. "No way," he said icily. "I *walk* out of here. You're not getting me into that damned contraption!"

The nurse clucked at him reprovingly. "Now, Mr. Bendicks," she scolded, "don't be like that. *Every* patient is taken downstairs in a wheelchair. Hospital rules."

"Not me," Harry said stubbornly. "I'm perfectly able to walk."

"Of course you are, Mr. Bendicks," the nurse humored him. "But we still have to follow hospital rules, don't we? I'll just have to wheel you down."

Harry's face was set. "No one's getting *me* into that damned thing," he stated flatly. "No one's going to push *me* around in a damned wheelchair."

"Now, Mr. Bendicks." The nurse's voice was getting slightly edgy. "We mustn't be unreasonable, must we? Why don't you—"

Quietly Leif interrupted her. "Nurse," he said, "I am Dr. Leif Bendicks. The patient is my father. Would it be all right if *I* took over the responsibility from you here and now and walked my father downstairs?"

The nurse looked at Leif dubiously. "Dr. Leif Bendicks." She tasted the name. "You aren't one of the doctors in this hospital, are you?"

"No, I'm not," Leif conceded agreeably. "But I am familiar with hospital rules, and you are entirely correct. However, under the circumstances, I'm sure you have the authority to make an exception."

The nurse hesitated. "Well," she said, "I suppose I—"

"Thank you so much," Leif said. "We'll be very careful." He turned to his father. "Come on, Dad," he said. "The elevators are just outside in the corridor."

Harry gave the nurse—and the wheelchair—a sour look, and followed Leif from the room.

One of the three elevators was already at the eighth floor as Harry and Leif came up to it. The door was open and an orderly was maneuvering a large, multi-tiered food cart into the elevator. Some of the heavy-wire shelves held plastic trays with the remnants of patients' meals. As he saw Harry and Leif approach, he smiled, stood aside and motioned them into the empty elevator.

They stepped in.

Harry was impatient to get out of the place—but he was suddenly aware of distant alarm bells clamoring in his mind. What? Something was out of kilter. Something had set them off. What?

The orderly.

He turned. The man had pushed the cart into the elevator after them. He turned it, effectively blocking Harry and Leif from the door. He pushed the lower basement button. Harry strained to figure out what had caused his sudden apprehension. He stared at the orderly. An elderly man. White shirt and pants. Gray hair closely cropped. Elderly? Too damned old to be an orderly.

The elevator doors started to close—and in the last moment the orderly quickly stepped outside.

Even as the doors closed, Harry flew into action. He pushed Leif aside and stretched across the cart in an effort to reach the button panel.

The elevator started down.

Almost at once there was a loud click and a brief grinding sound. The elevator jerked sharply—and suddenly there was no restraint in its downward plunge.

With a sickening screech that gathered in intensity—like a giant nail raked across a blackboard—the elevator hurtled down the shaft toward the basement eight floors below.

Straining across the cart, Harry managed to reach the emergency STOP button on the panel. He stabbed it.

It was dead.

The elevator continued its plunge.

Leif stood ashen-faced against the wall. His mind churned. His eyes sought his father's. The father he loved—and would never know. He felt deep sorrow clutch his chest. . . .

Suddenly Harry whirled on his son.

"Up on the cart!" he screamed at him over the screech of the plummeting elevator, even as he himself scrambled up onto the food cart. "Move! On your back!"

At once Leif clambered up. Side by side, holding on to one another, father and son lay flat on the sturdy metal-frame cart, waiting as the seconds flew by. . . .

And with pile-driving force the elevator hit.

The tiers of sturdy wire shelves collapsed, telescoping the food cart; the metal legs crumpled, taking up the bone-splintering impact, the cart flattening like a giant honeycomb. The metal floor of the elevator buckled as the pit-bottom buffers slammed into it.

Leif felt himself being pressed into the hard top shelf of the cart by a tremendous weight that seemed to crush him. Every nerve end in his body shrieked in pain. A cascade of brilliant light exploded before his eyes and he felt his mind wavering.

And there was silence.

With an excruciating effort Leif turned his head toward his

father—and met his eyes. There was no need for words. The concern one for the other was eloquent. . . .

Laboriously, every bone aching, every muscle protesting, the two men eased themselves from the crumpled food cart.

They had survived.

Grimly Harry looked at his son.

"Coincidence?" he asked.

Slowly Leif shook his head. "No, Dad," he said, his voice unsteady. "You were right."

"Goddamned bastard," Harry growled.

"The orderly? Who—was he?"

Harry looked at the accordion-crumpled food cart. "We'll damn well check him out," he said. "But I'll bet my black-and-blue ass that there's no orderly on the staff of this hospital that fits his description."

"Like—that studio worker . . ."

Harry nodded grimly.

"But how? How did they know *we'd* be taking the elevator? And when?"

"Easy," Harry said. "Anyone could find out my room number and the time of my discharge. Wouldn't be too difficult to rig the car for the right moment. That phony orderly just had to keep an eye out for the nurse and her damned wheelchair. Wouldn't take a mental giant to figure we'd be coming out soon when he saw her go in. And we sure as hell weren't going to walk down eight floors. All the bastard had to do was to use his food cart to hold the elevator and block anyone else from using it. Just—us."

"What's going on?" Leif asked. "What's it all about?"

Harry looked at him.

"Son," he said, "we no longer have a choice. It was just taken away from us. It's no longer a matter of our wanting to find out —to get *them*. If we don't—they'll get *us*. . . ."

They were suddenly aware of urgent voices outside. The elevator doors were slowly pried open.

Harry watched the pale, pinched faces appear in the opening. They looked frightened.

Dammit—he was frightened too. Up against something he didn't understand. That was the worst of it. Not knowing. He hated it. Three times, now, they—someone—had tried to kill him. And the certain knowledge that there'd be another try chilled him. He looked at his son. He raged against the decision he'd made to involve him. Too late, now, to undo that stupid mistake. They —whoever they were—would be after Leif, too. Better they stick together all the way.

It was obvious that he'd made himself some determined, resourceful and utterly ruthless enemies. But what the hell was it that made them so eager to get rid of him? And Leif? And there were still so many other unanswered questions. Simple, fundamental questions—such as *who?*

And *why?*

WEST-GERMAN NEO-NAZIS
LINKED TO U.S. GROUP

RHINELAND-PALATINATE, West Germany—According to a report by the Ministry of the Interior of the Rhineland-Palatinate, the most active international links of West German neo-Nazi groups with countries outside Europe are with the U.S.A.

16

It was not until the next morning, Thursday, March 16, that Harry and Leif were able to get to the King's Court.

The hospital authorities had insisted on keeping them overnight for observation, and for once Harry's grumblings and objections had come to naught.

There'd been reports to fill out and questions to answer. More reports, and more questions. As Harry had predicted—no one answering the description of the orderly worked on the hospital staff.

They had been X-rayed and examined. And they had been declared okay. Shaken. Bruised. Sore as hell—especially Harry's newly mended ribs. But they were okay. The friction as the elevator plunged; the shock-absorbing power of the strong oil buffers at the bottom of the pit, and, above all, the cushioning effect of the collapsing food cart had combined to save them from being badly injured. Or killed. . . .

The dismal lobby of the King's Court was deserted. The manager was not behind his desk. Harry hit the bell placed on the counter top, and presently the manager appeared from his office. His face soured as he saw who his visitors were.

"Good morning," Harry said pleasantly. "We're here to see Konrad."

The manager gave him a quick glance. "I don't know if he's in," he said sullenly.

"Oh?" Harry sounded slightly unbelieving. "When did you see him last?"

"Yesterday."

"Okay. What's his room number?"

"Three seventeen."

Harry nodded. "Don't bother to show us. We'll find it." He and Leif started for the stairs. Harry turned back toward the manager. "By the way," he said casually, "what's this Konrad's last name?"

The manager looked up quickly. His mouth tightened and flattened out and his eyes glinted malevolently behind his spectacles as he realized how Harry had played him.

"Wendkos," he said, his voice surly.

"Thank you," Harry said with exaggerated politeness. "Thank you very much!" He was enjoying himself.

"That was almost too easy." Leif grinned as he and his father walked up the stairs to the third floor, trying to ignore their protesting muscles. Tacitly they had avoided the elevator.

Harry snorted. "Yeah. The guy is hardly a motor mouth." He barked a little laugh. "I thought he'd shit little green apples when he caught on he'd been had."

They reached the third floor. Number 317 was down the hall to the right.

Stepping lightly, Harry walked toward the door. He eased his gun from its shoulder holster.

Silently Leif followed.

317 . . .

Gun in hand, Harry stepped to one side of the door. He kept

close to the wall. Leif took up a position on the other side. Harry reached over and knocked sharply on the door. He waited and listened, all his being in his ears.

Leif was conscious of his heart beating considerably faster than normal. He wondered if his father had the same reaction—after all these years. Who—and what—was Konrad?

He was suddenly aware of a faint, nauseating smell that seemed to seep out and rise from the crack between the closed door and the floor. He tested it cautiously.

There was no answer to Harry's knock. No sound came from behind the closed door. Harry knocked again. The sound was loud in the quiet. He glanced over at Leif.

Leif mouthed the words at him. "What's that smell?" He pointed to the door crack.

Harry looked down. He sniffed the air. Suddenly his eyes widened.

"Damn!" he spat.

He grabbed the doorknob and twisted it. The door was locked. He stood away from it. "Stand back!" he growled at his son.

He brought up his foot and delivered a savage kick to the locked door. He winced and automatically clutched his injured ribs.

The door held.

Leif took his father's place. "Let me," he said.

At his second kick the door flew open.

Harry was in the room before it hit the wall.

The man was in the middle of the room—hanging from a sturdy ceiling hook which once might have held a chandelier.

He had used piano wire for his noose. As he had kicked away the chair, the wire had cut the flesh on his throat and slid it up, bunching it under his chin, exposing a skinned, oddly elongated neck. He wore striped pajamas, sagging on him and streaked with brown-dried blood.

For a split second a vision of concentration-camp inmates in their striped, threadbare uniforms flitted through Harry's mind.

In the violence of death, the man's bowels and bladder had voided, the excrement running down his scrawny legs. Below his stiffly pointing toes the feces and urine, mixed with coagulated blood, formed a caked pool. The stink was overpowering.

Leif stared at the corpse dangling in the middle of the room. He could feel the rising bile burning in his throat. But he did not avert his eyes.

This was Konrad. SS Obersturmführer Ernst Helmut Müller's friend. The man they had come to question. He appeared to be in his late sixties—although, from his bloated, discolored face with its swollen tongue and bulging eyes, it was difficult to judge.

Leif heard a noise at the door behind him, and the manager's petulant voice: "What on earth do you think—" The rest of the complaint was cut off by a strangled gasp. And the sound of retching.

Leif turned.

The manager was staring at the dead man. His hands were clamped over his mouth. A spasm racked his body, and vomit oozed through his fingers.

He turned and fled.

Leif swallowed. It was difficult. He turned to his father.

"I—I suppose we should take him down," he said uncertainly.

"Leave him," Harry snapped. "Leave him to the coroner's boys."

Harry was rummaging about on a small desk in a corner of the room. A pair of eyeglasses rested on the desk pad as if carefully placed there to protect them from being broken. Glasses? Harry poked them thoughtfully. He picked up a bunch of newspaper clippings. He glanced through them and handed them to Leif.

"Look at this," he said without comment.

There were three separate clippings. One had the yellowed look newsprint takes on after even a few months, the others looked new. And there was a small dog-eared card. . . .

Thurs. August 4, 1977   Los Angeles Times

TASK FORCE FORMED TO HUNT
NAZI WAR CRIMINALS IN U.S.

WASHINGTON, D.C.—The Immigration and Naturalization Service Wednesday announced the organization of a special

unit to track accused Nazi war criminals
who have taken refuge in the United
States. . . .

and the story went on to explain the function and area of operation
of the new unit.

Tues. March 7, 1978   Los Angeles Herald

HOLLYWOOD MUGGING
VICTIM DIES

LOS ANGELES—Ernest H. Muller, a motion picture industry employee, was
robbed and killed in the street last night
only a few steps from his home in the
King's Court apartments on Jaymar
Street in Hollywood. Police Lt. Jack Stein
of the Hollywood Division promises an
early arrest. Mr. Muller was the four-
teenth victim who . . .

And the last clipping—only a day old . . .

Wed. March 15, 1978   Los Angeles Herald

NAZI WAR CRIMINAL
DEPORTED TO HUNGARY

WASHINGTON, D.C.—The Immigration
and Naturalization Service announced
yesterday that its special unit, formed to
track down accused Nazi war criminals
in hiding in the U.S., has closed its case
against Matyas Szolnok, the former
Hungarian Gestapo officer accused as a
mass murderer in his homeland. Szolnok was deported Monday to be tried
by a Hungarian court. His alleged
crimes include . . .

Across the clipping had been scrawled: *Am I next? I can run no more—*

Leif looked at the last item, the little card.

```
┌─────────────────────────────────────────────┐
│                                             │
│     Schutzstaffel der N.S.D.A.P.            │
│                                             │
│   ⚡⚡ Führer-Ausweiss-Nr.  280.271.         │
│   Partei-Mitglied-Nr.  3.307.519.          │
│                                             │
│      W e n d k o s ,   Konrad              │
│                                             │
│      geboren 5.7.1911                       │
│   ist ⚡⚡ - Oberstrumbannführer            │
│   im Sicherheitsdienst (SD)                 │
│                                             │
└─────────────────────────────────────────────┘
```

There was a small photograph that might have been a picture of the dead man in his younger days. It was impossible to tell. And along the side the signature:

Konrad Wendkos
Eigenhändige
Unterschrift

He turned the card over. On the reverse was the familiar bold signature, its letters ominous and sharp like pointed daggers:

Der Reichsführer-⚡⚡

H. Himmler

H. HIMMLER

Nathan Zuckermann's hunch about Konrad had been a good one.

But it had come too late. . . .

Harry took the document from Leif. "Two down," he said grimly. "How many more to go?"

EX-RUSSIAN IN MIAMI
TIED TO NAZI CAMP

MIAMI—The Justice Department Monday filed a civil suit to revoke the American citizenship of a former Soviet officer accused of helping the Nazis execute thousands of Jews in a World War II death camp. . . . The suit would ultimately lead to deportation and trial as a war criminal. . . .

17

"Look at his ID, dammit!"

Harry stabbed a finger at the Wendkos SS identification card lying on the desk. The imperturbable man sitting there watched him and Leif evenly.

"The man was in the SD. The Sicherheitsdienst. The intelligence branch of the SS. A major!" He held up two fingers. "That's two of them. Muller and Wendkos. Both SS. Both right here in LA. Doesn't that make you one tiny bit curious, for crissake?"

Agent-in-Charge David Rosenfeld studied the two earnest men sitting across from him. Father and son. A recently retired LAPD investigator—his shoulder holster still showing in brief flashes when he gesticulated—and his psychologist son. Crackpots? No. But certainly over-excited because of a few unhappy coincidences. Maybe you couldn't blame them, but they of all people should know that coincidence is the very fabric of life. He sighed inwardly. Ex-Nazis plotting to kill? Because of a mugging victim? And an old snapshot? Attempted murder by ex-SS men who turn out to be non-existent? . . . His mind flitted briefly to the stack of active investigations his office was handling at this moment. Investigating dead Nazis would have a priority of about minus twenty. Why beat a dead horse—especially when you can't find it?

"Mr. Bendicks," he said calmly, "investigating Nazi war criminals as such does not fall within the jurisdiction of the FBI. It would be most unusual for us to get involved. Neither do muggings or suicides. Perhaps Immigration and Naturalization can be of help?"

"INS has no records of either Muller or Wendkos," Harry said, doing nothing to disguise the disgust in his voice. "And there are no local records on either. Why the hell do you think we came to you? All we want are some names of characters—possible characters—that Muller and Wendkos associated with."

Rosenfeld slowly spread his hands. He shook his head regretfully. "I'm sorry, Mr. Bendicks," he said firmly, "but our files are confidential. By law. Information can be given only to appropriate and authorized agencies. I shall, however, disseminate the information you have given me."

"Thanks a lot," Harry said sourly.

Unruffled, Rosenfeld continued. "And I can suggest that you request information from the Bureau through appropriate channels."

"Such as?"

"You may request information under the provisions of the Freedom of Information Act." He opened a drawer in his immaculately orderly desk and took out a printed form. "This will instruct you in the procedure to follow." He gave the form to Harry. "Simply address your request to the Deputy Attorney General of the U.S. Department of Justice in Washington, D.C.—indicating in your letter that it is a Freedom of Information Act request."

Harry took the form. He glanced at it.

"Information may be made available to you—unless it violates the law, or someone's privacy. Or pertains to an active investigation." Rosenfeld indicated the form. "As you can see, you must furnish your name, place and date of birth, present and all prior residences, places of employment and dates, and so on, as well as all pertinent information which would be helpful in connection with your request—all of it notarized. This will initiate a complete check and facilitate the necessary file search." He sounded as if he'd delivered the exact same speech hundreds of times. He had.

He stood up. He handed the Wendkos ID card to Harry. Harry pocketed it. He had to get it back to Stein. He knew the lieutenant had let him "borrow" it to placate him, and he hadn't cared.

"I'm afraid I can't be of any further assistance," Rosenfeld said pleasantly. "But I promise you I'll see what I can do."

Harry and Leif glanced at each other. Both knew full well it would remain just that. A promise.

"Thanks," Harry said. "Sorry to have taken your time."

As they stood waiting for the elevator, Harry turned to his son. "You had a lot to say," he commented sourly.

"Would anything I could have said make a difference?"

"Guess not," Harry grumbled. He looked at the instruction form the agent had given him. He crumpled it into a little ball and dropped it in the cigarette-butt-littered sand of a standing ashtray.

Written requests. Check-outs. File searches . . . The hell with it. He knew they couldn't afford to wait for information through channels. They'd have to go it alone. By the time they might—*might*, that is—get anything through the bureaucratic red tape, chances were they'd either be successful . . .

Or dead.

Harry strode rapidly across the squadroom toward Lieutenant Stein's office. How many days had he been off the force? Three? He already felt nostalgic. Without knocking, he barged into Stein's office and threw a bunch of papers on the desk in front of the lieutenant.

"Jack," he said angrily, "that's a crock of shit!"

Lieutenant Stein glanced at the papers. They were the various reports of the hospital elevator incident. From the Building & Safety Department. The Hospital Engineer. The LAPD Injury Reports.

"Where'd you get those?" Stein asked.

"Pete."

"Figures."

"Accident, they say," Harry fumed. "They call it a fucking *accident!* Hell, Jack, it was a deliberate attempt at murder!"

Lieutenant Stein sat back in his chair. He frowned at the agitated man standing before him. "Harry," he said, "you're acting like a damned fool." He had trouble keeping his annoyance out of his voice. "If you were still on the force, I'd kick your ass."

"Have you read that crap?"

"I have. Competent, routine reports. *No* evidence was found of any deliberate tampering with any of the machinery."

"You buy that?"

Stein slowly nodded. "They're the experts, Harry."

"Don't hand me that shit, Jack!" Harry was thoroughly disgusted. "It's nothing but drivel from a bunch of arthritic brains."

Stein sighed.

"Harry," he said quietly. "Off the record?" He looked questioningly at his friend.

"Off the record," Harry grumbled.

"Off the record, I'm inclined to agree with you. But we got nothing to go on. Nothing concrete. Just conjecture—'hunches,' for crissake! And a stack of reports that say *accidents.*" He looked at Harry. "Mind you, I still think your Nazis are nothing but a bunch of old farts. And those young idiots playing with swastikas and Hitler worship are just clowns." He frowned lightly. "But I do admit, you're turning up too damned accident prone for it to be accidental—if *that* makes sense."

Harry was calming down. He sat on the edge of the desk.

"Look, Jack," he said earnestly, "I didn't put in thirty damned years in the department for nothing. I made my own inquiries."

"I'd have bet on it," Stein said dryly.

"I talked to the chief engineer of the elevator service company. Guy named Hogan. Let me put you in the picture." Harry was warming to his subject. "An expert in elevator engineering would consider it child's play to tamper with a car. Screw up the works good. Make it crash."

"And you think one of your mysterious ex-Nazis is that kind of expert," Stein said with a thin smile.

"Why not?" Harry snapped. "The Nazis didn't just *walk* upstairs. And the sabotage itself is damned simple. All he'd have to do is bypass the motor speed-control circuit and jump out the governor contacts. That's an emergency safety system. That would make the car plunge down, full speed. The mechanical governor —a sort of cable that travels with the car as it moves up and down

—wouldn't trip the safety device that should wedge the car to the rails in the hoistway and stop it in case of overspeed. And . . . *crash!*"

"Pretty tall order, isn't it?" Stein asked dubiously.

"No way. Listen to this. *All* the machinery and *all* the electrical controls in question are in the machine room overhead. If the guy knew what he was doing, he could sabotage a car in a few minutes. And it'd take him even less than that to remove all traces of his tampering!"

Stein slowly shook his head. "It's not easy to buy, Harry." He shuffled the papers on his desk. "The reports mention that the machine room is kept locked. At all times. A pretty complicated locking system at that. Only a very few people have keys. The building engineer. The inspector from the elevator service company. Like that. We checked them all, Harry. All of them. We can account for every key. And there was no—get that, Harry—*no* evidence of any tampering."

"Dammit, I told you there wouldn't be!"

"Granted, a combination of malfunctions that would result in the accident that happened—"

"No *accident*, Jack!"

"—is a million-to-one chance. More. But that's what we're stuck with. Officially. A freak accident."

Harry began to protest. Stein held up a hand.

"Okay, okay, I don't buy it either. But, dammit, my hands are tied." He looked closely at Harry. "Again—off the record. I haven't dropped the case. We're looking for that orderly of yours. The engineers are still working their asses off running tests and inspecting every dab of solder in the damned system. We'll come up with something, Harry. In time."

"But I don't *have* time," Harry said in exasperation. "I'm a goddamned target. I wish I knew the hell why! We *both* are. Leif and I. And your engineers won't find anything wrong. I'm telling you, the car was sabotaged. By an expert. My informant is definite on that."

"The guy from the service outfit? What the hell else would you expect him to say? He's a company man."

"Oh, shit!"

Harry reached for the reports on the lieutenant's desk. Stein put his hand over them.

"Let me handle it, Harry. Don't make waves."

"The hell I won't!"

"Look. I've already had one complaint. Harassment. Destruction of private property. You name it."

"The bastard didn't waste much time."

"Lay off, Harry. You're a private citizen now."

Harry bristled. "No one can keep me from asking questions."

"No one will. Just—just don't interfere with—police business. . . ."

Harry suddenly felt numb. For the first time it really hit him. *He was off the force.* Out of it. All at once he felt lost—an outsider in his own life. . . .

Again he reached for the reports. For a second Stein's hand tensed. He looked sharply at Harry—then he took his hand away. Harry picked up the papers.

"I'll take them back to Pete," he said. He turned to go.

"Harry," Stein said quietly, "I believe you. Something is *not* kosher. I'll follow through. Do what I can. But, Harry, I mean it. Lay off. Don't go looking for a bumper-sticker solution. You're no longer on the force, remember that. Don't get yourself in trouble."

Harry turned back. He looked at the lieutenant.

"Trouble?" he said. "Hell, Jack, I'm in it up to my ass already."

He left, closing the door quietly behind him.

For a moment Lieutenant Stein stared at the closed door. Privately he agreed with Harry. The arm of coincidence did seem to stretch too damned far. He'd hated to deal his friend that low blow —but he had to keep him from getting into a mess with no way out but trouble. . . . He felt strapped. He'd do what he could—but it was damned little. The accident reports so far were inconclusive. Until he could dredge up something concrete, they'd have to be accepted at their face value. As accidents. And how can you go looking for a villain in an accident case?

Harry made for the station locker room. He went into the john and sat down in a stall. Just sat. He needed to be alone with his thoughts for a while.

He looked at the papers in his hands without seeing them. Whoever invented the phrase *stone-walling* sure had a way with words. He felt solidly up against one.

Alone.

No. Not alone. There was his son. He felt suddenly strengthened. Leif was in fact busily making all the necessary arrangements to leave his practice for a couple of weeks or so. Together Harry and his son would try to find some answers to the mess of puzzles and questions. Together . . .

He frowned. It was a matter of survival—and the danger was *right now*. There was no time to wait for official action. He knew the delays of departmental red tape only too well. He'd have to rely on himself. And his son. He was convinced he was on to something. Something important. Big. Big enough to kill for.

He had an idea.

The snapshot.

The dog-eared snapshot showing the Bavarian forest cabin with *Jenbach* scribbled on it. It was his only lead. He began to feel the familiar excitement of being on a case. Reasoning out his course of action.

Why not go to the source? Start at the beginning? With the cabin. The raid on the cabin. He'd never known what the follow-up investigations had uncovered about that whole mess.

The reports of the Army Interrogation Center would still exist —and he knew where.

In the Military Division of the National Archives in Washington, D.C.

EX-SS NAZIS GATHER FOR OLD TIMES' SAKE

ROSENHEIM, West Germany—About 500 former members of the notorious Nazi "Das Reich" SS Division which massacred the population of the French village of Oradou-sur-Glane in 1944 met here Saturday to "preserve the camaraderie of the last war, sealed in blood."

TWO

Washington, D.C.

20–22 March 1978

I

Dr. Arthur Rosenberg sat back in his chair. It creaked in protest —an obviously familiar sound in the small office. He peered benevolently at his two visitors.

"We're always glad to help researchers who take the pains to go to the original source," he said. "The trouble is, too many don't. And once misinformation has been published, it perpetuates itself as *fact* and becomes virtually impossible to change." He gazed sternly at Harry and Leif, seated before him. "It is indeed an admirable rule never to accept the first available source of information. Whenever and wherever possible, one should go back to the original source. That, of course, is one reason *we* are here." He leaned back again, oblivious to the protesting creak of his chair. "Now," he mused. "You are interested in Third Army Interrogation Center, April '45. Of course. War Department, G-2 Division Files. I imagine those records are long since out of purgatory." He eyed his visitors expectantly.

Harry and Leif exchanged glances.

"Purgatory?" Harry was puzzled.

Rosenberg, a pleasant man in his sixties, balding, with a tendency to a paunch, smiled at him. It was exactly the reaction he'd been playing for. He loved to tell his little story. Never failed to elicit a chuckle.

"Purgatory," he said firmly. "We have a nationwide network of records centers. Fifteen of them. Josh Townes, my witty colleague in OSS Records, dubbed them *purgatory*. All kinds of documents are held there, pending a decision whether to *save* them or *destroy* them. The good ones go to the heavenly files in the Archives —and the bad ones to the furnaces below!" He gave a funny little cackle. "Josh has a way with words, don't you think?"

Harry and Leif chuckled politely. "I just hope the records we're looking for haven't gone up in smoke," Harry replied.

He settled back and looked around. No government waste here, he thought. Rosenberg's small, unprepossessing office was cluttered with cardboard boxes and filing cabinets neatly stacked with papers and books. It was more like a glorified hallway.

The taxi ride from the Hotel Jefferson on Sixteenth and M Streets to the National Archives Building on Pennsylvania and Eighth had been a little longer and a lot more expensive than he'd bargained for. Sleet showers had fallen on the city, and the traffic lights had washed alternating red and green streaks of glistening color across the wet and slushy street. The leaden afternoon sky threatened to open up with more snow and rain any moment. They had decided on the cab rather than risk being caught in a sleety downpour at a bus stop. It had been slow going, but they had finally made it.

They had quickly gotten their researchers' identification cards and had been shown straight to the office of Dr. Rosenberg, head of the Modern Military Branch of the Military Archives Division.

Rosenberg's chair creaked again. "What exactly are you looking for?" he asked.

"AIC documents, investigation reports, interrogation and arrest reports, follow-up reports," Harry answered. "Anything that has to do with an incident—an ambush—that took place April 21, 1945, at a forest cabin in a place called Kugelberg at the village of Fichtendorf near Kulmbach."

"Classified?"

"Originally. Probably *Secret*. Periodic Reports. But they should long since have been declassified."

Rosenberg pursed his lips. "A forest cabin," he mused. "Do you have any names? Investigating officers? Occupants of the cabin?"

"Negative. No idea. Only about the ambush itself. And I'm not interested in that. What I want to find out is what any AIC follow-up investigation learned about the cabin and its occupants. Names. Disposition of the case. Anything . . ."

Rosenfeld slowly nodded. "We have quite a few declassified documents from that period available for your perusal, Mr. Bendicks," he said. "Over two hundred million pages."

Harry looked startled.

Rosenberg smiled. "Digging out information about an obscure forest cabin—provided such information exists at all—might take a little doing, what? A needle in a haystack would stand out like a sore thumb in comparison!" He chuckled. "As you can see, I can mix metaphors with the best of them."

"There must be a way to narrow the search down," Leif said.

"Of course there is. We have a very extensive card-filing system. Indexed. Cross-indexed. Double-cross-indexed." Rosenberg gave his little cackling laugh. "I suspect it takes a little getting used to. I gather your need is rather urgent." He again pursed his lips in thought. "If your search indeed is as important as you claim, I'll venture to say you could use a little help?"

"You bet," Harry said fervently.

Rosenberg nodded sagely. He leaned way back in his chair, adding a new pitch to its creak, and turned his head toward an open door.

"Josh!" he called. "You got anyone free to lend a couple of gentlemen a hand?"

A voice answered from the room beyond. "Sure. Gannon's indexing. Some just declassified Nazi stuff. That can be put off."

"Gannon will do admirably, Josh. Thanks," Rosenberg called back. He turned to Harry and Leif. "You'll have to excuse our intercom system," he said. "Somewhat primitive, I fear. But it works." He leaned forward. The chair remained silent. "Now," he said, all business. "The records you want to consult can probably be found either here or at the National Records Center at Suitland in Maryland, just a short distance from here. Gannon will know. A daily shuttle service is provided, and—"

"This had better be a matter of life or death for the Republic, Arthur!" The sound of a woman's voice interrupted him. "I'm right in the middle of the 0.15 file and you—"

A young woman appeared in the open doorway leading to the domain of Josh Townes of OSS Records. She stopped when she saw Harry and Leif. "Oh," she exclaimed. "I didn't know you were busy."

Harry and Leif looked at her and she looked back at them from large, expressive eyes behind over-sized, gold-rimmed glasses. Her open face was cradled by short, softly cut auburn hair, and a generous mouth hinted at an easy smile. She seemed to be in her middle twenties.

"Ah, there you are," Rosenberg said. He turned to his visitors. "Gentlemen, this is Gannon."

"*Susan* Gannon," the young woman said pointedly. "Arthur

insists on calling me Gannon. He refuses to acknowledge that I have a first name." She smiled. "I suspect he can't face the fact that it's a *woman's* name!"

Harry and Leif stood up. Leif offered the girl his hand. "I am Leif Bendicks," he said. "This is my father, Harry. Very nice to meet you." He meant it.

He took her hand. Briefly his thoughts flitted back to a party in Hollywood where he'd shaken the hand of one of the screen's legendary beauties. Myrna Loy. He'd been surprised that her hand felt like the hand of any other woman. This girl's hand should have felt the same, but somehow it didn't.

"Sorry to take you away from what you were doing," Harry said.

"It's perfectly all right," Susan said. Leif could see in her eyes that it wasn't. "I'll do what I can to help."

"They're looking for some Third Army Interrogation Center records," Rosenberg interjected. "1945. Not much to go on."

"Any suggestions how we can best go about it?" Harry asked.

"Yes," Susan answered. "It would be a help if you would make a list of all names, dates and places known to you, pertinent to the subject you want to research."

"Can do."

"It's late in the day," Leif said. "Perhaps we could ask Miss Gannon to have an early dinner with us. We could explain our problem to her." He looked at his father.

"Great idea," Harry said. He turned to the girl. "Will you join us?"

"I'm afraid not," Susan said. "I'd better start closing up the files I've been working on so I'll be ready to help you first thing tomorrow."

Leif smiled at her.

"See you tomorrow," he said.

As they left the building, Harry, the habit of constant observation long since become second nature, took in the scene before them. The day was still overcast and dark, and the streetlights had already come on. On their left a delivery van was stopping a short distance away, and a little to their right three men in overcoats stood in conversation near a wall surrounding the grounds of the Archives building.

Harry and Leif walked toward the steps leading to the street. An elderly man was making his way up the steps, cradling a cardboard box in his arms. Suddenly he stumbled and almost lost his footing. In his effort to regain his balance, the cardboard box slipped from his grip and fell to the ground. It flew open, and file cards scattered up and down the steps.

Harry and Leif hurried up to the shaken man.

"Are you all right?" Leif asked.

The man nodded. He looked with dismay at the litter of file cards.

"We'll give you a hand," Harry said. He picked up the box and handed it to the old man. He and Leif began to collect the cards. A uniformed guard came from the building to join them, bending toward the scattered cards.

Harry straightened up with a handful. Out of habit, he glanced at them. They were blank. He looked around for the owner of the box. The guard and Leif were still busy picking up.

The man was gone.

So was the delivery van. And the three men at the wall.

A chill of alarm went through him.

"Leif!" he called sharply. "Did you see where that guy went?"

Leif looked around, puzzled. "No. I thought—"

"You?" Harry addressed the guard.

The man shook his head. "I didn't see him leave." He nodded toward the building. "Perhaps he went inside."

Harry nodded. He looked grim. "Perhaps."

He gave the guard the collected cards. "Here," he said, "take these. If the gentleman is inside, perhaps you'll give them to him."

The guard took the cards from Harry and Leif. "Sure thing," he said.

As they walked down the avenue in the gathering darkness in search of a restaurant, Harry felt acutely on edge. He remembered his first trip back to Germany after the war. 1949. Walking the streets of a German town, he had felt exposed, in danger. It had finally dawned on him that it was because he was unarmed.

He was without a gun in "enemy" country for the first time in years. . . .

He had the exact same feeling now.

Even the familiar feel of his gun in its shoulder holster did not allay his uneasiness.

A host of questions raced through his mind. . . . Who was the old man? Why did he disappear? What became of him? . . . And the guard. What would have happened if the uniformed guard had not joined them? Was that why the old man left? Was that an unforeseen interruption in a carefully orchestrated incident? If so—what had been the purpose? . . . He had a creepy feeling he knew. They had been set up. But—dammit—for what? And from where would the danger have come? The delivery van? The three men at the wall? Something he'd missed altogether? He frowned. What the hell could happen in the middle of Washington, D.C.? Was he getting paranoid?

He kept his thoughts to himself, but he couldn't shake his feeling of acute apprehension.

After all, he thought, just because you're paranoid doesn't mean they're not out to get you!

NEO-NAZI PUBLICATIONS AT ALL-TIME HIGH

WEST GERMANY—The circulation figures of the extreme right press give some suggestion of the strength of the neo-Nazis. There are indications of a growing public interest in the neo-Nazi movement, whose newspaper editions are now at their highest point since 1945. Some 102 weeklies are published with a combined circulation of 244,000.

2

Dates of Material	:	April—May, 1945
Originating Unit	:	Army Interrogation Center Third Army, U.S.A.
Subject Documents	:	Interrogation Reports and Follow-up Reports pertaining to AIC investigations involving the following: Ambush firefight at mountain cabin at Fichtendorf near Kulmbach, Upper Bavaria, 21 April, 1945.
Keys	:	Following names and place names may provide keys to requested documents.
Names	:	CIC Agent Harold NMI Bendicks CIC Det. 212, XII Corps
		CIC Agent Andrew William Dexter CIC Det. 212, XII Corps (Killed in action at cabin)
		Sgt. Jackson (First name unknown) (Killed in action at cabin)
		SS Sturmbannführer Sepp Knauer Leibstandarte Adolf Hitler (Killed in action at cabin)
Places	:	Kugelberg Fichtendorf Kulmbach
Possibles	:	Ernest Helmut Muller Konrad Wendkos

Nathan Zuckermann
and
Jenbach   (Unknown whether name of person or
place. NOTE: Several villages in Germany,
Austria and Switzerland bear the name; telephone directories from those countries include
several listings of the name.

Susan looked up from the list Harry had given her. "Excellent," she said, obviously pleased with its thoroughness. "I'll have it Xeroxed so we can all have a copy. It should be very helpful."

Harry grinned. "I haven't written a few hundred thousand CIC and PD reports for nothing. How do we get started?" He gave his son a quick look. "If you'll point me in the right direction, I'll tackle the records at the Suitland center."

"Fine," Leif said brightly. "Miss Gannon and I'll stay here."

Susan glanced at him. "Well," she said. She sounded hesitant. "Yes, I suppose we can do it that way." She turned to Harry. "There's a shuttle leaving in a few minutes. The guard downstairs will direct you. If you have any questions or run into any problems, you have the number here."

Harry nodded. "I'll yell for help."

Leif was watching the girl sitting catty-cornered across from him at the table, engrossed in the contents of a large file folder. Susan had given him a fast, concise and impersonal course in how to use the Archives' filing system, and had unhesitatingly joined him in the search. They hadn't exchanged half a dozen words during the three hours they had already spent searching through document lists, files and indexes, reference compilations and registers.

They had found nothing.

And they'd heard nothing from Harry.

Reluctantly Leif returned his attention to the card-index file he was going through—but it was only seconds before his eyes sought out Susan once again.

He let his eyes rest on her. A lock of hair had separated and fallen across the edge of her glasses. She looked utterly feminine

—and desirable. He frowned lightly. He had a disturbing feeling that she was trying to keep him at arm's length. Her response to his attempts at friendliness had been strict courtesy and professionalism. He thought it was deliberate.

With some surprise he admitted to himself that he was very much attracted to her. He recognized the feeling of mixed excitement and apprehension he remembered from his first schoolboy crush, and later in his relationship with Ellen. Would it always feel the same? No matter when it happened? He didn't know why he was reacting so strongly toward Susan. He only knew he was. And he was not about to analyze why. It was the first time in too many years he'd felt anything like it.

He glanced at his watch. Just past noon. He stretched.

"What do you say we take a break?" he suggested.

Susan looked up. She seemed startled.

"Oh," she said. She looked at her watch. "Of course."

"Fine. I'd like to take you to lunch. I hope you'll accept." He sounded more anxious than he'd intended—a far cry from the tone of nonchalance he'd attempted.

Susan's face clouded briefly. She hesitated. "No," she said quietly, "I—I don't think so. Thank you." She saw the look of disappointment on his face. She bit her lip. "It's—it's almost impossible to get in anywhere at this time of day—without standing in line forever." She gave him a hesitant smile. "But—maybe I can invite you to join *me?*"

"Accepted!" he said at once. "Is there a restaurant in the building?"

Susan stood up. Unconsciously she smoothed her dress. "Better than that," she said with a smile. "You wait here."

Almost at once she reappeared. He noticed that the stray lock of hair was now in place. She was carrying a thermos bottle and a white paper bag, and she placed them ceremoniously on the table.

"Lunch," she announced brightly.

Leif grinned. "I'm a brown-bagger myself. But *white-bagging*—that's real class!"

"I always thought it did make it more festive—without being altogether too formal." She gave him a smile. "We can use the

paper cups over there." She indicated a wall dispenser near a
drinking fountain. "Just use three at a time. That way the coffee
doesn't soak through so fast."

They settled down at the table.

Lunch was great. Leif had never eaten a better half-a-baloney-
and-cheese sandwich. The apple and the cookie had been a treat.
And he'd only had to change his paper cups once. And somehow
sharing the contents of the little white bag had thawed some of
Susan's reserve. They had talked, and he had found her easy to talk
to. When he told her about the reasons for their urgency, she had
shown genuine concern. And he had talked to her about Ellen. It
had seemed a natural thing to do. He suddenly realized it had
been easier to talk to her—than to his father. . . .

He looked at her. He felt good. Warm. So—why not?

"You know," he said, "in between examining file cards and
index lists, I've been doing another kind of examining—some
heavy analytical thinking, believe it or not."

A fleeting cloud showed in Susan's eyes.

"Oh," she said. "The psychologist at work and play? Have you
been—analyzing me?" Her banter sounded a little forced.

"No," Leif said. "Me."

He looked closely at the girl. "I find the study of love-at-first-
sight a fascinating subject. And I have a prime case to probe."

"Love, Dr. Bendicks?"

"Leif."

Susan looked at him, her eyes grave. She had sworn she wouldn't
let it happen again. It had taken too long, it had cost her too much
in suffering, sleeplessness, self-hate when Mark had told her it was
over . . . there was someone else in his life. Even now, she hurt
when she thought of him. She had been so much in love. She had
trusted him so completely. She had been so *sure*. And now—here
was this man. So unlike Mark, but she recognized the feelings that
stirred in her as they sat together. But it was no good. She could
never in her life go through all that again. Maybe she was a cow-
ard, but she couldn't take the chance. . . . But when she spoke, she
said—

"Leif."

And her voice was soft.

Leif was watching her. A strange look, he thought. Worried? Pleased? Annoyed? Amused? He could not tell. Perhaps all of them. Or none.

"Susan," he said.

The ring of the telephone was the most unpleasant sound he'd ever heard.

Susan answered it. "Yes, Mr. Bendicks," she said. She listened briefly. She turned to Leif. "Your father has found some AIC records from the period you're interested in. He—"

Leif was on his feet. "Tell him we'll be right over," he said.

She did. She hung up. She smiled at Leif.

"He said not to wait for the shuttle. Take a cab!"

There were about a dozen AIC documents which dealt with the follow-up interrogations and investigations of the cabin ambush. As Harry read through them, he felt as if it had been only yesterday—certainly last week—that he'd been immersed in CIC work himself.

It was only a sketchy picture that emerged. The investigation had taken place during the hectic and eventful days immediately before VE-Day, and had probably suffered in thoroughness because of it. The locals questioned had been uncooperative, which was certainly not unusual, and had given little concrete information.

The cabin near Kugelberg had been occupied by a couple and their son, a pre-teenage boy. The Fichtendorf villagers stated they'd had very little contact with the family. They referred to the man and his wife as the Kampers, with no first names supplied, and stated that they kept to themselves. Strangely—and that, Harry thought, might have been the reason for the original report by the snitch—two men also lived with the family. They could have been relatives. Or friends. Servants. No one knew. They were described as strong-looking, burly young men. They never showed themselves in the village.

The subsequent search of the cabin by AIC personnel had proven completely negative. The inhabitants had vanished—and not a scrap of paper or anything else that could shed light on their identities had been found.

Harry learned little from the reports, except the fact that the word *Jenbach* was nowhere mentioned.

He was going over the summary portion of the last document, a report of the interrogation of a Fichtendorf farmer and his wife. A middle-aged couple with little to say. One son—away at war. One BDM girl, helping out. No concrete information. But one thing caught Harry's attention. In his conclusion the AIC interrogator mentioned his feeling that the man and woman knew more than they let on. Harry respected that kind of hunch. He went back to the heading of the report to see who the subjects were.

He read the name.

A surge of excitement swept through him.

The names of the Fichtendorf farmer and his wife were—*Anna and Helmut Müller.*

As in SS Obersturmführer Ernst Helmut Müller—late of the King's Court in Los Angeles!

YOUTHS TRAINED IN IDEOLOGY
OF THIRD REICH

FRANKFURT, West Germany—Erwin Schoenborn, born in 1915, leader of the Neo-Nazi organization Kampfbund Deutscher Soldaten with a claimed membership of 1,000, trains youths in the ideology of the Third Reich and racial consciousness. The youngest KDS activist is 15 years old. Schoenborn proclaims loyalty to Adolf Hitler and calls him "Germany's greatest leader."

THREE

Germany

22–26 March 1978

I

Hans-Jürgen von Flatow replaced the receiver on the old-fashioned European telephone. For a moment he sat gazing out the lead-sashed window into the night. He felt a smoldering annoyance. It had been a taxing two days—and now *this*. He glared at the telephone. Tomorrow was already March 23. Time had a disconcerting habit of accelerating and at the same time dragging when a deadline drew near.

He drained the last few drops of brandy from his glass and looked toward the man cleaning up the small, well-stocked bar.

"Emil," he called. "Another brandy, please."

"Yes, sir."

The man at the bar picked up a bottle and walked toward Von Flatow.

The great hall of Rittersheim Estate near the village of Fichtendorf was spacious, high-ceilinged and opulently furnished, the walls hung with paintings and tapestries. At one end a fire burned in a huge stone fireplace flanked by hunting trophies mounted on the wall: heads of wild boars, stag and deer. Heavy brocade draperies hung at the tall, arched windows.

The smell of cigar smoke permeated the air. The estate had been the seat of two days' intensive briefing of twenty delegates from the four corners of the earth. They had come from Spain, Italy, Great Britain. From the Scandinavian countries and the Balkan states. From South America and the Middle East. From the United States of America. They had gathered in the old German mansion to deliver their reports and receive final instructions.

The master of Rittersheim Estate was a man in his sixties, tall, erect, with graying hair and clear blue eyes in an arrogantly intelligent face. His manner and bearing bespoke his familiarity with power and authority. Only since the end of the war had he called himself Hans-Jürgen von Flatow.

Emil poured a generous brandy. Von Flatow swirled it in the balloon glass cradled in his hand. He breathed the lingering aroma of the cigars. So different from the musty air in the Führerbunker, he thought; there only an occasional cigarette could be smoked in secret because of the Führer's aversion to such indulgences. He looked up at Emil.

"You are taking Herr Berger to the airport tonight, are you not?" he asked.

Emil nodded. "Yes, sir. At 2100."

Von Flatow glanced at his watch. "Ask him to see me before he leaves," he said.

The man who joined Von Flatow was slightly younger. He remained standing.

Von Flatow peered at him, his eyes cold. "Your Los Angeles *Kreis* has failed not once but repeatedly to complete a routine action, Berger," he stated flatly. "The removal of a petty nuisance."

Berger wet his lips. "There have been complications, Herr von Flatow," he said deferentially. "We had orders to make it look like an accident. Otherwise it would have been considerably simpler."

"Fact is, you failed in your assignment," Von Flatow said icily. "Had you not done so, had the order been carried out correctly the first time, the necessity of dealing with *two* subjects would not have arisen."

Berger remained silent.

Von Flatow raked him with a look that moved from his receding hairline to his polished shoes and back up to his pallid face.

The man was a newcomer. Not of the old guard, Von Flatow thought disdainfully. Not of Emil's caliber, for instance. Emil—not the brightest intellect, perhaps, but loyal. Emil had served under him in the war. He had carried a pair of pliers in the pocket of his SS uniform tunic. At all times. Used them to pry the gold teeth from bodies on the battlefields. Friend and foe alike. After the war he had financed his denazification trial with the proceeds. . . . This Berger was not in the same league.

"You will be relieved to know, Herr Berger," Von Flatow said, sarcasm acid in his voice, "that the task is to be lifted from your shoulders." He glanced at the telephone. "The subjects of your abortive attempts are even now arriving in Germany."

He sipped his brandy.

"When you make your report of our meeting here," he said,

"you will also convey my assurances that the matter will be taken care of. By me."

He gave Berger a withering glance.

"I want you to give me a detailed profile of both men," he ordered curtly. "Now!"

Berger's descriptions of Harry and Leif were faultless.

NEO-NAZI UMBRELLA ORGANIZATION

FRANKFURT, West Germany—Efforts have been made to assemble neo-Nazi groups into an umbrella organization. . . . A meeting held in Frankfurt for this purpose, organized by Werner Kosbab, brought together some thirty delegates from rightist groups and received greetings from all over Europe. This National Forum of the People's Socialist Movement of Germany defines its goals as: the separation of races, German reunification and the union of all Europe's national socialists.

2

It was no damned different, Harry thought with nagging uneasiness. The narrow forest road looked just as he remembered it—and the wheelbase of their rented Volkswagen didn't fit the deep ruts. As with the jeep thirty-three years ago. What the hell had they been driving on the damned trail? Roman chariots?

He and Leif were slowly making their way along the little-used side road. Harry was behind the wheel. He peered ahead. Any moment he expected to catch sight of the distinctive mountain formation called Kugelberg—and the clearing with the cabin pictured on the faded, dog-eared photograph in his pocket. . . .

They had arrived in Frankfurt that very morning, Thursday the twenty-third, had picked up their stick-shift rental car and set out directly for Kulmbach. Harry had carefully figured the cost of doing it that way as against using public transportation. Renting the Volkswagen in Frankfurt had been cheaper. Even with the sky-high cost of gasoline.

With some surprise and to his enormous gratification, Leif had discovered that his limited knowledge of German made it possible for him not only to understand but to communicate with the German people. It was his first real chance to use the language he had taught himself in order to read professional books and periodicals available only in German. Harry, of course, seemed equally at home in both German and English.

In the shoulder holster under Harry's left arm rested his service gun. He felt comfortable with it there, "whole." Not exposed and vulnerable as he had in '49. As a retired police officer, he was allowed by law to carry a gun. In California. He had no idea if it was legal for him to do so in Germany. And he was not about to ask. He honored the old Army axiom: Ask no questions and you'll get no answers you don't want to hear! He was just thankful the customs check of their luggage had been so cursory.

From Frankfurt they'd taken the E5 Autobahn, by-passing Würzburg. At the Höchstadt junction they'd left the throughway and traveled north on route 505, skirting Bamberg. As they neared Kulmbach, Harry began to recognize the names of towns and villages on the highway junction signs. They were entering the area that had been XII Corps territory during the war. *His* territory. His pulse quickened. . . .

Coburg . . . He had interrogated the feeble old Duke of Coburg at his castle high atop a hill overlooking the city. Coburg had capitulated after a night of continuous shelling, and a couple of castle wings were without roofs. The surrender of the town had been negotiated by the Duke himself, and the old man had still been shaken when Harry questioned him immediately after.

Kronach . . . It was here he'd learned of the death of FDR and had attended the memorial service for the Commander in Chief in the field behind the forward echelons of XII Corps HQ.

Brückdorf . . . The bullet had literally come within a hair's breadth of giving him a part on the wrong side of his head. He'd actually felt it pass through his hair. The boy who fired it was eight years old. Luckily. The recoil of the gun had knocked it out of his hand before he could take a second shot. He'd been hiding in the cellar of the house since the GIs took the place earlier that day. He and his five-year-old sister. He thought he was protecting her from the enemy monsters. Harry had taken off his helmet to use as a carrying basket when he went into the cellar. He'd been down there looking for booze—not a bullet.

They made the nearly 190 miles to Kulmbach in a little under four hours, and it was still early afternoon when they arrived. They decided to go on to Fichtendorf, only a few miles farther, and try to find a place to stay.

Fichtendorf's only street bulged in the center to form a village square, and here they checked in at Gasthof Hirsch. The inn doubled as the local *Bierstube* and boasted the only available accommodations. It had all of three guestrooms. Harry and Leif were the only guests. Their room had no running water, the hard beds were smothered by huge featherbeds and the john was down the bare-floored corridor. But—as Harry observed—it was close to the action. And cheap.

Harry had been impatient. Keyed up. There were still several hours of daylight left—and they set out for Kugelberg. Just to look around. . . .

The Volkswagen was jolting along the forest road, leaning to one side, two wheels in the deep rut, the other two up on the center ridge. The front wheel on the ridge hit a rock and the car spun against the side of the rut, scraping along before Harry coaxed it back to its precarious course.

"Damn this pregnant rollerskate!" he growled. "Handles like it had square wheels."

Leif pointed ahead. "Is that it?"

Harry looked. Through the trees he could make out the rounded form of Kugelberg. Exactly as he remembered. And exactly as it looked on the photo in his pocket.

"That's it," he said. "The clearing and the cabin should be just up ahead." He was conscious of his heart beating faster. His senses sharpening. It was just about here. . . .

The forest road led into a clearing nestled among the evergreens. Harry brought the car to a halt. He stared ahead.

The clearing was lush and green.

And empty.

There was no sign of the cabin.

Harry frowned. "It's gone," he said unnecessarily. "The damned cabin is gone."

"Are you sure this is the place?" Leif asked.

"Of course I'm sure," Harry snapped. Could he ever forget? He started the car up again. The trail wound across the clearing to enter the forest on the far side. Harry stopped by a large tree. He got out. He walked up to the tree. Leif followed.

Harry peered closely at the tree. He ran his hand over the bark. He turned to his son.

"Look," he said. "On the trunk. The scar. This is the tree. That's where that SS man crashed his motorcycle. Gouged chunks out of the wood." He touched the overgrown scars. "It's—healed now. But you can still see it," he said, his voice suddenly husky. For a fleeting moment he heard the staccato rattle of enemy fire, the roar of motorcycles; and felt the sticky warmth of Andy's blood. . . .

He frowned. "Dammit," he said, "this *is* where that cabin was!" He strode rapidly into the clearing.

He walked the ground. It was overgrown with grass and weeds. He tramped all over it. There was no sign of a cabin ever having stood there.

Harry glowered at the silent forest surrounding them, as if he held it personally responsible. He frowned in thought.

"The pump," he said suddenly. "The well. The bastards couldn't cart *that* away."

He began to walk back and forth, examining the ground, kicking clumps and tufts.

Leif joined him. He was searching the ground, testing it with his feet. Suddenly he stopped.

"Over here, Dad!" he called.

Harry hurried to him. He kicked the ground. He exposed the end of a heavy wooden plank, overgrown with moss and weeds. He bent down and took hold of it. He lifted, strained—and the plank broke loose from the turf. He pushed it aside. Beneath it was a black hole. Other thick, overgrown planks all but covered it, blending perfectly with the ground.

Harry picked up a stone. He let it fall into the hole. In less than a second they heard a soft splash.

Harry looked at his son, his eyes triumphant. He was about to speak when a gruff voice interrupted him.

"Was suchen Sie hier?"

They both whirled toward the sound. Automatically Harry fell to one knee, his hand flew toward his gun. In the last instant he checked himself—but he knew the gesture wasn't lost on the man who stood watching them at the edge of the forest, a shotgun cradled casually in his arms.

Harry was acutely aware of the shotgun. He knew the split-second motion it would take to bring it into firing position. He was itching to have his own gun in his hand—but at the same time he recognized the absurdity of the urge. This was thirty-three years later, for crissake! He had a fleeting thought. Could he outdraw the man with the shotgun? No way. Once, perhaps—but not now. Anyway, this was no *High Noon* contest.

But he couldn't shake the feeling that he and Leif were in enemy country. . . .

"I asked you what you are doing here?" the man repeated, his voice harsh with animosity.

"Why?" Harry countered. He stood up.

"This is private property," the man snapped. He did nothing to conceal his hostility. "You are trespassing."

"We were looking for the cabin that once stood here," Harry said. "When was it torn down?"

"There was no cabin here," the man said flatly. "Ever."

Harry was about to contradict him when a second man—also holding a shotgun—stepped from the woods and joined the first. He had on a green, embroidered wool jacket and gray knee breeches, heavy boots and a hat with a *Gamsbart* tuft ornamenting the hat band.

He glanced at Harry and Leif, then turned to the other man. When he spoke, his voice was curt and authoritative.

"What is going on here, Emil?" he asked.

NEW PUBLIC ATTITUDE
TOWARD THE THIRD REICH
IN GERMANY

WÜRZBURG, West Germany—One
sign of the new public attitude toward
the Third Reich is the meeting of former
SS units. Contrary to earlier practice,
these are now held without any attempt
to maintain secrecy. One such meeting of
the Horst Wessel and the French Charle-
magne SS Divisions took place in Würzburg and was attended by 300 former
members, including 50 Frenchmen.

3

Emil didn't take his eyes from Harry and Leif.

"I was telling them they are trespassing on private property,
Herr von Flatow," he answered. There was a certain eagerness in
his voice. It sounded dangerous.

Von Flatow looked at Harry and Leif. Berger's description had
been perfect, he thought. He stepped a little closer to them.

"Allow me to introduce myself," he said pleasantly. "My name
is Hans-Jürgen von Flatow. It is my estate—the hunting estate
Rittersheim—on which you, as our good Emil put it, are trespassing." He smiled engagingly. "May I ask who you are and what it
is you are looking for?"

Harry sized the man up with the speed born of years of practice.
Instinctively he distrusted him, although there was no obvious
reason for it.

He introduced himself and Leif. "We were looking for a cabin,"
he said. "It used to be right here." He looked at Emil. "Your man
there said—"

"Ah, yes," Von Flatow interrupted him easily. He felt a twinge
of annoyance with Emil. It had been stupid to deny the existence

of the cabin. "The cabin. Unfortunately, it burned down. Many years ago. Emil would not know of that. It happened before his time." He looked around the clearing. "I had all the debris removed. Long ago. This little *Waldwiese* is a favorite grazing spot for my best game." He returned his attention to Harry and Leif. "How did *you* know about that old cabin?" he asked with only polite curiosity.

Harry thought fast. He didn't know the man. Von whatever-his-name-was. No use laying the whole story on him. Use the golden rule: Give away as little as possible. Use a cover. But the best cover story still consists of as much fact and truth as possible, with only a necessary minimum of fabrication.

"I have been here before," he said. Defiantly he added, "During the war."

Von Flatow smiled. "But of course," he said amiably. "A sentimental journey. So many of your countrymen make sentimental journeys to their old fields of glory, do they not? You are perhaps showing your son such a place?"

Harry said nothing. He looked steadily at Von Flatow. The German stared back, his clear blue eyes penetrating. Harry had the creepy feeling that the man was trying to look through his skull and read his brain.

Von Flatow was watching the two Americans. Now? They were alone. Defenseless. It would be simple. A small amount of risk, of course. But that could be dealt with. His hand tightened imperceptibly on his gun. He felt Emil watching him intently, ready to follow his lead. . . . No. Not yet. There were too many questions unanswered. Why *had* they come? Surely not just to look at the old cabin. Had they learned something from the papers of that idiot Muller? If so—what? These things should be known. He relaxed. It might be amusing to play a little cat-and-mouse game.

Especially when the mice were in the cat's own sandbox. . . .

He made a slight bow to them. "Please," he said, "feel free to look around. As my guests." He turned to Emil. "Come," he said. "We shall show the gentlemen the courtesy of leaving them to their memories."

The two Germans walked into the forest.

For a moment Harry and Leif stood looking after them. Then Harry turned abruptly and walked straight for the car.

They were well away from the clearing before either of them spoke.

"Did you take a good look at that character called Emil?" Leif asked. "He looked as if he'd enjoy tearing you apart."

Harry grunted assent. "I'll give you odds that he once had an SS identification card. I've seen his kind before. They used to guard concentration camps. And enjoy it . . ."

For an instant kaleidoscopic images whirled through his mind. His first look at a newly liberated camp. The sights, the sounds, the smells of horror as he walked—his footsteps leaden—like a tourist through hell. . . .

"What do you make of Von Flatow?" Leif asked.

"Nothing," Harry said. "Yet."

Typical arrogant Kraut, he thought. Wouldn't trust him farther than I could throw his damned estate. But he said nothing. No use airing his prejudices. If they *were* prejudices—and not judgments based on grim experience . . .

"What time is it?" he asked.

Leif glanced at his watch. "Just past five."

"Okay. We'll go back to the *Gasthof.* Get a bite to eat. Tomorrow is Friday. First thing in the morning we'll drive to Kulmbach. The Records Office at the *Bürgermeisteramt* should be able to tell us where to find the Müllers."

They ate well: knackwurst, sauerbraten and boiled potatoes washed down with *Münchner Hofbräu.* Harry and Leif were the only ones eating dinner in the little *Bierstube* of the Gasthof Hirsch, although there were several others in the room, laughing, talking and drinking beer—and studiously keeping to themselves.

They felt pleasantly relaxed after the meal. The jet lag hadn't caught up with them yet and they were eager to get on with finding Anna and Helmut Müller.

"When we do find them, what then?" Leif wanted to know.

"I'll interrogate them," Harry said.

"*Interrogate* them?" Leif raised an eyebrow.

"Okay, question them. Find out what they really know about that cabin. What they were hiding when they were questioned before by the AIC officer. I'll get it out of them."

"How, Dad? You can't really interrogate them. Or even question them. Not if they don't want to talk to you."

"They'll talk to me," Harry said grimly.

"This isn't 1945, Dad," Leif said seriously. "You can't use the same—approach you did in the CIC. Or the LAPD, for that matter. This is different."

For a moment Harry glared at his son. Then he relaxed. He grinned. "Okay," he said. "I promise I won't slam them up against the wall or use my rubber hose. Will that do?"

"I guess I'll have to be satisfied with small favors," Leif said. He smiled back at his father.

"It'll work," Harry said confidently. "With no trouble. It had better."

"I certainly agree with that."

"*Any* conversation in a given situation is revealing," Harry said. "Something is always given away." He took a healthy draught of his beer. "The trick is to recognize it. Even the most ordinary, banal smalltalk contains a helluva lot of information, if you look for it." A glint of amusement crept into his eyes. "I'll bet you a beer I can get at least half a dozen facts or reasonable assumptions out of *anything* you can say to me!"

"Anything?"

"Anything. Just give me a situation and one short sentence."

"You're on!"

Leif thought for a moment. "Smalltalk, eh? All right—how about this? Two men on the street. One says: 'Good morning. How are you today?'"

Harry didn't hesitate a second. Ticking off on his fingers and automatically falling into officialese, he rattled off:

"*One.* Fact. Time of day. Morning. *Two.* The subjects have just met, therefore the greeting. *Three.* The person spoken to is able to hear, presumably he is therefore not deaf, nor—*Four*—mute, as a reply obviously is expected. At any rate, the subject is able to understand and communicate. *Five.* The person spoken to must appear to be all right. No visible or unexpected injuries or abnormalities are evident to the speaker, or the question probably would not have been asked—or a different phraseology would have been used. *Six.* The speaker and the person spoken to evidently know each other or have seen one another before, or the question probably would not have included the word *today.* *Seven.* It is obviously daylight and the speaker is sighted—that is, not blind—and so presumably is the man addressed by him—or, again, a different phraseology would have been used incorporating some sort of self-identification. *Eight.* It can further be speculated that the speaker is or wishes to be on a friendly basis with the addressee; that at least there is no animosity between them."

He finally paused for a deep breath. "As you can see, we already know quite a lot about both your subjects. That's for openers. Now, in addition—"

"Okay, okay," Leif laughed. He caught the eye of the girl serving beer at a table nearby.

"Zwei Hofbräu, bitte," he said in his best German. He turned to his father. "I could poke a lot of holes in that pretty speech," he said. "But you've certainly proved your point."

Harry finished his beer in anticipation of the round he'd just won. "Interrogation—asking questions and getting answers—is a funny business," he said expansively. "And I'm not talking about hunches," he added quickly. "I'm talking about all the signs, all the little indications that can help you spot a guy who's lying. By studying his face."

Leif nodded. "I agree."

"I'm not talking about the usual signs," Harry said, warming to his subject. "The sweaty palms. The shifty eyes. The beating artery at the temple. That sort of thing. The common indications of tension, apprehension—what have you."

The barmaid put two steins of foaming beer on the table. *"Zwei Hofbräu,"* she announced.

"Danke schön," Leif said.

Harry was oblivious to the interruption. "There's something else. Almost imperceptible gestures. You learn to watch for them. To recognize them. Tiny involuntary reactions that telegraph a lot of information that doesn't come out in words . . ."

"Micromomentary expressions," Leif said quietly.

"Yeah. Little facial changes that appear and disappear in a fraction of a second. A twitch of a nostril. Or a cheek. A lightning-fast frown. Or smile."

"The blinking of an eye so fast you can hardly see it," Leif said. He watched his father, a mischievous gleam in his eyes. "You more —feel it. . . ."

"Yeah."

"Or a sneer so fleeting as to have been almost non-existent."

"Exactly!" Harry reached for his beer. He stopped in mid-motion. He looked at Leif. With a sheepish little grin he shook his head. "You bastard!" he said. "You're putting me on!" He laughed. He looked at his stein. "Must be the beer."

"Not exactly, Dad," Leif said. He was enjoying himself. He hadn't felt this fully at ease with his father for years. "But what you are describing is something I am quite familiar with. The minute, quick motions—we call them micromomentaries—that appear and disappear on a person's face when under stress. They're believed to be split-second reactions released by the subconscious before they are literally wiped off by the conscious mind." He looked closely at his father. "I watch for that sort of thing, too, when I talk with my patients—my subjects. . . ."

"I'll be damned," Harry said. "Of course. It would have to be like that. We *are* in essence doing the same thing. Getting information. I—I never thought of it that way." He sounded surprised.

"Neither did I," Leif said quietly.

For a little while both men were silent, sipping their beer, savoring the moment.

Harry looked at his son. He had a momentary thought of Andy —and the gratification of being part of a goddamned good team. . . .

He finished his beer.

"Come on," he said. "Let's go fight those damned featherbeds. Tomorrow is going to be a heavy day. We'd better get some information out of the Müllers. With or without micromomentaries!"

MOCK "JEW BURNING" AT
ARMED FORCES UNIVERSITY
IN MUNICH

BONN—The newspaper *Frankfurter Rundschau* reported that eight to ten young army officers climaxed a drinking bout at the Armed Forces University in Munich last Feb. 16 by burning papers scribbled with the word "Juden" (Jews), exchanging Nazi salutes and singing a Nazi hymn.

4

The woman behind the wear-polished wood counter in the Kulmbach *Bürgermeisteramt* Records Office peered primly at Harry and Leif.

"Anna and Helmut Müller," she said, her thin lips pursed in that pinched pout of apparent distaste with which most German *Beamte*—civil servants—address the public and which is the mark everywhere of small people with a little power. "It is a very common name. Have you a previous address for them?"

"Fichtendorf," Harry said.

"I see," said the woman. Evidently the answer displeased her. "When—to your knowledge—did they live there?"

"In 1945," Harry said. "That is the last date we have."

The woman quickly looked up at him. Her eyes flitted to Leif and back to Harry. They grew veiled and cold. She put her bony hand to the tight bun of mouse-gray, lackluster hair at the nape of her neck.

"May I ask why you wish to locate these people?" she asked, her voice sharp with suspicion.

"It is a private matter."

"Are you related to them?"

"No."

"Your name?"

"Bendicks. Harry Bendicks."

The woman made a note on a pad. She looked at them, her eyes hostile. "You are not—German." It was more a statement than a question.

"No," Harry said. "American."

"So." The tone of voice was like the snapping shut of a book.

"We should very much appreciate any help you can give us in locating the Müllers," Harry said pleasantly. *"Fräulein—?"*

"Frau Wedemeister," the woman corrected.

"—Frau Wedemeister."

"I do not think that will be possible."

"Surely you have records?"

"Of course. But we can *not* allow our records to be examined without a valid reason. Especially not—" She broke the sentence off. Both Harry and Leif knew how she had intended to end it: — not by foreigners.

"It is a matter of some importance," Harry insisted. "A confidential matter. I'm sure you could make an exception."

The woman's lips drew themselves into a thin, straight line. In the process the faint growth of hair on her upper lip became more prominent. She shook her head.

"It is not possible." Her voice was final.

Harry nodded. He took out his wallet and opened it. Carefully he scribbled a note on a small pad, making sure the woman caught a glimpse of his official-looking badge. He put the wallet away. He looked at the woman.

"I wonder, Frau Wedemeister—" He pronounced her name meticulously. "Inasmuch as you are unable—or perhaps unwilling —to assist us, I wonder if you would be good enough to tell your superior that we should like to speak with him." His tone of voice was pleasant. Perhaps a little too pleasant.

The woman glared at him. "That will not be necessary," she snapped icily. "I am in charge of this department. I am perfectly able to take care of the matter myself. Be so good as to wait here." She turned abruptly and stalked away.

Harry glanced at Leif. They exchanged a minute smile. They looked around the office.

The wooden counter ran the full length of the room dividing the area set aside for the public from the office area. A few uncomfortable-looking benches shared the public side with a hat-and-coat rack and a rusty umbrella stand. A couple of glass-covered bulletin boards held pinned-up notifications, pamphlets and official proclamations. On the other side several people were working at desks placed in orderly rows.

The minutes dragged by. Harry did not allow himself to become impatient. He'd known the woman would punish them by making them wait.

Finally she reappeared carrying a large, dusty-looking ledger. She put it on the counter and opened it to a page where she had placed a paper marker.

"Müller, Anna," she read, flat-voiced. "Yes. Fichtendorf." She looked up at Harry. "This is the last official entry," she said. "1949. There is a note: *Current address unknown.*" She looked pleased with herself.

"Is that all?" Harry allowed himself to sound incredulous. "Are your records that incomplete?"

"Some entries—unimportant ones, of course—are not up to date," the woman said curtly. "Anna Müller may have left this *Amt* entirely."

"What about her husband? Her family? I'm certain the records kept by your department must have more information," Harry persisted.

"The husband of Anna Müller, Helmut Müller, died in 1947," the woman said without consulting the leger. "The Müllers had one son. Müller, Ernst Helmut. He was in the armed forces. He is listed as missing in action since 1945." She closed the book. "That is all the information I—or my superior—can give you, Herr Bendicks."

She left no room for doubt that the interview was ended.

"It makes damned good sense," Harry said to his son as they were walking down the broad stairs from the Records Office in the *Bürgermeisteramt.* "If Ernst Helmut Müller came from this area —and it sure looks like he did—he might easily have been assigned to an operation in his own backyard." He frowned. "We've got to find his mother."

"Yes. But—how?"

"We'll have to dig. The local newspaper morgue. Police files. The local burgers. Hospitals. Cemeteries. The works. It'll take time. A helluva lot of time. Always does." He sounded disgusted. It would be like every other damned investigation. Plodding. Plodding. Plodding. Only a helluva lot more difficult. In a foreign country. Without official status . . .

"We could try to go to a higher authority at the *Bürgermeisteramt,*" Leif suggested. "Perhaps the mayor's office?"

Harry nodded. "That, too."

They'd reached the bottom of the stairs when a voice called out: "Herr Bendicks!"

They turned.

At the top of the stairs stood a young woman. She glanced back over her shoulder, than ran down the steps to join the two men.

"Herr Bendicks," she said hesitantly, addressing Harry, "please forgive me. I could not help overhearing your conversation with Frau Wedemeister."

"Yes?"

"Please, you must understand her. You must forgive her. She is of an older generation. She was raised during the time of the National Socialists. During the war. It is difficult for her to deny her past. You must understand."

The girl looked quickly over her shoulder. Harry knew that look. He used to call it "the Gestapo glance." Making sure no one was close enough to overhear. He'd seen it countless times in the past as a CIC agent. His interest was at once alerted.

"Of course," he said.

"You were asking about the Müller family? Ernst Helmut Müller?"

"Yes."

"Ernst Müller was an officer," the girl said. "I know it from the old records. An officer in the SS." She looked frightened. Automatically she lowered her voice. "It was never certain what happened to him. He—disappeared. That is what Frau Wedemeister would not have you know." The young woman talked quickly, with frequent glances up the stairs behind her. "She feared you might be looking for him. That you might mean harm to him, should you find him. Please, you must understand. Frau Wede-meister—her loyalties may be wrong, but they are loyalties. . . ."

"We do understand," Harry said quietly.

"And then you must also understand, please, that there are many of us—the younger generation—who do not wish to—to cover up for what was done under the Nazis. We—all of us—must face up to the consequences."

"Do you know anything that might help us?" Harry asked.

The girl nodded. "Perhaps. I do not know Anna Müller. I do not know where she is. But I do know someone who might. A man. An old man. Close to eighty. His name is Anton Gerner. He would have known Anna Müller. I am sure of it. He may know where she is. He was the last Ortsbauernführer in Fichtendorf."

"The Nazi leader of Fichtendorf," Harry said softly to his raptly listening son. "Do you know where we can find this Anton Gerner?" he asked the girl.

"Yes. He is getting a welfare pension from the government," she said. "I work on the records." She pressed a slip of folded paper into Harry's hand. "I have written the address for you."

Quickly she turned and ran up the stairs.

Harry unfolded the paper.

Anton Gerner
Windgasse 79
Kulmbach

It was their first real lead.

GERMAN STUDENTS' VIEW
OF HITLER

BERLIN—The *Berliner Allgemeine Jüdis-che Wochenzeitung* published excerpts from school essays on the topic "What I Have Heard About Adolf Hitler."

The authors, aged 14 and 15, were born years after Hitler died in the ruins of Berlin in April 1945. Here are some examples of their hearsay reports:

"Hitler was strict with his people and
everybody had respect for him. . . .
The neighbors still wish sometimes that
he was back again. . . . He was great in
the war too. His soldiers were courageous and were laughing when they
went to war."

5

The sign stenciled in gold-edged black letters on the shopwindow formed a semicircle—

ANTIQUITÄTEN

P. GRAFF

Over the only entrance to the little house on Windgasse was the
number—79.

The display area behind the window was cluttered with a con-
glomeration of objects that had two things in common: age and
dust. There were a few good antiques, but most of it could best be
described as junk—charitably, perhaps, as curios. A few pieces of
cut glass; an old doll with a porcelain head; deer antlers; painted
regimental steins; and a few carved wooden figures which showed
a certain imagination.

Leif looked at his father. "Do you think she gave us a wrong
address?" he asked.

Harry grunted. He peered through the window into the gloomy
shop beyond.

"One way to find out," he said. Resolutely he opened the door.

A thin bell tinkled overhead as Harry and Leif entered the shop.

Behind a glass display counter holding trays of jewelry, watches and silver flatware, a plump woman raised her head.

"*Guten Tag!*" she greeted them with a friendly smile. "Please come in."

On the counter before her lay an old stereoscope and a pile of stereoscopic photographs. She held one of them up and looked at it.

"Remember these?" she asked. "I do. They were so very interesting. And so picturesque. Real three-dimensional." She shook her head. "I remember they used to be only a few pfennig. And now—I must get three marks for each." She looked up at her customers. "Times change, do they not?" She marked the price on the back of the photograph and smiled at Harry. "What can I do for you?"

"May we just look around for a moment?" Harry asked.

"*Bitte, bitte!*" The woman beamed. "Of course. There are so many wonderful things to see, is that not so? Please . . ."

Harry walked over to a rickety little sidetable. On it stood a small music box. Old and scratched, the painted picture on the lid all but chipped away. *Symphonion,* he read on the inside. It had a metal disc with an arrangement of holes. The disc could be rotated with a small handle. He tried it. A few delicate tones came from the box.

"Over a hundred years old, that is," the woman said. "Once the toy of some lucky *Kindchen,* no? One does not find many of those little treasures today."

"Very interesting," Harry said. He turned to the woman. "P. Graff," he said, nodding toward the shopwindow. "Is that the owner?"

The woman gave a little laugh. "It is," she said. "I am P. Graff. The P. is for Paula."

Harry smiled at her. "You have a fascinating place," he said.

The woman sighed. "Once," she said. "Once I had some very good things." Her face suddenly clouded over. "But this is many years ago. . . . In the war my husband was killed. In a bombing. Our house was damaged. Very badly. And then—when the Americans came—it was hard to make a living. Very hard." Again she sighed. "I had many of my lovely things from my home still. Undamaged. The *Amis* were always looking for things to send home. So —I began to sell my things. What good were they to me—without my husband?" She shrugged. "What else could I do? I had no skills. It was the beginning of my little shop. But now—today—it is not easy to find good things that can be sold at reasonable prices."

She brightened. "But I *do* have some very fine pieces. Do you have a special interest, perhaps? I could show you what I have." She smiled at him.

"That's very kind of you, Frau Graff," Harry said. "Actually—we came here to look for a man named Anton Gerner."

Leif was watching the woman. He knew what his father had been doing. Getting the woman to talk, off guard, before broaching the actual subject of their visit. He thought he saw her stiffen as his father mentioned Anton Gerner. But she caught herself at once.

"Anton," she said brightly. "Poor old Anton. He does not get many visitors these days. He will be pleased." She looked guilelessly at Harry and Leif. "You are friends, perhaps? I have not seen you before. And Anton has lived here many years. . . ."

"We are from America," Harry said.

Again Leif thought the woman stiffened.

"I—see," she said. Her recovery was not as instantaneous as before.

"The Records Office in the *Bürgermeisteramt* sent us here to see Herr Gerner," Harry said.

"Trouble?" The woman looked concerned. She nodded, answering her own question. "Nothing but trouble ever comes from the government." She looked up at Harry. "But Anton can do no harm," she said. "Not anymore. And he was such a little, unimportant man. Of course, he was a Nazi. You know that. Most everyone had to be." She shook her head. "I myself—and my husband—we could not agree with—We were never Nazis. Never." She looked solemnly at Harry. "Of course, we had to do what the authorities told us. We had no choice. It was so long ago. . . ." She bit her lip. "They—they sent us two girls. To help in the house. And in my husband's business. Two Jewish girls, they were. But I treated them well. Always. They ate the same as us. I treated them just like people. . . ."

She looked from Harry to Leif, satisfied that she had convinced them of her good-hearted nature and anti-Nazi past. After all, one can never be too careful with Americans. . . .

Harry found it difficult to continue to be civil. "There is no trouble, Frau Graff," he said.

The woman's ample bosom heaved in a deep sigh. "It is about his welfare pension, perhaps?" she asked. "It is little enough he gets. And little enough they give me for looking after him."

"It is not about the pension, Frau Graff," Harry assured her. "It is a personal matter. Could you tell me where we can find him?"

Frau Graff looked at him speculatively.

"Personal matter," she repeated. "You do not know Anton, do you? Of course not." She gave a little laugh. "Anton is an old man. He is *blim-blim.*" She tapped her temple. "From old age." She nodded toward a door in the rear of the shop. "He lives back there. Across the yard. You are welcome to go see him."

"You know, Dad, if the old man really *has* senile dementia," Leif said, "we are not going to get much from him—if anything at all."

Harry nodded. They were walking across a small cobblestoned courtyard in the back of the antique shop, headed for a little shed in the rear. The windows on either side of the door were covered with faded, gaily patterned curtains, and a pile of wood was stacked beneath one of them.

Harry knocked on the door.

There was no answer.

He knocked again. "Herr Gerner!" he called. Still nothing. He tried the handle. The door was unlocked. He opened it and stepped inside, followed by his son.

They both stopped short.

The place seemed to be a combination of workshop and living quarters. Untidy, cluttered and stuffy, it was still a place of magic. Intricate and imaginative wood carvings and sculptures—some finished, others in various stages of completion—crowded every corner, every available space in the squalid room. An infinite variety of subjects and shapes. Strong, honest expressions of man and his world. Scattered throughout, almost as an afterthought, were a few pieces of battered furniture. An unmade cot, soiled blankets bunched up; a rickety washstand with a cracked bowl; a couple of chairs partly held together with heavy string; a massive chest of drawers, its edges and corners whittled away. And over all, a layer of wood chips and shavings. Only one area was bare of the wood parings, the area immediately around a small, black, pot-bellied stove. A fire flickered behind the grate in the door.

Dominating it all, demanding attention, stood a figure nearly two feet tall carved from dark wood and directly facing the door.

It was a Christ. The traditional long hair, beard and flowing robe. In the time-honored gesture the arms were held at the sides, stretched forward, palms up. But—disturbingly—the feeling created was not one of comfort, serenity and love. Instead the sharp angles of the arms and hands and the stiffness of the body imparted a chill of terror. The face was blank—totally without features. Leif wondered uneasily what expression its creator saw in that empty visage. . . .

On a stool at a scarred table sat an old man, slowly whittling away at a piece of wood. He turned to look at Harry and Leif as they entered. Then he resumed his whittling.

"Herr Gerner?" Harry asked. "Anton Gerner?"

The old man did not react.

"Herr Gerner!" Harry said, speaking in a louder voice.

Without turning from his whittling, the old man answered irritably, "Yes, yes, yes . . ." He looked up at them. "Where is my soup?" he asked cantankerously. "I am supposed to get my soup." He turned back to his whittling. He put down the piece of wood on which he was working and picked up another. Vigorously he chipped away at it.

Harry stepped closer to him. "Herr Gerner," he said, "we'd like to talk to you for a moment."

The old man raised his head. He held up the piece of wood. He opened his mouth in a wide, toothless grin. "This one," he said happily. "Ah, yes. This one. It will be the best of them all." And again he took up his whittling.

Harry contemplated him. It was easy to believe the man was almost eighty. His sparse hair was a yellowish gray and his weathered face deeply wrinkled. His hand guiding the sharp knife into the wood was gnarled and big-knuckled. His head nodded almost imperceptibly as he worked away.

Suddenly he put away the wood. Laboriously he stood up. He looked surprisingly robust for his age. In a short-stepped, shuffling gait he walked over to the washstand. For a moment he stood there staring vacantly into space. Then he frowned in puzzlement —and started back toward the table. He caught sight of Harry and Leif and peered at them, looking crotchety. "Who are you?" he asked irascibly. "What are you doing here? Get out!" He shuffled over to the table, sat down on his stool and again began to whittle.

Harry walked up to him.

"Herr Gerner," he said, "please listen to me. I would like to ask you a favor. A question. One question."

The old man looked up at him, his eyes strangely unfocused. He said nothing. Harry put his hand on the old man's arm. Gerner stopped whittling—and stared at Harry's hand.

"Herr Gerner," Harry said firmly, "listen to me now. Frau Anna Müller. You know her."

The old man did not react.

"Anna Müller. From Fichtendorf," Harry pressed. "Do you know where she is? Where she lives now?"

Gerner suddenly looked up at him. Again he smiled his toothless grin. "Frau Graff," he said. "She sold my wood carvings. She told me." He frowned. He looked around. He picked up a fresh piece of wood and began to examine it minutely. The piece he had been working on fell to the floor.

Leif walked up to his father. "Dad," he said quietly, "I want to talk to you." He nodded toward the far end of the room. "Over there."

Harry followed his son. "It's no damned use," he said bitterly. "The old geezer *is* senile."

Leif looked thoughtful. "Perhaps," he said. He spoke in English, but he still kept his voice low.

Harry followed his example. In a half-whisper he said, "What do you mean?"

"Listen, Dad," Leif said earnestly, "I've been watching him. He could be faking."

"Faking?" Harry was startled. "Why the hell should he do that?"

"I don't know. Maybe to avoid answering questions."

Harry watched the old man for a brief moment. Then he turned back to his son. "What makes you think he's not senile?" he asked.

"There is a difference between senescence and senile dementia," Leif explained. "It's sometimes difficult to draw a sharp distinction. In senile dementia, certain association areas in the frontal, temporal and parietal lobes of the brain are atrophic, resulting in—"

Harry interrupted him. "In English, please!"

"It has to do with Mr. Gerner's symptoms of senility, Dad. They're different in the normal aging process from the advanced senility that's caused by a physical disorder of the brain—the kind of senile dementia Gerner apparently suffers from."

Harry looked sharply at his son. "Go on."

"He does exhibit some of these symptoms. His shuffling walk; his quick changes of mood; his difficulty in focusing attention; his lack of awareness of what's going on around him; his irascibility. They're all legitimate symptoms. So is his appearance. His wrinkled skin; the hair." He frowned. "But it's not the symptoms he *does* exhibit. It's the ones he *doesn't*."

He searched for words.

"He looks—too healthy. Normally, at his stage of senility there'd be a marked loss of weight. . . . And his hands. They're too steady —wielding that knife. None of the tremulousness that would be expected . . . And his movements are too—too coordinated." He looked at his father. "But there's one thing that really clinched it for me."

"What?"

"The stove." He glanced toward the little pot-bellied stove. "Look at the area immediately around it. It's being kept clean. It's free of the wood chips and shavings that would be a real fire hazard. A man with the advanced senile dementia exhibited by Mr. Gerner could not act that logically and consistently."

Harry stared at Leif. "I'll be damned," he said. He glanced toward the old man, who was apparently oblivious to them. "What do you suggest we do?" he asked.

Leif frowned in thought. "First—let me talk to him," he said. "That may do it. If not—think up something . . . something that

will be a shock. It may show us if he really can't relate to reality.
We'll play it by ear from then on."

Harry nodded. "Sold."

Leif walked over to Gerner. He pulled up a chair and sat down
opposite the old man.

Gerner looked up. He drew a work-hardened thumb across the
blade of his knife. "They don't make them like they used to," he
said plaintively. "Nothing is like it used to be. . . ."

"Herr Gerner," Leif said calmly, "you don't have to pretend
that you don't understand. We know you are as much in command
of your faculties as we are." It was a matter-of-fact statement.

Gerner said nothing. He bent over his wood, whittling furiously.

"I don't know why you are pretending," Leif continued. "And
I don't want to know. All we want is the address of Frau Anna
Müller, whom you know. Then we'll leave." He paused and looked
steadily at the old man.

Gerner remained silent.

"I am a psychologist," Leif said. "I *know*. It is not uncommon
for someone who wants to hide something to pretend not to understand. But it is difficult to carry off. And it never fools an expert." He looked closely at the old man. "I *am* an expert, Herr
Gerner."

The old man put the wood away. He sat quietly, staring vacu-
ously into space. He said nothing.

Leif stood up. He turned to his father.

"Dad," he said quietly.

Harry walked over and sat down on the chair. He picked up the
knife and began to whittle a piece of wood.

"It's a good pastime—whittling," he said pleasantly. "I used to
do a lot of it when I was a boy."

Gerner did not react. Harry glanced toward Leif. He kept on
whittling.

"Herr Gerner," he said, "what is that piece of wood going to be?
An angel? A Madonna? A Christ?"

A flash of interest showed in the old man's face. Was there a
micromomentary flitting of his eyes toward his sculpture in front
of the door? He picked up his piece of wood and reached for the
knife in Harry's hand.

"It is *my* knife," he said querulously. "I finish my work."

Harry held the knife out of reach. "Oh, no, Herr Gerner," he said. "*I* will finish mine. It will be my masterpiece. . . ."

He stood up. He walked over to the Christ figure. Gerner was watching him.

"It will be so much more beautiful than *this* one". Harry put the sharp knife to the base of the statue. "We might as well destroy this piece of junk. Right now."

The knife bit into the wood and sent a chip flying. Harry moved the knife to the blank face of the figure. "Finish it off for good!"

"*No!*" It was a cry of anguish.

Gerner had risen from his stool. He stood staring wild-eyed at Harry, his hand stretched out, imploring.

Harry stood frozen at the Christ statue. There was not a sound to be heard in the room.

Slowly Gerner looked from one to the other. Then he sank down on his stool and put his hands over his face.

Leif went up to him. "It's all right, Herr Gerner," he said soothingly. "We mean you no harm."

Slowly Gerner looked up at him, his face haunted and hopeless. "Why?" he whispered. "Who are you?"

Harry came over. "We only want some information," he said. "About Frau Anna Müller. Where she can be found."

Gerner looked frightened. "You—you are not—from *them?*"

Harry frowned. "Them?" he asked. "Who are they?"

Gerner looked desolate.

"Why don't you tell us, Herr Gerner?" Leif asked, not unkindly.

Gerner looked up at him, his rheumy old eyes bleak. "Perhaps," he whispered, defeat in his voice, "perhaps it no longer matters." He seemed to collapse a little within himself. "I am—old. Perhaps it is time. . . ."

"Would you like to tell us about it?" Leif asked softly.

"It—it has been so long," the old man whispered haltingly. "So very long." For a moment he sat in silence, his gnarled hands idle in his lap. He was alone with his thoughts.

"I—I was too young to be a soldier in the war of 1914. Only fifteen . . . But then—afterward—came the National Socialists. Adolf Hitler. And the Stormtroopers. And then I was old enough.

And I joined. . . . But when war came again—I was too old Instead of a soldier they—they made me a guard. In Auschwitz-Birkenau . . . Two years I was there." He shivered. "Then—I came home. To Fichtendorf. And I became the *Ortsbauernführer.*"

He looked up at Harry and Leif, his old face a mask of torment. "And the war was lost. And they wanted to arrest me—the *Ami* soldiers occupying my village. Because I was a Nazi leader."

He stopped. He took a deep breath. Yes, Harry thought, he would have been arrested by the CIC. As an *Ortsbauernführer,* he would have been an automatic arrestee. But he was small fry. He would have been processed—and let go.

Gerner spoke again. "They—they accused me of war crimes," he whispered. "Atrocities . . . in the camp." He gave a little sob. "They were right. But—I thought I had to follow my orders. So—I went into hiding . . . so many years of hiding. First from the *Ami* secret police. From hiding place to hiding place I went And then —later, when the *Amis* left—from the law . . . And now—from *them.* But now—I am too old to run. I had to—to hide in the open. Within myself . . . Except now I have lost my—my last hiding place. . . ."

He fell silent. He closed his eyes tightly, as if to shut out the intolerable world around him.

"Who are *they?*" Leif prodded gently.

"They are still the same," Anton Gerner said, his voice toneless and flat. "They have not gone away. They are still here. . . . The Nazis . . ."

"Why are you—hiding from them?"

The old man looked up at Leif. "They are—afraid of me," he said. "I *know*—things. . . . From the days in the camps. From my time as village leader. They are afraid I might—talk. . . . But they think as long as I am a foolish old man with the mind of a child no one would listen to me—even if I did talk. . . . Now, when they know, they will—" He left the sentence unfinished.

"No one will learn anything from us," Leif said.

"What about Anna Müller?" Harry asked. "Do you know her?"

Anton Gerner nodded. "She was from my village. Fichtendorf. She, too, was—afraid. I do not know why."

"Do you know where we can find her?"

Gerner looked up at Harry. Then at Leif.

"We mean her no harm, Herr Gerner," Leif said softly.

The old man nodded. "She lives here. Just outside Kulmbach. On the road to Bayreuth. In a little house they call the Schränklein . . . She is—" He stopped. He shook his head. "I don't know what it is she does now. But she is no longer Anna Müller. She has now the name Anna Hoffbauer."

The door suddenly opened and Frau Graff came in. She carried a bowl of steaming soup.

"Well, Herr Gerner," she said brightly, "are you enjoying your company?" Her eyes made a quick survey of the room. She put the bowl on the table. "Here is your soup," she said. "Nice and hot."

The old man paid her no attention. He was looking vacantly into the room, slowly rocking to and fro.

"I'm afraid we haven't gotten very far with Herr Gerner," Harry said regretfully. "You were right, Frau Graff. He is—eh, difficult to reach."

"I told you," the woman said. *"Blim-blim."*

"Yes. Well—we had hoped to commission some wood carvings from him," Harry said. "We had heard he did some beautiful work." He waved an arm around the room. "And it certainly seems to be true. Such a shame it—eh, couldn't have worked out." He turned to the old man. *"Auf wiedersehen,* Herr Gerner," he said.

Anton Gerner did not react.

"Auf wiedersehen, Frau Graff," Harry said. "And thank you for your courtesy."

The woman nodded. "I told you it would be a waste of time."

"Yes," Harry said. "You did." He gave the old man a last look. "And you were right," he said.

Outside, the day had grown darker under a threatening sky.

Harry and Leif were halfway across the little courtyard when a piercing scream tore the silence. Almost at once the door to the shack flew open and Frau Graff stumbled into the doorway, screaming.

Harry and Leif rushed past her into the room.

Sprawled grotesquely on the floor lay old Anton Gerner. Both his bony hands were clutched like talons at his throat. The knife had entered at the front and passed through his neck, its bright red tip gleaming through the ruptured skin. Blood, pumping sluggishly from a lacerated jugular vein, welled out onto the floor, coloring the wood chips crimson.

A faint, moistly gurgling sound came from the old man. For a split second his eyes met Harry's. A grimace distorted his wrinkled face—was it a smile?—and he was dead.

Ashen-faced, Frau Graff stood rooted to the floor, staring at the old man.

"He—fell," she breathed hoarsely, horror constricting her throat. "He picked up his knife and he walked toward that figure of the Christ . . . and he tripped."

She crossed herself.

"Josef Maria have mercy on his soul," she whispered.

GERMANS TRYING TO RE-ESTABLISH NAZIS

DÜSSELDORF, West Germany—A self-styled "combat group" that aims to re-establish the Nazi Party has been formed, headed by nine men. . . . They also formed a Bavarian wing called the "Adolf Hitler Combat Group." . . . The group's aims are to spread Nazi propaganda and collect weapons, ammunition and explosives.

6

The death of Anton Gerner created very little stir in official circles.

Frau Graff related the tragic mishap in lurid detail to a bored inspector named Krueger from the Kulmbach police department. Krueger's questioning of Harry and Leif was only cursory. After all, they had not been present during Gerner's fatal fall. In taking their statements he accepted at face value the explanation of having wanted to see the old man about his wood carvings.

As they drove their Volkswagen toward Bayreuth in search of the Müller-Hoffbauer house, they were both subdued. Harry felt vaguely uneasy about old Gerner's death. *Had* it been an accident? Or had Gerner deliberately taken his own life? There was a third possibility. Gerner could have been killed by the woman. But—why?

He refused to dwell on it. He would never know. . . .

His mind returned its full attention to the matter at hand. Schränklein—meaning *little wardrobe*—a strange name for a house. Of course, people did occasionally give their houses and villas some pretty odd names. Sahara Igloo and The Teatlark he'd run into. But Little Wardrobe? Had to be a reason.

His gloomy mood began to lift. He felt the familiar excitement sharpen his mind and senses. He was back on a case.

After a few kilometers—and several stops to ask directions—Harry pulled up in front of the Schränklein. The name of the house was painted in fancifully ornamental letters over the door. It was a tiny old house sandwiched in between two postwar buildings that had probably been built on empty lots after a shelling which had perversely left the "Schränklein" standing. The name fitted. The tiny house was dominated by its front door, which seemed vastly oversized for the job. Indeed, the little building did resemble a wardrobe.

A hand-lettered cardboard sign was propped up in the single window next to the wide door. STRICKZEUG—*Alles Handgemacht —Bitte Klopfen!* And the name *Anna Hoffbauer.*

Leif silently translated the sign for himself: KNITTING—*Everything Handmade—Please Knock!*

Harry lifted his fist and rapped on the door.

A woman's voice called from within. *"Herein!"*

Harry opened the door.

They were about to meet Anna Hoffbauer AKA Anna Müller. The mother of SS Obersturmführer Ernst Helmut Müller, late of the King's Court in Hollywood.

The small room was cozy and warm. One whole wall was lined with cubbyhole shelving holding skeins of wool yarn in many colors, mostly grays and greens, reds and whites. A large chart showing a great variety of knit patterns hung on the opposite wall, each pattern named: *Rib, Interlock, Tucked* and so on. Next to it was a board covered in gray cloth on which were fastened dozens of different buttons, from thick, arched silver to carved bone, all numbered and mounted in pairs.

On a small, low table lay a collection of illustrations from magazines and design books neatly mounted on heavy paper and showing men, women and children happily wearing an assortment of knitwear—sweaters, skirts and scarfs; mittens, hats and socks; even a small child wrapped in a baby-blue blanket.

In a corner stood a wooden stand with two "arms" stretched out, the smoothly worn pegs holding a looped skein of red yarn ready to be wound off into a ball; nearby a rack held several knitted garments in various stages of completion. Despite its size and the resulting congestion, the place looked neat and organized.

At the far end of the room a closed door led presumably to living quarters beyond. In a comfortable chair nearby sat a woman making what looked like a sleeve out of bright green yarn, her slender hands manipulating both ends of a large knitting needle bent into a circle.

She was not at all what Harry had expected, the rather corpulent, colorless peasant so common to the area, with coarse hands, lackluster hair drawn back in a bun and pedestrian clothes. Instead, Anna Hoffbauer—or Anna Müller—was a slight woman. Wavy hair surrounded a pleasant, surprisingly youthful face. Her fingers moved quickly, surely and gracefully, as if with a life of their own.

She put the knitting aside and stood up, smoothing her dress.

"Guten Tag, meine Herren," she said pleasantly. "What can I do for you?"

"Frau Hoffbauer?" Harry inquired politely.

"Yes."

"I am Harry Bendicks," he said. He indicated Leif. "This is my son."

Frau Hoffbauer inclined her head in a gracious greeting. "Welcome to my little shop," she said, smiling at them. "How may I be of service?"

Harry looked around. "You certainly have a—a colorful place,

Frau Hoffbauer." He looked at her. "And a charming little building. The Schränklein. So apt. Did you name it yourself?"

"My husband did." She smiled at him. "When the new buildings
on either side of us went up. We felt—rather like a cramped little
wardrobe." She looked at Harry. "My husband—God rest his soul
—had a small haberdashery here."

"Oh," Harry said. "Then you run this place all by yourself?"

She nodded solemnly. "I have been—for eleven years now. Ever
since I started it. When my husband passed on." She waved a hand
around the room. "Everything I make—with my own two hands."

"And beautiful things they are, *Frau Müller.*"

She looked sharply at Harry. "What?" She stared at him, her
face suddenly clouded over.

"Frau Müller," Harry repeated. "Frau Anna Müller. Is that not
correct?"

Her smile had vanished. "My first husband passed on in 1947,"
she snapped. "I do not see how this concerns you." She regarded
him warily.

"I know," Harry said. "And you left your farm at Fichtendorf to
come here to Kulmbach."

"Who are you?" Anna Hoffbauer demanded. "What do you want
here?"

"I am an American," Harry said. "An investigator." He stepped
closer to her. "During the war I was an officer in the CIC. You are
aware of what that means, I'm sure."

She shrank away from him.

"In 1945," Harry continued, "I was here."

The woman nervously wet her lips. "What—what do you want
from me?" she whispered, her face suddenly drawn.

"Information, Frau Müller," Harry said at once. "Information
you withheld from the U.S. Army interrogator when you were
questioned. Back in 1945. Information about a certain cabin in the
forest near Kugelberg."

Anna Hoffbauer stared at Harry as if she were seeing an appari-
tion from the past. Her eyes filmed over with fear. With visible
effort she rallied her courage and composure. She drew herself up.

"I—I have no intention of answering any questions," she said,
kindling a spark of defiance.

"I think you will, Frau Müller." Harry scowled at the woman. Slowly he moved toward her. "I think you had better."

Leif had been watching the exchange without interfering but with growing apprehension. His father seemed to be treating the woman as if he—and she—were still back in the war. He was about to speak up, to restrain his father, but something stopped him.

Anna Hoffbauer glared at Harry. "This is not 1945!" she flared. "You have no right—"

"Right!" Harry exploded. The woman flinched. Harry spat the words at her. "How dare you speak of rights? That bastard you worshipped. The unholy party you supported. *You!* You are responsible for millions of people being killed. No—not just six million Jews, Frau Hoffbauer. Sixty million! Sixty million people who lost their lives. Because of you and your like. *How dare you speak of rights?*"

The woman stared at him, wide-eyed.

"Do you deny you were one of them?" Harry shot the question at her.

She stood mute. But the answer flashed across her face in a micromoment.

"Or your husbands? Either of them. What were *they?* You don't have to tell me about your son."

Anna Hoffbauer's hand flew to her mouth. "My son?" She could barely wrench the words from her throat. She shivered. "What do you know of my son?" she whispered. "He was—a soldier. Missing in action . . ."

"Bullshit!" Harry spat. "And you know that as well as I!"

Anna Hoffbauer shook her head. Her mouth worked—but no sound emerged.

"An SS officer," Harry said brutally. "That was your son. SS Obersturmführer Ernst Helmut Müller. *That* was your son!"

She sank down in her chair. With terrified eyes she stared up at Harry.

"And not missing in action, Frau Müller. *Dead!*"

She drew in her breath in a sharp gasp.

"Your son, the SS officer, was killed. Only a few days ago. In Los Angeles. *Murdered!*"

"No!" It was a cry of anguish.

Relentlessly Harry pressed on. "You knew all along what he was, did you not? You knew all along that he was alive. That he was doing a putrid job for your putrid Nazi friends." The cringing woman lowered her head. "Dammit! Look at me!" Harry shouted at her.

She jerked her head up, her eyes fixed on the man towering above her.

Leif felt a chill go through him. It was not possible—but he was witnessing an interrogation that could have taken place thirty-three years ago. He was watching his father, CIC agent Harry Bendicks, breaking a subject. Battering her. Giving her no time to think . . . And Anna Müller? Once again she was the vanquished victim. Once again she was fighting to safeguard what she believed in. . . .

The questions hammered at her. She cowered under them. But she remained silent.

"Answer me, dammit!" Harry growled. He lowered his voice. The effect was that of a shout. *"Did you know about your son?"*

Anna Müller trembled.

"Talk!"

She started violently. He moved closer.

She nodded. "I—I knew he was alive."

"What else?"

"Nothing. Nothing else. I swear it!"

"Did you know *where* he was?"

"No."

"His friends. The people he associated with. Any of *them* still around? Here?"

"No. I—I do not know. . . ."

Harry contemplated her. Inwardly he exulted. She had answered her first questions. It was the beginning. Soon she would be talking her damned head off. . . .

Fascinated, Leif stood motionless. The regression was complete. His father once again the all-powerful conqueror. Anna Müller his subject. So total was the illusion that it clearly never entered the woman's mind that all she had to do was order them from her house. He wondered briefly what kind of mind could allow itself to be so easily deluded. A mind filled with suspicions and fears? Guilt?

"The cabin," Harry demanded harshly. "What do you know

about the Kugelberg cabin? On Von Flatow's estate?"

She shook her head like a marionette, her terrified eyes never leaving Harry.

"Answer me, Frau Müller. *Now!*"

She flinched.

Harry leaned down toward her, his voice ominously low. "I am waiting, Frau Müller. I can promise you, if you do not start to talk —right now!—you will regret it. Bitterly. I promise you."

Tears of terror welled in her eyes. "I—I am afraid, *Herr Offizier,*" she whispered. "Afraid . . ."

"Of what? Of whom? Von Flatow?" The questions were like shots.

"No. I—don't know. I do not know *who* they are. . . ."

They, Leif thought. Exactly what old Anton Gerner had said. *They* . . .

"You had better start being afraid of *me*, Frau Müller. Forget about *them*, whoever you think they are. Look at *me!* I am here!"

Casually, as if totally unaware of it, Harry brushed his jacket with his arm—exposing his gun in its shoulder holster. He held the woman's eyes in an inexorable stare.

"You do know about the cabin?"

"Yes."

"Who lived there?"

"I—I do not know."

"Did you ever see them?"

She hesitated.

"Well?"

She started as if from a physical blow. "Yes. Once."

"Go on. Out with it."

She opened her mouth, but she seemed too paralyzed to speak.

"Talk, goddamn it! Talk!"

"*Bitte, Herr Offizer* . . . Please. I—I am afraid. . . ." It was a whisper of abject fear.

"Of what? That *they* will kill you? As they killed your son? And your friend Anton Gerner?"

The shock sent a violent shudder through the slender body. She grasped her hands before her, clenching them, knuckles white.

"Anton!" she breathed, her face ashen.

"Yes. Anton. They killed him, Frau Müller. Only hours ago. Murdered him. As they murdered your son."

In shock and terror Anna Hoffbauer's eyes were fixed on the man before her.

Hardly daring to breathe, Leif watched her begin to fall apart. He watched his father, oblivious to anything but the shaken, tormented woman sitting before him. Hitting her with shock after shock, breaking her down systematically and relentlessly. A CIC interrogator, rough and single-minded, his ruthless attack getting results—when results were imperative.

"You think you are safe," his father said, his voice suddenly threatening, "if you keep quiet? Safe? After your—your *friends* find out you have been talking to me?" He sounded almost regretful. "And they will find out, Frau Müller. Be certain of that. They will."

Anna Hoffbauer shook her head, her bloodless face strained in terror. "But—but I have told you nothing!"

"Will *they* know that?" Harry snapped.

She started.

"Your only chance now," Harry went on, "is to tell me everything you do know. Right now. And we may be able to stop them, before . . ." Ominously he let the sentence die. He lowered his voice. "The cabin, Frau Müller. What about the people in the cabin?"

Suddenly the woman let out a wrenching sob. She buried her head in her hands. The thin shoulders heaved.

Harry ▮▮▮▮▮ t, looking down at her. His moments of triumph ▮▮▮▮▮ omplete. There was always that damned business o▮▮▮▮ y for the bastards he'd broken.

Haltingly she began to talk.

"It—it was so long ago. I—I did not mean to do it. . . ." She sobbed. She took her hands from her tear-stained face, and they fell into her lap to lie limply, empty of their earlier swift grace.

By now, Harry thought bleakly, by now she looks just like all of them.

When she spoke, her voice was toneless with despair. "We—we had our farm then, Helmut and I. It was not very far from

Kugelberg. I—I did not know I was getting so close to the cabin. We—everyone—always stayed away from it. But—I was looking for *Pfifferlinge.* Helmut liked them. They were his favorite mushrooms. So sweet, he used to say. . . ." She sighed—a sobbing sigh. "And then—then I heard it. A woman's voice. High-pitched. Alarmed. She called, 'Where are you? For God's sake, Karl, get him! . . . Dolfi! . . . Dolfi! . . . Where are you?' " She stopped. She seemed calmer. Once started the words came easier. "And—I saw him. He was at the well. A boy. Perhaps twelve. He wore *Lederhosen.* He was playing with the pump. And a man came running from the house. And he picked up the boy and carried him into the hut. . . ." She took a deep breath. "And—and then I knew . . . I knew who that little boy was. There had been rumors. Whispers. Anton Gerner had told me. . . . And I *knew.* . . ."

She stopped, seemingly lost in the enormity of her knowledge. She looked suddenly old, her pale skin stretched taut across her skull, the face of a woman already dead.

"Who?" Harry asked quietly. "Who was the boy?"

Anna Müller Hoffbauer looked up at him. "Dolfi," she said, her voice barely audible, "Dolfi means little Adolf." She closed her eyes as if to escape being present when she revealed her secret.

"The boy—the boy was the son of the Führer."

NEO-NAZIS OBSERVE HITLER'S BIRTHDAY

HANNOVER—Neo-Nazis observed A̶ Hitler's birthday yesterday by sme̶ swastikas and anti-Jewish slogans̶ Jewish cemetery and on public buildi̶ police in Hannover, West Germany, re- ported. Hitler would have been 88. . . . The Nazi symbol and slogans of the brown-shirted Stormtroopers were smeared during the night on Jewish gravestones, museums, pedestrian tunnels, the house of parliament and other public buildings in Hannover, the capital of the state of Lower Saxony. . . .

7

"The damned thing is," said Harry, "that it could be true. A lot of pieces would fall into place."

The rented VW was tooling along the road toward Fichtendorf and Gasthof Hirsch, Harry at the wheel.

It had not been an easy task to persuade Anna Hoffbauer that she was in no danger for having revealed her secret, but Harry'd thought he owed it to her. He'd told her the truth about her son's mugging. He'd told her that Anton Gerner's death was an accident. That no Nazi vengeance was involved. But even as he'd reassured her he'd had a nagging feeling of doubt.

She had finally accepted his assurances, but she had still been shaken and worried when they left.

"It makes sense. In a grim, crazy way." Harry ticked off his reasons. "The illegitimate offspring of the Führer kept hidden in the inaccessible forest cabin . . . The raid to rescue him and bring him to safety when we overran the area . . . Ernest Muller was probably one of the raiders, and he kept the snapshot of the place as a memento. . . . And last, but—dammit—not least, the attempts to knock us off after I stumbled on their tracks." He looked soberly at Leif. "If Hitler's son really *was* living in that cabin, and they're afraid we're about to find that out, no wonder Gerner's and Hoffbauer's *'they'* are hell-bent to stop us."

"Maybe," Leif said skeptically. "But it wouldn't be the first time some suppos̶e̶d̶ son of Hitler has surfaced. It was only—what?—six mon̶ ̶ ̶ ̶ ̶ome Frenchman, I think his name was—Loret, Jea̶ ̶ ̶ ̶ ̶d to be Hitler's son. Conceived during the First Worl̶ ̶ ̶ ̶at! Nothing came of it. Certainly no attempted murders."

Harry nodded. "I remember. An event of earth-shaking unimportance. And that's exactly what makes *this* damned set-up so puzzling."

"What do you mean?"

"Why go to such desperate lengths to keep *this* SOB a deep, dark secret? Dammit, we nearly got killed—just for being curious. Why the hell all the fuss? What makes *this* Hitler by-blow so different from all the others?"

"I see what you mean," Leif said thoughtfully. "Somebody certainly does seem anxious the keep his existence dark."

"So the bottom line is *why?* What are they so damned afraid we'll find out? And who *are* the bloody watchdogs?" He frowned, then answered himself with another question. "The neo-Nazis? The papers are full of their shenanigans. All over the world. More every day."

"Or survivors," Leif said. "The authentic Third Reich originals. There must still be a lot of them around. The JDL told me several millions. Of course, they're mostly old men by now."

"So are the men who run our country," Harry observed. "Our sterling Senators." He grew sober. "Anyway, if there really *is* a son of Hitler floating around, and they'll commit murder to keep his existence secret, where the hell is he? Or—a damned sight more important—*who?*"

Leif looked at his father. He felt a sudden, clammy apprehension. "Who indeed?" he said. "A politician? Industrialist? Military man? Someone with clout?"

Harry nodded. "And if it *is* a bunch of old Nazis going to such desperate lengths to protect him—why? What kind of threat could he represent? Now?"

Father and son looked gravely at one another, each filled with his own disturbing thoughts.

They drove on in silence. Father and son, pondering another father-and-son combination.

Fichtendorf was in sight when Leif broke the silence. "What about Von Flatow?" he asked. "What does *he* know? The cabin stood on his estate."

"If he owned it at that time," Harry said. "I   aps he knows a helluva lot."

"Should we try to find out?"

"As in 'go see him'? If he *is* involved, that might be like marching into the lions' den with a sign around your neck reading *Blue Plate Special!*"

Leif laughed. "But if he isn't, he might be able to give us a lead on what to do next."

Harry nodded. He had been thinking about Von Flatow. He'd come to the same conclusion as his son. Had he been alone or with a partner in the line of duty, he would not have hesitated. It would be a calculated risk, and some risks had to be taken in any investigation—if you wanted to get answers. But he was loath to take his son into a situation that might turn sour. Or worse . . .

"It's a possibility," he said. "Let's give it some thought."

They parked their car in the little courtyard behind the *Gasthof.* As they crossed the *Bierstube* on the way to their room, a man approached them.

It was the man called Emil.

"Herr Bendicks!" Politely he addressed Harry, his crude arrogance gone. "Herr von Flatow begs you to forgive him this late invitation, but he did not know who you were when he met you at Kugelberg last Thursday," he said, a dog-wiggle in his voice. "Herr von Flatow would be honored if you would dine with him and some of his friends at Rittersheim tonight. He begs you to accept."

He stopped and waited obsequiously.

Harry and Leif glanced at one another.

Harry grinned at his son. "Fate rears its ugly head."

He turned to the German.

"We accept," he said formally.

SS COMMEMORATIVE MARCH

MANNHEIM, West Germany—A commemorative march for SS Col. Jochen ____er brought out some 800 black-_d marchers. The date of the Mann-__march, coinciding with observ-_s in Germany of *Kristallnacht,* that __ght of terror and murder, masterminded by Reinhard Heydrich, when Stormtroopers and SS men ravaged the Jewish communities, was intentionally provocative. A memorial tablet intended for display in a public place bore the inscription: "Our heroes live in our hearts!" . . .

8

Hans-Jürgen von Flatow struggled with the studs in his dress shirt. They were diamonds set in onyx and mounted in white gold —and just a little too large for the buttonholes. They were a gift from Reichsleiter Martin Bormann, but there was nothing to identify them as such. The last stud finally in place, he walked to his dresser for his black tie. For the third time in the last hour he picked up the report lying there—the background report on his very special dinner guests.

He already knew every word in it, but he was still looking for an angle. That perfect denouement that would keep him wholly above suspicion. He glanced at the report.

The two Americans made an unusual team. Father and son. Nordic ancestry. Interesting. Both experienced in investigation, although on quite different levels. Both highly effective. The older man undoubtedly able to call upon assistance, if needed, by availing himself of connections through the "old boy" system—as efficient in law-enforcement circles as in the military. Perhaps somewhat of a bull in a china shop; more like a bulldog never letting go. His son obviously brought a special kind of knowledge to the team. They could turn out to be a real danger. That, however, would soon be a moot question. . . .

He placed the report in a dresser drawer. Grudgingly he admitted to himself that the U.S. organization had done a *prima* job. Every detail was there. A list of the son's consultative jobs for the Los Angeles police. The father's linguistic abi   ilitary record—even a notation regarding his sharps   from the police academy . . .

In front of the mirror he straightened his tie. He   forward to the evening.

As a hunter, he always enjoyed the stalk the most.

The kill was always a letdown. . . .

There were eight people seated around the festive table set up in the main hall of Rittersheim Estate. Besides Harry and Leif there were four guests and Von Flatow's daughter, Teresa, a woman in her early thirties. Two of the host's business associates, an Egyptian named Naha Ali Mahmud from Cairo, and a

Dane from Copenhagen, a Mr. Eigil Knudsen, had stayed over following a conference at the estate, and the group had been joined by a Dr. Josef Hartman from Kulmbach and his wife, Elsa, who looked slightly out of place in her chic Paris evening gown—as do so many German *Hausfraus*. Harry and Leif were the only men not in dinner jackets and black ties. Leif had been slightly uncomfortable at the beginning. Harry couldn't have cared less.

The excellent dinner had featured a marvelous saddle of venison—the deer had been shot on the estate by Von Flatow himself —cooked to perfection and served with a savory cream gravy and a superb Bernkastler 1949, Schlossgut Reichartshausen. Harry had enjoyed the meal enormously, Leif with less enthusiasm after Von Flatow had pointed out the head of the donor among the trophies adorning the walls. He'd been acutely aware of the beast watching him from above.

Von Flatow presided at the head of the table, Teresa sat at the opposite end with Leif on her left, while Harry was seated between Von Flatow and the Dane. He'd enjoyed practicing his Danish. The conversation had been general and pleasant, the mood mellow and relaxed, and there had been no opportunity for Harry and Leif to do any "pumping" of their respective Von Flatows.

Teresa was an attractive young woman, her honey-yellow hair full and loose, her pale blue eyes watchful. When she smiled, which was often, she showed a little too much pink gum above even white teeth. Leif found her an intelligent and quick conversationalist and a charming dinner partner. But his thoughts kept straying to Washington, D.C., and Susan Gannon. He marveled that he'd actually enjoyed his brown-bag—or white-bag—lunch with her very much more than the exquisite meal being served at the Rittersheim table.

Teresa was talking to him animatedly. "As a matter of fact," she was saying, "I have only been back home a few days after being away for over two months."

"Traveling?"

"I was at the Villeneuve d'Acq University at Lille. Taking a postgraduate course. In history."

"Lille," said Leif. "The birthtown of De Gaulle." He looked at her. "An interesting man. *He* certainly made a great contribution to history."

"Yes. Of course." Teresa sounded as if she wanted to believe it but couldn't quite make it.

"You are an historian?" Leif asked.

Teresa gave a little laugh. Was it slightly forced? "I really am not anything, Herr Bendicks, except interested. Interested in history. One can learn so much from history, do you not agree?"

"Indeed I do." He looked at her. "Are you home for a while now?"

"No," she said. "I leave again first thing Monday morning." She looked affectionately toward Von Flatow. "I really see much too little of my father."

"Where are you going this time?" Leif asked.

"Alassio," she said. "I want to find some good old lace." She gave Leif a sidelong glance. "In many ways I prefer the Italian Riviera to the French, don't you?"

"I think my favorite sea resorts are along the Oregon coast," Leif said ingenuously. "Don't you agree the sweep of it is truly majestic?"

Teresa laughed. *"Touché!"* she said mischievously. "You have me. *I* have not been *there."*

"But you obviously travel a great deal more than I do," Leif said. "How long will you be away this time?"

"Not long," Teresa answered. "I must be back home in about three weeks. By the middle of April. My father—"

She stopped.

"Oh," said Leif. "A special occasion?"

"No," she said. She flashed him a bright smi   ther will be here, too, at that time. It will give us   pend some time together. We find that time all too ra

She turned away to take a sip of her wine.

But Leif had noticed it. That tiny flash-reaction—like the flick of a snake's tongue—that whipped through her eyes, giving the lie to her words. Something special *was* scheduled for the middle of April. He was certain of it.

Von Flatow stood up.

"I hope you have enjoyed your dinner," he said. "I have an

excellent Armagnac, an Armand Dodet, if you would like an after-dinner brandy." He motioned toward a small, well-stocked bar. Emil stood there, stony-faced, chilling a bottle of champagne in a bucket of ice. "Or anything else you might wish, of course. Champagne?" He turned to Harry. "Will you join me in an Armagnac?" he asked cordially. "It really is excellent. It was bottled by Delord Frères-Lannepax thirty years before I acquired it, and I have had it for twenty. Fifty years, Herr Bendicks. Like liquid velvet and the finest aroma imaginable."

"I'll give it a try," Harry said.

They walked toward the fireplace with their drinks. The Armagnac *was* one of the best things Harry had ever put in his mouth, but somehow he couldn't bring himself to mention it to Von Flatow. He looked around the room. Leif was talking animatedly with the daughter, Teresa. Good. The shifty-eyed Egyptian had been cornered by the drab Frau Doktor Hartman, who was in the process of talking his ear off. He had that typical "cocktail-party look," pretending to be attentive to what the woman was prattling on about, while surreptitiously looking around for any acceptable excuse to escape. The Dane and the Kulmbach doctor were in earnest conversation, within easy reach of the little bar. Harry returned his full attention to his host.

"I must compliment you on your German," Von Flatow was saying. "Few non-Germans learn to speak our language as fluently and as free of accent."

"I've spent a lot of time here," Harry said. "Since the early thirties." He looked closely at the German. "And during the war."

"Of course," Von Flatow said, dismissing an entire world war with a shrug. "Perhaps you were here in 1936? The Berlin Olympics? One of the most spectacular and stirring spectacles ever put on by any country."

"As a matter of fact, I was," Harry said agreeably. "And I did attend the games. Some of the events, anyway."

"Our German athletes did exceptionally well," Von Flatow remarked. "I believe they broke a string of straight wins by the United States since the beginning of the modern Olympics in 1896."

"Yeah," Harry agreed. "But, you know, the greatest moment I

remember was when our man Jesse Owens won the hundred-meter dash. And so easily."

Harry remembered seeing Hitler at the games. He'd been sitting close enough to the Führer box to observe his crowing delight when a German won, and his glum displeasure when one lost. The reactions of a spoiled brat with not the slightest idea of sportsmanship. Hitler seemed to look upon each event as a war in which the Fatherland *had* to win. . . . And he'd seen him lose his cool when that Dutch woman broke through the ranks of Stormtroopers and planted a lusty smack on his puss. The Führer had been so rattled he'd stalked from the stadium. Harry kept the remembered observations to himself. Enough is enough.

He sipped his Armagnac. It *was* damned good. "It's quite a place you've got here," he said. "Is it a family estate?"

"No. As a matter of fact, I took over the estate in 1946. The—the former owner, for various reasons, was not in a position to maintain it."

I bet, Harry thought. Anyway, that answered that question. Von Flatow had not been in residence during the war, during the time the boy and the others had lived in the cabin.

"It is a beautiful estate," Von Flatow went on. "I wish I could show it to you. It includes a most picturesque lake nearly four kilometers long and large areas of excellent hunting. And it has a quite fascinating history." He gave Harry a quick glance. "All sorts of legends and—rumors."

One of them about a son of Adolf? Harry thought. Maybe Von Flatow did know something, after all. . . .

The German walked to the wall between th   ental gun-display cases painted with bright Bavaria   rge, colorful map set in a massive, carved oak frame   wall. "Let me show you," he said.

He pointed to the various places as he talked. "Here is the village, Fichtendorf," he explained. "Rittersheim is here, slightly to the southeast at the northern end of the lake—unimaginatively called Fichtendorf Lake."

Harry looked at the map. He was at once able to orient himself. His map-reading courses in the CIC had been thorough. And he had not forgotten.

Fichtendorf Lake was shaped like a fat sausage or half-moon with a long, narrow finger protruding from the inside curve. It was surrounded by forest land except at the northern end, where the estate went down to the shore.

"The entire area constitutes the Rittersheim hunting preserve. And the hunting is splendid." Von Flatow turned to one of the cabinets. "Let me show you some of my guns."

He produced a key from his pocket and unlocked the cabinet. He swung the glass doors open.

"I am quite proud of my little collection," he said. "I have some very fine pieces."

Harry inspected the guns. He ran his fingers over the intricately carved stock of one of the shotguns. "That's a beauty," he said admiringly.

"A Boss, twelve-gauge, over-and-under," Von Flatow said. "French walnut stock." He pointed to another gun. "Here is another of my favorites," he said. "A Holland and Holland, twelve-gauge, side-by-side, single-trigger, Royal Ejector Model. A very satisfactory gun." He took out yet another gun, handling it with the touch of a caress. "This one, Herr Bendicks," he said almost reverently. "This one is the pride of my collection. An English gun. A Purdey, twelve-gauge, side-by-side, thirty-inch barrels with full choke, both barrels." He stroked it lovingly. "I wouldn't part with it for fifteen thousand dollars."

"That's quite a gun."

Von Flatow looked at him. "Are you a hunter, Herr Bendicks?"

"Not really. I've done a little duck-shooting some years back. I know enough to understand my swing and how to time my trigger to it."

Von Flatow gave him a quick look. This was what he had been looking for. The angle.

"How extraordinary," he said brightly. "I have planned a duck shoot for tomorrow morning. We have some fine Mallard on the lake. A small party, really. Just my guests and a couple of hunters from the village. Men only. You and your son *must* join us. I shall not accept your refusal! . . . We shall have a picnic lunch and a campfire afterward. Sit down and exchange hunting yarns, that sort of thing." He smiled at Harry. "You will enjoy it, I am sure."

Harry's thoughts raced. He was torn. It would be a damned good opportunity to sit down informally with Von Flatow and maybe pump him a little about those—rumors. . . . On the other hand, if the German did have anything violent in mind, a hunting accident could so easily be arranged. Okay. *One* accident. But—*two?* Both him and Leif? Hardly. No one in his right mind would buy a *double* accidental shooting!

Before he could decide, Von Flatow went on as if the matter already had been settled. His way.

"You can take your pick of my guns," he said expansively. "You might like the Churchill, twelve-gauge, over-and-under, or the J. P. Saur, side-by-side, one of the really fine German-made guns." He pointed to two guns standing together. "Or perhaps you would feel more at home with the Winchester, Model 21, or the Remington, Model 32? Both also twelve-gauge."

"I'll take the Winchester," Harry said. "My son may want the Remington."

Okay . . . If after talking it over with Leif they decided the risk was too great, they could always cancel.

Somehow he knew they wouldn't. . . .

NEO-NAZI SLOGANS ON LILLE UNIVERSITY CAMPUS

PARIS, France—For the first time in its existence the campus of the University of Villeneuve d'Acq at Lille was covered with racist slogans. Not only were me ing insults painted on the walls, but authors felt the need to give vent to Nazi convictions. Swastikas were dra In large black letters one could read: "Glory to Hitler!" and "Glory to the Waffen SS!"

9

It was barely dawn.

The full-throated growl of the powerful outboard motor of the tow boat intruded crassly on the misty stillness that lay over Fichtendorf Lake. Behind, the string of four small skiffs moved steadily across the quiet water toward the southern end of the lake. In the tow boat Emil was at the controls; another man from the estate held two magnificent, eager bird dogs of a breed unfamiliar to Harry. Von Flatow had called them *Deutsche Drahthaar*—German Wirehairs.

The skiff directly behind the tow boat held two dour and taciturn men from the village. They had merely nodded when introduced to Harry and Leif. In the next skiff sat Knudsen, the Dane, and Dr. Hartman; Naha Ali Mahmud and Von Flatow were in the third, and in the last one, Harry and Leif. They would be the first to be dropped off, Von Flatow had explained. Theirs would be the choice spot. First chance at the ducks.

The morning was overcast and raw, and Harry was glad he and Leif had borrowed a couple of heavy coats along with their shotguns. Everyone had a shotgun—except Emil and the man with him.

Harry and Leif had discussed at length the pros and cons of accepting Von Flatow's invitation. Two things had finally persuaded them that whatever risk was involved was worth taking: Von Flatow's hint of old rumors about the estate, and Leif's conviction that something was scheduled to happen at Rittersheim the middle of April, only three weeks away. Their desire to get information on both points had outweighed their reservations.

Harry's eyes traveled along the string of skiffs. A colorful crew, he thought. Von Flatow himself in red, as was the Dane. The doctor was in blue and the Egyptian in yellow. Both he and Leif were in bright orange. Only the villagers were clad in drab green. His eyes came to rest on Emil in the lead boat, handling the tiller of the outboard motor. He wore a jet-black jacket. All it needs is the swastika armband, Harry thought. He admired the outboard motor. It seemed to tow the four skiffs effortlessly.

"That's a great little outboard," he said to Von Flatow, a few feet away in the boat ahead. Might as well establish a nice chatty relationship, he thought. For later . . .

"It is quite satisfactory," Von Flatow agreed. "A British Seagull." He patted his Purdey shotgun. "I seem to be partial to good English products." He smiled and nodded toward the lead boat. "It is a Forty Plus, long-shaft outboard," he said, "with a tilting tiller and a four-bladed Hydrofan propeller. It is really quite powerful."

The pitch of the motor lowered as Emil began to slow down.

"Ah," said Von Flatow, "here we are. Position one. Your position, Herr Bendicks." He pointed to a narrow slough cut into the rushes and reeds growing thickly at the edge of the lake. "Take your boat in there." He peered up into the leaden sky. "You should not have too long a wait."

Harry put out the oars.

"By the way," Von Flatow said, "our Mallards have had quite a bit of gun education. They are wary fellows." He cast off the tow line from Harry's skiff. "A piece of advice. If you see him circling and he suddenly breaks, by all means shoot. He is not coming any closer. *Weidmanns Heil, die Herren Bendicks!*"

"Thanks." Harry began to row the skiff toward the slough. "And Hunter's Luck to you too, Herr von Flatow."

The pitch of the motor increased again, and the caravan moved on.

The skiff fitted the slough like a hand in a glove. As the sound of the outboard motor faded in the distance, Harry took the Remington shotgun Leif had borrowed. He examined it minutely before giving it back. Then he went over his own borrowed Winchester. He nodded with grim satisfaction.

"Okay. Both of them," he said. "No funny business." He patted his voluminous, bulging jacket pockets. "And plenty of shells. We'll just keep our eyes open." He felt better. They were not without protection. He took his own gun from its shoulder holster. He checked it. It was habit.

Leif watched him. "Always carry it, Dad?"

"Always. Long time ago I decided never to be without my gun." Long time . . . My God. It was—thirty years?"

"Why? What happened?"

"You really want to know?"

"Yes. I do."

"Well—I guess we've got nothing better to do." For a moment Harry sat silent.

"I was a rookie," he began. "I was off duty, and I thought carrying a gun spoiled the lines of my suit. I was dating your mother. One night I'd taken her home after a movie, and I decided to walk home. It was pretty late. I was passing an alley when I heard a noise. I stopped and looked in. It was pretty damned dark in there, but I could make out someone standing over what looked like a body. I started into the alley. The guy heard me coming. He whirled around—and he had a long switchblade in his hand. I was damned sure he knew how to use it."

He paused, and gave a little snort. "So—I reached for my gun —but it wasn't there. And the guy started for me. I took a chance. You've gotta use what you got. I counted on the darkness—and the guy being just as scared as I was. I stuck out my right hand, two fingers pointed forward, and I grabbed it with my left, put my left index finger on the right-hand fingers bent into my palm, and held both arms straight out in front of me as if I was holding a gun. I crouched down in the firing stance they'd taught me and shouted, 'Police! Stop or I'll shoot!' The guy stopped. He couldn't make it out clearly, but he thought I had a gun pointed at his guts. I never moved. I told him to drop the knife, turn around and put his hands on his back. He did. And I put the cuffs on him. *Those* I had in my back pocket. And right then and there I decided I'd always carry my gun, too."

Leif looked at his father. How many, many things he had not known. He wondered if *he* could have reacted that quickly. Make that kind of use of what he had.

"I don't blame you," he said.

Harry grinned. "Your mother heard the story. She never ever complained about my frayed shirts or out-of-shape jackets. . . ."

Suddenly they became aware of the sound of the outboard motor in the distance. It seemed to be getting louder . . . and nearer.

Harry picked up his shotgun. He motioned for Leif to do the same. They waited.

The outboard throttled down.

"Herr Bendicks!" they heard Emil call. "Herr Bendicks!"

Harry frowned. Dammit! What was up? It was no use playing possum. Emil knew where they were. If . . .

"What is it?" he called.

"Herr von Flatow requests that you move one position farther up," Emil shouted. "He wants to tighten the pattern."

"Okay," Harry called back.

He motioned for Leif to keep a lookout. He took one of the oars and slowly, carefully, punted the skiff toward the mouth of the slough. He stopped. Through a stand of cattails he could see the boat. Emil sat at the idling motor, the other man on the seat in the center. Both still seemed to be unarmed. The dogs were gone.

Harry placed the oars in the oarlocks. Slowly, warily, he rowed out from the slough into open water.

Suddenly the powerful motor roared to life. The boat seemed to leap in the water. It hurtled straight for the skiff. Harry had a glimpse of the man sitting in the middle, white-faced, holding on to the sides.

And it struck.

The skiff splintered—the crash echoing over the still lake.

Harry found himself floundering in the water, battered by debris and weighted down by the shell-filled jacket. He was aware of Leif struggling in the wreckage next to him. Both guns were at the bottom of the lake. . . .

A new sound suddenly intruded upon his awareness. The outboard.

And he saw it.

The boat had been turned around.

Emil's companion was sculling it forcefully into position, backing it toward the two men flailing about in the wreckage-strewn water.

Emil stood at the stern. He had tilted the propeller shaft up out of the water. It whined viciously as it came straight at them.

In a flash of clarity Harry understood. It would not be a shooting accident. Drowning! Plausible. Drowning after a collision. After being cut to ribbons by the whirling propeller!

He fought to reach his gun in its shoulder holster. The heavy, wet jacket glued itself to him. He tried to struggle out of it. There was no time. His hand found the gun. He drew it out—and the boat struck the wreckage. Desperately he dodged the deadly propeller. It flashed within inches of his face as Emil sliced the shaft upward. Thrashing to avoid the whirling blades, Harry struck his arm on a piece of wreckage. The gun flew from his grip and disappeared. His head ducked below water and he gulped a mouthful. He came up coughing and sputtering.

The boat was at once sculled into position for a second try. Harry's consciousness was filled with the deadly whir of the blades.

Where was Leif?

There. Only a few feet away.

And the murderous blades bore down on them again. . . .

Leif was struggling in the water. He'd been aware of a sharp blow to his left leg when the skiff was rammed. He felt nothing now. His heavy, weighted jacket was pulling him down. He was almost out of it when the boat came bearing down the second time, the spinning blades reaching to rip them apart.

He saw the raised propeller shaft headed straight for his father. The high-pitched whine became a shriek in his ears. He saw his father struggling to move away, his exertions made sluggish and ineffective by his water-logged jacket.

The jacket!

With a superhuman effort Leif lifted his own soggy jacket out of the water and hurled it at the oncoming propeller.

Emil saw it coming. In the last split second he tilted the shaft, whipping it up to prevent the jacket from hitting the propeller and snagging it. The jacket hit high on the shaft—and clung. The propeller blades were free.

Quickly Emil leaned over to tear the jacket away so that it would not slide down and foul the propeller when he lowered it for his attack. One of his feet slipped on the wet wood. He swayed and fell headlong from the boat, his face striking the slashing blades.

There was not even time for a scream. . . .

Emil's faceless body slid along the shaft as it dipped back into the water, rapidly churning it to a deep red froth.

Ashen with horror, the other man grabbed the tiller and headed out onto the lake at full throttle, leaving the mangled body of his comrade floating in the crimson water.

Harry and Leif made it through the slough to the shore. Spent

and shaken, they crawled up on land. For a moment they lay
silent, trying to exorcise the horror.

Harry turned to his son.

"That was—fast thinking," he panted. "Damned fast thinking
. . . Leif . . ."

He stood up. Automatically he touched his shoulder holster. He
knew it would be empty.

Leif rose to his feet. His left leg buckled under him and he
almost fell. With surprise he touched it. He looked up at his father.

"Dad," he said, "I think I've injured my knee."

"How bad is it?" Harry's voice was tense. "Can you walk on it?"

Leif put his weight on the leg. He walked a few steps. He limped
badly.

"I can make it," he said.

"We've got to get out of here," Harry said with quiet urgency.
"Von Flatow has shown his hand. He's got to play it out. He has
no choice. Now . . ."

He looked out over the lake. The sound of the outboard motor
was distant. He heard it sputter. And die. Involuntarily he shivered.

Too damned close . . .

Grimly he took stock. He and his son were unarmed. They were
up against six hunters armed with powerful shotguns. Five miles
from the village and their car.

And his son could hardly walk. . . .

NEO-NAZIS TAKEN
SERIOUSLY

BONN—The formation of paramilitary
right-wing groups with members carrying pictures of Adolf Hitler and the Nazi
bible, *Mein Kampf,* is fact. One discovered here recently consisted of a dozen
persons who had built up considerable
stores of weapons and spent their time
taking target practice. . . .

10

Harry recognized the feeling of deadly urgency. He had felt it before, and he hoped it would spur him on, hone his wits to their ultimate sharpness. As it had before.

He tried to dismiss the nagging suspicion that this time there *was* no way out.

He was not entirely successful.

"Sit down," he said to his son, his voice taut. "Massage your knee. Gently. Get the blood flowing. Your leg's cold from the water." He had no idea if it would help, but it might appear to, and that was something. It couldn't hurt.

Leif sat down on the ground. He began to rub his knee.

"We'll have to make a run for it," Harry said. "But not without knowing what the hell we're doing. No use tearing around like a couple of chickens with their heads cut off." He concentrated. In his mind he visualized the map he'd seen in Von Flatow's place. The village. The estate. The lake. The German would remember that. He'd know that Harry had some idea of the terrain. He'd act accordingly.

"We have a number of choices," Harry said crisply. "We can make for the village by the west shore of the lake or by the east, where we are now. That's the long way around because of that damned inlet. But if we keep close to the water, we can't get lost in the forest. . . . We can stay put and hide in the underbrush until they get tired of looking for us." Or find us, he thought. "Or— there's a main road a couple of miles to the east of here. We could make for that and hope to flag someone down.

He frowned in thought. "Von Flatow will handle this like a military operation. I'll bet on it. He'll cover all the possibilities. He'll have to split up his men. Probably into three groups. Two men to each. One pair headed for that main road. One staying around here, to look for us and cut us off from reaching the other side of the lake, which would be the short route to the village. The last pair following the east shore as fast as possible to catch up with us before we reach the village if we should take that route. One thing is damned sure. The bastards can't afford to leave us here alive if they do catch up with us." He looked at his son. "Any comments?"

"I think staying here and hiding is out," Leif said firmly. "Getting to the other side of the lake would be pretty impossible. It'll have to be either the main road or the long way around to the village."

Harry nodded. "Agreed." He frowned. "As it is, Von Flatow and his men are probably no farther from that road than we are. We could never get there in time to flag someone down before they turned up. Anyway—the risk is too great. There's no guarantee anyone *would* come along. In time." He looked up the lake. "I think we're stuck with the lake route to the village. The long way. It's a good five miles." He looked with grave concern at Leif's leg. "Can you make it?"

Leif nodded. "Yes." He wasn't at all sure he could.

"Okay. Now—empty your pockets. Let's see what we have that might be of use."

Their joint belongings—beyond the normal handkerchiefs, keys and wallets—afforded only one item of possible use. A small penknife on Leif's key chain.

Harry held it in his hand. If it wasn't so damned ridiculous it'd be funny, he thought. A two-dollar penknife against a fifteen-thousand-dollar shotgun! Great odds! So, a shotgun didn't have the range and accuracy of a rifle—it was deadly just the same. . . .

He shrugged out of his bright orange jacket. No use making himself a fucking target for the bastards.

Suddenly—from the far distance—harsh, shouted commands intruded on his thoughts. He turned to Leif.

"How's the leg now?" he asked, urgency making his voice strident. "Ready to travel?"

Leif stood up. "Ready," he said.

"Wait here," Harry said.

He scampered up the shore embankment. He ran a few steps into the forest. A narrow path—a game trail?—seemed to run along the lake. He called to his son. "Up here!"

Leif scrambled up after his father. Pain from his knee knifed through his leg with every step he took. He stiffened himself. He was determined not to let it get him.

Together they began to run down the trail, Leif hobbling badly.

The path was obviously little used. Weeds and shrubs were encroaching on it. The forest was dense. A mixture of evergreens and various deciduous trees with heavy undergrowth. Branches and small tree limbs reached across the trail, making the going difficult and precarious.

But they kept on.

After the first guttural shouts they had heard no sounds at all; no signs of pursuit. It worried Harry. He had no way of knowing where—how far back—their pursuers were.

But he knew with absolute certainty that they were there.

Leif stumbled. A little moan escaped him. His leg was on fire.

"Don't stop!" Harry warned. "Keep going. Or the damned leg will stiffen up on you."

He ran close to his son. "Here. Put your hand on my shoulder. Take some of the weight off."

Leif did.

Awkwardly they ran on. But the going was slow. Harry knew the hunters had to be gaining on them. His back began to crawl. Would the blast from the shotgun strike without warning? When? Now? *Now?* He had to fight the urge to look back over his shoulder.

The forest thinned as they were stumbling down a slope. Harry's apprehension increased. They were easy targets here. They reached the bottom of the depression and started up the far side. At the top the forest once more became densely overgrown.

Suddenly Leif fell. He tried to get up at once. He winced with pain.

"Stop," Harry cried hoarsely. "Rest. Massage your calf. Your thigh. Don't let that knee stiffen." He turned and peered back anxiously. He could see across the shallow dale to the other side.

Nothing.

The forest was still; no sound or movement.

He sat down beside Leif. He was deeply worried. His son was obviously in great pain. He cursed his own age. He knew he could not carry Leif. Not for long. He was winded already.

He glanced back across the little valley—and stiffened.

Two men were emerging from the denser forest and starting

down the slope. Both carried shotguns. With an easy gait they loped down the trail. One of them wore a yellow jacket. Yellow? The Egyptian, Naha Ali Mahmud. The other red. The Dane, Knudsen? Or Von Flatow himself? They were too far for recognition.

Harry sprang to his feet. He reached a hand to his son. "Okay," he said, his voice low. "We're off."

They started down the trail. Harry's thoughts were bleak. It would be only a matter of time before the hunters caught up with them. Desperately he cast about for a way out.

There was none.

Could he leave Leif behind? Make it alone? Hide his son and hope the hunters wouldn't find him? Their only chance was to get to the village before Von Flatow and his men—and on to Kulmbach. To the authorities. That police inspector. Krueger? If he could make it alone, he could come back after Leif. If . . .

Even as the thoughts streaked through his mind he knew he could never leave his son behind. Angrily he shook himself. There *had* to be another way. . . .

They trotted on. Leif in obvious agony, his pale face drawn with pain.

Ahead the forest grew lighter again. Harry realized they were nearing the long inlet that they had to get around. A sudden thought chilled him. The hunters knew the area. Had they cut across the forest? To lie in ambush for them as they skirted the inlet? Was that why he had heard nothing for so long? He glanced at Leif, feeling heavy with regret that he had allowed events to involve his son.

The shore of the lake was in sight, and the trail turned sharply to the right, following the inlet.

Leif stumbled. He fell to his knees. Suddenly he called, "Dad!" He pointed. "Look! Is that a skiff?"

At once Harry bent down and looked ahead. Half hidden in the rushes, a small flatboat was lying overturned just above the water line. "We could cross the inlet," Leif said. "We—wouldn't have to go around. . . ."

Harry raced down to the flatboat. His eyes flew over it. It seemed seaworthy. He tugged at it. It moved. He turned it over.

He strained to push it into the water. Leif joined him. The little boat slid off the shore. It was waterborne. Harry piled in. Two oars lay in the bottom, wedged under the seat. He broke them out. Leif slid over the side. He collapsed in the bottom of the boat. Harry stood up. With one of the oars he pushed off, and the flatboat floated out into open water.

Hurriedly Harry sat down. The oars were in place—and with every ounce of his remaining strength he began to row. With every powerful pull the little boat jerked through the water. To Harry it seemed to drag in molasses. The inlet was only a few hundred feet across, but they had to make it before their pursuers reached the shore. Harry knew their guns were the best to be had.

He kept his eyes glued on the forest edge on the receding shore. Wasn't the boat making any headway at all? The shore seemed to be no farther away, no matter how fast he rowed.

Suddenly there was a sharp jolt. Harry almost pitched off the thwart. They had reached the other shore. At once he leaped from the boat and helped Leif ashore. The short respite seemed to have restored some of Leif's strength. Harry glanced back.

A glimpse of red appeared among the shrubbery on the far shore, and then Harry saw two flash points appear almost simultaneously. Instinctively he pulled Leif to the ground, even as the loud reports reached them and rolled thunderously over the lake. At once they heard a sharp rattle as of a sudden hail squall as the shotgun pellets tore through the shrubbery and leaves above them. Too far, Harry thought automatically. Too damned much spread and dissipation of power.

He stood up. Without looking back, he put his arm around Leif and they started off once again.

Harry felt elated. They'd bought time. Twenty minutes at least. They might make it.

A few minutes later he knew they would not.

They had slowed to nothing but a fast walk. The trail was badly overgrown, the light was murky and they were getting cut and scratched by branches and shrubs that stretched out over the trail.

Harry was looking at a grim fact. Their pursuers would catch up long before they could reach the village. If they were to save their lives, they'd have to speed up. Speed up considerably. Or—

Suddenly he stopped. He looked back along the narrow path. Grateful for the respite, Leif massaged his knee.

"We've got just one chance," Harry said grimly. "Boom or bust. If we are going to reach the village before those bastards get within gunshot, we've got to stop them. At least slow them down."

"How?"

"Booby-trap."

"Booby-trap?" Leif was startled. "But—we'd need explosives! Trigger mechanism. We don't—"

Harry interrupted him. "We do!" he said quickly. He looked back down the path. "I have an idea. I saw what we need back there a little way." He started to run back the way they'd come.

"We're going *back?*" Leif was aghast.

"Come on, dammit!" Harry snapped. "I'll need your help." He started back down the trail. Leif followed. "Just do what I tell you. Fast!"

"All right."

They were running down the trail in the direction they had just come from. Harry was looking intently at the trees as they ran past.

"Balatik," he puffed. "I remembered it from a CIC course I took. On booby-traps. Took it before we knew if we'd be fighting the Japs in the jungle. After VE-Day. It's a native Philippine trap. I think I remember it. I think we can—jury-rig it. . . ."

He stopped abruptly at a tree growing at the edge of the trail. "Here it is!"

It was a young tree, little more than a sapling, with long, slender branches reaching for the light high above.

Harry sat down on the ground. He pulled off his shoes. "I figure they are about twenty minutes behind us," he said hurriedly. "We've got to rig this damned thing in fifteen. Tops. That means —*move!*" He threw his shoes at Leif. "Pull out the laces," he said. "From your own shoes, too. Tie them all together. Then take our handkerchiefs. Both of them. Rip them into strips."

Leif asked no questions. He at once set to work.

"Give me your penknife," Harry said.

Hurriedly Leif snapped it off his key chain. He threw it to his father.

Harry turned to the tree. About five feet from the ground a long, supple branch reached out over the trail. He remembered having had to duck under it as they ran past. Quickly he began to strip off all the twigs and leaves, leaving the branch a long, naked bough.

He took the little penknife and cut off three lengths of wood. He whittled them clean into strong, pointed pegs, leaving a fork hook at one end of each where a smaller twig joined it. Two were sturdy and thick, the third one longer and slender.

He selected three more strong sticks about ten inches long and sharpened one end of each to a dagger point.

"Ready!" Leif called.

Harry threw the knife to him. "Cut four lengths of about three inches each off the line," he ordered. "Enough to tie the top eyelets of our shoes together so they'll stay on. Put them in the shoes." He grabbed the shredded handkerchiefs and quickly knotted the strips together into three pieces. With them he cross-tied the three sharply pointed sticks securely to the naked tree branch, their dagger ends pointed back down the trail.

"Okay!" Leif called.

"Give me the knife," Harry said. "Take a strong stick. Pound it into the ground. Over there. Use a shoe." He pointed to a spot on the opposite side of the path from where the tree stood and a couple of feet down the trail.

"Right."

Harry shrugged out of his empty shoulder holster. With the knife he cut away the strap buckle. He kept the metal buckle ring and threw the rest away far into the shrubbery. He looked at his watch.

Nine minutes . . .

The sense of another time washed over him—abruptly shattered by Leif's—

"Done!"

Harry ran to him. He took the shoelace line and tied it securely to the stake Leif had pounded into the ground. He gave the loose end to Leif. "Hold this," he said.

He ran back across the trail. Opposite the stake with the string tied to it he pounded the two sturdy pegs into the ground about five inches apart at a right angle to the path. The one farthest away from the edge faced its fork hook down the trail, the nearest one the other way.

"Bring the line over here," he called to Leif. Again he looked at his watch. Eleven minutes. Despite himself, he listened for the sounds of pursuit.

Leif handed him the line. He measured it to the nearest peg and cut it. He gave the rest of the string to Leif. "Tie it to this ring," he instructed him. He tossed the strap-buckle ring to his son. "Double-knot it." He bent down and tied the loose end of the stake line to the slender forked twig and placed it horizontally, resting in the forks of the two pegs in the ground. He stretched the string taut so that it ran across the trail a couple of inches off the ground. A short piece of the smooth end of the horizontal stick protruded at the other end of the far peg in the ground.

"Give me the ring," he said.

He put the ring on the end of the stick. He gave a light pull on the line that ran across the path. The horizontal stick was pulled from the fork rests. The ring fell to the ground.

"Okay," he said. "I wish to hell I had a better trigger pin. But this'll have to do." Again he glanced at his watch.

Thirteen minutes.

Any second he expected to hear the roar of a shotgun.

Or—perhaps to hear nothing at all. . . .

He ran to the strong, resilient branch on which he had fastened the needle-sharp pieces of wood.

"Put the ring back on the pin," he called to Leif. "Hold the string ready."

He took hold of the branch. He started to bend it around to the back of the tree trunk. He strained. He tested the resiliency. He fought to bring the branch as far back as possible, to give it the greatest springlike tension possible—without breaking it.

At last the branch had been bent back in an arc of more than 180 degrees.

"Now!" Harry puffed, straining to hold it. "Bring the string over. Tie it to the end of the branch."

Leif did.

"Pray the damned laces hold," Harry whispered fervently.

Gradually he eased up, letting the branch go, now held back only by the string.

It held.

Harry looked at his watch.

Fourteen minutes and thirty seconds . . .

His mind flashed to the illustration in the MIS textbook. He had it. It would work.

"We've got to test the damned thing," he said. "Stand clear."

He ran to the trip line running across the trail.

He tripped it.

The line pulled the trigger stick from the forked pegs. The ring slipped from the end, and with a hissing whoosh the taut branch —suddenly released—savagely whipped across the trail. For a brief moment it lashed back and forth, shaking its needle-sharp and lethal stiletto sticks.

Leif looked, wide-eyed with shock, at the deadly trap.

"My—God!" he whispered.

"Come on! We've got to reset it. You do the pin."

Harry ran to the branch.

Once again he struggled to pull it back. . . .

It was done.

Quickly they threw some leaves over the stakes and the trip line. They placed a cut branch so the stiletto sticks were hidden from anyone coming along the trail.

And they started off once again, running at a limping trot down the path.

Sixteen minutes had gone by.

They were about halfway to the village. . . .

NEO-NAZI PARAMILITARY TRAINING

BAVARIA, WEST GERMANY—Police searches have revealed several hoards of weapons, including military types, that have been squirreled away by neo-Nazis for future use. One of the oldest and largest of the militaristic organizations is the

> Wiking Jugend (Viking Youth). Their
> clandestine training camps are attended
> by youths from France and Belgium as
> well as Germany, with sometimes as
> many as 1,000 of them coming together.
> . . . In Bavaria the young people march
> with pistols and carbines, and use ca-
> mouflage-colored trucks with SS skulls
> painted on the doors. . . .

11

Von Flatow was coldly furious. That *verdammte* Emil. His blunder had complicated the plan needlessly. Now it would be necessary to destroy the Americans any way he could and worry about
explanations later. No longer did he have the protection of a perfect accident. Damn that Emil! Just as well he had paid for his
failure.

The master of Rittersheim was loping along the trail around the
inlet. It was irritating that the Americans had stumbled on the
flatboat. But it only meant a small gain in the time they would live.
He had not the slightest doubt that he'd catch up with them. Long
before they could reach the village. Obviously, one of them—or
both—had been injured in the abortive collision or he and Ali
would not have gained on them as rapidly as they had. It was
annoying that he could not have sent the boat back to the estate
with a warning. But the damned motor had apparently been damaged in the action. It had quit. And they had not been able to
repair it in the time available.

He changed his grip on the gun. It was getting heavier. Nonsense! He was simply more conscious of it. He was aware that he
was breathing in shallow gulps. He'd kept himself in good condition, but he was not as young as he used to be. He kept on running,
getting his second wind.

He was leading the way down the trail, Ali close behind him.
Grudgingly he admitted to himself that he was enjoying the chase.

He felt stimulated, eager, savoring the inevitable outcome.

His thoughts went briefly back to another pursuit through another forest. Many years ago. Three prisoners of war had escaped from the *Stalag* he had been assigned to as his first SS duty, taking part in the Gestapo secret surveillance of the camps. The prisoners had tunneled under the barbed-wire fence. An unimaginative effort—but it had worked. They, too, had been Americans. He and a detail of SS troops had pursued the prisoners through the woods surrounding the camp. It had been an exciting chase—and he had loved every minute of it.

He had brought the fugitives back, of course. All three of them.

But they had not been alive.

It would be the same now. . . .

He increased his speed slightly, spurred on by the remembered pleasure.

He was also vastly gratified that it was *he* who had found the two meddlers. Of course, he had reasoned it out that way. Still, he'd had to play it safe. Hartman and one of the Fichtendorfers had gone to the Kulmbacher road, and Knudsen had kept the two others to search the area around the lake and prevent their quarry from doubling back.

He had tried to put himself inside the heads of his adversaries. Deduce what course of action they would take.

He was enormously pleased that he had succeeded.

It would be he who would dictate the end of the chase. . . .

It felt to Leif as if he had no foot, no leg. Only a knee, the site of a searing pain. With every step a lance of agony shot up his side to his pain-racked mind. He dreaded each instant when his leg would hit the ground again . . . and again . . . and again. . . .

He wanted desperately to stop. Stop the stabbing, pounding pain. He knew he could not. He hobbled on. He knew his father would not go on without him. The knowledge was bleak. Together they would never make it.

And there was no hope alone. . . .

Exhausted, he sought comfort in thoughts of Susan—lovely, warm Susan—but found none. Instead, a wrenching, overwhelming sadness enveloped him. A profound regret at all the things that would never be. Never to hold her in his arms. Never to breathe her scent. Never to caress her, know her in total merging . . .

He stumbled and fell heavily to the ground. The shock jarred him back to terrifying, pain-racked reality. He was conscious of his father helping him to his feet. From some place deep within himself he found the strength and the courage to go on. And in a limping half-run he stumped on down the trail. . . .

Harry was hardly aware of helping his son to his feet. He was driven by one single, all-obliterating thought. They—must—go—on. . . . His feet were leaden. His lungs on fire. But—*they must go on.* . . .

His mind swam with fatigue, reality and memory mingled in a blur. They could not stop. Soon. Soon they would reach their own lines . . . and safety. Soon . . . But—hurry! The enemy—the Krauts —were gaining. And Andy was . . . Andy? No. Not Andy. *Leif.* His son. His son who had saved his life. . . . He shook himself. Think. Think of only one thing:

Go on.

They had reached the bend in the trail where it turned away from the inlet to follow the lakeside to the north. Von Flatow had briefly considered the idea of cutting across the forest, but had at once dismissed it. It would be slow and difficult going through the thicket. The trail was longer—but faster.

He was loping down the path a good ten meters in front of his companion. Ali was obviously played out. His breathing was labored, his steps heavy. Von Flatow's face grimaced in contempt as he thought of the Egyptian. Those people had no stamina.

The forest was getting denser, the trees grew closer to the path and the going was more difficult. But Von Flatow kept up as fast a pace as possible. He found himself searching the trail ahead with his eyes.

It would not be long now. . . .

Harry was profoundly worried. Their flight along the forest trail had slowed to a limping, shuffling gait hardly faster than a walk. And even that pace was an agonizing effort to keep up. Time itself was beginning to blur in his mind. How long had they been running? One hour? Two? Four? It seemed forever. The forest had swallowed up their world. Nothing else existed. He refused to despair. They plodded on, continuing their nightmare flight.

In some deep recess of his mind Harry knew the end would come soon. . . .

Von Flatow was getting annoyed. That idiot Ali was falling farther and farther behind. He was about to turn and rebuke the man when he heard a quick whooshing sound, a dull thud and, immediately, a piercing scream and the roar of a shotgun being discharged. He whirled around—and froze.

Behind him on the trail stood Ali, his face twisted in agony, his eyes wide in shock. His hands were clawing desperately at a naked branch clinging to his chest—blood welling over his writhing fingers. On the path lay his gun—fired in his convulsion as the stilettoes slammed into him. Even as Von Flatow watched, the man sagged to his knees, pulling the resilient branch down with him. A chilling, ululating wail came from his open mouth.

Von Flatow ran back to him. At once he knew. His eyes flew over the evidence. The trip line. The deadly spring-powered branch. A trap . . .

The stiletto sticks cross-tied to the bough had struck Ali full in the chest. One of the daggers had penetrated his lung just below the collar bone. Another had pierced his upper arm.

Von Flatow shuddered. A paralyzing thought shot through him. *He* could have been hanging there. Mangled. His life slowly oozing from him. Only seconds before, *he* had run across the trip line. *His* foot would have been within a fraction of an inch from tripping the murderous trap. He suddenly felt cold.

Ali looked up at him, eyes burning, his face ashen beneath the sheen of sweat. "Help . . . me . . . ," he rasped. He coughed. Blood seeped from the corners of his mouth.

Von Flatow put one hand on the man's shoulder. With the other he grasped the branch and jerked the daggersticks from Ali's chest and arm. The man gave a harrowing scream.

Von Flatow let go of the branch, averting his eyes from the pointed sticks quivering moist and red on their lethal perch. He eased the injured man to the ground.

"Help . . . me . . . please . . . ," Ali pleaded, his voice a gurgle.

Von Flatow looked down at him and then glanced up the trail. His quarry was gaining time. Getting away . . .

Face set, he turned to his injured aide.

"I can do nothing for you, Ali," he said, his voice flat. "I shall send help." And without waiting, he turned and began to run down the trail.

He stopped. For a moment he stood stock still. A thought flashed into his mind. The stiletto spring might not be the only trap! What—else . . .?

He dared not take the chance. He dared not run down the path as fast as he had before. He had to go slow. Watch. Check. Be cautious. His quarry would have time to get away.

He raged.

There *was* another way. He would not use the trail. He would run parallel to it. It would be difficult. Slow. But he might still have a chance to overtake the Americans.

And even as he crashed into the thicket he was making plans. Deciding what to do if he did not catch up with them, considering other means of silencing them. . . .

Harry and Leif had heard the distant shot.

"The trap!" Harry exclaimed. "They hit the damned trap!" They stopped and looked back, knowing they would see nothing.

Leif shuddered. In his mind's eye he could see the wicked dagger-pointed branch. And the hideous injuries the trap would have inflicted.

"That'll slow them down," Harry said wearily.

But hope had been rekindled. They might make it. They moved on. . . .

Forty minutes later the village of Fichtendorf came into view.

The last few steps to Gasthof Hirsch were the hardest. Now that relief and rest seemed within their grasp, their ordeal intensified. They dragged along, hanging on to one another, oblivious to the frightened stares of a couple of peasant women watching open-mouthed before ducking into a house.

At last they hobbled into the little courtyard in back of the

Gasthof. Their car was still where they had left it. They limped to it.

Harry opened the door. "Get in," he panted. "Wait. I won't be long." He hurried into the *Gasthof* as best he could, through the back door.

Laboriously Leif crawled into the VW. Every muscle in his body ached. His leg was one mass of pain. Gently he massaged his swollen knee. The relief was undetectable. . . .

Harry made straight for their room. Only essentials. Passports. Tickets. Shoes. A change of clothes for each of them. Leave the rest. It would more than make up for any unpaid bill. Helter-skelter he stuffed everything into one suitcase and ran from the room.

The little Volkswagen started up at once. Harry wheeled it out of the yard into the village square. At once he put on speed and raced down the main street toward the road to Kulmbach. Leaving the square, he glanced into his rear-view mirror. At the far end of the square a small group of young men emerged hurriedly from a side street behind a large barn and made for the Hirsch. There were maybe four or five of them and he caught sight of a flash of red. He saw them stop and look after the car. . . .

Twenty-four minutes later, on the outskirts of Kulmbach, Harry stopped at a gas station. While the VW's tank was being filled up, he and Leif used the men's room to change out of their torn and soiled clothing. The attendant gave them directions to the *Polizei-hauptamt*—the main police station—and they drove on immediately. If they could only reach Krueger with their story . . .

The rest had renewed them both. Leif's leg ached. But the sharp pain had subsided.

Empty parking spaces were as difficult to find in Kulmbach as in LA. After they first spotted the police station, Harry and Leif had to drive two blocks before they found a space where they could squeeze their VW in. It was a restricted zone, but they disregarded the sign. Quickly they made their way back to the station.

The self-important sergeant at the desk was not to be hurried. "Your name?" he asked Harry.

"Bendicks," Harry answered, "Harald Bendicks."

The sergeant spelled out the name as he wrote it. "B-E-N-D-I-X." Questioningly he looked up at Harry.

"Please. It is important. May we see Inspector Krueger?" Harry said urgently.

"x?" the sergeant asked.

"C-K-S."

"Ah." Meticulously the man erased what he had written and substituted the correct letters.

"Sergeant," Harry said, "is the inspector available?"

The sergeant turned to Leif. "Name?" he asked.

"Bendicks, Leif," Leif answered at once. "Same spelling."

The sergeant wrote. Slowly.

Harry fumed inwardly. Goddamn that Teutonic thoroughness, he thought. Questions. Forms. Records. Hell could freeze over before someone got permission to turn on the heat.

"Sergeant," he said, with a deliberate calm which somehow sounded strained, "may we *please* see Inspector Krueger? It is urgent!"

The police factotum looked at him, and back at Leif.

"L-E-I-F?" he asked.

"Correct."

The man nodded. He wrote. He picked up a large ledger and opened it to a marked page. He looked back over his shoulder at a big clock on the wall and entered the time in the ledger. Carefully he copied the two names into the book. He looked up.

"State your business," he ordered.

Harry gave him an ugly look. He wished he could nail the supercilious bastard's balls to the wall!

"We are here to see Inspector Krueger," he said. It was an effort to sound civil.

"Do you have an appointment?"

"No," Harry answered. "But it is a matter of grave importance. An urgent matter. The inspector knows us," he added.

The desk sergeant nodded. He picked up a phone and dialed a three-digit number. He waited.

Herr Inspektor? . . . There are two gentlemen here to see you. Their names are—" he consulted his ledger—"Harald Bendicks and Leif Bendicks. They say it is a matter of importance." He sounded apologetic. He waited. *"Jawohl, Herr Inspektor,"* he said. He hung up. He pointed down a corridor. "Second door on your left," he said. "Inspector Krueger's name is on the door."

Harry and Leif hurried down the corridor. They knocked on the door. A voice called: *"Herein!"*

They entered. Inspector Krueger stood behind a large, battered desk overflowing with neat stacks of papers and documents. Flat-eyed, he regarded Leif and Harry.

"Come in," he said.

"Inspector Krueger," Harry said quickly, "you may remember us from—"

"Of course," Krueger interrupted him.

"Good. We are here to report a—"

"I know," Krueger again interrupted him. "I have just been on the telephone with Herr von Flatow."

"Von Flatow!" Harry was startled.

"Yes. He told me in detail everything that happened," Krueger said. There was an edge of wary hostility in his voice. "I am gratified that you elected to turn yourselves in," he said coldly. "I was just about to issue an order for your arrest. . . ."

NEO-NAZIS LED BY YOUNGER MEN

WEST GERMANY—In West Germany a "Hitler wave" is cresting. . . . Some of the old Nazis have collected small militant groups around themselves, but for the most part the extreme right organizations in West Germany are led by men of a younger generation. . . . Some of these groups claim to have as many as 1,000 members. . . .

12

"Arrest!" Harry exploded. "What the hell do you mean, *arrest?*" He took a step toward the desk.

Krueger stood his ground. But his hand reached toward a button on the desk.

"Wait a minute, Dad," Leif said quickly. "Perhaps we should ask the inspector why he wants to arrest us." He turned to Krueger. "Would you mind telling us, *Herr Inspektor?* What did Herr von Flatow report to you?"

Krueger shrugged. His eyes were flat. He brought his hand back. "I see no reason why I should not do so," he said. "It is your right to know."

He sat down behind his desk.

"Inspector, I have injured my knee quite badly," Leif told him. "Would you mind if we sat down?"

Krueger nodded. *"Bitte,"* he said. Curtly he indicated two chairs in front of his desk. Harry and Leif sat down.

"What did Von Flatow tell you?" Harry asked.

"I shall be brief," Krueger said. "Herr von Flatow reported that during a duck shoot arranged for his guests this morning, disregarding specific safety instructions issued to you, you caused a serious boating accident. Instead of remaining at the scene of the accident and rendering assistance, you fled, leaving behind you one man dead, and one man critically injured by splinters from the shattered boat." He looked from one to the other. "Have you anything to add?" he asked.

"You're damned right!" Harry growled. "It's a pack of lies!" His eyes flashed angrily.

"Really, Herr Bendicks?" Krueger fixed him with an icy stare. "Yet—you are here. Alone. That would seem to corroborate Herr von Flatow's contention that you—eh, left the scene of the accident without facing your responsibilities—moral as well as legal." The threat was unmistakable.

"You are taking this Von Flatow's fairy tale at face value?" Harry demanded. He was unable to keep a tone of belligerence from creeping into his voice. "Without an investigation?"

"Oh, I shall investigate, Herr Bendicks. Of course. But Herr von Flatow has made no *criminal* charges. Yet. He is a reasonable man. He realizes that you may have—eh, panicked. He merely requests that we detain you here until he and his witnesses can arrive and a further inquiry can be conducted. It should not be too long a wait. Herr von Flatow informed me that he would be leaving his estate directly."

"Detain us!" Harry could not keep his anger in check. They had endured all the agonies of their ordeal only to land right in the hands of their enemies. "Who the hell *is* this Von Flatow that he can tell you to detain us?"

"Herr von Flatow *tells* me nothing, Herr Bendicks. But he is a respected, an influential man in this region. When he makes a complaint, I listen. I would do the same for anyone else." Krueger's voice was calm and controlled. But there were brass knuckles inside the velvet glove.

Leif had been following the tense exchange and its escalating hostility with growing concern. He realized they would have little chance of coming out alive if they allowed themselves to fall into Von Flatow's hands. He did not know if Krueger was in the man's pocket or merely a policeman doing his job as he saw it. It made no difference. The result would be the same if they did not get away before Von Flatow and his men arrived. Quite obviously Krueger had no intention of letting them go.

He knew the anger his father felt. The same anger smoldered in him. But anger was not the lever with which to pry them out of the dilemma. He turned toward his father. "Dad," he said, "perhaps we ought to tell Inspector Krueger *our* story. From the beginning."

"What the hell for?" Harry snapped. "If it comes to that, whose version do you think they'll believe? Ours? Or his? Backed up by his cronies?" He sounded angry and bitter.

Leif tried to catch his father's eye. He did. He let a flicker of warning flit through his eyes. He prayed his father understood. "If you don't mind," he said, "I'd like to tell him. Everything."

Harry gave his son a quick glance. Something alerted him. What was Leif trying to convey? Bleakly he realized that he didn't know his son well enough to *know*. To know with absolute certainty.

The way it had been with Andy. Even with Pete . . . And yet—he had the exact same intuition he'd had in so many cases that his partner had a plan. Did his son? . . . He decided to play it that way.

He shrugged. "Go ahead."

Leif turned to Krueger. "Do you mind, *Herr Inspektor?*"

Krueger contemplated him. He was a good enough investigator to know that you never stopped a suspect from talking. Always, in even the most irrelevant ravings, there were kernels of useful fact to be gathered. Often at such times information would be given which the most grueling interrogation would not pry out. And there was, of course, Von Flatow. He would undoubtedly wish to know as much about the Americans as possible.

"Not at all," he said.

Leif moved his chair a little closer to the desk. He pointed to a pack of cigarettes lying on it.

"Herr Inspektor," he said, "it has been an ordeal. I am certain you understand. May I have a cigarette? It would greatly help to calm my nerves."

"Bitte," Krueger said. He pushed the pack of cigarettes over.

With slightly trembling hands Leif lit a cigarette.

Harry felt himself tense. His heart beat faster as adrenalin pumped through him. He was wholly alert. He knew. Leif did have a plan. He'd have to be ready to act instantly when the moment came.

He watched Leif pull greedily on the cigarette. And he was certain.

His son never smoked.

Leif reached over and pulled a half-full ashtray a little closer. He flicked the ashes from his cigarette into it. He began to talk.

"It all began in Los Angeles, *Herr Inspektor*. A man was mugged in the street. He was killed."

He looked shaken. He took another deep puff on his cigarette. Any second now. He wished he could give his father some sign. Had he understood? Would he be ready? But he dared not even look at him. He had to keep his attention wholly on the German. He puffed again and flicked the ashes into the ashtray.

"My father is a retired police investigator," he continued. "From the Los Angeles Police Department. His last case before retiring was the investigation of that street murder."

He took another deep draw on his cigarette. Krueger was listening intently. He *was* learning something.

"It was a curious case, *Herr Inspektor.* A case with a very startling outcome."

He reached over and picked up the ashtray. He stubbed out his half-smoked cigarette in it.

Suddenly, with an explosive blast of air, he blew the accumulated ashes into the German's face. Blinded, the man instinctively threw both his hands up to his face. A bellow began to build in his throat, choked to a gagging sound by the gritty ashes.

With only a millisecond between impulse and action, Harry leaped from his chair. In the same motion he delivered a savage blow with the edges of his stiffened hands to both sides of Krueger's neck. The cry died unborn in the man's throat and he slid from the chair, unconscious.

Leif was on his feet. He ran silently to the door. He listened. No one had heard. No one came.

Harry examined Krueger. The man was out. No way of knowing for how long.

A subtle change had crept into the way the two men were working together. Neither Harry nor Leif was aware of it, but it was there. Men who are not used to working together, who have not built up an automatic trust of one another, express awareness of each other in their actions, their expressions and body motions, whereas familiar partners act as if each were alone. There is no need for conscious confirmation of the other's readiness. Without checking, Harry and Leif each did what seemed important, each automatically relying on the other.

Harry joined Leif at the door. "Let's get out of here," he said in a near-whisper.

Unhurriedly they walked past the desk sergeant.

"Thank you, Sergeant," Harry said pleasantly. *"Auf Wiedersehen."*

The officer nodded. He pulled over the large ledger, checked the clock on the wall behind him and signed *die Herren Bendicks* —with *cks*—out. . . .

Their Volkswagen had a parking ticket on it. Harry laughed in relief.

They got in and started up.

"We'll make straight for Frankfurt," Harry said. "Get the first possible flight out of there."

"Will they try to stop us, do you think?"

"Don't know. I doubt it," Harry opined. "I'm hoping they won't have time enough to alert everyone—if—*if*, indeed, Von Flatow and his crew can afford to take the chance of an international inquiry." He looked in the rear-view mirror. "If we can just get out of this damned burg . . ."

He drove cautiously, careful to observe all traffic regulations. But the moderate pace made him tense and impatient. He felt they were as conspicuous as two bagels in an Easter basket. Any second he expected to hear the wailing, two-tone horn of a police car.

But nothing happened.

Soon they were barreling along the E5 Autobahn toward Frankfurt. . . .

The grainy brown sky swam in and out of focus in Krueger's vision. Gradually he realized he was lying on the floor staring up at the underside of his desk drawer. His head throbbed. His eyes smarted. His mouth was gritty.

He moved—and winced with pain. His neck was tender and sore. He suddenly remembered. How long had he been out? He glanced at his watch. It could only have been a matter of minutes. Silently he cursed himself.

He'd been watching the older man. The obvious professional. It had been a mistake. . . .

Laboriously he struggled to his feet. He waited for his head to clear completely before he took any steps. He could not afford another blunder. Gently he wiped his watering eyes. He hawked and spat saliva, gray with cigarette ashes, into his handkerchief. *Verflucht!* The young Bendicks had taken him by complete surprise. Despite himself, he felt a grudging admiration. The young man had thought quickly—and with imagination. He wondered briefly what was going on between Von Flatow and the Americans. He was quite certain it was not what appeared on the surface. He dismissed it. He did not look forward to having to tell the master of Rittersheim that he had allowed the two Americans to escape. Especially after Von Flatow had personally requested him to detain them. He had long since learned it was not healthy to displease Herr von Flatow. He considered himself a good policeman. He was paid to take chances. But he was not paid to be an idiot. And he did not wish to become involved with Von Flatow. In any way . . .

He reached for the telephone. There might still be time to bottle the Americans up before they could leave his jurisdiction.

As his hand touched the receiver, the phone rang shrilly. Involuntarily he jumped. He picked it up.

"Krueger," he said crisply. He listened. "Send him in," he said. He hung up. He leaned back in his chair. He sighed.

Von Flatow had arrived.

Hans-Jürgen von Flatow regarded the police inspector icily. The incompetent nincompoop had ruined everything. He ached for the pleasure of tearing the idiot apart—but he kept himself coldly aloof. It was too late. He could not afford to make a major issue out of the case. Not at this stage.

"Very well, Krueger," he said, the contempt in his voice devastating. "It is of no importance. Under the circumstances I prefer that you do nothing. Nothing, understood?"

"Yes, Herr von Flatow. Understood, Herr von Flatow."

Von Flatow turned away. When he spoke again, he did not deign to look at the inspector.

"I want to use your telephone, Krueger. Your private line."

"Of course, Herr von Flatow," the inspector said subserviently. He indicated one of the two telephones on his desk. *"Bitte.* It is at your service."

Von Flatow said nothing. He looked at Krueger. Just—looked.

"Of course, Herr von Flatow," the man said uncomfortably. He rubbed his eyes. "You will want privacy. Please excuse me." He got up to leave his office.

Von Flatow waited until he was alone. Then he sat down in the inspector's chair. He picked up the private phone.

"Operator," he said, "I want to place an overseas call. To Los Angeles. United States of America. It is to be charged to the following credit number—" he recited a long code number—"in the name of Heinrich. Please expedite. It is an emergency." He listened for a moment. "I shall wait," he said.

He replaced the receiver. He sat immobile behind the large desk, staring at the phone.

It rang.

He picked it up.

"Heinrich," he said. He listened. "The goods are undamaged," he said. "They are being returned to the United States. I await instructions."

He listened.

"Understood," he said. "Washington, D.C. I shall leave here first thing tomorrow morning." He paused. "I suggest you have Berger meet me. The problem is greater than anticipated. I shall need all the assistance I can get."

MOURNERS GIVE NAZI SALUTE AT KAPPLER RITES

SOLTAU, West Germany—Nazi salutes by several mourners marked the burial of convicted Nazi war criminal Herbert Kappler in this north German town where he died of cancer after fleeing an Italian prison. . . . The German authorities refused to send Kappler back to Italy and afforded him heavy police protection. . . . Critics of this action contend that the German democracy is a façade and that *the needs of Nazism remain in the German spirit.* . . .

FOUR

Washington, D.C.

5–9 April 1978

I

"Listen to this, Dad." Leif looked up at his father sitting across the table in the little reading room of the Modern Military Branch at the National Archives. "It's from an editorial in *The New York Times.*"

Harry looked up. "Yeah?"

"They're evaluating the Nazis in Germany. Trying to assess if they constitute any kind of threat," Leif said. "Federal authorities estimate the strength of the Nazi forces at little more than one thousand, and this is how they evaluate them." He looked at the papers before him. " 'Persons better fitted for the comic opera stage than for a serious effort to overthrow the government'!"

Harry snorted. "Underestimating them just a little, I'd say," he said dryly.

"More than you think, Dad." Leif held up the document from which he was reading. "That particular article was written in November—*1923!*"

"I'll be damned," Harry said.

"I've been reading news stories from the years just before Hitler seized power," Leif said soberly. "To get some kind of picture. They all say the Nazis are not to be taken seriously. Pretty much what we're running up against now." He picked up another paper. "Here's one. As late as 1933. 'Hitlerism is on the downgrade and slipping fast. As a real menace, it is finished.' " He looked up. "That was *The New York Times* too."

"Their crystal ball must have had a cloudy day," Harry observed.

Harry and Leif had been back from Germany nine days. It was Wednesday, April 5. Teresa von Flatow had let slip that the middle of the month would be a fateful time. And the middle of April was approaching. Fast . . .

Immediately upon their return they had made full and detailed reports to what Harry referred to as the Washington alphabet boys, the CIA, the FBI, the NSA, the DIA, and even the IADB—the Inter-American Defense Board. They'd talked to representatives from the State Department and the Defense Department.

And they'd taken their case to the Immigration & Naturalization Services' Special Unit, formed only a few months before to track down Nazi war criminals in the U.S.

Everywhere their story had been met with polite skepticism. It had patiently been pointed out to them that they had little concrete information that would justify the launching of a sensitive investigation of international scope. Their allegations would be looked into, they were assured, but it would of necessity take time. Any inquiries would, of course, have to be made discreetly. As for a possible living son of Adolf Hitler, it was of dubious interest and even less importance—best described as historical trivia.

Pointedly they had been asked if there really were some big, international—eh, plot afoot, why had it not been discovered by the agencies specifically set up to monitor such activities? The CIA? Or the British Intelligence Services? The answer was, of course, simple, but hard for the bureaucratic mind to swallow. Harry and Leif had not been trying to discover anything—they'd simply stumbled on it.

And become involved . . .

Grimly they had realized that they could not let go. They had to follow through, and that meant digging. Digging deep into the records at the Archives in Washington and through the captured German documents at Alexandria.

There were several possible subject areas to probe. Where there were a *son* and a *father* there must also have been a *mother*. Who was the mother of the boy in the Kugelberg cabin? Her identity, if they could find it out, might provide a clue. Were there indeed documents to be found that referred to a Hitler son? . . . And Von Flatow? Would *he* show up in any of the captured documents? Or in CIC records? If so—as what? Or were there any papers pertaining to a possible plan to resurrect the Reich? There were many questions the answers to which might hold clues.

And, of course, there was *Jenbach.* . . .

So they dug. And dug deep.

For many days they had submerged themselves in work. At first they had been looking over their shoulders constantly.

Harry was convinced that they would not be safe until they had gotten to the bottom of the whole mess. Or until whatever was planned for the middle of April had occurred. But nothing had happened—and they were beginning to relax. They had rented a small car, and—since they spent their time partly at the Archives on Pennsylvania and partly in Alexandria—rather than staying at the Jefferson again, they had taken a room in a motel, the Riverview, on the Virginia side of the Potomac, just off the road to Alexandria south of the Rochambeau Memorial Bridge.

Leif had returned to Washington with a special nervous excitement of his own. What would it be like seeing Susan again? Was she as wonderful as he remembered her, or had his imagination embroidered her picture while he had been away—missing her? The answer had been abundantly clear. His imagination must have been completely dormant. He had remembered only half the wonderful things about her.

Susan was no longer free to work exclusively with him and his father. But whenever she could she helped them out with information and with her knowledge of the archives. The white-bag lunch had been repeated a few times—each more enjoyable than the one before—and Leif had taken Susan to lunch once, a disappointing experience, locked into a tiny space at an even tinier table crowded by a noisy, impatient throng of Washington lunchers.

Leif readily admitted to himself that he was becoming preoccupied with the girl. He found his thoughts wandering to her at all hours. He couldn't help it—and he didn't try to. One thing did bother him: He could not make up his mind how Susan felt about him. She was a private person.

He determined to find out.

Harry stretched. "I've been doing a little reading myself," he said. "I feel as if I'd just raided a particularly sleazy porno shop on Santa Monica."

Leif looked at him. "That bad?"

"That bad. Our Adolf—did you know the women called him *der schöne Adolf?*—the handsome Adolf? Well, he sure wasn't the puritanical ascetic his propaganda machine made him out to be." He pulled over a thick book, bound with many pages of typescript and carbons. "Here's a little titbit from the OSS *Hitler Source Book*. It's from an interview with some movie director who used to work for the UFA studios in Neubabelsberg in Berlin. He was required to supply Hitler's Chancellery with starlets and chorus girls for some bunk calisthenics—God, does that sound familiar. One of them was a rather well-known actress named Renate Müller."

"Müller," said Leif. "Seems we're being haunted by Müllers."

Harry snorted. "This one might well be doing some haunting," he said. "Listen to this." He began to read:

"Renate told him that she had been sure that Hitler was going to have intercourse with her; that they had both undressed and were apparently getting ready for bed when Hitler fell on the floor and begged her to kick him. She demurred, but he pleaded with her and condemned himself as unworthy, heaped all kinds of accusations on his own head and just groveled around in an agonizing manner. The scene became intolerable to her and she finally acceded to his wishes—and kicked him. This excited him greatly and he begged for more and more, always saying that it was even better than he deserved and that he was not worthy to be in the same room with her. As she continued to kick him, he became more and more excited and, as a final climax, masturbated before her. He then suggested that they get dressed and thanked her warmly for a pleasant evening."

Harry looked at his son. "Not long thereafter," he said soberly, "Renate Müller committed suicide. Threw herself from the window of a Berlin hotel."

Leif's thoughts briefly flashed to another woman killed in a fall from a window.

Sarah Zuckermann . . .

"As a matter of fact," Harry said, "suicide—or attempted suicide—seems to be par for the course after a go-around with the beautiful Adolf. There are close to a dozen documented cases in here. His niece, Angela Raubal—Geli, he called her—shot and killed herself after a hot-and-heavy with her uncle. Unity Mitford, his English girl friend, Lord Redesdale's daughter, tried to kill herself—and so did Eva Braun. Twice. Out of jealousy. Once she shot herself, aiming for the heart. She missed. Once by taking an overdose of sleeping pills. The Führer's love life makes a pretty sleazy picture. He seems to have been a whole sexual disaster area all by himself. Some writer who knew him put it this way: 'Most loath-some of all is the reeking miasma of furtive, unnatural sexuality that fills and fouls the whole atmosphere around him, like an evil emanation. . . .' "

He pushed the book away and pulled over a large yellow pad filled with notes.

"Okay," he said. "Let's see what we've got."

He consulted the pad.

"Item. Adolf liked the girls—but his sexual appetites were bi-zarre, to say the least. I've come up with more than fifty—count them, *fifty*—women with whom he supposedly fooled around, whether he got into their pants or not.

"Item. A dozen or so of these women apparently were quite important to him. He sure had the hots—but bad—for his little niece, Geli. She was apparently his great love. He's supposed to have had a collection of wildly pornographic drawings of her to feast his eyes on. She was probably pregnant by him when she killed herself with a shot through the heart."

He looked up. "Of course, some citizens of the Third Reich were of the opinion that *der schöne Adolf* shot her himself. After all, it was one of his Walther guns that was used."

He returned to the pad.

"Next on my list of bedmates: Jenny Haug. She was the sister of his first chauffeur. That was back in 1923. She and Adolf were supposed to have been engaged. But nothing came of it. . . .

"And there was Henny Hoffmann, the daughter of Hitler's offi-cial party photographer and, according to reports, little more than a whore whom anybody could have for a few marks. Apparently Hitler just indulged in some kinky sex with her.

"Then we have a girl from Berchtesgaden named Maria—or Mizzi—Reiter. She, too, tried to knock herself off. There seems to be little doubt that Hitler screwed her. Last time probably in 1938. . . .

"He was also enamored of a good-looking broad named Erna Hanfstaengl, the sister of his good friend Putzi, and with several ladies of more or less established fame. Among them Siegfried Wagner's widow, Winifred; the opera diva Margrete Slezak; our friend Renate Müller; and another actress, Jenny Jugo. He rewarded *her* with a villa near Wiesbaden for her—eh, contribution. . . .

"And then, of course, Eva Braun—queen of the group."

He looked up. "And that brings us to the interesting part. Which of Adolf's various centerfolds might have had a kid by him?

"Item. Apart from a lot of claims by out-and-out crackpots, there are several reports that warrant closer scrutiny."

He turned over a page of the pad.

"Let's take the case of little Eva first. From the newspaper stories that appeared in 1945 we know she's supposed to have given birth to two children, a boy and a girl, both fathered by Adolf, and both supposed to have been spirited to safety toward the end of the war."

"When did they say the boy was born?" Leif asked.

"1938. He would be the right age," Harry answered. He went on.

"I don't put much stock in the story that one of Martin Bormann's kids was actually an illegitimate son of Hitler by some girl named Uschi and was adopted by the Bormanns. No, I think I'll put *my* money on Eleonore Bauer, Sister Pia, the nun who became so smitten with *der schöne Adolf* that she was excommunicated. There seems to be quite a bit of evidence that she made it to Adolf's bed and the resulting brat was reared by a special, secret party fund. He *could* be our little Dolfi from the Kugelberg cabin."

He turned another page.

"The two people still living who claim to be Hitler's offspring are, of course, out of the running. That Frenchman Jean Loret, dug up by Maser a few months ago, and Gisela Heuser, who keeps writing magazine articles claiming she has proof that Adolf is her daddy. We can forget about them."

He looked up at his son.

"But—fact is that a child fathered by Hitler most certainly is no far-fetched notion. Maybe a kid by someone else who never made the history books. If we *have* run across an illegitimate Hitler heir, it's been a well-kept secret for a long time—and it took some punk kid in LA to blow the lid off it. . . ."

He snorted. He turned his attention to the pad once again.

"Item. Someone is going to a hell of a lot of trouble to safeguard the knowledge of his particular Hitler bastard. Why?"

He looked at Leif. He paused. He flipped a page of the pad. Leif was listening. He was spellbound.

"Item. The world—especially Germany—is experiencing a sharp, resurgent interest in Hitler and the Nazis. More and more incidents involving Nazi activities are reported in the world press every week. Is there a central control for all this? If so—why? And by whom? And has it anything to do with that boy in the cabin?

"Item. There are still a lot of old-time Nazi leaders around to guide any neo-Nazi movement—like that arch-bastard Josef Mengele, the Angel of Death from Auschwitz-Birkenau. Wiesenthal says he's in hiding in Paraguay. Just consider this. Germany as a nation lost some forty percent of its fighting men in the war—but the Nazi party leadership lost only about two and a half percent! What does that tell you?"

Harry thumbed through his notes.

"Okay," he said. "Put it all together and—what the hell *does* it spell?" He held up his hand as Leif was about to answer. "Don't tell me," he said. "I've got the answer. Trouble!"

He glanced toward the door as a man carrying a small stack of books entered the little reading room. They had seen him several times before, always studiously absorbed in whatever research he was doing. The man gave Harry and Leif a quick look and took a seat well away from them. He busied himself with his books. Harry and Leif lowered their voices.

"Nobody's bothered us since we got back," Leif pointed out. "Maybe they've decided to leave us alone."

"Maybe." Harry looked glumly at his pad. "Might as well," he said. "We sure aren't getting anywhere."

Dr. Rosenberg came into the room. He nodded pleasantly to Harry and Leif and walked over to the newcomer engrossed in his research. He placed a large envelope tied with a wrinkled ribbon before him.

"Here is the special material you requested," he said. "I hope it will be of help."

"Thank you, Dr. Rosenberg," the man said. "I appreciate it." Rosenberg nodded amiably. "My pleasure, Mr. Berger."

NAZI OFFENSIVE IN ROSKILDE

ROSKILDE, Denmark—The brown ghosts of Nazis surfaced in Roskilde, where posters demanded "ruthless persecution" of Marxists and Zionists . . . and laws to prevent the mentally retarded from "multiplying." The posters are distributed by Denmark's National-Socialist Youth (DNSU) and are adorned with SS script and with a big swastika.

2

Outwardly the ivy-covered house of Clayton Parks did not dis tinguish itself from the other well-groomed residential building on the street on the outskirts of Washington, D.C. Neither did it occupant.

A confirmed bachelor, slight, deceptively meek-looking, Clay ton Parks was in his late fifties. He had emigrated from Argentin; to the U.S. in 1954 and had become a naturalized citizen, changin; his name from Klaes Packmayr. He was a successful CPA with ; well-earned reputation for highly "creative" accounting abilities It was therefore not surprising that he counted among his client a good many officials with influence.

At the moment Clayton Parks had a houseguest. One Hans Jürgen von Flatow.

The excellent dinner, provided by a caterer of known discretior who had already left the premises, had been an unqualified suc cess. It was not a dinner Clayton could legitimately deduct on hi; Form 1040, but he would undoubtedly find a way to do just that None of his seven male guests was a client and only one held ; government position—although all were successful and influen· tial.

They sat around the table comfortably smoking and sipping an excellent Sandeman port as they chatted urbanely. Yet the genial and seemingly relaxed atmosphere was slowly being invaded by expectant tension.

When the faint ring of the doorbell was finally heard, the conversation stopped at once, and the men watched in taut silence as Parks himself rose to answer it.

Von Flatow also stood up. There was no need for him to tap his teaspoon on his glass for attention, but habit is stronger than need, and he did. The men turned toward him.

"Gentlemen," he said quietly, "he is here. *SS Standartenführer Dr. Franz Schindler!*"

The door to the dining room opened and a man entered. As one, the guests all rose and stood facing him, ramrod straight.

The years had been neither kind nor unkind to Dr. Franz Schindler. His hair had grayed and his clean-shaven face no longer had the smooth glow of youth. But he was still lean and carried himself erect and with authority. Flanking him, a little behind him, two burly, grim-looking men stared at the assembled guests with hard, hooded eyes. Clayton Parks stayed in the background.

"Welcome, *Herr Standartenführer,*" said Von Flatow. He indicated the chair at the head of the table, vacated by their host. "Please."

Schindler nodded. Slowly, deliberately, he walked to the chair. He remained standing.

"Please, gentlemen," he said, his voice firm and full, "sit down."

The men took their seats. They watched the man standing before them. With the exception of Von Flatow, none of them had seen him before. But they had all heard about him. To them he was a living legend, one of the Führer's few remaining intimates. Their leader. Their hope for a future passionately and ruthlessly yearned for by each of them.

For a moment Schindler stood silent. He let his penetrating eyes move from man to man, resting a moment on the face of each in turn.

"Gentlemen," he said, his voice laden with portent, "in exactly two weeks your lives will change. Dramatically. And forever. I am confident you are prepared to accept the grave responsibilities that will be thrust upon you."

He paused. He looked around the room.

"Each one of you will be responsible for a *Gau*—a major section of the North American Reich." Again he looked from man to man as he spoke. "The Northeastern States. The Southeastern States. The Midwestern States. The Southern States. The Northwestern States—and the Southwestern States. Six *Gauen.* Each of you will have complete authority in his own territory and be answerable only to me. Each of you will have specific tasks to perform at the appointed hour. You are aware of them. Specific strings to be pulled—to make specific puppets dance to our tune!"

Again he paused. The men watched him raptly—in utter silence.

"At long last," Schindler said. "At long last we have come full circle. The young Siegfried, sleeping, awaiting the time to rise again, is ready to be awakened. Ready to forge the sword that will destroy his enemies. *Our* enemies . . ."

Eyes burning with fanatic fire, he stood for a moment staring fiercely at the listening men. "That sword, gentlemen, will soon strike its first blow. The target area has been chosen." He paused dramatically. "It is the Middle East!"

There was a rustle of reaction around the table.

"The Middle East is a seething caldron," Schindler went on. "We shall overturn that caldron and spill its destructive contents across the world. Even now our strike forces are moving into place. Wherever in the world German-speaking, German-thinking people exist—there is Germany. Greater Germany. And there our preparations are now entering the final stage. Even as they are here. Tonight . . .

"It is all according to the ultimate plan of the Führer, Adolf Hitler, the legacy *he* handed down to me. To us. Before his ultimate self-sacrifice. Nothing shall alter it. In his political testament Adolf Hitler prophesied: *'There will rise the seed of a glorious rebirth of the National Socialist movement.'* The German Reich! . . . So be it."

He paused to let the men recall for themselves the stirring words of their Führer.

"The Führer realized even then that only through conflict, through cataclysmic upheaval, through another world war, can our Reich, a Nazi Germany—a Nazi world!—rise again. But this time the sacred soil of Germany herself shall not be the battlefield. No. The battle between East and West that will erupt shall be fought on alien soil, and to that end we shall—at first—ally ourselves with certain nations. Arab nations."

Again a reaction stirred around the table.

"Do not misunderstand," Schindler said. He looked grim. "In so doing, we are faithfully following the Führer's plan. To touch off the worldwide conflict that will be the breeding ground for our rebirth, the Führer ordered us to find and use a world trouble spot. Certainly the Middle East is such a spot today. The Arab nations with their abundance of oil constitute one of the richest, most 'power-filled' areas of the world. We can put those riches and power to good use. Yet—these nations are backward, unstable, without coherent leadership."

Again his eyes swept the men at the table.

"Of course, we shall not genuinely ally ourselves with an inferior, Semitic race. We shall merely *use* them. We shall follow the Führer's own advice as he wrote it in *Mein Kampf:* 'Without the possibility of using lower human beings—without the help of suitable beasts he knows how to tame—the Aryan would never have been able to take his first steps!' . . . We, gentlemen, shall heed that admonition laid down by our Führer, Adolf Hitler, in taking *our* first step. Two weeks from today!"

He smiled a thin, cold smile.

"After all," he said, "we do have something in common with them. The desire to destroy the Jewish state and to achieve the final annihilation of the Jewish people. Neither the Arabs nor we Aryans can rest easy as long as the abomination that is Israel is permitted to exist. Again, this was prophesied by the Führer himself in his political testament: 'There will burst forth anew the hatred for the people who alone are ultimately responsible—the Jews!' *We* shall fan the flames of that hatred."

Von Flatow listened and watched intently. He contemplated the scene before him. Not all violence is physical, he thought. He smiled to himself.

"Already," Schindler continued, "already our cooperation with the PLO has been effective in laying the groundwork.

"Once again," he said, looking around the room, letting his eyes rest briefly on each of the raptly listening men in turn, "once again we shall be following the Führer's example. *He* knew the importance of using the right trigger to set off the desired reaction. Forty-five years ago he needed an extreme event to rally the German people around him and give him the powers he needed. The burning of the Reichstag was the trigger. An inspired, an audacious conception of the Führer, brilliantly planned by Dr. Goebbels and carried out to perfection by Goering. It served its purpose superbly."

He sipped his brandy. All eyes were on him.

"And the scapegoat, *meine Herren,*" he continued. "We must not forget the scapegoat. They used the Dutch Communist, the half-wit arsonist Van der Lubbe. He was their scapegoat. . . . And Germany belonged to Adolf Hitler."

He paused.

"But *our* target is not merely Germany. It is the world. *Our* trigger must be world-shaking. It is. . . . Adolf Hitler called the burning of the Reichstag a beacon of light from heaven. *Ours* will be a bolt of fire from hell! And at this moment our trigger is being readied."

SS Standartenführer Dr. Franz Schindler drew himself up. "Events are moving swiftly," he said. "And we must adhere to our timetable. It has been carefully laid out. It cannot be changed at this late date. Too many factors in too many places the world over. Preparations too complicated to alter now."

He looked around at the listening men.

"Gentlemen. In exactly two weeks, on April the twentieth, the birthday of Adolf Hitler, we shall trigger events that will change the world. Forever!"

He picked up his glass.

"I proudly repeat the words of the Führer, spoken as he watched the Reichstag burn. *'There can be no turning back, no mercy. Whoever gets in our way will be struck down!'*"

He stood ramrod straight and lifted his glass.

"Heil!" he said. "Our watch is nearly done. *Sieg Heil!* The Fourth Reich!"

As with one voice the men echoed, *"Sieg Heil!"*

They filed from the room. Schindler turned to Von Flatow. "Hans-Jürgen," he said, "please stay." He addressed Clayton Parks. "Leave us," he said.

The two men sat down at the table. Schindler poured them each a glass of port. He sipped his with obvious enjoyment.

"Hans-Jürgen," he said, "what is the status of the Bendicks affair? What are they doing?"

"Floundering, *Herr Doktor,*" Von Flatow answered. "We have followed your instructions. We have monitored their actions. Kept them under surveillance, but left them alone. As you ordered. They have made no discoveries of importance."

"Excellent. As long as they do not, you will continue merely to keep them under observation. In two weeks they will know!" He laughed unpleasantly. "But should they run across any vital information, information that can in any way endanger our operation or ourselves—you know what to do."

"Of course, *Herr Doktor.*"

Schindler sipped his port. "When will you leave for the target area?" he asked.

"I want to be there two days ahead," Von Flatow replied. "On April eighteenth."

Schindler nodded. "Good. By then it will be too late for anyone to do anything—whatever they may discover."

He looked searchingly at Von Flatow. "Yours will be the vital task," he said gravely. "Do not fail. . . ."

His mind flew back to another time, another place, when he had admonished a subordinate not to fail. In a stinking storage room of the gym in an abandoned boys' school in the ruins of Berlin. Then—his order had been followed. To the letter. He had no doubt it would be the same now.

He sat back in his chair. He contemplated the deep, rich color of his port.

"You know, Hans-Jürgen," he said, a cynical little smile on his lips, "the unimaginative, the pedestrian thinkers of this world might look upon all this as rather far-fetched."

His eyes glinted.

"So many things are far-fetched," he said. "Until they happen!"

NEO-NAZI, ARAB
CONNECTION

HAMBURG, West Germany—When police in Hamburg arrested Udo Albrecht
for illegal possession of weapons that
included hand grenades, he was identified as a member of the little known
Freikorps Adolf Hitler. This organization and its affiliate Freikorps Ara-
bien (Free Corps Arabia) have as their
primary goal the destruction of Israel.
Albrecht is reported to have recruited
over 500 German mercenaries for
training with the PLO for attacks on
Israel.

3

Dinner had been a quick ham-and-cheese on white toast and a
cup of coffee in a little fast-food joint on Eighth, and Harry, Leif
and Susan had returned to the Modern Military Branch reading
room at the Archives for a couple of hours' work before the offices
closed at ten P.M. Susan had finished her working day and was
helping out. The three of them were alone.

Earlier in the day Susan had brought Harry a fat file folder
marked: ADOLF HITLER: SUPERSTITIONS & ABERRATIONS.

"It's a long shot," she'd said, "but there might be something
there. It's worth a quick look."

Harry had agreed. He'd already spent several hours looking
through the records and documents, some of them in English,
some in German.

He sat staring at the document in his hand, an analysis of the
Führer's persecution mania. He shook his head. His mind swam
with his newly acquired knowledge of Hitler. Anyone who says a
madman can't get to run the insane asylum is crazy, he thought.

Hitler was into every absurd superstition, every nutty half-science, every cracked occultism you'd care to mention. From phrenology to graphology. Clairvoyance and palmistry. Physiognomy and spiritualism. Pornography. Fetishism. You name it. And ever since his early exposure to the sometime astrologer, sometime fortune-teller Erik Hanussen—of course—astrology. While forbidding others to dabble in it, Adolf himself was hooked. Big. Locked away in his library they'd found hundreds of large envelopes with astrological charts and pictures, horoscopes and projections, all meticulously marked in the Führer's own hand. Harry remembered being told in the CIC school that *we* had a bunch of astrologers telling *us* what Hitler's astrologers probably were telling *him!* To the very end a couple of out-and-out fortune-tellers had been his frequent guests. God only knew how much stock he put in their advice.

Even his racial theories seemed to have come from an occult magazine, a Viennese publication called *Ostara,* an erotic, mystical sheet filled with pseudo-scientific mumbo-jumbo. Hitler's "knowledge" of the Aryan race apparently came from *Ostara* and its publisher, one Lanz, who warned that the pure Aryan race was being threatened by an inferior, apelike race. The Jews.

And Adolf had put his faith—the care of life itself—in the hands of an obscure doctor. A quack! A guy named Theodor Morell, who shot him full of all kinds of weird and poisonous concoctions and stuffed him with pills—some of them laced with generous doses of strychnine and belladonna, for crissake!—and had him forever munching magic lozenges.

The Führer was convinced that secret, mysterious forces surrounded and guided him. Hell, he even heard "voices" imparting the secrets of the universe to him. If *anyone* had foretold that a king-sized crackpot, ridden by such demented superstitions and such lunacy, one day would come close to ruling the world—he'd have been laughed right into the nearest funny-farm. . . .

Harry put the report aside and picked up another from the file folder—one of the last remaining. He read:

REICHS-UNIVERSITÄT STRASBOURG
INSTITUT DER RASSENKUNDE

Ahnenerbe
Abteilung der Schädellehre
Dr. August Hirt, Direktor   Strasbourg, den 17.11.43

There were several schematic views of a human skull pictured from the top and from the sides, with many notations and measurements, lines, angles and planes pencilled in. And the words

Subjekt: Der Führer u. Reichskanzler Adolf Hitler, Geb. 20.4.1889.

and the prominent, black stamp: GEHEIM!
SECRET!
Harry showed it to Leif.
"What do you make of this?" he asked. It comes from the University of Strasbourg, the institute of racial sciences. *Ahnenerbe*—ancestral heritage. Division of—skull science. What the hell is *skull science*? I guess it's the skull of Adolf they're talking about."
Leif took the document. He looked at it. "Division of craniology," he said.
"Big help," Harry said dryly.
Leif laughed. He showed the document to Susan. The three of them studied it briefly.
"Craniology is the science dealing with the variations in size, shape and proportions of the cranium—the skull," Leif explained. "It's normally used to characterize the variations in the different races of man. Some also consider these variations inheritable on an individual basis."
"And those markings?" Harry asked. *"F—pr—gn—ba* . . . What do they mean?"
"Measurements for the cranial index," Leif told him. "The precise measuring of the cranium is the central technique of craniology. It's called craniometry." He pointed to the date at the head of the document. "1943. In this case, actually cephalometry—when the measurements are taken over the skin on a living person."
He looked up at his father. He pointed to two stylized sketches

of a human head. From the right. And left. The area of the skull was divided into sections, much like a butcher's plan of a side of beef showing the various cuts, each section numbered. "According to these charts, they used phrenology, too," he said. "There seem to have been a lot of studies made. Apparently not so much to learn as to justify preconceived ideas."

"I ran into that phrenology bit," Harry said. "What exactly is it?"

"It's a kind of pseudo-science," Leif said. "It's based on the belief that the contours of the skull minutely conform to the highly specialized portions of the brain lying directly beneath. By measuring these protrusions—bumps, if you will—a system was developed to chart a person's character traits and abilities. Some years back it was very popular. It has no scientific support."

Harry looked at the charts. "You mean this is a complete map of all the bumps on Adolf's head?"

Leif nodded. "Something like that. Certain contours and traits were believed to be inheritable and quite unique."

He turned the page. Clipped to the second page of the document was a copy of a tightly written note penned in Gothic script. Leif gave it to his father.

"That's beyond me," he said. "Anything?"

Harry began to read it. He grew visibly pale. In silence he finished the note. He looked up at Leif and Susan.

"Jesus," he said.

"What is it?" Susan asked.

"It's a copy of a note," Harry said. His voice sounded strangely constricted. "From that Dr. Hirt on the letterhead. The director of the place." He looked down at the note. "He wants a bunch of skulls in good condition for his studies. For comparisons. So he— he requisitions them from the Auschwitz-Birkenau concentration camp—with explicit directions on how to severe the head from the useless trunk without damaging it—after the selected victim has been put to death."

He paused. He looked angry. Leif and Susan watched him, their faces gray.

"Soon that wasn't enough for the bastard," Harry said. "So he puts in a big order for his damned skulls. And so the goods'll arrive nice and fresh and undamaged, they're sent to him on the hoof!

Almost two hundred of them." He looked at Leif and Susan. "Then
they were gassed with cyanide," he said, his voice low. "An efficient process that did not damage the—the specimen, and then
they were prepared under supervision of Hirt himself."

He looked at the piece of paper in his hand with visible loathing.

"There's a little note added when this copy was made," he said.
"Dr. Hirt disappeared after the war. He was never caught. Not the
slightest vestige of information about what happened to him has
ever been found."

He threw the document on the table in angry disgust. "For all
we know, the bastard may have himself a nice little practice under
some new name in some German burg—making house calls and
patting little kids on *their* heads," he growled.

Leif picked up the pages. He them, his eyes incredulous. He looked at the signatu d of the craniological
report—the record of ancestral he Führer, Adolf Hitler.

Hirt.

Suddenly his eyes widened. He looked closer.

"Bingo!" he whispered.

Harry looked at him sharply.

"Look," said Leif quickly. He pointed to a faint notation in the
lower left-hand corner of the craniological report.

Harry read it.

Betr. Jenbach

It was the first time they'd seen the word—except for the Muller
snapshot. Harry felt a surge of excitement. His hunch had been
right. Jenbach *was* of importance. Enough so to command copies
of the personal, secret records of the Führer himself.

But—why?

He stared at the notation. "Concerns Jenbach," he read. "Why
the hell should a map of the damned bumps on Hitler's head
concern Jenbach?" He frowned.

"Whoever Jenbach is," Leif said.

"Or what," Harry said. "Or—where . . ."

Harry pulled the rental car into the parking area across from the
motel unit that was his and Leif's. Number 9. The Riverview Motel

was made up of several individual bungalows, each with two units. Harry and Leif were in the fifth unit away from the larger office building with the red neon sign blinking VACANCY. The other room in the bungalow was empty.

He killed the motor and turned off the headlights. For a moment he sat in the dark, thinking. After the Archives had closed for the night, he'd left Leif and Susan in town. They'd wanted to relax over a drink, they'd said, and he'd dropped them off at the Embassy Lounge on Massachusetts Avenue not far from their old haunt, the Jefferson, and on the way to Georgetown, where Susan had a small apartment. Harry grinned to himself. He had a hunch the drink was the least important ingredient in what his son and Susan were cooking up. He v   pleased. Susan was a helluva girl.

He himself had want⌐⌐   ⌐n in. Relax his own way. Go to sleep—and let his silen   ⌐a little work, for a change. He'd come to regard his s   mind as a separate partner. A partner who kept o   ⌐xing problems while he himself slept, and who'd come up with some sort of solution, some ideas. Most of the time. Somewhere in all the incoherent information and unrelated happenings in the Muller case was a key. Go find it, partner. And good luck . . .

He stepped out of the car. The night was cold. He hurried toward the bungalow, fishing his key from his pocket. Or, rather, Leif's key. He'd had to borrow it from his son. He'd left his own key in the pocket of his other jacket that morning. Getting absent-minded with the years, he thought. Great for an investigator. He had a momentary twinge.

Ex-investigator . . .

He unlocked the door and stepped inside. The bungalow was cozy and warm.

He looked forward to a quiet rest. He needed it.

"I agree," Leif said, an amused little smile on his face. "I agree with you one hundred percent."

Susan looked at him with surprise. "Agree? I didn't say anything," she said, puzzled.

"Not with words," Leif said. "But there are other ways to communicate."

"What are you talking about?"

"Unspoken language," he said. "Body language." He watched her, his eyes twinkling. "And your body language is shouting!"

"Oh? What about?" She was intrigued.

"That singer." Leif nodded toward a piano bar where a girl was doing strange and wondrous things to an old standard. "You don't like her. You'd rather talk than have to listen to her. I agree."

Susan looked at him. She blushed. "How did you know?" she asked. "Are you a mind-reader as well as a psychologist?"

Leif laughed. "You were telling me," he said. "In body language. Your fingers were tapping the table—but not in time with the music. Your eyes kept flitting toward that backstage entrance over there. Your message was clear. You were yelling Impatience!"

Susan took her hand from the table. "My God!" she said with mock indignation. "Is nothing sacred?"

"Not much," Leif said. "Freud once said: No mortal can keep a secret. If his lips are silent, he chatters with his fingertips. Betrayal oozes out of him from every pore."

Susan smiled. "Looks like I was both chattering and oozing."

"We all do. All of us communicate all the time, and not just with words. The *way* we say the words. How often have you heard someone explaining: It wasn't *what* was said, it was the *way* it was said?"

"How true. I've often had a compliment that sounded like an insult."

"Exactly. And all the little actions we think are unimportant and incidental. Every movement. Expressions. Glances. Gestures. Positions. They all form a language even more important and revealing than the language of words."

Susan eyed him. "I think I'll just sit perfectly still and stare straight ahead," she stated.

"Loudest body-language shout of all!" Leif told her. "I hardly dare tell you what *that* means."

Susan laughed. The singer had stopped singing and just noodled pleasantly on the piano. Susan took a sip from her brandy Alexander.

"I suppose I'm communicating all kinds of dark secrets by doing this," she said. "I guess I'll just throw caution to the winds and make snappy patter in body language."

"I'll be listening—third ear and all." He sipped his own drink. He looked at the girl over the rim of his glass.

"You know," he said, "the real meaning of any communication depends only to a relatively small degree on the actual words used. There's even a formula for it—developed by a psychologist named Mehrabian: Seven percent verbal. Thirty-eight percent vocal— your tone of voice. And a whopping fifty-five percent body language!"

"*That* you've got to prove to me," Susan said skeptically.

Leif gave her a quizzical look. "All right," he said. Slowly he leaned over and put his face close to hers. He gazed directly into her eyes. He placed his hand over hers. "I—hate you," he said quietly, his voice soft, intimate and gentle.

Susan's cheeks colored. She looked away—then she recovered herself and returned her eyes to his.

"Well?" he asked. "Which do you believe?" He sounded perhaps a little more serious than he'd intended. "The seven percent? Or the ninety-three percent?"

Susan gave him an enigmatic little smile. "What made you become a psychologist?" she asked.

"A Viking." Leif gave a little laugh. It was pleasant to remember. "A children's book about a young Viking."

"Must have been an unusual book."

"It was. It was called *Leif the Lucky*. It was about Leif Erikson and his discovery of America. I thought it was about me. I was seven."

He had. He'd identified so strongly with the Viking boy in the pictures. He could still see them. . . .

"You mean Leif Erikson not only discovered America, but psychology as well?"

Leif laughed. "Not quite," he said. He looked into the soft face of the girl sitting so close to him. "I remember there was an illustration in the book," he told her. "It showed Leif and his Vikings aboard his ship. Everyone was enveloped in a thick fog. All you could see through it were Leif's eyes and his arm sticking out of the fog, pointing ahead." He smiled at the remembered scene. "I remember it said that Leif could see better and farther than all the others, and that his eyes pierced the fog and he could point the way. I wanted to be able to do that." He looked into Susan's eyes. "I've always remembered that picture. Isn't that what psychology is?"

"So now you're pointing your patients toward their own personal Vinlands."

"I try. It's all too easy to get hung up on the rocks, or find yourself ashore in a barren wasteland. . . ."

For a moment he looked at her. Both were silent.

"And you," he said. "Never married. Why?"

"Possibility never arose," she said.

But she knew at once. She knew that that ninety-three-percent non-verbal communicating must have given her away. She'd felt her voice go flat, the tightening around her mouth—even as she glanced away.

There had been Mark. . . .

She looked back at Leif. "No," she said. "There was—someone. Once. It didn't work out."

Somehow it didn't hurt anymore.

Leif took her hand in his. Their eyes met.

"Susan," he said. "Dear Susan."

She said nothing.

In words . . .

He did not ask the taxi driver to wait. It seemed perfectly natural.

Susan's little apartment was warm and friendly. He hardly noticed.

Her face was grave and soft and lovely before him.

He took her in his arms. Her silken hair lay gently against his cheek, and the sweet scent of it embraced him.

They kissed.

And there was nothing else. . . .

Susan felt his arms press her to him—and she knew there was no turning back. She knew she would give herself in all ways to this man who held her so tightly and yet so tenderly in his arms.

Give—and take . . .

NEO-FASCISTS GAIN
STRENGTH
IN ARGENTINA

BUENOS AIRES—In this romantic city a
new nationalist movement sworn to combat Marxism and Zionism has emerged
with a recruiting slogan, "The best
enemy is a dead enemy." . . . Slogans and
symbols on posters are reminiscent of
Hitler's Nazi Party. An emblem of the
Argentine condor stamped on them re-
calls the eagle used by the Nazis. The
party is admittedly based on European
Fascist ideology.

4

Harry and Leif were crossing Pennsylvania Avenue on their
way back to the Archives from the FBI Building. They'd spent
most of the morning at the Bureau. Harry'd pulled some "old
buddy" strings and a friend of his at the International Association
of Chiefs of Police had persuaded someone at the FBI National
Crime Information Center to run a search of the criminal identification records on the name *Jenbach.*

No dice.

Harry was disappointed—but it had been a long shot.

Out of the corners of his eyes he glanced at his son. They had
not discussed the very late—or rather early—hour Leif had returned to the motel. There had been no need. Harry knew the
look. Great . . .

He huddled in his coat. It was a raw and cold Friday in Washington.

There were two other people in the Modern Military Branch
reading room when they entered. The elderly man who had been
there doing research for the last several days, and whom Dr.

Rosenberg had addressed as Mr. Berger, and a young girl. She looked bored. Probably a college student paid to do research for someone else. Both looked up when Harry and Leif entered, then returned to their respective activities.

Harry and Leif took seats at another table.

"Well," said Leif. "Where do we go from here?"

Harry looked glum. "Damned if I know," he growled.

"Perhaps *I* do!"

The voice came from the door.

They turned toward it.

It was Susan. She stood in the doorway. Her eyes looked radiant with excitement. She carried a document in her hand.

"Where have you been?" she scolded. "I've been waiting for you all morning."

Quickly she walked over to Harry and Leif.

"Look," she said. "I was indexing some British intelligence records they just got around to declassifying and—look what I found!" She handed the document to Harry.

He and Leif examined it—

Harry stared at the document. He'd seen the word at once.

JENBACH!

His eyes flew over the report.

Jenbach was a *town,* dammit! A little town in Austria. Near Innsbruck. Hall. And Wörgl. Right smack in the middle of the National Redoubt. In the dead center of Hitler's Alpine Fortress. He knew the area. Well. It had been considered impregnable during the war. One of Ike's greatest headaches. A fortified Nazi bastion that could have been defended forever.

Suddenly all the pieces fell into place: Hitler's son and heir kept hidden and guarded in the Kugelberg cabin. The eleventh-hour mission by the SS—including SS Obersturmführer Ernst Helmut Müller—to get the boy out after the area had been overrun. Get him out and take him to safety in the new unassailable Führerbunker at Jenbach! The destination penciled on Muller's snapshot of the cabin the boy had been rescued from. Jenbach . . . The craniological report on the Führer from the Institute of Racial Science in Strasbourg—and probably other Hitler family records

FROM CPM   0147622

Report No. FWIS(H)/KP/658   S E C R E T   / FÜHRERHAUPTQUARTIER /

FILE

REPORT ON INTERROGATION PW KP/229264 Geb. Jäg.
KEREK, Stefan - KEMPTON PARK CAMP - 14 APR 45

1. PREAMBLE   MAY 3 1945

PW is a 28 year old Pole, very willing and co-operative. In civilian life he was a musician and is endowed with a lively imagination. The infm given in this Report is, as indicated, only based on rumour.

2. POSSIBLE LOCATION OF FÜHRERHAUPTQUARTIER

Whilst travelling by train from WÖRGL to INNSBRUCK early in Feb 45 PW noticed on the right hand side of the line (facing in the direction of INNSBRUCK) three or four adits leading into the mountain. PW thinks they were somewhere near JENBACH and states they were definitely on the WÖRGL side of HALL.

These adits were between 100 and 200 m distant from the rly line and in front of them was a levelled space which PW thought had been concreted. He did not notice any roads leading to it.

The adits were about 2 m high and about 1 m wide, the top being curved in the form of an arch. On the left of these three entrances were three or four steel doors or hatches about 150 cm x 80 cm. These did not reach to the ground, the top of them being about level with the top of the adits.

Near the rly line was a sign which stated "Luftschutzkeller für ....." (the followed the name of some firm which PW does not remember). He stated, however, that his compartment was full of local inhabitants, and they stated that it was being prepared for the Führer HQ.

On his arrival at INNSBRUCK PW states that he saw an abnormal number of cars bearing party flags and that these seemed to be travelling in the direction of HALL.

DECLASSIFIED   Authority NND   Chinac Leg
BY WHC   Major,
SIO Kempton Park Camp.

Kempton Park Camp,
Sunbury on Thames,
Mddx.
15 Apr 45
gs

RECEIVED 2 MAY 1945

Distribution: -
    SHAEF (PW & R) - 5
    FWIS(H)   - 51 (50 to MI19(a))
    CSDIC (UK) - 3
    MIRS
    LDC

—collected at Jenbach. To be kept safe with—and for—his son and heir!

Dammit—it all fitted!

Perhaps now they could find the answer to the big question that remained: Why? *Why* was it so damned important to keep the knowledge of Jenbach and the existence of Dolfi a secret? After thirty-three years?

And the damned watchdogs—who the hell *were* they?

He turned to Susan. For a moment he looked into her shining face. His son was a damned lucky man, he thought.

"You *did* it!" he said. He was proud of her.

He slammed his hand down on the document on the table. "Now," he said vigorously. "*Now* we go to work!"

Leif glanced at his watch. "I'd better go call the motel first," he said. "They wanted to know if we want to keep the room for a few more days. Before one o'clock. I guess the answer is yes."

"You're damned right," Harry said crisply. "We've got to contact someone in British intelligence records. In London. I suppose Rosenberg can help us there?" He looked questioningly at Susan. She nodded. "I want *anything* they have on the Jenbach place. Records. Documents. Who was involved with it. Names. Any Nazi big shots. What was found. The works!" He turned to his son. "You and I'll keep digging here—now that we know exactly *what* we're digging for. We'll wait for whatever information the British can come up with." He looked at the document. "We'll start with this," he said. "You go over it word for word. See if you can find any further clues. I'll talk to Rosenberg. Get things rolling."

"Fine," Leif agreed. "Let me make my call first."

"I'll do that," Susan said. "Do you have the number?"

Leif took the motel key from his pocket. He handed it to Susan. "It's on the tag," he said. "Thanks."

For a moment their eyes met and held. Then Susan turned and hurried off.

Leif sat down. Carefully he began to read the PW interrogation report. He felt excited. Things were happening. In *their* favor.

At last.

He was not aware that the little man at the other table had collected his research material and quietly left the reading room. . . .

It was after dark when Harry and Leif pulled into the parking area at the Riverview Motel. Harry was driving. He'd been too keyed up to be merely a passenger. It had been a hectic day. Rosenberg had pledged his cooperation—but, due to the time difference, it had been too late to contact anyone in London.

First thing tomorrow . . .

Leif put his hand in his pocket. "Oh, great," he said. "In all the excitement I forgot to get my key back from Susan."

"Use mine," Harry said. He suddenly swore. "Shit! I *still* didn't get the damned thing from my other jacket!"

"That's all right," Leif said. "I'll go down to the office and borrow the passkey from the manager. Won't take long." He got out of the car.

"Okay," Harry said. He felt chagrined—but not enough to spoil his good mood. "I'll lock the car. Meet you at the bungalow."

He took the flashlight they kept in the glove compartment, stepped out of the car, locked it and walked over to the bungalow. The whole court was quiet and dark, except for the faint lights burning over the unit doors. He stopped at Number 9. He looked after Leif. His son was just entering the office building.

Harry sighed. He found it hard to relax. He waited. His mind was filled with thoughts. Facts. Ideas. Conjectures. The myriad bits and pieces that make up an investigation . . .

He suddenly felt uneasy. The edges of his mind began to itch.

He looked around quickly, fully alert.

Nothing.

Yet—something had set off the alarm.

What?

He grew tense. He began to investigate his immediate surroundings. Something was wrong. He felt it. Crawling on the flesh of his back . . .

He tried the door. It was locked.

He looked at the window facing the court. The faded, dirty-yellow curtains were drawn.

The curtains!

That was it. They had left the curtains open when they'd gone out this morning. To let a little sunlight into the room. Now they were closed. The maid? Probably . . .

The nagging feeling of danger did not leave him.

He looked closer. He played his flashlight all around the window. At the bottom in a corner on the inside the curtain had been caught. A small patch of dark blue showed in the flashlight beam.

Blue?

The room towels were blue.

He had a sudden thought. Had someone ransacked the place? He ran to the back of the bungalow. Beneath the rear window were several deep footprints in the moisture-softened earth—as if someone had jumped out.

Here, too, the curtains were drawn, the window closed. But a narrow slit where the curtains met in the center remained open. Harry played the beam from his flashlight through it into the room beyond.

Icy realization instantly etched the scene upon his mind: The towels stuffed around the window and door cracks. The missing faint-blue glow of the pilot light in the gas wall-heater!

His flashlight beam came to rest on the door. He moved it down the edge to the floor. At the doorhandle side the towels had been kept away for a stretch of several inches.

His light beam stopped—and he froze.

With the incongruity of sudden shock he saw himself as that bionic character on television, his eyes zooming in on the small device fastened to the bottom of the door.

Two wooden matches taped to the door itself, their heads just reaching below the bottom edge—resting on the striking surface of a matchbook cover!

Open the door a mere fraction of an inch and . . .

Viciously he smashed the flashlight against the windowpane. It shattered. Instantly he was enveloped in a cloud of gas.

Suddenly an icy thought shot through him.

Leif!

His son had gone to get the key. Any second he would . . .

He raced around the bungalow. He shouted. "Leif! Don't . . ."

A few feet and he would be able to see the front door.

The thunderclap explosion lifted him up bodily and slammed him into the ground. A blinding fireball flared from the rupturing bungalow. Harry lay sprawled on the ground. The wind was knocked out of him. His head swam. He refused to black out.

He fought to his feet. Every step a lance of agony, he ran to the front of the blazing bungalow.

The figure thrashing and writhing on the ground was a mass of flames. Its head a hairless, charred orb, slit open by a black hole that screamed and screamed . . .

Harry raced to him.

"Leif!" he shouted in torment. "Leif!"

He ripped his jacket from his aching body. He beat at the devouring flames. With it. With his hands. He rolled the blazing body on the ground, savagely trying to smother the fire. And all the time the black hole screamed. And screamed . . .

Suddenly the screaming stopped.

The silence knifed through Harry like a white-hot spear.

Leif!

The greedy flames made the charring limbs twist and jerk.

But with searing certainty Harry knew it was a macabre dance of death.

The screaming came from his own throat this time.

"Leif! . . . Leif! . . ."

5

He was dimly aware of many voices, of many hands tearing him away from the smoldering body.

And suddenly a voice rising above the others.

"Dad! . . . Oh, my God, Dad!"

He lifted his head. Through a distorting mist his burning eyes saw someone running toward him.

It was his son.

It was Leif.

And he slipped into blackness. . . .

The siren cut sharply into his mind. Painfully his eyes began to focus. Abruptly he tried to sit up. Two hands held him down. He turned his head. He looked up into the face of his son.

"Easy, Dad," it said quietly. "Easy. You are all right."

He did not understand. It didn't matter. The swaying motion of the speeding ambulance dizzied him. He let himself drift away. . . .

Harry stood at the American Airlines Gate 43 at Dulles Airport. Flight 77 to Los Angeles was about to leave. The place was crowded. The Sunday flight was always filled. He was watching Leif and Susan saying their goodbyes.

He looked at his bandaged hands. They would heal quickly. The burns were superficial. Involuntarily he shuddered as his thoughts strayed to the charred corpse on the ground outside the blazing motel bungalow. The body of the night manager.

The man had not wanted to trust Leif with the motel's passkey. He had been right. But that had not saved his life. Instead he had gone to open the door himself—while Leif went across the street to get an evening paper.

It had been called an accident. Of course. Harry's thoughts were bitter. He had not bothered to mention the matchbook trigger he'd seen. Only to his son. No one would have believed him. He knew that from experience now. Not without evidence. And no matches, no tape, no matchbook cover could have survived the blast and the flames. Likely as not people would have thought it a wild story to cover up his own negligence.

So—a tragic accident.

He and Leif had decided to return to Los Angeles. It had been Leif's idea. They could take care of Harry's hands better at home, he'd said. Harry had agreed. But he'd known Leif wanted them to get away from Susan. For now.

Their presence quite obviously could be a danger to her.

Rosenberg had promised to forward any information the British came up with. He, Harry, had no intention of giving up his quest.

He was determined to stick with it. Now more than ever.

A woman's voice over the public-address system interrupted his bleak thoughts.

"American Airlines Flight 77 to Los Angeles now boarding at Gate 43," it announced.

Hollywood, here we come, he thought.

It was the end of Act Two. There were bodies all over the damned stage. Muller. Wendkos. Gerner. Emil. And the night manager of the Riverview Motel.

He had no idea what Act Three would bring.

All he knew—the damned curtain was about to go up. . . .

NEO-FACIST TERRORIST GROUP CLAIMS RESPONSIBILITY FOR BOMBING

BOLOGNA, Italy—A neo-Facist terrorist group in Italy called the Black Order left a note in a phone booth in Bologna claiming responsibility for the bomb explosion that took 12 lives on an express train traveling through a tunnel between Florence and Bologna.

FIVE

Los Angeles

15–17 April 1978

1

Helan går! Helan går!
Hej hop faldera hurrah! Hurrah!

The lusty Scandinavian drinking song rang out in the banquet room, bawled enthusiastically by the group of men sitting around a large table.

Harry downed his schnapps in one big gulp as tradition demanded. He could feel the warmth of it going down.

He had decided to attend the regular meeting of the Danish Luncheon Club of Los Angeles after all. He usually did whenever possible. And he had to do something—or he'd disintegrate with frustration.

His hands were almost healed, but the burns *had* curtailed his activities. He was restless and on edge with impatience.

He took a good pull on his beer chaser. He wished he hadn't come. He found it hard to keep his mind from wandering. He usually enjoyed the monthly luncheons, the easy camaraderie with other Danish-speaking men; eating good Danish food washed down generously with Carlsberg beer and Aalborg aquavit accompanied by the appropriate vocal exercises.

But—today was April 15. The middle of the month.

Nothing had happened. Nothing, that is, outside the usual mayhem and crises. But—if he and his son were right—somewhere, something was about to blow.

And here he sat, dammit, fat-assed, eating umpteen kinds of herring and other goodies from the Danish cold table.

Usually the club met every second Monday of the month. But this luncheon meeting had been postponed to Saturday, to accommodate the special speaker who would only be in LA over the weekend. The man promised to be interesting—and probably worth changing a few habits for.

Harry watched him sitting across the table in animated conversation with the club president. White, bushy hair. A ruddy red face and ham-sized fists. He looked more like a Danish farmer or fisherman than what he was: Gunnar Jensen, a professor at the University of Copenhagen and the successful author of several books based on his own exploits and experiences as a leader of the Freedom Fighters during the Nazi occupation of Denmark. His talk would undoubtedly be fascinating. And he had brought along some film clips to go with it.

Harry contemplated the man. Would *he* believe the Nazis were still around? In force? Would *he* believe the bastards were out to get him, Harry, and his son? Would *he*—

Angrily he looked away. Dammit—he had to take himself in hand.

He concentrated on the Danish plaice they were going to have. With browned butter and parsley potatoes. It was one of his favorites. To hell with the Nazi bastards . . .

Professor Jensen was being introduced. Harry listened without hearing.

There had been no word from Rosenberg. Had he heard from the British? Had they found out anything about Jenbach? Anything at all? Dammit—time was being pissed away. He decided to call Rosenberg first thing in the morning. No. That would be Sunday. First thing Monday morning. Damn this weekend business anyway. Everything always came to a screeching halt. . . .

He was suddenly aware of what Jensen was saying.

". . . and the record of the Danish resistance is a proud one indeed. The Gestapo chief of Copenhagen bitterly complained that it was the most difficult resistance encountered by German occupation forces in Europe. It was so varied. He never knew what to expect next. And that's exactly the way we wanted it!

"As a result, vast numbers of Nazi troops were kept from fighting on Germany's main fronts by Danish sabotage of railroads, factories, airfields, military depots—and targets where the enemy could be hurt. You name it—we weren't choosy. The resistance groups were supplied with huge quantities of arms, ammunition, explosives and equipment by Allied air drops. So efficient were the recovery operations that only six percent of this vast quantity of supplies was lost. This relentless sabotage also had the effect of sparing the Danish population from the large-scale air attacks the Allies had, of necessity, to inflict on other European cities. The saboteurs and Freedom Fighters did the job on the ground. Their valiant efforts were described by Field Marshal Bernard Montgomery as *second to none!*

"As far as the Danish police force was concerned, they . . . "

Stein had come up with nothing, Harry thought. Zero. You couldn't blame him. Every available man on the force had been pressed into an all-out effort to apprehend the vicious killer who'd terrorized the city for months, raping and murdering young girls. The Hillside Strangler . . .

He was startled when the room went dark. Jensen was going to show some of his film.

"When the day of liberation did arrive," he said, "the Danish underground press had published a total of twenty-five million issues of illegal newspapers. Almost half a million feet of film showing actual sabotage raids and resistance operations had been shot by the Freedom Fighters under the eyes of the Gestapo. Believe it or not, we had our own cameramen along on most missions to record them. What I am about to show you is one such action. The sabotage of a factory taken over by the Nazis for their war effort."

The film—grainy, scratched, black-and-white footage—illuminated the screen. The obviously hand-held camera showed a large factory building shot from a high vantage point.

"The raid began at exactly eight A.M. on a Sunday morning," Jensen commented, raising his voice above the whir of the projector. "The Danish workers would be off . . . "

Harry had a sudden idea. He looked toward the speaker—a dark figure next to the projector. The man was an expert in his field. It was worth a try. He'd buttonhole him once the program was over.

He returned his attention to the screen.

Suddenly the entire roof of the main factory building shot skyward in a blinding flash. Huge pieces of equipment and machinery sailed through the air as smoke and fire billowed forth. The roof crashed down, leaving an entangled heap of mangled beams, twisted girders and shattered masonry.

"We made our getaway on bicycles," Jensen was saying. "At the first side street the first one would leave the group—and so on at each street until we were all thoroughly dispersed. Pursuit was almost impossible. . . ."

Harry literally had to pry Jensen away from the group of Danes all talking to him at once.

"Professor Jensen," he said, "I need your help."

Jensen shot him a quick glance. He nodded crisply. "Outside," he said. He turned back to the men around him and excused himself.

In the lobby outside the banquet room he studied Harry. "Bendicks, wasn't it?" he said. "You sounded serious. What can I do for you?"

"I don't know," Harry said. "Perhaps nothing." Now that he'd collared the man, he felt stupid. Like the European who meets some guy named Smith from New York and says: Hey! Then you must know my cousin, Joe Smith. He lives in New York too. . . .

"Let's give it a try," Jensen said.

"Okay." Harry formed his sentences carefully. "A few weeks ago I met a man. In Germany. He was a Dane. Big. About our age. I had the feeling he might have been, shall we say, sympathetic to the Nazis if he'd been in Denmark during the occupation. I was wondering if in your activities in the resistance you had perhaps heard of him. It's a pretty common name, though. The man's name was Knudsen. I can't remember his first name."

As he said the name, he remembered the conversation—in Danish—he'd had with Knudsen at Von Flatow's table.

Jensen frowned in thought. "This man," he said, "it is important for you to know about him?"

Harry nodded. "It is."

Jensen asked no more questions. "You are right," he said. "Knudsen is a common name." He stroked his nose. "Knudsen," he mused. "Knudsen . . . The Knudsen that first comes to mind wouldn't be your man," he thought aloud. "He was the Berlin correspondent for one of the largest Danish newspapers, *Berlingske Tidende*—until the Nazis threw him out in '43. But—first of all, he was very much anti-Nazi and, secondly, he'd be too old. Close to eighty now. His name was Helge."

Harry shook his head.

"There was another Knudsen," Jensen said. "He was the leader of a small sabotage group. He was called Mads. Mads Knudsen. I did not learn his last name until after liberation day."

Harry shook his head. "No," he said. "It wasn't Mads."

Jensen thought for a moment. "Another Knudsen I remember," he said, "was a collaborator. He became a leader in the notorious Schalburg Corps, the Danish SS troops. He disappeared after the war. No one knows what became of him. His name was Eigil. Eigil Knudsen."

"That's it!" Harry exclaimed. "Eigil!" Eagerly he looked at Jensen. "What else do you know about him?"

Jensen shook his head. "Nothing much," he said. "The man was a merchant seaman. Of course, he may have changed his name. A lot of them did."

"No," Harry said, "I don't think this one did. . . ."

Eigil Knudsen, houseguest of Hans-Jürgen von Flatow and quite obviously involved up to his ass in whatever shenanigans Von Flatow had planned—Eigil Knudsen had been a merchant seaman and a Nazi collaborator during the war. If the two Eigil Knudsens were indeed the same man . . . Another tiny part of the puzzle had been put into its proper slot.

It didn't make the picture any clearer.

The persistent ring of the telephone bored into his sleep-numbed brain.

He fumbled the receiver to his ear.

"Yeah," he growled.

"Harry. This is Susan."

He was awake at once.

"Susan," he said. "You heard from the British! They contacted Rosenberg?"

"No, Harry."

"No?"

"It's something else." She sounded urgent.

"Are you all right?"

"Of course. In fact—very much so. I am arriving in Los Angeles tomorrow."

Harry was startled. "Does Leif know?"

"No. I called you, Harry. I was afraid Leif would try to talk me out of it. I—I know how he feels. I know his concern. But—I do think it's important."

"What is?" Harry asked. "Why? Why are you coming out?"

"I—I don't want to discuss it on the phone," Susan said. She sounded strained. "I don't think that would be a good idea—in view of everything." She paused. "Besides, I am bringing something along."

"What?"

"Something I think you'd want to see for yourselves. As soon as possible."

"Something—important?"

"It could be even more than that." She sounded frightened.

Harry thought fast. If Susan did have some information—information of real value—she might well be in danger. It was obvious that he and Leif somehow had been under observation even in Washington. Did that surveillance extend to include the girl? Perhaps she *would* be safer where he and Leif could keep an eye on her. On the other hand—if she got herself really involved—

"Listen, Susan," he said. "I think you—"

"Don't!" She sounded firm. "I'm coming out. If you want to meet me at the airport, perhaps you should take down the information."

He did.

NATIONALISM NEW EAST GERMAN FORCE

BERLIN—German nationalism, a centuries-old force which has regularly disturbed the peace of Central Europe, is on the rise in an unlikely place—Communist East Germany. . . . Last month, thirty-three years after the defeat of the Nazi Third Reich, three people were killed when youths rioted and started to shout, "Germany Awake!"—an old Nazi slogan. . . .

2

Harry's home on Poinsettia Place between Fountain and Sunset was a pleasant, two-bedroom, single-family house in the California Spanish style so popular in the late twenties, much like many others in the neighborhood. The spacious porch with its arches and massive columns seemed to promise more house than was actually there.

Harry and Edith had bought the house when Leif was eleven. From there he had gone to Le Conte Junior High and later Hollywood High only a few blocks away.

Father and son had decided Susan should stay at Harry's. Earlier that afternoon Leif had been very much aware of his eager anticipation as he and his father waited at the airport gate for the Washington passengers to deplane. It had seemed perfectly natural for both of them to embrace and kiss Susan when she arrived, and Leif had felt wonderfully *right* holding her in his arms again.

They had driven directly to the house from the airport, and the three of them were sitting in Harry's living room. Susan had brought only an overnight bag, which she'd carried aboard the plane. Nothing had been said of her reason for coming out, but she was noticeably tense.

"All right, Susan," Harry said soberly. "You said you had something—important to show us."

Susan nodded gravely. "Yes," she said. "I don't know—but I think it opens a whole new avenue of investigation for you." Carefully she took a folded document from the large leather bag with a shoulder strap she had been clutching ever since they saw her. She looked at Harry. "You remember that list you gave me with the various dates and places and names of people to look for? Your original research objectives?"

"I do."

"Well—I kept it with me, and I kept checking whenever I worked on document classification or filing."

She looked seriously from one to the other.

"There was a name on that list," she said. "A man's. You told me about him, but we didn't discuss him." She handed the document to Harry. "Then—I found this."

Harry took the document and unfolded it quickly. He stared at it. His eyes widened.

"I'll be damned," he said. "I'll be double-damned. . . ."

"What is it?" Leif asked. He reached for the document.

"Wait," Harry said. He looked at his son. "Didn't you tell me that Zuckermann, the guy from the Militaria, the one who told us about Konrad Wendkos—didn't you tell me he showed you his concentration-camp number tattooed on his arm?"

"Yes." Leif looked puzzled. "He did."

"Do you remember the number?"

Leif shook his head. "No," he said. "It had a lot of digits in it." He frowned in concentration. "It started with an A. For Auschwitz, I suppose. The two last digits . . . I remember the two last digits. Three-nine. I remember because I thought: That was the year the war began—'39."

Soberly Harry handed the document to his son. "Look at it," he said.

Leif took the paper. Even though it was partly printed and partly handwritten in Gothic script, he at once knew what it was. It was unmistakably a copy of a page from the Auschwitz-Birkenau Concentration Camp Death Register. The last page for the day of 17 February 1945. One entry had been circled:

Nr. 5792. Z U C K E R M A N N, Nathan, Jew, 31
Nearest living relative, Zuckermann, Sarah, wife, emigrated.
Other living relatives—none.
KZ Nr. A22839

Nathan Zuckermann, the proprietor of the Militaria, *died* February 17, 1945! At the age of thirty-one . . .

Leif looked up from the document. "Zuckermann," he said. "But—how is that possible?"

"How?" Harry said grimly. "I'll tell you how. Once you suggested to me that Muller might not be *Muller.* We should have asked: Is Zuckermann—*Zuckermann?*"

He looked soberly at his son.

"I suggest we do that. Right now!"

It was already dark when Harry and Leif arrived at the Militaria. They parked in front of it. They had instructed Susan to stay put in Harry's place until she heard from them.

There were no lights on in the shop, and a tall, solid, wooden fence prevented them from seeing the windows in the rear of the house, but there was a car in the carport.

Harry banged on the door.

They waited.

Presently a door in the back of the shop opened, spilling a broad streak of yellow light across the floor. Silhouetted in the doorway stood Nathan Zuckermann, peering into the dark shop. He reached for a switch on the wall—and the lights came on, revealing the old man's miniature armies and ceremonial weaponry. He shuffled across the shop toward the front door.

"Yes?" he called. "The Militaria is closed on Sunday. What do you want?"

"We want to talk to you, Mr. Zuckermann," Harry called back through the door. "Just for a moment."

The old man stuck his head close to the glass in the door and squinted at his visitors. He saw Leif.

"So," he said. "It is you." He looked puzzled. He glanced at Harry and back at Leif. "Yes. Yes. I remember you," he said.

"May we come in?" Harry asked.

"Oh? Yes. Yes, of course." Zuckermann reached up and pulled down a dead bolt. Laboriously he bent down and pulled another one up from the floor. He unlocked the door and opened it.

"Come in," he said. "Come in."

Harry and Leif entered the shop. Zuckermann closed and locked the door behind them. He shuffled behind his counter and screwed up his eyes at his visitors.

"It is late," he said. "What is it you want from me?" He sounded tired. Beat.

Harry took the Auschwitz Death Register page from his pocket. He unfolded it.

"Mr. Zuckermann," he said gravely, "can you tell me what this is?"

He placed the document on the counter in front of the old man.

Zuckermann glanced at it. For a split second his eyes blazed and in the same instant his hand shot toward a drawer in the counter.

"Don't!" Harry's voice was like an explosion.

Zuckermann froze. He looked up—and stared squarely into the muzzle of Harry's gun.

"Stand very, very still, Zuckermann," Harry said, his voice dangerously low. His eyes bored into the man. His finger curled around the trigger.

"You are less than a one-pound pressure from joining your damned Führer!"

NEO-NAZI PLOT TO FREE RUDOLF HESS

WEST BERLIN—A plan by neo-Nazis to free Hitler's former deputy, Rudolf Hess, from West Berlin's Spandau Prison, where he is serving a life sentence imposed at the Nuremberg war crimes trial in 1946, thirty-two years ago, has been revealed. Five members of a Neo-Nazi group, which operated under the guise of a shooting club, have been detained and a hunt launched for up to 20 others. . . .

3

Mesmerized, the old man stared at the gun in Harry's hand. His face was gray and pinched with fear.

Please," he whispered. "Please don't hurt me." He looked at them, pleadingly. "I will give you all the money I have. Anything you want. But—don't hurt me. Please!"

"Who are you?" Harry shot the question at him harshly. "You are *not* Nathan Zuckermann. Who the hell *are* you?"

Zuckermann's eyes widened. He looked down at the document

on the counter before him. Suddenly oblivious to the gun in Harry's hand, he picked up the paper and peered myopically at it. He gasped. He looked at Harry. "You—know!" he exclaimed in grim astonishment. "How? Where did you get this?"

"Never mind," Harry rasped. "Who—are—you?"

Zuckermann looked at him, fear pulling at his face. "Why, I— I *am* Nathan Zuckermann."

Harry scowled at him. Imperceptibly the gun moved. Zuckermann held up his hands in a gesture of supplication.

"Please," he breathed. "I beg of you. Please let me explain." In a rush he went on. "I—I had a friend in Auschwitz. A *Kapo*—an inmate who helped the SS guards. So he could stay alive. He—he put *my* name on the Death Register—instead of that of another *KZ'ler* who had died. It was a trick, don't you see? The SS would not look for me to—to eliminate—if I were dead! It was toward the end. I hid—among the others. And—I survived." He looked beseechingly at Harry and Leif. "Don't you see?" he whispered. "Because *my* name was substituted for that of a dead man—I was *already* dead! And safe . . ."

Harry nodded toward the drawer in the counter. "What do you keep in that drawer, Zuckermann—or whoever the hell you are?" he asked bitingly. "Not jelly beans. Let me guess. A gun?"

Frightened, Zuckermann nodded. "Yes—but—"

"And you went straight for it when you saw that document!"

Zuckermann shook his head. His whole body rocked back and forth in apparent anguish. "But—you must understand," he said. "I—was confused. I did not know what the document was. I could not read it. I do not see that well. I—I thought you had come to rob me. Once before—they did that. They came in with something. Something to show me. And when I looked at it—a fine war flag, it was—they hit me. And robbed me." He looked from Harry to Leif. Miserably his eyes pleaded with them. "Don't you see . . . ?"

Leif watched the frightened old man. My God, he thought, it could be true. The old man has lived a lifetime of horror and grief —and we are adding to it. . . .

Even as he thought it, he did not accept it. He had an unshakable feeling that the German was lying to them. A hunch? Like his father's? Or was it that microsecond of someone else showing in the old man as he whirled toward the gun drawer? He looked at his father. He was about to say something when Harry spoke.

"Bullshit!" he said roughly. "I don't believe one word of it. You *knew* my son. You recognized him. Why the hell let us in if you thought we were going to rob you? Bullshit!—that's why. You didn't have any such idea until you saw that damned document. You're lying. Lying through your goddamned teeth. I don't believe you, get that? And I am not going to let go until I've put you through a wringer that'll squeeze every damned drop of truth from your hide!"

He stopped just long enough to catch his breath. He glared at the German. "Now," he said, his face and voice tense. "For the last time. *Who—are—you?*"

The old man looked at him. Nervously he licked his thin, bloodless lips. When he spoke his voice was barely a whisper.

"I am—Nathan Zuckermann. . . ."

Suddenly Harry felt uncontrollable rage erupt in him. He saw red. Literally. He saw everything through a blood-red haze . . . Muller's lifeless body, its head bashed in . . . The bony corpse of Wendkos dangling from the piano wire above a pool of stinking blood and feces . . . The pitiful ancient mouth of Anton Gerner gurgling crimson froth . . . The mangled flesh that was Emil's face as he hit the whirling propeller . . . The writhing, blackened hulk that was once the night manager of the Riverview Motel . . . Rage overtook him. He could not—did not want to—stem it. He slammed his gun down on the counter, shattering the glass top into shards.

"*Damn* you!" he growled, his voice hoarse with fury. "*God damn you!*" He glowered at the German, his eyes wild. "Not *one* more lie! Or, so help me, I'll shoot your fucking Kraut head full of holes!" He gulped a breath of air. It didn't interrupt his stream of words. "You bastards have tried to crush me with a fucking beam. Run me down. Kill us in an elevator shaft. We've been shot at—nearly slashed to bloody ribbons—and almost burned to a cinder! And we don't know the hell why! I want to know, dammit, and I want to know *now!*" He took a firmer grip on his gun, pointing it unwaveringly at the German's gut. "*Who are you?*"

His finger twitched on the trigger.

The German looked at Harry. Slowly he drew himself out of his stoop. His hands stopped their trembling. The entreating fear in his eyes died, replaced by a hard, steady gaze. His face turned grim. The change was subtle, but it was chilling.

"I believe you," he said evenly. His voice was calm, controlled. Resigned. "You will not let go."

He shrugged—but no longer was it the elaborate gesture of an old Jew. It was the arrogant shrug of Teutonic hauteur.

"I knew someday the truth would have to be told." He made a slight bow to Harry. "Let it be today."

"And right now," Harry said icily.

The German inclined his head, an almost imperceptible smile of disdain on his thin lips.

"What I told you," he said, "was quite correct. Up to a point. I did take the identity of one Nathan Zuckermann. A Jew." He managed to make the word sound dirty. "I was an officer in the SS—assigned to duty at the Auschwitz-Birkenau work camps. As a loyal officer, I carried out my duties." It was a self-evident fact the way he said it. "Although I did not foresee your—ah, *'war crimes'* trial at Nürnberg, I did realize that, once the war was lost, world Jewry would insist on exacting its vengeance on us and demand its pounds and pounds of flesh."

He pursed his lips scornfully. He seemed almost to be enjoying himself and his callous tale.

"From the material available to me in the camp I selected a— a Jew my own age with no relatives still alive to identify me. The man was—disposed of, and I took his name. His identity. His past —and his future. I had his KZ number tattooed on my arm—and my own SS blood-type tattoo removed. It took only a little time for it to look completely authentic."

He touched his upper left arm on the inside, perhaps unaware of the gesture.

"No relatives," Harry said coldly. "Zuckermann had a wife. Sarah."

The German once again shrugged, dismissing the fact. "She could have identified me, of course. And I would have had to confront her."

"*You* had her killed!" Anger made Harry's voice harsh.

"I merely turned a liability into an asset. It was necessary for my safety. The plan had to be absolute to work." He looked directly at Harry. "What would you have done if you were I?"

"I hope to God I never become you!" Harry snapped.

"Of course, I was thorough," the German continued, a hint of perverse pride coloring his voice. "I learned Hebrew. Yiddish. I familiarized myself with Jewish customs and Jewish religious practices. I adopted Jewish gestures. I learned what I had to know about Nathan Zuckermann, the Jew, from our camp records. They were complete enough. The American authorities accepted me without question."

Harry could well believe it. They had probably even felt sorry for the bastard, he thought bitterly, helped him as best they could. . . .

"I spared myself no indignities," the German went on. "Even to that distasteful mutilation enforced on male Jews. I became—a *Jew*. I became—Nathan Zuckermann. To survive."

He drew himself up.

"And I did survive. When others lost their freedom—or their lives—*I* remained free." He fixed his disturbingly cold eyes on Harry. "Until now."

Harry remained silent. His mind boiled. What was wrong with the picture? he thought. What?

The German turned to Leif.

"I congratulate you, Mr. Bendicks," he said. It was difficult to tell if he was being sarcastic or merely overbearing. "You were persistent. We gave you Konrad Wendkos. We sacrificed a good man to your—persistency. In an effort to protect my respectability. We thought that would satisfy you."

Yeah, Harry thought angrily. You "gave" us Wendkos, all right. Strung up like the Jewish victims of the Gestapo in the pictures he'd once found on an SS man—naked men and women strung up on butcher hooks and stamped *Kosher Meat!*

The German inclined his head toward Leif. "I do congratulate you. You did not—let go. You sniffed out a—a 'war criminal' who has successfully remained hidden for decades."

Leif shivered. The ruthless sacrifice of Konrad Wendkos *had* worked. He *had* believed Zuckermann to be above suspicion. He had a fleeting pang of guilt. The man would not have lost his life in so hideous a manner had it not been for his, Leif's, interference. He dismissed the feeling at once. Wendkos was a victim of his own beliefs, his own chosen associates. . . .

The German turned to Harry. He nodded resignedly. "I shall have to face it," he said. "I shall have to submit myself to an official investigation. Here—and in my own country." There was a trace of a mocking smile on his lips. "Probably years of investigation, judging from past performances. And then? Perhaps deportation? Possibly internment? It remains to be seen, does it not?"

He drew himself up.

"I shall cooperate," he said stiffly. "It is too late for me to start to—to run again." He made another slight bow toward Harry. "I am at your disposal."

Harry was studying the man. His CIC intuition was working overtime. Something *was* wrong. He'd run into this kind of prick before. This mixture of bravado, contempt and all-too-eager cooperation. It was usually when the bastards had something to hide. Something more important than was readily to be seen.

What was this one hiding? What made him accept his role as an unmasked war criminal so readily?

"Not so fast, Buster," he said unpleasantly. He glanced toward the door to the rear of the house. "First we take a little look around."

A shadow of a frown flitted across the German's face. "Search my home?" he asked. "Is it not customary to have a search warrant for such an invasion of privacy?"

"Search warrant?" Harry scoffed. "I have a search warrant." He gestured with his gun. "Right here. You want to quarrel with it?"

The German inclined his head. His eyes reflected his hostility. "It will be an illegal search," he said, flat-voiced. "Whatever you may find cannot be used against me. That, I believe, *is* a proper restraint placed on police operations."

"True," Harry agreed. "Very true. You're a regular latrine lawyer." His voice grew hard. "But this is *not* a police operation. I am *not* a police officer. I'm just goddamned mad. And I'm curious, see? And I want to get to the bottom of this fucking situation right now!" He gun-gestured toward the door. "Move your ass, Buster! Now!"

The German turned toward the door. "I can assure you," he said calmly, "you will find nothing. I, however, will have an excellent reason for legal action. . . ."

The one-story house was comfortably furnished in a no-frills fashion. The man obviously lived alone, but Harry noticed evidence of a woman's presence. The German shrugged it off. He was not yet old enough to be celibate. . . .

Harry and Leif made a cursory search of the place.

They found nothing.

They were standing in the kitchen, which faced out on a spacious backyard surrounded by the high wooden fence they had seen from the street. The darkness outside prevented them from seeing the area clearly. It seemed to be mostly lawn, with a few shrubs and what looked like a birdbath or dead fountain in the center of an unkempt flower bed. A rusty table and two paint-peeling chairs stood outside the back door. On one side of the kitchen was a small service area with an old washer-dryer and a wicker basket half filled with laundry. On the other was a door.

Harry tried it. It was locked.

"What's in there?" he asked.

"It is a storeroom," the German said disinterestedly. "I keep unsorted stock in there."

"Open it," Harry ordered.

The German hesitated.

Harry looked at him, a cold smile on his face. "My son has a helluva right foot," he said. "Would you prefer that *he* opens it?"

The German glared at him. He brought a set of keys from his pocket, unlocked the door and stood aside.

"After you," Harry said, gun-gesturing the man through the door.

He went through.

Harry and Leif followed him into the room beyond. Leif flipped a light switch just inside on the wall. They stared in astonishment.

It was a cutting room. A well-equipped, orderly editing room such as Harry had seen at the studios. For editing film or tape.

There was a workbench with rewinds, a viewer and several splicers. There were racks of cans and rolls of tape. There were bins and a small bookcase crammed with technical books. In one corner stood a large-screen TV set with a video cassette recorder hooked onto it. The expensive equipment seemed oddly out of place.

Harry held the tight-faced German at bay. He nodded toward the TV. "Turn it on," he said to his son.

Leif switched on the set.

The screen came to life with pulsating light, swirling color and flickering lines. Suddenly a picture steadied on it.

Harry and Leif stared at it in shock.

In front of a huge swastika flag covering a wall stood a massive desk, flanked by two burly, scowling men in black trousers and black shirts without insignia or ornamentation. Behind the desk in a high-backed chair sat a young man, perhaps twenty years of age, clad in a plain brown shirt. He stared out of the screen—a strange, indefinable look of tension on his face.

It was that face more than anything that shocked Harry and Leif. It bore an uncanny likeness to the face that had scowled at the world for two decades.

Adolf Hitler.

Harry was stunned. Was this Hitler's son? The boy from the Kugelberg cabin? Impossible. The son would be twice the age of this young man. Then—who? An actor? What *was* this tape? A movie? Recorded from some B-film? A TV show? Hollywood make-believe?

A cold feeling in the pit of his stomach told him it was not. . . .

Suddenly the young man spoke. From the screen his eyes burned into his listeners.

"I am Adolf Hitler," he rasped in a chillingly familiar voice. "I am the grandson of our immortal Führer!"

The picture on the screen cut to a huge close shot of the flag on the wall—the twisted black cross in its white circle on the field of blood red.

Then back to the young Hitler.

"I am the heir of Adolf Hitler," the strange young man intoned. "I who bear his name; I charge you—*the time has come!*"

NAZI FOOTSTEPS ECHO LOUDER

LOS ANGELES—There is a new, current thrust to American Nazism.... According to observers, neo-Nazi groups "are suddenly active as hell. Too many things are happening at once, and it is not by accident.... Something is stirring. There is a whole new cadre built around old ex-Nazis, who are clever enough not to flaunt swastikas." ... It may be 1977, but the theme is repeated all over the nation....

4

Spellbound in astonishment, Harry and Leif watched the screen and listened to the shocking speech.

"Rise with me!" the young man cried, his guttural voice hoarse with excitement. "Together we shall purge the world. In the spirit of the Führer—my grandfather—we shall begin anew the realm of a thousand years!"

As the young man spoke, the images on the TV screen changed constantly: a few spectacular scenes from the mammoth Nazi rallies of the Third Reich; the stony-faced, black-uniformed guards flanking the young speaker and the huge blood-red swastika flag on the wall; brief close shots of young Hitler staring intently from the screen, ranting on.

"The world is on the brink of chaos," the tirade continued. "The world *must* have strong leadership or mankind will perish. *I*—the grandson of the Führer, Adolf Hitler, the greatest leader the world ever had—*I* will provide that strength! And with me—with *us*, the heirs of the Führer throughout the world—with us a new and glorious Germanic National Socialist world shall rise!"

Harry and Leif listened incredulously.

"I come to you now, at this specific time, because of the catastrophe that has just occurred—an act to be condemned by all mankind. The time for us has come. It is *now!*... I stand ready to serve the world, as did my grandfather. *I*—your new leader—guided by the wisdom and knowledge of my mentor, the confidant of my martyred grandfather and my own father, the true son of the immortal Führer, Adolf Hitler, whose life was taken from him long since in the struggle to the death against the foul Jewish-Communist powers—my trusted advisor, the *Herr Doktor Franz Schindler!*"

The image on the screen cut to a close shot of a stern, gray-haired man. Icy-blue eyes in a strong, clean-shaven face looked directly at the viewer from the screen. Harry and Leif froze in shock. The face on the screen was the face of the man standing motionless before them. The ex-SS officer who had usurped the name and the life of Nathan Zuckermann.

Once again the face of young Hitler filled the screen. His mouth was working, but no sound emerged.

And the screen went dead.

Harry stared at the German. His mind whirled.

Schindler! Dr. Franz Schindler. High on all the mandatory arrest lists of the CIC. One of Hitler's trusted personal physicians, reported to have had the Führer's most intimate confidence to the last. The youngest of the infamous triumvirate of Nazi doctors: Mengele—Rasher—and *Schindler!*

And in his charge the grandson of Adolf Hitler—the Führer's heir.

They stared at the German, the change in him now complete. No longer the self-effacing, gentle old Jew enveloped in his mantle of suffering like a prayer shawl draped over his frail shoulders, he was now openly the icy SS officer. Looking ten years younger, he stood before them stiffly, his hands held rigidly in front of him, one clamped on the other, like a deadly Dr. Strangelove.

Harry's eyes bored into Schindler. Calmly the man answered his unspoken question.

"You were correct, Herr Bendicks," he said. "The boy in the Kugelberg cabin *was* the son of the Führer. He was taken to safety at the fortified bunker at Jenbach in the Alpine Fortress—and later exfiltrated via O D E S S A."

"What happened to him?"

"He died," Schindler said tonelessly. "In South America. Brazil. In 1956. Only months before the birth of *his* son."

"You were there?"

Schindler nodded. "It was—an accident. *He* had been destined to be his father's heir. His death made it necessary for us to wait. To let time go by. Wait for the grandson to reach maturity. He has. *He* will now be the rallying point for the rise of the new Reich. The magnet to attract our followers the world over."

"You're nuts!" Harry snorted.

Schindler looked at him, a sardonic half-smile on his lips. "I realize that by that singularly maladroit expression you mean to convey that in your opinion we shall not succeed," he said. "But I also realize that the peculiar paucity of words in the English language forces you to use such vulgarisms."

"Nuts?" Harry said. "I thought you would be especially familiar with that one. After Bastogne . . ."

Schindler looked away.

Harry nodded toward the TV screen, silent but still awash with a jumble of color. "You may have a rough time palming off that punk as Hitler's grandson," he said.

Schindler looked back at him. "Not at all," he said confidently. "We possess irrefutable and unalterable proof that the boy's father *is* in fact the true son of Adolf Hitler. The Führer's flesh and blood. All such documentation is safe—in a Swiss bank vault."

"Sure it is. . . ."

"Proof," Schindler repeated firmly. "Proof that no one can gainsay. No one disprove. Sworn birth-record affidavits. Photographs. Fingerprints. Statements in the Führer's own hand."

Harry and Leif stared at him.

"Genealogical and biological studies that cannot be contradicted." His thin, cynical smile touched his lips again. "You yourself discovered one of them," he pointed out. "An excellent study made by a colleague of mine."

"That craniological report . . ."

"Precisely. I admit, it might have been easier for us if the son himself had lived. We should not have been forced to wait so long. Till the last possible moment . . ." He shrugged in his disdainful manner. "But time had to go by. Time for the boy to become a man, mature enough to inspire the same deep loyalty his grandfather inspired before him. Time for Germany herself to grow strong—strong enough to dominate a world in chaos. Perhaps it was for the best. These things *have* happened. There has been time for the world to forget the lies about us perpetuated by the Jews. Today—new and fertile fields of acceptance beckon."

Harry shook his head. "Let me get this straight," he said. "Adolf Hitler had a son. . . ."

"Correct."

Harry looked at the German. "He also had a daughter, right?"

"He did."

"Then, you say, his *son* had a son—born in Brazil. In '56. The character on the TV."

Tight-lipped, Schindler answered. "A grandson was born in 1956. Correct."

"So you got yourself a Hitler grandson," Harry shrugged. "Big deal. And Adolf's daughter? Where is she?"

Steadily the German looked at them.

"She," he said calmly, "is the mother."

ANTI-NAZI TV PROGRAM RECEIVES HEAVY HATE MAIL

LOS ANGELES—NBC is receiving heavy hate mail over its scheduled broadcast of "Holocaust," a dramatization of Nazi persecutions of Jews to be aired on four consecutive nights beginning April 16, 1978. The hate mail condemns the program as Jewish propaganda. . . . According to a spokesman, "the views expressed are sickening."

5

Harry and Leif were too shocked to speak. The eyes of father and son regarded the Nazi with incredulity and revulsion. Schindler seemed oblivious—or at any rate indifferent—to their reaction.

"The Führer left a legacy with me," he said. "A legacy I have considered a sacred trust. His children . . . The seeds of the glorious rebirth of his ideals and his plans, of which he speaks in his final charge to his people—his political testament." He straightened in pride as he continued. "The Führer's son was born in 1933, his daughter four years later. They were of different mothers—it is unimportant who. They were reared apart from one another, not knowing of each other's existence. *I* was charged with the safety and care of these children. To watch them and guard them. And with them to create a dynasty. A Hitler dynasty."

He paused to give weight to his statement. Harry watched him, hardly daring to breathe. He did not in any way want to deflect the man's inclination to talk. He hoped Leif would understand and keep quiet, too. Schindler's revelations were not to be missed. He would listen as long as the German would talk. He disregarded the little "whys" that gnawed at the edges of his mind.

"My course of action was, of course, clear," Schindler said. "I had to create a pure, new generation. The dynasty had to be perpetuated. And in the purest way possible, as the rulers of ancient Egypt for centuries perpetuated theirs. And thus the grandson of Adolf Hitler was conceived and born to fulfill his destiny—by the mating of the Führer's own children—the purest Hitler blood."

He looked at Harry and Leif, his steady eyes a brazen challenge. "The seed has been sown."

Leif stared at the German. The man's depravity was abysmal. Or was he totally unaware of right and wrong?

"When he was imprisoned in Nürnberg awaiting his—ah, trial, Reichsmarschall Hermann Goering said, 'In a hundred years Hitler will again be the symbol of Germany!' He was quite correct. But he was pessimistic. He underestimated us. The heir of Adolf Hitler is here—the symbol of Germany, of world Nazism. Ready. Today!"

Like a serpent's egg ready to hatch, Harry thought. He gazed directly into the cold eyes of the German.

"Where is he?" he asked. "Where *is* this grandson of Adolf Hitler—this great-white-hope of Nazidom?"

A mocking smile wormed its way onto Schindler's grim face. "Quite obviously, Herr Bendicks, not here," he answered, a trace of gloating in his voice.

For a moment the three men stood in speculative silence. Then Leif walked over to the TV set and turned it off.

The soft hissing sound which had flowed from it stopped. The quiet was complete—except . . .

Upon the silence a faint, almost inaudible sound intruded. A low hum that had been drowned out before by the TV.

A whispered, muffled hum.

Harry cocked his head, listening. The window. Open to the garden in back of the house. Through it the muted hum drifted into the room.

Harry turned to Schindler. "What's that?" he asked.

Stony-faced, Schindler shrugged. He did not say a word.

Harry gestured with his gun. "Let's go take a look, shall we?" He motioned the German to the back door.

They went out into the garden.

As their eyes adjusted to the dim light, they saw it.

In the far right-hand corner of the yard was a large grass- and weed-grown mound of dirt. It had obviously been there a long time. Set into it was a heavy, slanted metal hatchway.

Harry knew at once what it was. One of the backyard fallout shelters built during the early '60s, their construction peaking in late '62 during the Russian/Cuban missile crisis. They'd been a pain in the ass after the scare died down and the shelter craze abated. Hangouts for weirdos, traps for kids and a soggy mess after the first heavy rain. "Blackout swimming pools," the department had dubbed them. They'd been right on.

The hum had stopped.

Harry looked at the shelter entrance. The hum could have come from there. An air-intake motor? A gravel path led to the slanted door.

He motioned Schindler toward the mound. "Let's go take a look at your private bunker over there, *Herr Doktor,*" he said. "Lead the way."

Wordlessly Schindler turned toward the shelter entrance. He walked the gravel path stiffly, as if his legs were encased in invisible splints. Harry and Leif followed.

As they came closer, they could make out two hooded pipes that protruded from the ground, looking like huge iron mushrooms. Air-intake and exhaust pipes?

Schindler stopped at the hatchway.

"Open it," Harry ordered.

The German lifted the heavy door. It was not locked. A black hole appeared behind it. A steep flight of cement stairs could be seen leading down into the darkness.

Harry peered into the hole. He suddenly felt chilled. "Any light?" he asked.

Schindler did not answer. He took a couple of steps down the shaft and flipped a light switch on the wall. Two feeble light bulbs came on. One about halfway down the slanted stairwell, the other at the bottom.

"After you," Harry said.

Schindler started down.

It was difficult to tell exactly how far down the stairs led. Harry estimated about fifteen feet. That would mean something like seven or eight feet of dirt on top of the underground shelter. One of the deepest he'd ever run across.

At the bottom, facing the stairs and leaving only a narrow space, was a massive cement-block wall, moldy and blotchy with age. That would be the entrance-shielding wall, Harry thought. To the right stood an old dented garbage can—empty; to the left the shielding wall ended, leaving a space wide enough to provide entrance to the shelter area beyond.

"Go on," Harry ordered.

Schindler turned toward the gap. On the wall before him was another light switch below an open pipe coming down from above. Air exhaust? He flipped the switch. A dim light shone through the opening. The three men stepped into the shelter area.

It was a dark and depressing place. It had obviously not been used for years. A rusty metal rack of shelves stood against the shielding wall. A broken army cot, the canvas rotted and decayed, lay before it. On the wall facing them a heavy pipe ran down from the ceiling. It ended in a pumping device with both a manually operated crank and an electric motor attached. In one corner was a pile of debris and a broken garden chair, and against the wall on the right stood a wooden storage cabinet, its door hanging loose on one hinge to reveal rows of dirty, empty shelves inside.

Harry motioned Schindler to the far right corner. "Over there," he said curtly. "Sit down, legs crossed, facing the wall. We don't want any surprises while we look around. Move!"

Schindler gave him a withering look. He did as he was told.

Leif looked around with curiosity. He'd never been in one of these dismal anachronisms before. He walked over to the pile of rubble and picked up an old can. It was unopened—still full. EMERGENCY DRINKING WATER, he read, *U.S. Coast Guard Approval No. 160.026/18/1.* He tossed it back on the pile. The dull thud sounded oddly forlorn. On the broken chair lay a soiled, crumpled pamphlet. He picked it up. *The Family Fallout Shelter* was the title. *Office of Civil and Defense Mobilization. 1959.* It seemed so much longer ago. . . .

Harry made for the air-intake pump. He cranked the handle on the manual device. It creaked with disuse. He fingered the tag on it. *This handblower provides 50 CFM to every 45 revs.* Nice to know . . . He felt the electric motor. It was cold and slightly damp. It had obviously not been running recently. The hum they'd heard could not have come from it. Then—from where?

On the wall next to the intake pipe hung a faded, torn Civil Defense flyer. *A Message from Governor Edmund G. Brown,* it proclaimed, dating it better than any calendar. *"Survival is possible if we act sensibly and calmly,"* he read. And in bold red letters the admonition: "PLAN TO SURVIVE!"

Unconsciously he took a firmer grip on his gun. He was planning on doing just that. It had always been his personal SOP.

He glanced toward the German sitting silently in the corner, staring at the bare wall, then let his eyes roam the oppressive place. The air was dank and stale. A stagnant hole in the ground as obsolete as Nikita Khruschev.

His eyes were getting used to the dim light. He could make out the ancient cobwebs, the water-seepage streaks, the dirt on the cement floor. The shelter held no secrets.

He was about to order Schindler to get up when something stopped him. He had a sudden uneasy feeling that he'd just seen something. Something that set off an alarm deep in his mind. He strained to conjure it up. No go . . .

He stood still. Once again he let his eyes roam through the dismal shelter. The shelf, the tumbledown cabinet, the broken pieces of furniture and the other debris; the air-intake equipment, the faded flyer on the wall . . . Nothing alerted him.

The dim light bulb overhead, the corner cobwebs, the water streaks, the dirty floor . . .

Suddenly he knew.

He stared at the floor.

It was dark with tracked-in dirt and grime, but across it ran a narrow trail, different in color, faint but unmistakable. It ran directly from the entrance gap to the broken-down cabinet standing against the wall.

A use path.

Someone had been walking from the entrance to the empty cabinet. Many times.

Why?

In two steps he was at the cabinet. He wrenched the one-hinged door aside. He glared at the shelves behind. All were completely empty.

He tugged at one of them.

The cabinet rocked.

With a violent shove he sent it crashing to the floor—and found himself staring at a small door set into the cement-block wall!

It was closed.

He whirled toward Schindler.

"On your feet!" he barked. "Up! Over here!"

Schindler stood up. He glared at Harry, venom in his eyes. He started toward him. Then stopped, tensed—a coiled spring. For a split second Harry thought the German was going to jump him— but the man stood motionless.

"What's in there?" Harry demanded. "Open it!"

The German did not make a sound—nor a move.

Harry stepped away from the door. He covered the German with his gun. "Leif!" he said.

Leif went up to the door. He felt enormously keyed up. He had the feeling that they were finally going to come face to face with the enigma that had plagued them—almost killed them.

The door seemed sturdy. To break it down would not be easy —if, indeed, he could do it at all. He glanced at Schindler. The man stood rigid, his face drawn, his eyes closed.

Cautiously Leif tried the door.

It was unlocked.

He threw it open.

At once bright light streamed from the opening, blazing into the dark shelter—momentarily blinding them.

It was what Schindler had been waiting for. Instantly he threw himself at Harry. The impact was sudden, violent—and utterly unexpected.

The gun flew from Harry's hand and skittered across the floor. Schindler whirled to get it.

But Harry had recovered himself. He knew he could not let the German get hold of the gun. He grabbed him and clung to him, oblivious of the furious hands trying to pull him off.

"Leif!" he yelled. "The gun! Get the gun!"

Leif, too, had been startled and blinded by the sudden glaring light. But his eyes were adjusting. Desperately he looked around the shelter.

There! Near the old army cot. He dived for it; whirled at the struggling men.

"Stop!" he shouted. "I have the gun! Stop it!"

Schindler only doubled his efforts to free himself from Harry's grip.

Leif aimed the gun. His hands trembled. How could he be certain of hitting the German and not his father? He dared not take the chance.

He took hold of the gun barrel. He stepped close to the grappling men, waited his chance . . .

Now! Schindler's head was turned toward him.

With all his might he crashed the gun butt down on the man's head in a killing blow. But—instinctively—in the last possible split second he pulled his punch.

The German collapsed without a sound. Harry let him topple to the floor. Panting, he stared at the unconscious man.

"Pretty cute," he puffed. "Pretty damned cute." He was winded. Disgusted because of it. God damn it, he was getting too old for this kind of crap. . . .

Leif handed the gun to his father. "Here," he said. "You take it."

He knelt beside the motionless body on the floor. Was the man dead? Had he killed him? Sudden nausea threatened in his throat. Quickly he felt the artery in the German's neck. He peeled back his eyelids and examined his pupils.

"Well?" Harry said. "Will the bastard live?"

Leif nodded. "He's out. Will be for a few minutes."

He stood up. He was surprised to find that his knees were weak and his legs trembled.

Together they turned to the open door, stepped into the room beyond—and stopped dead.

The room was quite large, brightly painted and well lit. Leif's first impression was of a big nursery—except for one thing: the huge swastika flag on one wall with a massive desk and a TV taping camera in front of it.

On the floor in the middle of the room a young man sat, awkwardly playing with a jumble of toy soldiers—a Nazi band and torchlight parade.

It was the young Adolf Hitler.

He turned and looked at Harry and Leif—eyes dull and vacuous, yet disturbingly tense. When he grinned at them, saliva dribbled onto his brown shirt. His hand shot up in a clumsy Nazi salute. *"Heil Hitler!"* he cried in a high, childish voice, adding delightedly, "That's me!" He giggled—then abruptly grew petulant. "Mutti?" He pouted. "Dolfi want—Mutti. . . ."

Harry and Leif stared at the pitiful figure on the floor.

Dr. Franz Schindler's abominable experiment had exacted its price. The grandson of Adolf Hitler, the greatest "superman" of them all, was an imbecile. . . .

NAZIS BOMB THEATER

BEVERLY HILLS, Calif.—An exploding gas bomb forced about 800 people, choking and gasping for air, to flee from a Beverly Hills theater, Monday night, before a premiere of a film about Dutch Christians who hid Jews during the Nazi occupation of Holland. . . . Investigators from the Beverly Hills Police Department discovered a Nazi swastika emblem on the bomb canister.

6

They dragged the unconscious Nazi into the room and propped him up against the desk. He made a rasping sound as the air was forced from his lungs. Young Adolf watched them without interest and returned to his toy soldiers, standing them up and gleefully knocking them down.

Harry took in the room. Besides the TV staging area with the Nazi flag and the big desk, it contained a bed, full size, but with side panels, like those on a child's crib, that could be lowered or raised. There was a battered toy chest containing mostly broken toys and a bookcase with children's picture books. Several crates and boxes were stacked in one corner, and against the wall to the left stood a refrigerator and a large freezer, both with locking devices. On the opposite wall two closed doors presumably led to other rooms of the underground warren, and in the far right corner an air-intake pipe entered the dugout from above. Harry estimated it would be just below the "birdbath" in the garden. That figured. The electric pump for the air intake had a heavy wire screening around it, locked in place, probably to keep young Adolf from tampering with it. There were also wire cages around the three lights set into the ceiling behind thick glass covers.

Leif was watching the young man on the floor. He frowned. "Dad," he said, "it's impossible!"

"What?"

"We saw that tape. We heard it." He nodded toward young Adolf. "*He* could not possibly have made it."

"But he did."

Leif shook his head. "I know. I saw it. But—it is impossible! That young man probably has a Binet mental age of four? Perhaps five? An IQ of between twenty and fifty? A syllogistic result of the—inbreeding." Earnestly he turned to his father. "Dad, he could not possibly have mastered the technique nor the concentration to make that tape we saw. To say nothing of the delivery."

Thoughtfully Harry contemplated young Hitler. "Perhaps he didn't," he said. "Not in the ordinary way." He looked at Schindler. "But I have an idea how it might have been done. Pretty wild . . ."

The German twitched. He gave a small moan. His eyelids quivered erratically.

"Let's check it out with our sleeping beauty there. I think he's about to rejoin us."

The German moved in little spasms. He opened his eyes—and gave a violent start as awareness flooded in on him. He jerked to get to his feet—and stopped as dizziness hit him. Slowly he rose, steadying himself on the massive desk. With cold hate he glared at Harry and Leif.

"Take it easy, good buddy," Harry said. He brought up his gun. "We don't want any more fun and games."

The German turned away from him. His eyes fell upon young Adolf playing with his Nazi soldiers, oblivious to everything else.

Harry followed his look. "Yeah," he said. "We know. Your would-be Führer is a loony!" He smiled sardonically. "I'm surprised at you, Schindler." He shook his head. "You of all people should have known better. Your—experiment was bound to come out a bust. What the hell did you expect? A super-Aryan? Out of incest?"

Schindler was gathering his strength. His eyes grew calculating. They flitted toward one of the doors in the far wall, then quickly came back to Harry.

"You are an expert on inbreeding?" he asked sarcastically.

"Enough to know that it usually produces defective offspring," Harry snapped.

The Nazi smiled his thin, disdainful smile. "You are in error, of course," he said overbearingly. "The primary effect of inbreeding is to increase genetic purity."

"Not always a desirable effect," Leif interjected. "In fact, as a rule not."

Schindler turned to him. "Ah, yes," he said. "The Doctor of Psychology." He made it sound vaguely distasteful. "Then you should also be aware that many inbred individuals are totally free of undesirable effects. Are, in fact, highly accomplished."

"It is a chance you had no right to take," Leif said angrily.

"Really?" Schindler looked at him, cold-eyed. "Let me remind you, Doctor, that inbreeding permits the offspring to inherit the same qualities as those of his sire. To resemble that sire genetically as well as in appearance. *Any* risk was justified in order to perpetuate the basic units of inheritance—the genes of the Führer, Adolf Hitler!"

"You sure made a mess of it," Harry said. "Just as well."

Schindler gave his disdainful shrug. "Unhappily, the modifications of the hereditary potential were for the worse rather than for the better," he said airily.

Harry glanced at young Adolf. "I'd say!"

"What *is* his condition?" Leif asked.

"He has the mental capacity of a four-year-old," Schindler said.

"Then it would have been utterly impossible for him to have made that tape," Leif said firmly.

The German said nothing.

"That tape, Schindler," Harry said. "It's doctored, right? You pieced it together in some way, right? Dubbed it?"

Schindler looked at him, his eyes hooded. A slight frown whisked across his forehead. His eyes flitted toward the young man on the floor—or was it toward one of the closed doors? He hesitated just a beat before addressing himself to Leif.

"You see, *Dr.* Bendicks"—he made the title sound like an insult —"nothing is impossible with a little imagination and perseverance." He nodded toward young Adolf. "Of course he is totally incapable of making the tape you saw. But *I—we*—are not. And *he* could still be used. That was, of course, imperative." He looked at Harry and Leif, a mixture of pride and contempt on his face. "You can teach even a stupid dog one simple trick," he said. "The same goes for a mental defective." He pointed to the desk. "The boy would sit behind the desk and do the only thing he is capable of doing. Mouth gibberish and baby-talk—and try to imitate me. I simply placed myself directly at the camera and read the lines, bit by bit, over and over. Adolf imitated me as best he could, knowing he would be rewarded for his efforts."

Monkey see, monkey do, Harry thought grimly. It was as simple as that.

"Of course it took time. Thousands of feet of tape to get segments that showed Adolf at his most convincing. Then these cuts were edited into a whole sequence with other clips, as you saw, and the speech itself was dubbed by an actor, one of *my* men, who is thoroughly familiar with the delivery and voice of the Führer." He looked at Harry. "As you surmised. It is, after all, hardly a new concept. Rather a Hollywood specialty. And effective. Exactly the method used in dubbing a foreign-language film into English, am I correct?" He looked back at the child-man on the floor. "Adolf came to enjoy being dressed up in his uniform, playing the leader of his toy army. . . ."

Looking at the ill-starred young man on the floor, Harry had an uneasy feeling in the back of his mind. Why was Schindler so damned willing to talk? It worried him. He knew enough about motion-picture making to realize that what the German had said was entirely possible. The tape could have been made exactly that way. But—why make it? For what purpose?

He suddenly remembered something on the tape that had registered only briefly in the shock of seeing it. He spoke sharply to Schindler.

"On the tape your boy said something about a catastrophe *that had just happened!* What the hell does that mean? What catastrophe? Where did it happen? When?"

Schindler looked steadily at his two adversaries. "When?" he said. "It has not happened yet. But it will. And it will trigger destiny."

"What the hell is that supposed to mean?" Harry asked.

Schindler shrugged. "There is no reason you should not know," he said. "Even with your—ah, success in exposing me and discovering young Adolf, the Führer's ultimate plan will go forward. It is inevitable. We all know that nothing you can say or do will be in time to make any difference. The fuse has already been lit. There is nothing you or anyone else can do to stomp it out!" He paused for a moment. His voice was calm and determined.

"There will be war," he said. "This time a world war in the true meaning of the word. A war from which we, the heirs of Adolf Hitler, the inheritors of the vision for which he himself offered up his life and death, shall emerge triumphant."

Harry and Leif looked at him in disbelief.

"You're a bunch of goddamned maniacs!" Harry finally sputtered.

Schindler's pale lips stretched into an icy smile. "Are we, Herr Bendicks? Consider the actions of these maniacs. Losing the war in 1945 was only a temporary setback. Already then the Führer had formulated his plans for his heirs—led by his own flesh and blood—ultimately to take full control of the world. The entire world. For years our people have been gradually placing themselves in positions of influence. Everywhere. Keeping—as you say—a low profile, contrary to many others of the Führer's loyal followers. Waiting for the time . . ."

He looked steadily at the men listening horrified to his every word.

"In *Mein Kampf* the Führer outlined step by step how he would exalt himself and his cause and seize power." Again he smiled at Harry and Leif, a smile that never reached his eyes. "Then, as now, he and his followers were called madmen. His plan, lunacy. Yet—he followed that plan. To the letter." He paused. For a split second he seemed to listen, but he kept his eyes locked on Harry and Leif.

"There is now a further plan," he continued. *"Der Kampf der Zukunft*—the Battle of the Future. A document given me by the Führer himself. In it he leaves us a legacy of unrivaled genius. A plan to *win* that battle. The Third Reich is not dead, the Führer wrote. It is merely dormant, awaiting the fitting time to rise again." He paused once more. His eyes drilled into Harry and Leif.

"And the future is here," he said quietly. "The conditions outlined in the Führer's charge are present. To wit: There is general dissatisfaction throughout the world. Two major ideologies are at each other's throats. There is no strong leader anywhere. And a powder-keg situation exists in the most sensitive part of the world."

The Middle East, Harry thought bleakly. The Arab-Israeli struggle—already bloody and implacable. The bastard's talking about the Middle East.

"The time is eminently ripe for us to launch our mission," Schindler said. "There will be a major act of provocation that will lead inevitably to total war. Exactly as the Führer planned it. A war between East and West, spreading over the whole world and leaving it spent and ready for the New Reich. A new order to rally around the new, young Adolf Hitler! The time has never been more propitious. The time is *now!*"

"That's a crock of shit!" Harry said. "There have been other times in the last thirty years when the world was just as unstable as it is now. You could have made your move before. Why did you hold off?"

Schindler motioned toward young Adolf. "He is one reason," he said. "The more important reason is one of historic fact. The world had to be ripe for a full-scale war—and such a war cannot follow too closely on another."

Despite himself, Harry felt chilled to the bone. He could see one more reason. It was the last gasp—the last chance for the old-time Nazis to strike for power. And a "last chance" is always the time to take outrageous risks if necessary. There's nothing to lose. He looked at the German. Calmly, steadily, Schindler returned his gaze. Harry felt a deep, angry frustration. The man was not easy to dismiss.

His mind jumped back to another time he had been confronted with a madman. That one had called himself the Fifth Angel—the angel from hell. He, too, plotted to start a total war. A racial war of annihilation. And when the antagonists had beaten each other to their knees, *he* would take over and rule the Earth! A madman, yes. But one who *acted* like a madman, easy to dismiss as mad. Charlie Manson . . .

But Schindler could not be dismissed that easily. His visions were real.

Harry glared at him. "And how are you going to start World War III, Schindler? It's not done by throwing a switch!" he said. "Provocation—bullshit! They've been up to their asses in provocation for years in the Middle East. And the world still hasn't blown up!"

Schindler inclined his head. "You have the area correct, Herr Bendicks. But you utterly fail to realize our capacities."

He changed his position at the desk slightly. Again his eyes flickered toward the closed doors.

The micromomentary glance was not lost on Harry. The man had let his eyes stray toward those doors once before. Was he expecting the marines to come charging through? Was that why he was so damned talkative? Stalling? Buying time? For what? Casually he positioned himself so that he could cover the doors as well as Schindler himself. He had no intention of looking for trouble behind those doors if that was what Schindler had in mind by subtly, yet deliberately, drawing his attention to them. Making him suspicious. No way. If trouble were to come, he'd rather meet it on his own terms. He looked at the German. Who was trying to con whom?

"You're a prime candidate for the funny-farm," he mocked. He shook his head. "No *provocation* is going to start World War III."

"Really, Herr Bendicks?" Schindler mocked him in return. "Not even a—*nuclear* provocation?"

DANGER OF NUCLEAR
TERRORISM GROWS

WASHINGTON, D.C.—In the more than three decades since 1946, four tons of nuclear materials, enough to make 530 bombs, have been listed as missing, much of it feared stolen, possibly by terrorist groups. . . . A Congressional Study recently released concluded that there was a "clear possibility" that such an organization could build a nuclear bomb. . . . Construction of an atomic bomb no

longer requires access to secret information. . . . It is no longer absurd to imagine
a terrorist group of any persuasion manu-
facturing an easily transported and exploded nuclear device. . . .

7

For a moment there was utter silence in the room. Only the
sound of young Adolf's tumbling soldiers could be heard.

Schindler nodded. "Yes, Herr Bendicks, a nuclear explosion,"
he said as calmly as if he were talking about a minor traffic accident. "The Israelis are known to possess nuclear capability.
They have already in the eyes of the world established a reputation for over-reacting and for the use of outlawed weapons. It
will be perfectly in character, and the nuclear event will be
staged to look like an Israeli retaliation. We will make certain
that the blame falls upon them, and the evidence will be totally convincing. *Their* final solution, if you will." He smiled—a
ghoulish grimace. "*Our* nuclear capability may not be as impressive as theirs," he said, almost apologetically. "But I assure
you it is perfectly adequate. Throughout the years we have acquired a more than sufficient supply of material for our scientists to construct a satisfactory nuclear device. It may not be
clean—but it most certainly will be effective!"

Again that cold, disturbing smile. "A nuclear weapon is surprisingly easy to construct, Herr Bendicks. Especially if you are not
overly concerned with maximum efficiency." He pursed his lips.
"We shall achieve at least a ten-percent yield, I estimate. Somewhat more powerful than the Hiroshima bomb."

Harry found it difficult to harness his thoughts. *This* was no
impossible pipe-dream. This could become hideous reality. No
matter how outrageous, how improbable, how illusionary Schindler's sick dream of ensuing war might be, no matter what the end
result, he and his gang *could* set off a nuclear explosion. Anywhere
they chose!

His mind hop-scotched across a grim pattern of sobering truths, starting with the fact that everyone who has attempted to design a nuclear bomb since Hiroshima has been successful, including a couple of college kids. All the necessary information could be gotten from government pamphlets. And building the damned thing would be feasible for any half-assed technician. The material can easily be had. Enough of the stuff has disappeared or been stolen over the years to blow up half the solar system. Insane or not, this was the ultimate in terrorism.

Schindler was watching him closely. "You must admit our timing is perfect," he said. The Middle East is seething—the turmoil carefully provoked and nurtured by us, I assure you. At this moment, decades of painstaking preparations will bear fruit. Armed cadres of our followers in every major city of the world will make certain that the holocaust we seek *will* erupt!"

The German smiled at his antagonists. "The—provocation will succeed, rest assured," he said. "Staged incidents have served us well in the past. The fuse of war has been ignited by provocation before."

Harry finally trusted his voice. "When?" he asked. "When will this happen?"

"In four days," Schindler said. "On April the twentieth it is the anniversary of the Führer's birth." Again the thin smile. "Draw your own conclusion."

"Where?"

Schindler shook his head. "That," he said, with mock regret. "That you will have to learn with the rest of the world."

Harry felt cold. It was a madman's scheme. It would never come to pass. . . .

But doubt persisted. That the nuclear explosion could be set off was a certainty. Could it *all* work? Schindler was right. It had before. The *Maine.* Sarajevo. Czechoslovakia. Even World War II had begun with a staged provocation. A faked attack on a German radio station by SS troops dressed up in Polish uniforms. . . .

Leif had been following the exchange, totally engrossed by the "logic" of a deeply irrational mind . . . even to the point of missing the danger signals in Schindler's expansive behavior.

"There is a flaw in all this," he said. He glanced toward the young Adolf. "How can you possibly hope to use that unfortunate young man as a—a rallying point? Surely he would be more of a detriment than an asset."

Schindler favored him with one of his glacial smiles. "Not so, *Dr. Bendicks*," he said. "It is precisely for that reason we made the tape. You see, the nuclear explosion will be the signal for the next phase of the operation. The phase that will announce our cause to the entire world. That phase will begin right here."

He was slowly regaining his confidence. He allowed himself to admit that earlier he had been rattled. It had been important, of course, to keep the two Americans contained as long as possible. As soon as they removed him from the premises and involved the authorities, too many of his options would be lost, and he himself would have little chance of remaining free to carry out his part. That, of course, was imperative. He was pleased with himself for having succeeded. Of course, he'd had to give away some information in the process, but it hardly mattered at this stage. As long as the crucial facts remained buried. And they would. And there was always the strong possibility that neither of these two would ever be in a position to pass on their knowledge. In the meantime every minute was a gain, buying him time in which any of his options might eventuate. He no longer had any serious doubts that he would prevail. In fact, he was actually beginning to enjoy himself. It was amusing to observe their reactions as he unfolded the plan.

He continued.

"We will simply take over one of the major television studios here. By force. We have the manpower and weapons necessary. It is admittedly not a novel idea. It has been done by activist forces before. But it *is* effective."

Uneasily Leif remembered the several huge secret arms-and-ammunition caches discovered at several sites in Southern California in recent months. Tons of material, enough to equip a small army, hidden by presumably militant groups. At least one of these groups had been Nazi-oriented.

"And, of course," Schindler went on, "we have the necessary inside help in the studio."

"Even if you do run the tape," Leif said, "what good will it do you? You cannot possibly produce your new Adolf Hitler."

"True—as far as it goes," Schindler agreed. "But there is more to our little scenario. One of the studio property men—a friend, incidentally, of Ernst Müller—is *my* man." He tapped the desk with his hand. "There exists in the property department of the studio an exact duplicate of this whole set.

"Adolf will be brought to the studio. He will sit in his familiar chair in front of his familiar flag. His guards will be at his side— and he will watch the camera and me, as he is used to—waiting for his game, and his reward."

He studied the Americans.

"The tape will be run—broadcast to the world via satellite. Even young Adolf's grandfather did not reach so vast an audience. And the instant the tape has run we will cut to the picture of young Adolf in the studio. No one will know it is not a continuation of the taped speech. No one will know it is not *all* a live transmission."

"Until he opens his mouth," Harry said dryly.

Schindler looked straight at him, his eyes terrible. "But he will *not* open his mouth, Herr Bendicks," he said. "Before he can speak at all—he will be shot! Assassinated. Live, I believe the terminology is, live on screen. In full view of the entire world!"

He leaned imperceptibly closer to Harry, eyes locked with his. "By a *Jew*—of course!" He gave his chilling smile. "It may be melodramatic," he conceded. "But that is how the masses are reached. The Führer proved that."

There was a sudden, sharp metallic click from the back of the room.

Even before he whirled toward the sound, Harry cursed himself. The doors! So completely had he been taken in by Schindler's diabolic plot he'd forgotten about the goddamned doors.

It was a woman. Drab. About forty. Dull, dirty-blond hair pulled back from a pale, drawn face devoid of make-up. Brooding eyes fixed on the three men.

Nothing about her was in the least noteworthy.

Except the Walther 7.65 pistol that pointed straight at Harry's guts . . .

NAZI ARMS AND
AMMUNITION
CACHES DISCOVERED

LOS ANGELES—The huge illegal arms
and ammunition dumps recently found
in Southern California may be the secret
arsenal of extreme right-wing militants.
. . . The American Nazi Party may have
been involved in hiding the arms and
other war material such as explosives,
grenades, mines and including ground-
to-air missiles and mortars—enough to
equip a 200-man army. Also found in the
secret caches were right-wing, anti-
Semitic literature. . . .

8

She was no stranger to firearms, Harry thought as he stared
at the gun held steady in the woman's hand. She had her middle finger on the trigger and her index finger laid stiffly along
the barrel to give added stability and accuracy. It was an old
trick.

His eyes sought her face. It was closed, without expression, as if
she had taken a deep breath and submerged within herself. Her
somber eyes stared straight ahead. But not at him. At Schindler . . .

Harry's eyes shifted rapidly to the German. Was there a hint of
uneasiness on his face? He returned his attention to the woman,
but his gun never wavered from Schindler. He nodded at the
Walther automatic in the woman's hand.

"Use it," he threatened, "and you've got yourself a dead Nazi!"

The woman seemed not to hear him.

Schindler spoke, an edge to his voice. "Geli," he said. "Do not
do anything rash. You must understand. We must all do—what is
best for the cause." His eyes flicked toward the child-man on the

floor. "Drop your gun, Geli." There was quiet authority in his voice. But a troubled shadow in his eyes . . .

For a moment the woman stood motionless. Then, her expression unchanged, she slowly let the hand holding the gun fall to her side.

"Leif," Harry breathed softly.

Calmly Leif approached the woman. She did not move. He removed the gun from her unresisting hand.

Harry watched tensely. He still felt chagrined. He'd been snowed. But good. In his time he'd met some smooth operators, guys who could con you out of your parachute on the way down during a jump. But this character was an expert. Of course, the bastard *did* have first-class material. . . .

"Cover him," Harry said. He gave his son his own gun and took the Walther. With part of his mind he noticed the finely intricate ornamental carvings of the steel; the inscription plaque on the grip. An *Ehrenwaffe*—an Honor Weapon—that rare gun given by the Führer himself only to close friends and high-ranking Nazis. Schindler's own? The plaque would tell. He did not look. It was of no consequence.

For a moment he considered giving the gun to his son. But Leif was unfamiliar with firearms, would certainly be with a German gun. It might turn out to be more of a handicap than an advantage, and he had long since developed a healthy respect for guns in the hands of the untrained. Instead, he removed the clip from the gun and emptied the chamber. He cocked the gun, and with a sharp blow on the edge of the freezer chest he knocked off the hammer. He threw the useless weapon and the ammunition on the concrete floor and retrieved his own gun from his son.

Schindler had watched without reaction.

Harry glanced at the woman still standing at the door. He knew who she was—but he asked—

"Who the hell is she?"

"She is Angela—Geli." The German pronounced the name with a hard G. "Young Adolf's mother."

Hitler's daughter. Harry gave her a quick look.

Suddenly the child-man on the floor began to whimper. He stretched his arms toward his mother and whined plaintively.

Without looking at the men, Geli spoke. "He is hungry," she said, her voice toneless, her delivery monotonous. "He needs his milk." She suddenly turned her head and looked straight at Harry, her eyes haunted. "Surely you cannot vent your hatred for us—on him?"

Harry nodded. "Go ahead."

Geli turned back to her son. For a moment she gazed at him, her eyes unfathomable. She brought her hands to her mouth and trembled. Once. Quickly.

Harry watched her uneasily. Inside his head an alarm went off. Why?

Every nerve alert, he covered the woman as she walked heavily to the refrigerator. She unlocked the latch and opened the door. Harry positioned himself to cover both Schindler and the woman and he watched to see that all she took from the refrigerator was milk.

Geli poured a plastic mug full of milk. She closed the refrigerator door and carried the mug to her son.

For a brief moment she stood gazing down at him. Then she gave him the mug.

Young Adolf grabbed it eagerly and began to slurp it down.

His mother straightened up. She stood rigid, staring glassy-eyed at her son, her eyes dark and terrible.

And suddenly Harry knew.

Even as he called out, young Adolf gagged. The mug clattered to the floor. He screamed—a gurgling shriek of uncomprehending agony and terror. His eyes bulged from their sockets. He crammed his fingers into his mouth, ripping the corners in a frenzied attempt to tear out the searing pain. Convulsions shook his body, contorted his limbs. Briefly he writhed on the floor, crushing his toy army beneath him. And he was dead.

Bitterly Harry cursed himself. He should have known, dammit. The woman had put her hands to her mouth. It should have been a dead giveaway. He'd seen the gesture before. In Germany in 1945. Young Adolf's mother, like most other Nazi bigwigs, had a cyanide capsule hidden in a tooth. She had worked it loose and crushed it in the milk she had given her son.

Schindler had not moved. Grim-faced, he stood staring at the dead young man crumpled on the floor. Deeply shaken, Harry and Leif watched the woman.

She sank to the floor beside her dead child. Almost absentmindedly she cradled him in her lap. Gently she pushed his eyelids down over his protruding eyes and wiped the bloody spittle and milk from his face with her skirt.

She rocked slowly back and forth as she talked, gazing down into the still face of her son. "I could not let them, Dolfi," she whispered into the unhearing ears. "I could not let them. . . ." Without looking up, she raised her bleak, toneless voice. "You never told me, Franz," she said. "You never told me the full truth."

Suddenly she looked up. Her eyes were pits of torment as she gazed at the three men.

"Did you think I would let my son become an object of ridicule to the world? Of curiosity? Of shame? My *father* destroyed himself to escape such a fate. Should my *son* deserve less?" She fixed her terrible eyes on Schindler. "You would have had him killed! Murdered—to thrill the rabble of the world. Better for him to die now —in my arms—if he was never to fulfill his destiny."

As she talked, Schindler had unobtrusively edged closer to the end of the big desk. Suddenly he made a quick move toward a drawer. Harry stopped him with a barked command.

"Hold it!" He gun-gestured the German away from the desk. "Back off! Move!" He looked sharply at Schindler. He was surprised at the man's clumsiness.

Schindler shrugged and moved away from the desk toward the corner. He held his hands up and gave his disdainful little smile.

Suddenly a guttural gurgle rattled through the room, followed instantly by a small, startled scream.

All the men looked toward the ghastly sound.

Geli had tried to move her dead son. The air in his lungs had been forced through his throat and given him voice. A last outcry. The voice of the dead . . .

Only for an instant had Harry's eyes left Schindler.

It had been enough.

Even as he looked back, something hit the concrete floor at his feet. A small, metallic object. He knew at once what it was.

The pin pulled from a grenade.

Schindler stood beside the pile of crates and boxes in the corner. The lid of one had been pushed aside, and in his hand he held a hand grenade, his fingers holding down the detonater handle!

His face was hard, his voice harsh. "Kill me," he said, "and we are all dead!"

Realization raced through Harry's mind with the speed only thought can achieve. He knew at once what had happened. Schindler's clumsiness had been deliberate. He had used the feint toward the desk drawer and Harry's command to back off as a dodge to move closer to the crates and the hand grenades they contained. And he'd grabbed the first instant of momentary distraction, knowing it would come—somehow. Should Harry have known? Should he have seen through the ploy? It was immaterial now. All he knew with absolute certainty was that killing Schindler and sacrificing their own lives would accomplish nothing. The terrorist action would take place without him. Only knowledge could stop it. Knowledge Schindler possessed. Therefore he could not kill the Nazi before he knew the full plan. And the most vital piece of information about that plan was still missing.

Where was the bomb set to go off?

Where would the holocaust begin?

He held his fire.

In command, Schindler's bearing changed drastically once again.

"Geli!" he snapped. "The gun."

Obediently the woman rose. She went to Harry. Without a word he gave up his gun and she brought it to Schindler. He took it with his free hand.

"The pin," he ordered. "Get the grenade pin."

Again the woman did as she was ordered. She quickly found the pin on the floor. Schindler inserted it and put the grenade in his jacket pocket. He gestured with Harry's gun.

"You two," he ordered. "Empty the freezer." To the woman he snapped, "Unlock it."

She did. Harry and Leif piled the frozen food on the floor.

"Geli," Schindler ordered. "Lock the doors to the back. Both of them."

The woman moved to obey.

Dimly Leif wondered why. Why lock the doors? Thoughts jumbled and flashed through his mind. Only one stood out clearly. Time. They needed time. Just a little time. His father would think of something. If they only had time . . .

The freezer was empty.

Again Schindler gun-gestured.

"The body," he said. "Place it in the freezer. Move!"

Startled, Leif glanced at the German. A thin smile of triumph stretched across the man's narrow lips.

That was it!

Excitement surged through him. That was it, he thought with sudden insight. It was a chance. Perhaps their only chance. Schindler would want his defeated adversaries to *know* without a doubt that he had succeeded. Before killing them. His ego, once triggered, would demand it. Leif suddenly felt clinically calm.

As he helped his father heft the lifeless body of young Adolf, he spoke, a slightly derisive tone in his voice.

"Your scheme will not work now, Dr. Schindler," he said. "It has just been destroyed."

Schindler barked a sharp laugh. "Has it?" he said. "Why?"

Harry and Leif were carrying Adolf's body to the freezer.

"Because of him," Leif panted. "You no longer have your— rallying point."

"You are naïve, *Dr.* Bendicks," the German said scornfully. He was enjoying himself. "Did you think we had not realized that something might happen to him? Before he could be—used?"

"What if you did?" Leif retorted. "He is just as dead."

They placed the body in the freezer. Schindler was watching them.

"We have an alternate plan," he said. "Obviously. We will run the tape. We will *stage* the assassination. With an actor, seen only from the back. It is a simple matter. Such seemingly realistic action is repeatedly shown on your television shows."

Harry and Leif had finished their gruesome task. They closed the freezer lid and stood back.

"The people of the world *will* believe," Schindler continued. "Those we need. Because they want to believe. . . . And we will give them proof that the young man murdered by a Jew was indeed the Führer's flesh and blood." He nodded curtly toward the freezer. "And we do have his body."

Harry and Leif stood before the gloating German. The woman had silently joined him.

Leif watched Schindler intently. The man was, of course, mad. His dreams of a world in chaos ready for the Nazi plucking was an insane fantasy. But he, Schindler, believed it. A lifetime of living in a world of nightmare self-deception, cut off from reality, feeding—and being fed by—that one obsession, had driven reason from his mind.

But you are just as dead when you've been struck by a bullet fired by a madman. And the heinous scheme of exploding a nuclear device *was* reality.

Schindler smiled icily at the two men standing before him. He had a last little bombshell to drop—a final surprise. It could not be missed.

"Everything is in readiness," he said crisply. "Awaiting only the final word from me." With evident self-satisfaction he looked from one of his adversaries to the other, settling his gaze on Harry. "As you saw and heard on the tape, Herr Bendicks," he said, "the Führer's heir already has passed the Hitler mantle to me, his trusted mentor. The Hitler dynasty is not dead. It will go on— through me. And through his daughter." He smiled his cold, cynical smile. "My wife!"

He paused, savoring every second of triumph as if it were a vintage wine. "Even now the woman is again with child," he said. *"My* child. A true grandson of the Führer. A worthy scion who *will* be strong . . ."

Harry's mind was awhirl. They were down to the wire. In minutes Schindler would kill them. He had not the slightest illusion of any other outcome. He would have to act. Now.

What could he do?

"And the world *will* be ours," Schindler declared, a note of finality creeping into his voice. "We *shall* succeed." His eyes blazed. "If not . . . Dr. Josef Goebbels wrote in his diary: 'If our leap to great power should fail, we shall leave our conquerers a heritage that will destroy them!' . . . *I,* Franz Schindler, promise you if we are not now successful, we shall make certain that the world goes down with us to absolute annihilation. That, Herr Bendicks, you may call *my* final solution!"

Harry was totally alert, every nerve taut, every muscle tense. His brain devoured every minute detail of the situation confronting him.

Himself—his son—the woman—Schindler—and the gun . . .

He was suddenly back in the CIC. There was—something.

The gun.

Schindler did not hold it locked against his abdomen, but extended slightly before him. Not the CIC way. There *was* a move Harry could try. A man attempting to hit a laterally moving target must swing his gun arm, if the gun is not locked and he can move his entire body. It is very difficult not to swing too far and overshoot, almost impossible to hit a moving target with the first shot.

With lightning speed he made his calculations. He and his son were about ten feet from the German. Schindler only had to overswing by half an inch to miss him. The Nazi was not a young man. How quick were his reflexes? How much control did he have? They would soon know. His move was to make a sudden sideways motion—at once reversing it. The man with the gun would swing his arm and overshoot, and . . .

Would Leif understand? Would he act? As Andy would have? Their lives depended on it.

He also knew the deadly countermove to his action. Did Schindler? He dismissed it. It was—now. He froze his eyes on the Nazi.

Suddenly he made his move. Almost in the same instant Schindler fired. Harry felt the bullet rip through his sleeve, grazing his arm a fraction of a second after he'd reversed his lunge . . . and Leif hurled himself at the German. The impact was violent. The gun flew from Schindler's hand and skittered under the massive desk.

In his quick turn Harry wrenched his knee. He felt a sharp pain lance through his leg. He cursed himself for being fifty-seven. He pulled himself up to lunge at Schindler, who was struggling with his son.

Leif, untrained in close combat, could find no hold. Suddenly Schindler pushed him violently away. Leif stumbled back, colliding with his father.

Schindler grabbed the woman. He pushed her through the door to the outer shelter and plunged after her.

In the last second before slamming the door shut, he rolled his hand grenade into the room.

The detonator handle flew off.

Harry stared at the ugly object of death.

They had five seconds to live. . . .

BRITISH ANTI-NAZI
LEADER
TARGET OF MAIL BOMB

HIGH WYCOMBE, England—A bomb in the form of a parcel exploded Wednesday in the face of a member of the British Anti-Nazi League. . . . The Anti-Nazi League was formed in late 1976, about 18 months ago, to counter the rise of the extreme right-wing organizations in Britain. . . .

9

In a micro-instant the scene etched itself on Harry's mind with terrifying clarity.

He saw with a shock that the door to the outer shelter *had no handle!* To keep young Adolf from blundering out, no doubt. . . . The two doors to the back rooms were locked. . . . There was no accessible cover in the room—except the desk; scant protection in that confined area, even if they both could take cover behind it before the explosion.

The live grenade lay on the floor at his feet.

There were four seconds left.

He sprang into action. He scooped the grenade up from the rough concrete floor, unmindful of scraping the skin from his knuckles.

"The lid!" he screamed at his son.

Leif understood at once. In two strides he was at the big freezer. He tore the heavy lid open.

At once Harry lobbed the grenade into the freezer, and Leif instantly slammed the lid down.

As they were diving for cover behind the desk, the grenade detonated.

The explosion rocked the room, but the heavy freezer contained the deadly hail of fragments—even as the lid flew open and, off its hinges, crashed against the wall in a crimson spray of blood.

Suddenly the silence was total.

Painfully Harry struggled up from the hard floor. He was dazed. There was a pulsating ringing in his ears. Vision blurred, his eyes searched for his son. The light in the room had grown dimmer. Two of the three ceiling lights had gone out.

Leif was on his feet, steadying himself against the desk. His face was bloody.

"Leif!" Harry called. "You're hurt."

"Just a nosebleed," Leif said thickly. "The concussion . . ." He began to stanch the blood with his handkerchief. "Are you all right, Dad?"

Harry nodded. It made his head swim. His son's voice came to him through a wad of cotton. He shook himself. He had to clear his mind.

The door! They had to get the hell out of there. They could still catch up with Schindler.

He hurried over to the handleless door. His hands explored it.

"We've got to get this damned thing open," he said. He pushed it. It would need a key.

He turned to his son. "My gun," he said crisply. "Under the desk. Get it."

Leif hurried over. Quickly he knelt down. He felt for it. There! He ran back to his father and gave him the gun.

Harry stood away from the door. "Out of the way," he said. "Behind me."

He aimed his gun at the lock and fired three rounds into it in quick succession. Resounding in the confines of the concrete room, the reports sent waves of pain to their already abused ears. Again Harry tried the door.

The bullets had shattered the lock, but the door would not budge. It would open in—not out. If at all.

"Shit!" Harry strained against the door with all his might. It did not move. Angrily he kicked it.

"It's the damned doorway," he said. "We've got to pull it."

He tried to jam his fingers into the bullet holes and get a grip. It was impossible.

"We need something," he said, looking around the room, knowing he'd find nothing. "Something to stick in there and pull with."

"The refrigerator!" Leif said suddenly.

He ran to it, averting his eyes from the horror in the nearby freezer, threw open the refrigerator door and yanked out one of the metal wire shelves, scattering food all over the floor. He inspected the shelf, then put it under his foot and pulled. Slowly it bent. Some of the thinner wires burst from the heavier supporting frame. He pried them out of the way, placed the thick frame in the refrigerator opening and closed the door on it. Straining, he curved the wire into a hook and ran back to his father.

"Here," he said. "Try this."

Harry grabbed the twisted shelf. He rammed the wire hook into one of the holes, twisting it tight. Together they pulled.

With a sudden, grating screech the door flew open.

Schindler had replaced the camouflage cabinet in front of the opening. Harry kicked it aside. Together they ran for the steep shelter stairs.

They burst from the stairwell into the garden. It was bathed in a flickering red-orange glow. Behind the kitchen windows, flames were writhing and leaping.

They raced for the house.

The editing room was an inferno. Tongues of fire shot out through the blazing doorway. Schindler had made sure no evidence would survive.

Harry didn't waste a glance at the work tapes going up in flames. He knew the Hitler tape would not be one of them.

They raced past the burning room, through the dark shop and burst from the front door.

A car—Schindler's car, which had been parked in the carport—was backing out of the driveway. It made a tire-screeching turn and careened down the deserted night street.

Harry and Leif rushed to their car at the curb. They threw themselves inside, Harry behind the wheel. It would not be his first chase. They slammed the doors, and in the same instant the car lurched forward and sped in pursuit.

"The fire," Leif called to his father. "Shouldn't we report it?"

"We will," Harry snapped. He gunned the car—hunched over the wheel. "We've got to stay on his tail. We can't afford to lose him."

He leaned on the car horn as he hurtled down the street. The din was ear-splitting in the night. He glanced in his rear-view mirror. Lights were going on in several houses behind him.

"They'll report it," he said.

Ahead of them Schindler's car screeched around a corner, side-swiped a parked car and caromed down another street.

Harry roared after it. He was going as fast as he could and still keep the car under control. He was not gaining.

He glanced around for a black-and-white. Where the hell were the cops? Never around when you need them. He fixed his eyes on the distant taillights of Schindler's car and stomped on the accelerator. He was determined not to lose his quarry. He'd stay on the bastard like a damned wetsuit.

Schindler made another high-speed turn, bouncing over the curb, bucking violently. He did not slow.

Harry took the corner on two wheels and careened into the street. Far ahead he could see the bright lights of a main crossing and the occasional headlights of passing cars.

Schindler apparently had seen it, too. At once he made another sharp turn, and was momentarily lost from sight.

Harry rounded the corner, barreling around it. He and Leif recognized the street at the same moment.

"Dad!" Leif called out. "This is the street to the studio back lot. The Spread!"

"Yeah." Harry slowed down. "It's a dead end!"

In the distance ahead they could see Schindler's car coming to a halt.

"We got him boxed," Harry said. "But we need help. He may be armed. He might have a gun in the car."

"I'll go after him," Leif said at once. "You get help."

"*No!*" Harry exploded with sudden vehemence. "That bastard is mine!" He stopped the car.

"Get out, Leif," he said urgently. "Get to a phone. Call Stein. Or Pete. Get *somebody* here. Right now!"

Leif tumbled from the car. "Be careful, Dad," he begged.

"Yeah." Harry gunned the car and roared down the dead-end street toward the gate to the studio lot.

He brought his car to a rubber-burning stop next to Schindler's. It was abandoned. Gun in hand, he leaped from his car, took cover and peered through the semi-darkness toward the gate. Suddenly he saw movement at one side of the fence. Two figures climbing down the wire fence on the inside. He ran toward the spot.

Schindler and the woman were disappearing into the shadows of the back lot, running fast.

Harry began to scale the fence. . . .

Leif banged on the door. It was the house nearest to where he'd gotten out. A two-story frame house. Like the others on the street, it was dark.

He called. "Open up! Please!" He banged as loudly as he could.

A light came on in an upstairs window. Leif stood back. He turned his blood-smeared face toward the light. "Open up!" he called. "I need help!"

The window opened. A man stuck his head out. "What do you want?" he called angrily. "Get the hell off my property!"

"I need help," Leif cried urgently. "I need to use your phone!"

"Are you out of your mind? It's the middle of the damned night. You gotta nerve waking us up like this!"

"It's an emergency!"

"Take your goddamned emergency somewheres else," the man called. "Don't bother me."

"Please! Listen to me!" Leif pleaded desperately.

"Look, you creep," the man said, his voice ugly, "I'm wise to your kind." Threateningly he pulled a shotgun into sight. "You get the hell away from here or I'll blast your ass full of extra holes!"

Bleakly, Leif realized that another appeal would do no good.

He turned and ran toward another house.

Please God that he would find someone to listen.
And help. . . .

Harry ran silently down the empty, dirt-surfaced street of the Western set, hugging the shadows of the hollow houses. His gun was in his hand, his eyes searched the distance for signs of Schindler and the woman.

The street seemed eerily different in the pale light cast by a cloud-mantled half-moon, and he recognized only a few of the false-front buildings. The open smithy, the hotel, the clapboard structure with the LIVERY STABLE sign, all barely distinguishable. He came to the corner and carefully peered to his left.

Ahead the faint light hit an open area. He could make out two figures running. They stopped. They seemed to exchange a few urgent words. Then the smaller of the two ran off to one side, the taller one in the opposite direction.

Schindler!

Harry knew exactly where the man was headed. The back-lot set of the war-scarred German town with its fire-gutted, shrapnel-shattered ruins, streets pockmarked with shell craters, heaps of rubble and debris, its crippled equipment, damaged church tower, grenade-blasted Town Hall—and the long-dead Nazi slogans. The make-believe relics of past violence—sought as a haven by a madman who would himself unleash the ultimate fury.

Harry started after the German, then slowed down. Schindler would not let himself be taken easily. He would fight back. He knew how. And killing him was out. Harry would crowd him. Follow him and crowd him. If possible, corner him and hold him. Wait until Leif arrived with help.

Cautiously he began to make his way into the war-ravaged Bavarian town. . . .

The door was opened a mere crack. A heavy chain kept it from opening any farther. A man peeked cautiously out at Leif.

"What do you want?" he asked suspiciously.

"Please," Leif said earnestly, "I need your help. I need to use your phone."

"You—want to get in?" The man sounded frightened.

"What is it, Verne?" a woman's voice called from inside. "Who's there?"

The man turned toward the voice. "It's a man," he called. "He —he wants to use the phone."

"Don't you let him in, you hear?" the woman cried in alarm. "Don't!"

"Please," Leif said quickly. "If you don't want to let me in, call the police for me. Ask for—"

"What's he want now?" the woman called.

"He wants us to call the police for him."

"Verne! You tell that man to go away! We don't want to get involved. We don't want to get involved in *anything!* Just tell him to go away."

The man turned to Leif. "Look," he said. "Try someone else." He closed the door. . . .

Ex-Standartenführer Dr. Franz Schindler hurried down the battle-razed street, picking his way through the offal of war, past dismal personal messages of anguish scrawled on bullet-scarred walls and boastful slogans and swastikas chalked on scorched ruins.

He had stopped running. He was winded—fighting a sting in his side.

He had an eerie feeling of *déjà vu,* the memory of another desperate nighttime flight through devastated Berlin.

But he knew exactly where he was. Müller had told him about the movie the prop man was working on. And the back-lot set. He knew about the prop boxes. The guns. And the live ammunition.

When the Bendicks father and son had come charging out of the burning house, he'd known he would not be able to shake them. Coldly he had calculated that he would have to kill them—at least one of them—in order to lose himself in the city and remain free until the hour he would be needed.

But he was unarmed.

And Bendicks had a gun.

He had made his plan instantly. And he had raced for the one place where he could find the means and the opportunity to carry it out.

Once before, this reincarnated fragment of the wartime Reich had served as the chosen instrument to eliminate an enemy. Then it had failed. Now it would serve again, successfully.

He scurried through a charred doorway where Müller had said the prop boxes were kept. On the wall was a torn propaganda poster just as Müller had described it. A German armament worker handing a cluster of grenades to a front-line soldier— WAFFEN FÜR DIE FRONT! it read. The aptness of the slogan was not lost on him. In the gloom he looked around for the prop boxes. He would have no difficulty forcing the locks.

The area behind the false front was open to the night sky. Supporting beams and struts cast a web of shadows across the dirt floor. But the place was empty. The prop boxes were gone.

In sudden unbridled rage he knew. The production was finished. The shooting done. The equipment removed. *Verflucht!*

He turned back to the street. For a moment he stood motionless, listening, trying to penetrate the darkness.

All seemed quiet.

Had Bendicks lost him? Followed Geli instead? It was unlikely. He had gained too much respect for the American's resourcefulness. Where was the son? Gone for help? Yes. That would have been the move. There was little time. . . .

Across the street loomed a big building. With a tower. A church. Although damaged, it was still largely intact. It would afford better protection than the half-open space behind the false front and a better spot for an ambush.

Quickly, silently, he crossed the street and entered the church.

For a moment he stood inside the doorway stock still, getting used to the deeper darkness within. He let his eyes roam the big open space, the stacks of battered old church pews, the clusters of light stands, piles of paint cans, rolled-up electric cables, boxes and rubble strewn about everywhere.

He walked on. At the tower end he could make out an almost vertical ladder reaching up into the gloom above.

He started toward it and froze. He whirled back toward the doorway through which he had just come.

In the opening, silhouetted against the half-light outside, stood a huge dog. A low, menacing growl rumbled deep in its throat.

A guard dog. A magnificent German shepherd.

Bitterly he cursed the dead Müller. The idiot had said nothing about dogs guarding the studio lot at night.

Without a moment's hesitation he turned and raced for the steep ladder. He sensed rather than heard the watchdog streaking after him.

He reached the first rungs, threw himself at the ladder, scrambled up—skinning his shin badly. Below him the dog leaped after him. But he was out of reach. He clambered up to a platform high above and lay panting. He'd played the feeble old man too long, he thought ironically. He looked down. The dog was standing, stiff-legged, its paws on the ladder. Snarling and growling, it stared up at him, its wild eyes glinting with malevolence, its long fangs gleaming wetly in the faint, narrow rays of moonlight filtering through rifts and cracks in the walls.

Schindler stared back. In his mind he also saw the sharp teeth of failure waiting for him below. The presence and actions of the beast would give him away at once. The instant Bendicks saw the enraged dog.

He had to eliminate it. Fast.

But how?

It would have to be done quickly, without any noise. Could he drop something down on it? Something heavy? Crush it? He dismissed the idea. If the beast was not killed at once, it would start to howl, bringing his armed hunter on the run. Anyway, the deadfall itself would make noise.

His eyes darted around the platform. Forty or fifty feet above ground, it was set in the shell-torn tower of the church. Part of the steeple walls had been shot away. In the center of the platform several large pieces of lighting equipment had been collected— studio spotlights and reflectors, scoops and broads and a quantity of "C" clamp hangers. A few heavy cables lay coiled near the right wall. The platform gave onto a railing-enclosed walkway running around the exterior of the tower and partly shot away, a portion of it extending precariously out into black nothingness. An electric-power panel and some mechanical device consisting of metal tubing were affixed to the right wall. Several electric cords, stapled to the wooden wall, ran across it.

The wires . . .

Quickly he tore one of them from the panel and ripped a length of it from the wall. The cord ran down the wall toward the ground below. It had to be cut. He tried to break it. It was impossible, and he had no tools. He glanced down at the intent dog bristling at the foot of the ladder, teeth bared in a snarl. They had one thing in common. Teeth!

At once he began to gnaw through the cord. The metal core cut his gums. He disregarded the bleeding.

The wire parted. He had a length about twenty feet long.

It would do.

Working feverishly, he fashioned a slip noose at one end of the wire, climbed down the steep ladder until he was about ten feet above the beast and hooked his arm around a rung. While the guard dog watched him with growing fury, Schindler dangled the noose above its head, wrapping the other end around a rung of the ladder. The beast looked as if it had the strength of a full-grown wolf.

He lowered the slip noose closer and closer to the animal, which snapped at it in rage. But its attention was fully and ravenously fixed on the man above.

Carefully Schindler worried the noose closer to the dog's head. It slid over the slavering jaws. Caressed the alertly pointed ears—and slipped around the neck.

Instantly Schindler yanked up on the wire with all his strength. The noose tightened around the dog's throat, and its feet were jerked from the ground.

Schindler strained to hold the wire. It cut into his hands. He ignored it.

Below, the dog twitched and kicked as life ebbed from it. A low whine came from its tortured throat; its tongue bloated grotesquely as it hung between its bared teeth; and the huge, dark eyes, filled with panic, slowly glazed over.

The convulsions stopped. To make certain, Schindler let the dead beast dangle for a moment. Then he unfastened the wire from the ladder and lowered the corpse to the ground.

He began to climb down. And froze.

A figure stood outlined in the doorway to the street.

Noiselessly, deliberately, Schindler climbed back up the ladder to the platform. He knew it would take a few seconds for Bendicks' eyes to adjust to the deeper darkness inside. He would not be seen.

He lay prostrate on the platform, watching his enemy, gun in hand, move slowly into the empty shell of the church below. . . .

Leif was back at the corner of the dead-end street to the lot. Frantically he looked for a likely house. In the distance two bright headlights were bearing down on him. He ran into the roadway. Waving his arms, he flagged down the car.

As it came closer, he saw it was a taxicab, but the vacancy light on top was dark. He placed himself directly in its path, still waving his arms, forcing the cab to stop.

He ran to the driver's side. The man rolled his window down an inch.

"What the hell do you think you're doing?" he growled. "Are you crazy?"

"I need help," Leif panted. "I need—"

"I'm off duty."

"Listen!" Leif cried desperately. "It's an emergency. I must contact the police!"

"What?" The taxi driver looked at him, startled.

"You have radio contact, haven't you? With your dispatcher?"

"Sure."

"Would they relay a message? To the police?"

"I guess so."

"Thank God!" Leif leaned against the cab. "Tell them they are to contact the LAPD communications division. Tell them this. . . ."

Cautiously Harry started into the church shell. He remembered the place. He felt enormously keyed up. He'd moved through the war-torn town. The motion-picture equipment was gone. The shooting over. The set deserted. More than ever, in the darkness of night, it looked and felt to him like the real thing.

He searched the gloom with his eyes. Any shadow could hide the Kraut. He'd seen his quarry slip inside. Was he still there? He had to make sure. He moved on in a slight crouch, his gun locked against his abdomen, ready to whirl his body toward any threat.

The place looked bigger, emptier, than he remembered. The portable dressing rooms were gone. That was it.

Where the hell was Leif?

He made his way toward the tower end. The dirt floor was still littered with debris, and stored equipment and heaps of stuff were still piled against the walls. The lighting stands still stood grouped in silent conference.

He was near the ladder leading up into the steeple. Suddenly he stopped, staring at the still, crumpled form lying at the foot of the ladder.

He approached it cautiously.

It was a dog. A German shepherd. Dead.

He felt its belly where the coat was thin. Still warm.

Schindler . . .

Quickly he glanced up the steep ladder. Was the bastard up there? He had to make certain.

He considered the ladder. No way could he climb it unnoticed. Nor without becoming vulnerable.

Wait. The memory burst upon him. The catwalk. The narrow catwalk he'd seen when he was here before, running around the wall just below the roofline, encircling the whole area and joining the higher platform. It could be reached by another ladder in the opposite end of the church.

He moved away. Slowly. Deliberately. He did not look back up toward the platform.

Schindler watched him slowly walking away from the ladder. He frowned. The man had found the dead dog. What had he thought? That his prey had left the church? Why didn't he search the platform? He watched Harry move toward the far end of the church, cautiously looking around, disappearing into the darkness.

Silently Schindler got up and moved toward the wall. He sat down, leaning against it and keeping his eyes on the doorway to the street. If Bendicks left the way he'd come in, he'd see him. But he had a nagging feeling that the American was up to something. It would be in character.

He'd wait. . . .

Harry reached the ladder to the catwalk. He replaced his gun in its shoulder holster, climbed up and stepped out onto the narrow walkway. He took a tentative step. Would the damned thing squeak? The sturdy catwalk was made with iron pipes, designed to hold heavy spotlights. It did not give. Slowly, silently, hugging the wall, gun locked before him, Harry moved toward the tower and the ladder leading from the catwalk to the platform. He found himself breathing in shallow gulps—and listening to the oppressive silence.

Where the *hell* was Leif? He should have heard the police sirens long ago. Or was his sense of time distorted? How long *had* it been?

He was at the ladder. He kept his gun in his hand. Rung by rung, he climbed. He was at the platform. Cautiously he lifted his head.

Thanks to the shell-blasted holes in the walls, the light on the tower platform was a few degrees brighter than the gloom of the area below, and Harry took in the scene at once.

In the center, across a pile of electrical equipment, a figure could be seen standing against the far wall, empty hands held out.

Schindler.

"I am unarmed, Herr Bendicks," the Nazi said evenly. He stood motionless.

Harry kept Schindler covered as he himself climbed onto the platform. He walked around the heap of equipment in the center, keeping the inside of the platform with the ladder to the ground clear.

"Just keep your hands where I can see them," he called. He gestured with his gun. "The ladder," he ordered. "Move!"

Schindler held out his hands. "I have no weapon," he said. He took a step toward Harry.

Harry at once took a couple of steps backward. "Hold it!" he snapped. "Right there! Keep your distance." Part of his mind was acutely aware that behind him the shell-damaged platform ended in a drop to the ground far below. He'd take no chance of a rush and a push. "The ladder," he ordered.

Schindler shrugged. He turned and walked along the wall toward the ladder, his back to Harry.

Suddenly he stumbled on one of the coiled cables. He reached out to steady himself—and hit a lever on the tubular steel contraption on the wall.

Instantly Harry felt the platform give way under him. He felt himself plunging down. Instinctively he reached with both hands for a hold, his gun flying from his grip to spin down into the darkness below. His head hit the hard edge of the platform as his fingers miraculously found a purchase. He felt his nails rip, but he held on, precariously suspended on a part of the platform that had given way.

He saw Schindler take a step toward him.

The Nazi had him. Where was Andy? Where were the others. Leif? . . . His mind swam in an ocean of half-remembered realities and present danger. Which was which?

Schindler looked down at him, a thin, triumphant smile stretching his lips.

"They call it a breakaway, Herr Bendicks," he said, his voice silken with malice. "It was built for the motion picture Ernst Helmut Müller worked on. I understand that in the story an American soldier—a GI—falls to his death when a shell hits the tower. A stunt, of course. Müller told me about it."

He motioned toward the steel contraption fastened to the inside wall.

"It works in two stages, Herr Bendicks." His cold smile matched his voice. "You have experienced the first. Your reactions were admirable," he mocked. "You would have made an excellent stunt man, I am sure."

Harry was beginning to understand his words. They found their way into his consciousness, colliding and spinning like radio cars in an amusement-park ride. His fingers sent waves of pain to his disoriented brain. But he held on. . . .

"The second stage is activated by *this* lever," the German explained, as matter-of-factly as if he were demonstrating a vacuum cleaner. He turned to the control device. "It releases the entire section of the platform that has been rigged to form the breakaway. It—and, of course, you—will crash to the ground below!" The SS officer was obviously savoring the moment.

He took a step toward Harry. "You have a choice to make, Herr Bendicks," he snapped. "You, I cannot help. But I will promise you not to dispose of your son if you will answer two questions for me. Now."

Harry stared at him through a hazy red mist. Not for a second

did he believe the man. He said nothing. He felt his grip weaken-
ing. . . .

"First," Schindler said impatiently. "Do you know *where* we will
strike—either by direct knowledge or deduction? Secondly. If so
—*who else knows?*"

Harry felt a great weariness overtake him. The game was played
out. There were no more jokers in the deck.

Suddenly there was a small noise from the darkened platform
behind Schindler.

The German whirled toward it.

A figure stepped into view, holding a gun.

Harry's gun.

"Geli!" Schindler exclaimed. He stared at the woman.

She stood motionless, gazing at the scene before her.

Schindler regained his composure. "You have his gun," he said
crisply. "Good. Give it to me."

The woman held out the gun toward him—and fired.

The shot caught Schindler full in the chest.

He was dead before he hit the floor.

Harry stared in horror. Only one thought shrieked in his mind.
The woman had killed Schindler. And his knowledge with him—
and the untold millions doomed to die in his nuclear plot . . .

Geli walked toward Harry like a somnambulist, without a glance
at the crumpled body of Dr. Franz Schindler, her husband.

She stared at Harry, but it was impossible to tell what her dead
eyes saw. The gun was pointed at his head.

Suddenly she spoke. To no one—not even herself. As if the
words were simply there, seeking to escape.

"I did not know," she said, her voice lifeless. "He never told me
Dolfi's father was my own brother. The seed was bad. We—did not
know. . . ."

With sudden vehemence she hurled the gun away from her and
walked steadily toward the edge of the platform high above the
ground.

She did not stop. . . .

Harry dug his pain-racked fingers into the wood. With a last,
desperate effort he inched himself up the breakaway to the safety
of the platform and hurried to the ladder.

Geli was still alive. Sprawled on the ground, one leg crushed beneath her at an impossible angle, blood seeping from one ear, she opened her eyes and gazed up at Harry as he gently called her name.

"Geli," he said softly. "If you can hear me, please answer. Where is the explosion going to happen? *Where?*"

He looked down into the gray face of Adolf Hitler's daughter, the woman who had chosen not to carry a second bad seed.

"Where?" he pressed. *"Where?"*

He was aware of screaming sirens in the distance. He paid no attention.

"Where?"

Geli's lips moved.

He bent to listen.

It was hardly audible. "Sa . . . id . . ." she breathed.

It was her last breath.

With an icy chill Harry straightened up.

Said. The target of Schindler's nuclear explosion. Port Said. The Suez Canal . . .

CAIRO "NEW NAZI CAPITAL"

LOS ANGELES—During a press conference at the Greater Los Angeles Press Club today, an authority on Middle East and German affairs stated that Cairo is the new Nazi capital of the world. "There are from 400 to 500 strong former Nazis who now live in Cairo," he declared. . . .

10

Harry barged into the office of Lieutenant Jack Stein and closed the door resolutely behind him, his face set in a determined scowl.

"Jack," he said, "I've got to have your help."

Stein looked up at him with mild surprise. "Come in," he said dryly.

Harry ignored the sarcasm. In two strides he reached the lieutenant's desk and sat down on a corner.

"I've spent most of the damned day filling out forms and reports," he said with disgust. "Leif too. You know the routine."

"Nothing I can do about that, Harry."

"I know that, dammit!" Harry snapped impatiently. "Listen to
me." He looked Stein straight in the face, his eyes desperately
earnest. "You know me well enough to know I'm not a nut. We
both know all my reports and triple-copy forms might just as well
be lining the drawers in the closet of some little old lady in
Pasadena, for all the action they'll get."

"Harry—"

"Hear me out, Jack. I'm goddamned serious."

Stein shrugged resignedly.

"I *know* it all sounds crazy. But, Jack, *I believe it!*"

Stein stared at him with a small frown.

"Something big *is* about to go down," Harry insisted.

Stein nodded soberly. "I heard. I haven't seen all the reports
yet." He shook his head. "Pretty wild. I—" He looked at his friend,
the man with whom he'd worked closely for so many years. Something in Harry's face made him abandon the deprecating remark
on his lips. Instead he said: "What is it you want to say?"

"There'll *be* a terrorist attack, Jack. A nuclear attack. An atomic
bomb will be exploded. We must prevent it!"

"Where? Where's this attack supposed to take place?"

"Port Said."

"Port Said!" Stein looked at him incredulously. "In Egypt?"

Harry nodded. "The Suez Canal."

"Are you out of your skull? How the hell can I—can *we* do
anything about what happens halfway round the world?" He
shook his head. "Who's supposed to pull this stunt? Your Nazis?"

"Yeah. *My* Nazis," Harry said bitingly. "The same fucking Nazis
who've strewn DBs all over the damned place—apparently unnoticed by the department! The same bastards who've knocked
themselves out to kill me and my son!"

He slammed the flat of his hand on the desk. It hurt. He grimaced at his fingers. The tips were yellow-brown with disinfec-
tant, as though with the nicotine stains of some super chain-

smoker. Hell of a note for someone who quit fifteen years ago.

Grim-faced, Lieutenant Stein studied him. "Look, Harry. We've known each other long enough for you to know I won't play games with you," he said quietly. "But let me play the devil's advocate."

"Shoot."

"Granted, you and your son stumbled on some neo-Nazi organization. A crackpot Nazi cult. Nothing new."

Harry began to protest. Stein held up his hand. "Now you hear *me* out," he said firmly. Harry shut up. "Granted, we found the— remains of a dead man. Reportedly murdered by his fellow Nazis. Again—nothing new. They bumped off Rockwell—and that guy Tomasi right here in El Monte a few years back."

He ticked off his points on his fingers.

"Granted, we found an old fallout shelter, expanded to house this Nazi kook cult and some of the members. But we found *nothing* down there or in what was left of the house that gave us the slightest indication it was *not* just an oddball outfit. . . . We found a mess of burned and scorched video recording tape and some equipment. Hell, lots of people dabble in videotaping without plotting to destroy the world! And we found a tape in a car with some guy acting like a poor man's Hitler, raving about resurrecting his grandfather. Easily the work of a bunch of weirdos—until proved otherwise. And any link between the guy on the tape and the body in the shelter *is* unproved so far. Identification was impossible. . . . Finally, you chased some citizen the records show to have been a harmless old man onto a movie set, where he was shot, with your gun, by a woman we haven't been able to identify. Strange? Yes. A case to be investigated? You bet. But hard evidence of terrorism on a world scale? No. . . ."

Again Harry started to interrupt. Again Stein silenced him. *"Despite* your documentary evidence, Harry. Which is over thirty years old, for crissake! And despite the fact that we both know our own nuclear experts consider something like this overdue . . ."

Harry could contain himself no longer. "That's exactly it," he exclaimed. "The whole damned plot *is* crazy. I admit it. But it *could* be true. *I* think it is. Sure it's irrational. But—as my son says —you can't expect rational thinking from irrational people."

"We've waltzed around like this before, Harry," Stein said. He sighed. "What do you want from me?"

"Okay. Perhaps my official reports will finally be acted on. Perhaps not. It's too damned hard to get a bureaucrat off his fat ass. And a desk is a piss-poor place from which to keep tabs on the world."

He looked searchingly at Stein.

"Jack," he said. "I know *something* will happen. Three days from now. April the twentieth. Hitler's birthday. I firmly believe it *will* be a nuclear action and that the bomb will be exploded in Port Said. You can figure the consequences yourself." His voice became angrier. "But I haven't a stinking inkling as to who'll do it—or exactly when or where! Jack, I'm going over there. To Port Said."

Stein gaped at him. "You *are* out of your mind," he said. "You can't take off like that. You can't run out on an ongoing investigation."

"I'm doing just that, Jack."

"Technically you're a suspect."

"I know. I told you my plan because I need help. Not hindrance." He took a deep breath. "I don't know what the hell I'll be looking for. But, whatever it is, I can't do it on my own. I need help. I've got a damned slim chance to stop it. But it's the only chance."

"And if you don't?" Stein asked soberly.

"No one else is going to do a fucking thing about it," Harry said angrily. "In time. It'll take too long to convince anyone with clout to interfere in the Middle East, and you damn well know it."

Stein stared at him incredulously. He said nothing.

"Jack. I want you to contact Interpol for me. In Cairo. I'm not asking you to suck up to anyone. Just clear me with Interpol."

"I could have you arrested, Harry," Stein said quietly.

Harry nodded grimly. "I know."

For a moment the two men stared at one another.

"This is not just something that's going on here, Jack. And in the Middle East. It's all over the goddamned world!"

The intercom on Stein's desk buzzed. He flipped the switch. "Yeah?"

"There's a Dr. Bendicks and a Miss Gannon to see you, Lieutenant."

Stein glanced at Harry. "Send them in," he said.

Leif went straight to his father.

"Dad," he said, obviously excited, "we got it!" He turned to Susan. "Tell him."

"Arthur called," she said. "The British came through."

"What've we got?" Harry asked at once.

"Documents. They're sending us copies." She took a small notebook from her purse. "I made some notes." She referred to the little book. "Several Hitler heritage studies—like the craniological report we found, all marked *Betr. Jenbach.* A document referring to a top-secret party project—also concerning Jenbach. Confirmation of the Jenbach bunker construction in the National Redoubt." She looked up. "And a document covering a special mission under the personal control of Adolf Hitler which involves his political testament and SS Standartenführer Dr. Franz Schindler!"

Harry turned to his son.

"Leif," he said, "I'm going over there."

"*We,*" Leif corrected him firmly. "*We* are going, Dad."

Harry looked at his son, his face grave.

"It's a long shot," he said. "A damned long shot. If we don't make it—we'll be sitting right in the middle of the bull's-eye."

Instinctively Susan moved closer to Leif. He looked down into her upturned face.

"I want to go with you, Dad," he said quietly. "And—I want to come back."

"We'll have to find out how to get there," Harry said. "As fast as possible."

"I thought that's what you'd want," Leif said. "I have the information." He pulled a note from his pocket. "We are booked on TWA Flight 904. We leave tomorrow morning. Nine fifteen A.M. our time. They're ten hours ahead of us out there. We'll arrive in Cairo at one fifty the following afternoon. It will be April the nineteenth."

"That gives us one day . . ."

"And one night."

Harry turned to Stein. "Jack?"

Stein sighed. He shook his head. He picked up the phone. "Get me Washington," he said. "Interpol."

NEO-FASCISTS PLANNING "EURO-RIGHT" MOVEMENT

ROME, Italy—Giorgio Almirante, leader of the neo-Fascist Italian Social Movement, announced Monday that rightists parties of Italy, France and Spain will take part in the organization of a "Euro-Right" movement in Europe. . . . Almirante wields growing influence. Already in 1976, two years ago, his Neo-Fascist party got 6% of the vote in Italy's general election. . . .

SIX

The Target

19–20 April 1978

1

For the fiftieth time Harry looked at his watch. The grim fact remained the same. They were already over one hour late.

It was seven minutes to three on the afternoon of Wednesday, April 19.

Impatiently he looked out the dirt-streaked window of the plane. The city of Cairo lay below, crowded on both sides of the Nile and on two large islands in the river. He had been prepared for the tall minarets, from whose birdcage cupolas the muezzins summoned the Moslem faithful to prayer, and the colorful, domed mosques—but not for the startling contrast of large modern buildings and skyscrapers, dominated by a huge circular structure with a massive, square tower in the center. The Cairo TV studios, according to the stewardess. Somehow the new buildings seemed disturbingly out of keeping with the three majestic and ancient Giza pyramids guarded by the Sphinx, visible on a desert plateau not far from the city.

He turned to Leif. "Dammit," he growled, "I wish we could get out and push. This damned crate—"

He was interrupted by the mellifluous tones of the stewardess announcing their imminent arrival at Cairo International Airport.

As Harry and Leif deplaned, a small, wiry man in civilian clothes approached them.

"Mr. Hari Ben-Deeks?" he inquired, giving Harry's name a decidedly Arabic flavor.

"Yeah. Bendicks," Harry said. He looked down into the man's swarthy face. His skin was like the leather of a well-worn shoe, and a small jet-black mustache perched under a prominent nose.

"I am Inspector Mustafa Hamid Osman," the Egyptian said formally. "Cairo Police." He did not offer his hand.

Harry nodded. "My son." He glanced at Leif.

"Are you armed?" Osman asked.

"Two guns," Harry answered. "In our luggage."

"I will get them through customs," Osman said. He looked interested. "Follow me."

They hurried toward the airport checkpoints.

"We have to get to Port Said," Harry said urgently. "As quickly as possible."

"I am assigned to your needs," Osman said. "I will be at your service." He sounded resentful.

"Is there a connecting flight?" Harry asked. "How soon can we leave?"

Osman shook his head regretfully. "Air travel is not possible," he stated. "Bus, yes. Railway, yes. But it takes long. Four hours. At least." He gave Harry a sidelong look. "I have official car. I can drive you to Port Said. Get there as fast as possible." He looked away. He shrugged. "But perhaps you will wish to wait for the train. The money for the car," he said, "it will be charged to you."

Harry said nothing. It was a moot question if *anyone* would be footing the bill. . . .

Inspector Osman's official car was a black 1974 Ford sedan. With the Egyptian at the wheel they left the airport and picked up the road going north.

With nonchalant skill Osman threaded the car through the flow of automobiles, bicycles, pushcarts and donkey-powered drays, fender-brushing the arms and legs of unconcerned pedestrians and liberally adding the clamor of his raucous horn to the general din. Harry thanked his lucky star that they didn't have to go through downtown Ciaro itself, with its old, narrow streets alternating with new, broad avenues and its hanging-room-only buses.

Soon the traffic thinned, and they sped on toward the strategic Canal city of Port Said.

Osman broke the silence.

"Port Said," he said. "What do you seek in Port Said?" He glanced at Harry sitting next to him. "I have been told nothing of your reason for being here." It obviously annoyed him. "Interpol requested that we cooperate with you. Strongly, they requested this. But—no details." Again he glanced at Harry. "What is it you seek? If I am to help, I must know."

Harry thought quickly. How much should he tell this little man in order to ensure his maximum cooperation? He appreciated Interpol's discretion. If word had gotten out of the true threat to the city, panic would most certainly have been the result. And to no avail. Time was the unbeatable enemy. And panic would have made *any* action on their part an impossibility—at best.

"We have information," Harry said carefully. "Reports that a terrorist attack is planned for tomorrow. In Port Said."

"This I know," Osman said. "Interpol told us that they would inform the appropriate high authorities here. But—they gave us no details." He gave Harry an inquiring glance.

Harry wondered briefly how many cockeyed stories, how many false alarms of terrorist actions the Egyptian authorities had to contend with under present conditions. Probably one hell of a lot, judging by LA standards. Would they give extra-special credence to a couple of nuts from the States? Why should they?

"It is a bomb," he said quietly. "A bomb hidden somewhere in Port Said. A bomb that could wreck the Canal—should it be exploded."

He saw no reason to tell the Egyptian that it was a nuclear bomb. Not yet . . .

Osman looked uneasy. "You—do not know where?" he asked.

"We don't."

The little man moistened his lips. "It is a big place, Port Said," he said. "How will you—look for it? How will you find it?"

"We've done a little brainstorming on that one," Harry said crisply. Osman gave him a quick look, but he asked no questions. "What we *know*. What we can assume."

"The bomb itself," Leif said. "It would have to have some bulk. We guess at—oh, two or three feet by four or five."

"And weight," Harry said. "It would have to be shielded. It—" He caught himself. "Several hundred pounds, we think. Nothing you'd haul around in a briefcase."

"The device undoubtedly would have been constructed somewhere else," Leif said. "Not in Port Said."

Harry turned to Osman. The Egyptian, watching him, looked disturbed. "How does freight—bulky freight—usually arrive in Port Said?" Harry asked.

"By rail," the little man answered at once. "But most often by ship. Port Said has excellent harbor facilities."

"I'd bet on a ship," Leif said. "A lot fewer transportation problems."

Harry nodded. "And a lot less chance of discovery during some inspection or other."

"Ships arrive in Port Said every day," Osman contributed. "Many ships. Either from the Mediterranean or through the Canal."

"So—where do we start?" Leif frowned in thought.

"Manifests!" Harry exclaimed. "Cargo manifests. Records. Destinations. Ports of departure. That sort of thing. Are such records available anywhere in Port Said?" he asked the Egyptian.

Osman nodded. "The Suez Canal Authority," he said. "Very powerful. The Harbor Master's office would have all such records."

"That's where we'll start," Harry said firmly.

It was close to six o'clock when Osman drove his dusty Ford sedan into the city of Port Said.

Situated on a narrow sand spit between Lake Manzala and the sea, the city teemed with activity. During the six-day war with Israel it had become virtually a ghost town as Israeli artillery blasted the waterfront and turned the Canal into a useless ditch, and in the years that followed, the once-thriving gateway to the Mediterranean and northern guardian of Egypt's vital waterway had lost its significance. But after the Canal had been cleared of debris and reopened, the derelict city and its extension on the east bank of the Canal, Port Fuad, had exploded into a metropolis of more than two million people. It now boasted new buildings, hotels, restaurants and clubs, a broad, safe harbor and a bustling shipyard. It was once again a vital sea-route center between East and West.

As Osman guided his car at a snail's pace through the crowded, colorful streets toward the Canal quays, Harry watched the ragged children romping along with them, white teeth flashing in sun-browned faces, huge, dark eyes gleaming with mischief. He looked at the peaceful hustle and bustle of the people sweeping through the street. And he knew that over it all hung the imminent threat of instant annihilation.

He looked away from the children. In his mind's eye he suddenly saw them as mangled, charred little corpses. . . .

The Canal Administration Building was glorious with purple

bougainvillaea—and closed tight as a satiated Venus flytrap. Osman was not surprised. He shrugged.

"Government offices close at two o'clock," he stated. "No one is here."

It was obvious.

"We've got to get to those manifests," Harry urged. "The records. Someone will *have* to let us in."

Osman frowned dubiously.

Harry looked at him, his face grave. "Inspector," he said, "if you have ever done anything of importance in your life, find a way for us to get in. Now!"

They located a telephone in the back of a little tourist shop. Osman began calling.

Harry and Leif watched tensely as the little man talked on the phone. They did not understand one word. The Egyptian began by being harsh and authoritative, almost dictatorial. When apparently he was switched to someone of greater importance, he became more civil and polite. Finally he must have reached someone in real authority, for he practically genuflected before the telephone. At last he hung up. He turned to Harry and Leif. He was sweating. Big, pear-shaped drops trickled down his nose to get caught in his bristly mustache.

"We will wait," he said. "Fifteen minutes." He looked pleased with himself. "The files will be opened for you."

Gray daylight was seeping into the office at the Canal Administration Building. Inexorably, April 20 was making its arrival known.

Eyes smarting with fatigue, Harry looked up at his son, who, with Osman's help, was also poring over the papers brought them in a steady stream by Osman and a surly administration clerk.

They had examined the manifests and all the other records of every ship of every nationality of every size that had entered or passed through Port Said in either direction for the last seven days, most of them carrying oil shipments from the Persian Gulf to Europe. A few had seemed to offer vague possibilities because of errors in the manifest or minor irregularities, but none was suspicious enough to warrant action.

They'd kept on looking. . . .

Wearily, Harry pulled the file of yet another ship from the diminishing pile before him.

The S.S. *Morroc Bay.* Of Liberian registry, a tanker of 70,000 deadweight tons loaded with crude oil and bound for Marseille from the Persian Gulf.

He pulled out a yellow telex copy. It was a request for berth facilities for the purpose of making minor emergency generator repairs, received six days before, on April 14. The S.S. *Morroc Bay* had moored at Berth Number 3 and had paid the applicable Suez Canal Authority dues for Tug Assistance with Maneuvering in Port and Mooring Fees. Departure date was set for April 20. The request had been authorized by the tanker's Chief Engineer . . .

Harry suddenly sat bolt upright.

In a lightning montage of images he saw the man before him— sitting at the dinner table at Rittersheim Estate; sipping his drink in the main hall in earnest conversation with a doctor from Kulmbach; perched on the seat of a skiff on Fichtendorf Lake, his shotgun cradled in bright red-jacketed arms.

Was this the same man?

Was this, the Chief Engineer of the tanker S.S. *Morroc Bay,* Von Flatow's Danish dinner guest? The man the Danish Luncheon Club speaker had identified as a merchant seaman?

The name on the request was Eigil Knudsen!

2

Inspector Osman's official-looking identification and his sharp, authoritative manner got them past the two suspicious armed guards at the gate and on to the shipyard wharf. They made straight for Berth Number 3.

Berth Number 3 was located on the first pier down. The rectangular basin was about 2,500 feet long and contained four mooring berths, two on each side. The near side held Numbers 1 and 3, the far side Numbers 2 and 4, both occupied. The S.S. *Morroc Bay* was moored at the inside berth, bow toward the channel from which the basin cut in. The berth in front of her, Number 1, was unoccupied. On the wharf across from the tanker were workshops and transit sheds.

Osman parked his car in the shade against the corrugated-iron wall of a workshop, and the three men hurried toward the single gangway to the S.S. *Morroc Bay.*

The tanker was not a big ship as tankers go, but to Leif she looked gargantuan. Over 800 feet long, she lay deep in the water, her boot topping covered, the wavelets lapping against the summer line. She was secured to massive bits on the wharf by several arm-thick Poly-Dac hawsers. At her stern, over the engine room below, squatted the superstructure—like a white-robed Arab astride his donkey, perched on the rump over the hind legs.

The metal gangway slanted up from the pier to the deck of the loaded tanker at a shallow angle, making it uncomfortable to negotiate the angular ridges meant for a steeper climb.

At the head a scowling seaman barred their way.

"What do you want?" he growled, eyeing the three men warily. "No one is allowed on board." He spoke English with an indeterminate accent.

Osman whipped out his impressive identification. He thrust it at the man. "I am Police Inspector Mustafa Hamid Osman," he said imperiously. "This is police business. Stand aside!"

The man gaped at him.

"Who's on board?" Harry asked.

"Eh, me. I'm on watch." The man was thoroughly cowed. "And the bosun."

"Who's in charge?"

"In charge? Eh—Jackson, I guess. The bosun."

"Where is he?"

"In the lounge—I guess."

"Lead the way."

"Me? But—I can't leave my post."

"Move!"

The man draped in an easy chair in the lounge was engrossed in a book, but he came to his feet with startled alacrity when Harry and the others came marching into the room. His angry eyes confronted them.

Bosun Jackson was even taller than Harry—a good six feet two —and built like a veteran iron-pumper; a formidable adversary as he stood glaring at them.

Harry watched him. He looks exactly like that black actor, what the hell is his name, he thought irrelevantly. Always so damned good . . .

With baleful eyes the big bosun fixed the seaman. "Banczek!" he snapped. "What the hell is this? Get your fucking ass back to your post!" He was unmistakably American. His voice was deep and resonant—and obviously used to giving orders.

Talks like him, too, Harry thought. Just like that actor. What *was* his name?

Jackson glared at Harry. "What are you doing here?" he barked. "Who the hell are you?"

"Who I am is of no consequence," Harry said quickly. He nodded toward Osman. "That is Police Inspector Osman."

"I don't give a shit if he's King of Sheba," Jackson growled. "Get the hell off the ship before I throw you off." He took a menacing step toward Harry.

Quickly Harry drew his gun from its shoulder holster. Steadily he pointed it at the big man's gut. The black stopped. He stared at the gun.

"Sorry, Jackson," Harry said, his voice tense. "There is no time for explanations. Just do as you're told, and you won't get hurt."

The bosun's eyes were fixed on Harry's gun. "Jee-sus," he whispered. He backed off.

"Now," Harry said crisply. "Who's on board?"

"Just me," Jackson replied. He gave a short nod toward the seaman. "And him. The relief mate. Banczek . . . And two men below."

"Who?"

"The Chief Engineer. And his First."

Harry felt a quick surge of excitement.

"What's the Chief's name?" he snapped.

"Knudsen."

"Only four men?" Leif asked. "Is that a normal watch for a ship as big as this?"

Jackson looked uncomfortable.

Peters, Harry thought suddenly. Brock Peters. That was the name of the actor. Brock Peters . . .

"Naw," the big man said. "Sort of skeleton watch. This was the last night in port. Captain gave everyone permission to go ashore. We've had a rough few days. Damned repair work." He looked at the men. "What's this all about, anyway?"

"Not now, Jackson," Harry said. He felt time slipping by. "Why are both the Chief Engineer and his First Assistant below?"

"Beats me." Jackson shrugged. "Guess they wanted to check out the repair work. We're scheduled to leave at noon. Captain and crew's due back at eight."

"You are ready to sail?" Harry couldn't keep his surprised concern out of his voice.

"Both boilers are warmed up," Jackson said. "On the line. I guess they'll warm up the turbine when the Captain comes aboard. Then we'll be on stand-by. Ready."

Harry thought fast. *Was* the bomb aboard the S.S. *Morroc Bay?* Did they want to detonate it in the Canal itself? It did not make sense. It would make no difference where the hell they set it off; in any event, it would certainly wipe out the tanker and the crew. Then why go on stand-by for departure? A ruse? Had the Captain and the crew taken off not intending to return? What about Knudsen? And the others on board? *Was* the Knudsen below Schindler's man? He suddenly felt cold. If not . . .

He turned to the bosun. "The two men below," he ordered. "Get them up here."

Jackson stared at him. "Me? How, man?"

"You figure it out."

"They ain't going to both leave the engine room, Mister."

"Try!"

Jackson shrugged. "I've gotta phone."

"Do."

"Nearest phone is in the pump room."

"Lead the way."

The cargo-control room was one long console of dials and meters, switches and levers. But there was a phone.

Jackson picked it up.

"Chief," he said, his voice suddenly urgent and frightened, "I gotta have some help up here. Banczek fell. I think he's broke his back."

He listened. "Yeah . . . I got him in the lounge. . . . Okay."

He replaced the receiver. He looked at Harry. "He's sending his First," he said.

Back in the lounge, Harry and the others waited in tense silence, Osman holding Jackson and the relief mate at bay. They had closed the door to the hallway outside.

Suddenly they heard hurried footsteps pounding down the passageway. All eyes were riveted on the door. It flew open and a man burst into the lounge.

He stopped short, staring in shocked astonishment at Harry's gun aimed straight at him.

Harry's eyes grew wide.

"Von Flatow!" he exclaimed.

Both he and the German recovered their composure at almost the same time.

"Put your hands on your head," Harry snapped. Without looking at his son, he ordered: "Frisk him."

At once Leif searched the German, careful not to get in his father's line of fire.

"He's not armed," he said.

"Okay, Von Flatow. You can take your hands down."

With a cold, thin smile the German complied. He nodded toward the two crew members who stood gaping at him.

"You are confusing Bosun Jackson, I fear," he said. Somehow he made even the man's name sound like an insult. "He knows me as First Assistant Engineer Werner Heinrich, who mustered on only yesterday when the former First had an—ah, regrettable accident."

"All right, Von Flatow, cut the comedy." Harry was conscious of the fact that he sounded desperate, and he hated himself for it. With a conscious effort he controlled his voice. "Your game is lost. That should be obvious to you." He glared at the German. "Where is it?"

Von Flatow gazed at him. "Where is what, Herr Bendicks?" he asked with icy calm.

Harry had to contain himself to keep from bashing the man's

face in. His voice was murderous. "Listen, you goddamned Nazi bastard," he growled. "You're playing watchdog over an empty junkyard. We *know* about your crazy scheme to get back in power. We *know* about your lunatic attempt to start a war. We *know* there's a bomb aboard this ship—a bomb that's supposed to be the trigger to your whole stinking plot. We *know* about the miserable imbecile you planned on using. Thank God the poor bastard is dead and can't be part of your abomination!"

For the first time Von Flatow was shaken. Young Adolf dead? With lightning speed his mind calculated the ramifications of this intelligence. . . . The plan could still be successful, but he, Von Flatow, would no longer be part of it. He had a fleeting pang of regret. But the cause was the important issue. Schindler? What about Schindler? Had he been caught? Or was he free to guide the new developments? Dead? He dared not ask. He hardly heard Harry finish his vehement outburst.

". . . and we *know* the bomb you've got aboard is an atomic bomb!"

Leif was watching the two crew members and the Egyptian police inspector. Jackson and the relief mate were staring at Harry and Von Flatow, obviously having trouble understanding the full significance of what they were hearing. But just as obviously they fully understood that their lives might well be in danger.

Mustafa Hamid Osman understood, too. His rich *café-au-lait* complexion had changed drastically. It had lost all its *café* and only the *lait* remained.

"You have indeed been busy, Herr Bendicks," Von Flatow remarked, totally unemotional, "since our little—ah, run-in at Rittersheim." He nodded his head stoically. "You are quite correct, of course. There *is* a nuclear bomb aboard. It *will* explode. The timing device has already been armed—and nothing you can do will disarm it." He drew himself up. "When the rest of the world sees the devastation that once was Port Said, our *action provocante* will trigger the fulfillment of Adolf Hitler's prophecy."

"When?" Harry shot at him. "When is it set to blow?"

Von Flatow smiled icily.

"Where is it?"

Von Flatow just looked at him, his smile unchanged.

"And you," Harry rasped. "You weren't going to blow *yourself* up, I bet. How were you—and your crony Knudsen—how were you going to get away?"

Von Flatow took a deep breath. "Come now, Herr Bendicks," he said condescendingly. "You do not actually expect me to answer your questions?"

Harry turned away from him. He knew he would be wasting his time trying to persuade the German to cooperate. But he'd had to make the attempt. He looked at the three shaken men watching the scene being played out before them. They were his only immediate allies. They—and Leif. He knew what had to be done. He formulated the details of his plan as he spoke.

"Osman. Jackson. Banczek," he said, urgency constricting his throat. He looked directly at each man in turn. "Do you understand the situation? It is critical. This bastard has hidden a bomb aboard the *Morroc Bay*. It is *somewhere* here. God knows where. It is a nuclear bomb. If it is detonated, it will destroy all of Port Said. All of its sister city, Port Fuad—and miles and miles of the Canal. The loss of human life will be incalculable. And there is *no* escape. None! The bomb could go off at any time. Even as we talk! Running away now would be utterly useless. We'd never make it. We couldn't get far enough away. Only one thing might save us—and the city. Find the bomb. Find it—and disarm it!"

He looked at the two crew members. "We need you," he said. "You know the ship. Will you help? Jackson?"

The face of the big black bosun was a sickly gray. He nodded. "Banczek?"

The relief mate shot a glance at his big companion. He bobbed his head.

"Good." Harry turned to the bosun. "Jackson, you stick with me." He nodded to the relief mate. "Banczek, you go with my son. Right now. We can't waste a second. Look in every place you think a bomb might be hidden. My son will tell you what to look for. Stay in the after end of the ship. Jackson and I'll take the forward section."

At once the two men started off. "Wait!" Harry called. "Leif. You have your gun?"

Leif nodded. He took the gun from his pocket. He held it awkwardly.

"That other Nazi bastard, Knudsen, is still aboard," Harry said. "We can't waste time searching for him—but watch out. If you see him, shoot. At once. Try not to kill him. He *might* talk. But don't take any chances. Understood?"

"Yes."

"Go!"

Harry turned to Osman. The little man had been listening without a sound. He looked petrified.

"Osman," Harry said, "we have to rely on you to go for help. We can't pull this off alone. I don't care what you have to do, but get *someone* to listen to you!" He looked sharply at the silent man. "You do understand the desperate urgency," he asked.

Osman nodded. He swallowed—with obvious difficulty.

Harry turned to Jackson. "Get something to tie this guy up with." He nodded toward Von Flatow. "Move!"

Without a word the bosun ran from the room. Harry turned to Osman. "We'll get him tied," he said. He pointed to a chair fastened by a chain below the seat to a ring in the deck. "You finish securing him to that chair—then take off. And come back with the marines. Understand?"

Osman nodded.

Jackson came running with a length of signal line. At once he and Harry trussed up the unresisting German. They placed him in the chair. Harry took a couple of hitches around him, then gave the line to Osman. "Finish it," he ordered. "Then get going!"

With Jackson he hurried from the lounge. . . .

Eigil Knudsen's palms were getting sweaty—and it wasn't just the heat in the engine room. Von Flatow was cutting it too close. They should be on their way to the airport pretty damned soon if they were to be sure of being far enough away when the explosion took place. The plane wouldn't wait forever. He hated leaving no margin for error. Especially when his life was on the line. Damn that clumsy Banczek anyway. . . .

He frowned. Von Flatow had been gone too long. What was going on? He wouldn't stay away that long without reporting.

He was suddenly aware of the cold sweat trickling down his armpits. Something was wrong.

He decided to find out. At once he turned to the Bridge Controls on the console. He put the Control Selector Switch to the central position. Quickly he moved to the breaker panel and placed the two steering-gear circuit-breakers in the open position. The ship was now completely controlled from the engine room. The bridge had been by-passed. Knudsen was a man who played it safe.

At a run he started up the steep stairs toward the decks above. . . .

Leif and Banczek were racing down the passageway to the stairway leading to the top levels of the superstructure. They'd work their way down.

"The bomb is probably the size of a four-drawer filing cabinet," Leif called to the crewman. "More or less. Anything that size around? Anything unusual? Anything that doesn't belong?"

"Nothing I know of," Banczek answered. He suddenly stopped. "Yeah!" he said. "The crate."

"What crate?"

"There's a crate. Up on the bridge level. It's a big one. They said there was some kind of radar equipment in it."

"Show me."

They ran up the stairs.

On the open level stood a large wooden crate. It had caution signs stenciled all over it and was marked RADAR. On the bulkhead nearby hung a big fire ax. Leif pointed to it.

"Break it open," he called. "Use the ax."

Banczek tore the ax from the wall. He struck a few powerful blows at the crate. The wood splintered.

A large piece of intricate-looking equipment could be seen inside, covered in heavy protective plastic. Leif ripped it away.

The radar equipment looked like a big, complicated control console.

It was big enough. It *could* hide a bomb.

Leif made up his mind.

"Smash it!" he said grimly.

Banczek gaped at him. "Are you crazy?" he exclaimed. "That thing costs thousands of dollars!"

Leif grabbed the ax from him. He dealt the machinery a hard blow. He struck again. The side burst in. He ripped it loose.

The inside was a maze of multicolored wires, electronic gear, condensers and resistors—shattered by the blows.

There was no bomb.

Knudsen cautiously stuck his head past the door at the head of the stairs leading up from the engine room. He listened.

Suddenly he heard the crashing sound of splintering wood coming from above. He started.

Then he knew what it was. Someone was breaking into the radar-gear crate.

Instantly he put it all together. They had been discovered. Or betrayed. That's why Von Flatow had not returned. Or reported. Someone was aboard—searching for the bomb!

He knew they would not find it—certainly not in time. But he had to get off the ship. He had to get to the plane. Von Flatow would have to fend for himself.

Quickly he ran from the superstructure to the fantail.

He could make it ashore down one of the aft mooring hawsers. . . .

Harry ran out onto the vast expanse of the deck, following the bosun. He tried to keep his churning thoughts in check. How long *did* they have? Hours? Minutes?

The huge deck was criss-crossed with a labyrinth of cables and pipes, ranging from a few inches to more than a foot in diameter; bisected with slatted steel walkways and dotted with heavy mooring bits and raised access hatches to the oil tanks below. Several massive mooring winches were set both to port and starboard, and a row of red-and-yellow-painted foam monitors for fire-fighting marched irregularly from stem to stern.

He looked around in deep dismay. The task seemed impossible. How could they hope to locate the damned bomb on this huge ship? They didn't even know what the hell the thing looked like.

And any second the world could blow up.

He pointed to one of the tank access hatches.

"How do you get into the tanks?" he asked the bosun.

"Knock the hatch bolts open. Swing it out on the davit."

"Could something be hidden down there? Even with the tanks full? Something big?"

"Sure. You could hang it from the ladder. Or dump it." Jackson scratched his head. "Depends on how big the thing is."

"How long does it take to open?

"Ten, twelve minutes."

"How many hatches are there?"

"One for each tank. She's got six main tanks, each divided into a port, a center and starboard tank. Eighteen."

It was impossible. If the bomb *was* hidden in one of the tanks, there was no way for them to get at it. They were already dead. . . .

He took heart at the fact that it would be equally inaccessible to Von Flatow and his accomplices. He dismissed the hatches as a possible hiding place.

He looked around for a more plausible place of concealment. . . .

Leif was following Banczek down the stairs to the engine room. They had found nothing, and time was racing by. The steps down were so steep he had to walk on his heels, clinging to the railing with his left hand, clutching the unfamiliar gun in his right.

Where was Knudsen? This was his domain.

He was descending into a world of noise and heat. A tangle of tubes and pipes wrapped in asbestos shielding snaked around the huge central pit at the bottom of which squatted the massive, white-painted turbine. Narrow steel catwalks with single-bar railings ringed the hole. Two gigantic boilers seemed to watch their invasion, each with a cyclops eye flickering malevolently: the round, protectively tinted view window monitoring the inferno inside.

They came to the control board. It was deserted. Deep down, the lowest level was murky and indistinct.

"What's down there?" Leif shouted at Banczek.

"Shaft alley," Banczek shouted back. "The shaft of the screw runs through there."

Leif peered down into the half-light of the shaft alley. Massive steel struts and bulkheads honeycombed the area, shoring it up. He thought he could make out several black holes cut in some of them.

"What're those openings?" he cried.

"Just—holes." Banczek shrugged.

"What's behind them?"

"Nothing."

Could one of them hide a bomb?

It could.

But it would be a herculean task to wrestle an object weighing many hundreds of pounds down there.

No. It would not.

He looked up.

High above he could make out a pulley hoist beam. Heavy equipment could be lowered into the pit. Of course . . .

He started down the steep stairway.

"Let's take a look. . . ."

Harry was running along the deck, hurdling cables and pipes, closely followed by the bosun. He looked ahead. A low housing occupied the very bow of the ship. Before it—lashed to the deck —lay a gigantic ship's screw. Harry pointed ahead.

"What's that?" he called.

"Spare screw," Jackson answered.

"No. The housing?"

"That the fo'c'sle."

"What's in there?"

"Nothing. Storage."

"Who goes in there?"

"Everybody."

Suddenly he saw it. "If you've lost your mule and want to go find it," the saying goes, *"think* like a mule—and you will." He was certain. He *was* thinking like a mule. He felt no surprise. No elation. Just a sharp, clean clarity of mind. It was the old maxim again: The best hiding place is the worst; the place where no one will look because it is too obvious.

He hurried past the colossal ship's screw and stepped into the fo'c'sle storage room. For a moment he stood in the gloom, acclimatizing himself.

Cans. Heavy hawsers rolled up. Crates. Boxes. And drums. Many huge drums, lashed to steel-railed bays or around several metal stanchions that ran from deck to overhead.

Some of the drums were marked: AGUANEX . . . MAGNUS MARITECH. Others: DIESEL FUEL . . . KEROSENE.

Fifty-five-gallon drums.

Large enough to hide a small nuclear bomb!

"What's in the drums?" He shot the question at Jackson.

The bosun looked puzzled. "Cleaning chemicals. Degreasers," he said. "Diesel fuel—for the generators. Hydraulic oil—for the winches."

Harry pointed to half a dozen drums lashed to a stanchion in the back. Large letters MT had been chalked on them.

"What does that mean?" he asked.

"Empty," Jackson said. "They're just empty drums."

"Get 'em loose," Harry snapped.

Together they tore the lashings away. The drums stood free.

At once Harry began to tilt the empty containers.

The fourth one he tried stood rooted to the steel deck with heaviness. He could not budge it.

He'd found the bomb!

It was simple. Unless every member of the crew was part of the conspiracy—and that obviously was not the case—the bomb on board would have had to be hidden from them, too. And who would look in an empty degreaser drum in a place accessible to everyone at all times?

He stared at the drum.

He imagined he could feel it on the verge of exploding. His flesh crawled. He was staring at death itself.

He whirled on Jackson.

"Get the other drums away from that one," he ordered. "Make room around it—but don't touch it! I'm going to get that German bastard!"

He rushed off.

The rage in him was cold and total. He was determined to force out of the Nazi the trick of disarming the timing device—if he had to break every finger of both the bastard's hands to get him to talk!

The several hundred feet along the deck from the fo'c'sle to the superstructure seemed like miles.

At last Harry reached the passageway. He raced for the lounge. The door was closed. He threw it open.

Osman was gone.

So was Von Flatow!

3

Von Flatow listened.

Only the normal sounds and background noises of the ship reached his ears. He was crouched on the bridge.

As soon as Bendicks and the bosun had left the lounge, the greasy little Egyptian had taken off, giving himself time for only one desperate question: Where was the plane that was supposed to take Von Flatow to safety? He had to respect the little *Gauner* for having deduced that he would have a plane waiting.

Of course he had not told the man where. . . .

It had taken him far too long to get out of the ropes with which he'd been tied, even though the Egyptian had turned tail without finishing the job. But he had finally succeeded.

From the bridge he'd seen the elder Bendicks and the big black crewman enter the fo'c'sle. Intently he waited. And watched . . .

Suddenly he saw Bendicks hurrying from the storage room. He knew at once.

The bomb had been found.

He clenched his teeth.

It did not mean it would not detonate.

Soon.

He frowned.

Why had he not heard from Schindler? He'd armed the timing device on his own—as agreed, if Schindler could not get through to him.

He was resigned to the fact that escape was now impossible. It was already too late. Less than an hour's time. But he decided to try to reach Schindler. The Standartenführer should be apprised of the situation. He ran for the communications room, locking the door behind him.

He was thoroughly familiar with the COMSAT General MARISAT system. He sat down at the communications console. He set the selector switch for VOICE and pushed the REQUEST button. Within seconds an operator answered.

He gave the telephone number of the Militaria in Los Angeles. In less than half a minute he heard the telephone ring. . . .

In the dark shop, permeated with the stench of smoke and wet, charred wood from the fire, the telephone rang. . . .

No one was there to answer it. Ring after ring traveled some forty thousand miles from the dark shop to the impatient man huddled over the satellite communications console half a world away. . . .

Harry came bounding into the fo'c'sle storage room. He was winded. He made straight for the drum. He examined it. There seemed to be no opening into it—except the capped bunghole.

He turned to Jackson. "Go find my son," he snapped.

The bosun took off at once.

Harry let his hands travel all over the drum's surface. He could feel no joint, no seam that would betray an access port to the inside. He tried the cap, straining with all his might to unscrew it. Pain from his still tender fingers shot through his arms. The cap would not budge. He looked around. A wrench. He needed a wrench. . . .

There!

He clamped it around the metal cap. He pushed against it—

Suddenly he stopped.

He let go the wrench.

It clattered to the steel deck.

He stared at the drum.

He was suddenly back in the war. Booby-traps. You never knew. The very steps you took to disarm them safely could set them off.

It would be the same now.

He knew with chilling certainty that he would be instantly vaporized before he even knew he'd made a mistake. He—and a whole city.

And fear flooded his mind.

He had known fear when he crouched beside his dead comrades at the Kugelberg cabin. Fear had coursed through him when the massive beam came crashing down on him in the studio back lot. When the blinding lights of the oncoming car bore down on him in the police parking area. When he was hurtling down the elevator shaft in a runaway car. When he stared into the whirling, slashing propeller on Fichtendorf Lake. When a live grenade was tossed at his feet. When he clung with slowly tearing fingers to a trap high on a make-believe church tower.

Fear?

Not until now had he ever known real fear. It paralyzed him.

For the first time in his life he did not know what to do.

He was suddenly aware of Leif standing at his side. He grabbed his son's arm, dimly conscious of the fierceness of his grip, and for a moment they stood—father and son—staring at the obscene black object which was death.

All at once a growing roar of activity intruded on their despair. They ran from the storage room. On the wharf below, several trucks roared up, disgorging Egyptian army troops. The soldiers rushed, weapons ready, to take up positions sealing off the area. Egyptian police officers swarmed over the adjoining workshops and sheds, and four men—one a civilian—burst from a car and raced for the gangway of the S.S. *Morroc Bay.*

Harry stared at the organized bedlam. *Finally,* he thought. Finally someone has gotten off his bureaucratic ass and made things move. Osman? He only hoped it was not too late.

He hurried to meet the men tramping up the gangway. Leif, Jackson and Banczek followed.

Even as he stepped from the gangway to the deck, the civilian barked at them. "I am Kamal Hassan Hamza," he said. "Harbor Master's office. Have you found the nuclear device?"

"In the fo'c'sle storage room." Harry pointed.

The civilian turned to an army officer. "Captain!" he snapped.

At once the officer, followed by two men carrying equipment boxes, raced for the fo'c'sle.

"Jackson!" Harry called. "Show them."

The bosun sprinted after the sappers.

"Captain Ahmed Mukhtah Sadek is an expert," the civilian said, his English clipped and precise. "Bomb disposal. He will disarm the bomb." He paused. *"In Sha'Allah,"* he added softly. "If God wills . . ."

Their eyes were on the fo'c'sle.

Eternal seconds oozed by, their every fraction an agony in Harry's mind.

He was not aware of breathing. He was not aware of anyone around him. Any thing. The world consisted of a black hole, a hatchway into a storage room, where hell itself lurked in a fifty-five-gallon drum. . . .

Crouched behind a window on the deserted bridge, Hans-Jürgen von Flatow watched the same black opening.

It was possible. Now. It was possible they might be able to disarm the bomb.

But not the plan!

He felt totally without emotion. He knew exactly what he had to do. His engineering knowledge—from outboard motors to tanker power plants—was expert.

He would still give his comrades their awaited trigger!

Cautiously he made his way from the bridge, headed for the engine room far below. . . .

On deck no one had moved from the spot at the gangway.

Staring at the fo'c'sle, trying to penetrate the very steel walls, they waited.

Suddenly Captain Sadek emerged. He held a small object up high over his head.

"Disarmed!" he shouted. "I have it! The initiator." He held the triggering mechanism aloft in triumph.

Kamal Hassan Hamza glanced at his watch. "Twelve minutes," he said with exaggerated calm—belied by the sweat that ran down his gray face. "Excellent!"

Harry let go. He felt himself begin to tremble. He did not attempt to stop it.

Captain Sadek joined them.

"How much time was left?" Harry asked.

"Seventeen minutes," the Egyptian officer replied. "Not too much leeway . . ."

Von Flatow had reached the engine-room control level. It would be a matter of less than two minutes.

Disengage the turning gear . . .

Done.

Open two main steam stop valves . . .

Done.

The control selector switch was already set on Central Control.

Throttle to forty revs . . . then sixty . . .

A fleeting thought. The turbine had not been warmed up. It was cold. It would be damaged.

Zum Teufel damit!

He turned the throttle control. . . .

Harry felt better than he ever had in his whole life. He grinned at his son.

"We made it," he said, his voice unsteady. "We made it, dammit!"

Suddenly a monstrous shudder shook the *Morroc Bay*. The entire ship at once began to vibrate violently. From the stern a growing roar rent the morning quiet. Instantly every mooring hawser was jerked taut as a bowstring as the huge ship strained to leave the wharf.

Terrified, the men looked toward the thundering noise The deck under their feet quivered and throbbed with restrained power as the ship's gigantic screw churned the oily harbor water into a white froth.

"The power!" Hamza shouted, eyes horrified. "Someone's cutting in the power!" He began to race for the superstructure. Harry and Leif followed, Jackson close behind.

The thunderous rumble from the laboring screw suddenly increased in pitch. A spasmodic tremor shot through the ship.

The men pounded along the quaking, rattling deck.

With a sudden, sharp report the first hawser ripped apart. Explosively it cracked across the deck.

"Get down!" Harry screamed.

The men hit the deck.

With a loud clap another hawser was torn apart by the titanic force exerted against it—instantly to shoot back over the deck.

With the piercing screech of tortured metal one of the massive mooring winches began to rip from the steel deck to which it was bolted—before the mooring line broke with the sound of a sharp explosion.

The turbulence whipped up by the full-throated labor of the huge screw spewed foaming, frothing water into the air.

Almost simultaneously the rest of the mooring hawsers snapped in a barrage of sharp reports, whipping through the air.

Like an iron sea monster, the leviathan shook herself in unbridled rage, tore away from the dock and leaped forward as if a giant fist had suddenly propelled her from the wharf.

The metal gangway slammed into a boom mast on the pier, wrapping itself around it with the grinding, grating noise of twisting metal, before being ripped from its clamps on the ship's railing.

Free of her fetters, the *Morroc Bay* plowed from her berth through the basin toward the channel ahead.

Hamza jumped to his feet. "The bridge!" he shouted. "We have got to shut her down!"

He drove for the superstructure, followed by Harry.

Jackson turned to Leif, suddenly authoritative. "You!" he shouted. "Get to the number-one foam monitor!" He pointed toward the bow. "Up there. Open the valve. The red turning wheel at the base. I'll get the foam going. Douse the entire bow!"

Without waiting for Leif's acknowledgment, he sped after the others toward the superstructure.

Leif ran for the fire-fighting aparatus.

Hamza burst onto the bridge. His hands flew over the controls. He swore a low oath. "No power," he cried. "Control has been taken away from the bridge."

He looked out the window—and blanched.

Wordlessly he pointed.

The *Morroc Bay* was churning through the water toward the mouth of the mooring basin, steadily gaining speed. Ahead was the channel, and along the far wharf, broadside to the oncoming *Morroc Bay*, another tanker lay moored.

They were on a collision course!

Harry grabbed a pair of binoculars resting on the sill. He brought them to his eyes. The other tanker suddenly seemed only a few yards away. It startled him. He searched for the name. There—

"The *Marinha Grande*," he said. "Portuguese? Do you know her? Hamza! Do you know her?"

Hamza shook his head. He seemed numbed with horror. "I—I do not remember," he whispered.

"What will happen if we ram her?"

"There will be—an explosion." The Egyptian shuddered.

A flash of remembered catastrophes—ships exploding in crowded harbors, leveling entire city blocks, killing hundreds— surged through Harry's mind.

Schindler would get his hell-born provocation yet. . . .

He shivered. He was riding a torpedo.

Hamza shook himself out of his paralysis. He grabbed the binoculars from Harry.

"Light draft," he said. "She is empty." He sounded bleak.

"Better that than loaded, too," Harry said.

"No." Hamza's voice was the sound of despair. "Loaded, she might burn—not explode. Empty, her tanks are filled with explosive gases. Detonation is inevitable."

Harry had a sudden, icy thought. Could the explosion detonate the nuclear bomb still sitting in the fo'c'sle? He didn't know. "And we?" he asked.

"We will catch fire. Burn . . . " Hamza said.

He studied the tanker through the binoculars. He bit his lip. "Unless . . ." he said tensely.

"Unless?"

"If she has been moored there a long time—undergoing extensive alterations—she *may* be gas free." He put the glasses down. "There is no way of knowing. . . . May it be the will of Allah . . ."

"What the hell can we do? There must be something. . . ."

Even as he spoke he saw a thick stream of white foam shoot from the forward monitor. He saw his son hanging on the forked steering bars like a gunner in the arm of a World War II anti-aircraft Bofors gun, directing the jet of foam toward the bow—inundating it in a white, gleaming mass.

"Cut down the danger of fire," Hamza said. He peered ahead, a determined look on his perspiring face. "Four minutes," he said. He spoke fast, tensely, in short staccato sentences, seemingly to himself. "Less. And we collide. No chance of stopping her. Inertia too great. Even if we could cut the power. Must be doing five knots by now. . . . She'll have a tendency to veer right with her rudder locked. Even the hydraulic lock will not prevent it entirely. Right. Not enough to miss . . ."

Suddenly he turned and ran from the bridge. "Come on!"

"Where?" Harry raced after him.

"Engine-room control. If I can work the steering from there, we might miss the Portuguese."

They clattered down the stairs to the level of the main deck. Three minutes . . .

Hamza rushed for the door to the engine-room stairs.

Suddenly a man came hurrying into the passageway from a side corridor—and stopped dead.

Von Flatow.

Hamza didn't stop. He disappeared through the engine-room door.

For the flick of a snake's tongue Von Flatow and Harry stood staring at one another.

Then Harry ripped his gun from his shoulder holster, and in the exact same instant Von Flatow turned and dove for the closest door. He tore it open. Even as Harry brought his gun up into firing position, Von Flatow plunged through.

At once Harry started after him. He pounded up to the open door and flung himself through.

He screamed.

But even before the first sound tore through his throat, to be drowned out by the noise of the laboring engines, the scene before him was seared into his mind.

The door led nowhere.

It was the access to the hoist beam. A tiny platform with a chain railing—the front broken—perched five levels above the huge turbine far below!

He tried to stop his headlong rush. In vain. He felt himself topple from the ledge. In a flash he saw the dark, twisted form sprawled in grotesque death on the white-painted turbine below.

Von Flatow.

The broken chain hung from a rail post. Wildly he grabbed for it, letting his gun fall into the void.

His hands found the chain and locked around the knobby links. The flesh ripped on his palms—and he dangled below the tiny platform.

His hands burned. He hadn't the strength to haul himself up. Blood from his torn skin made the chain slippery. He felt himself slide down. . . .

His mind clouded with agony and despair. He turned his eyes to the rim of the shelf so close above him—and yet unreachable. The sweat of pain ran into them, blinding him.

But through the haze of torment he saw his son's face. Strong hands grabbed his wrists and he felt himself slowly dragged back to safety.

Deeply exhausted, father and son lay side by side on the platform. Abruptly Harry sat up. He looked down toward the engine-room control.

Hamza stood before it, staring at the console, arms hanging slack at his sides.

Harry strained to look.

The hand wheels of the steering control and the throttle had been dismantled—and removed.

There was no way to alter the collision course of the *Morroc Bay*. And there was less than one minute left. . . .

Harry struggled to his feet. He stumbled into the passageway and staggered for the deck, Leif at his side.

They stopped—aghast.

Looming directly ahead of the foam-covered bow of the *Morroc Bay*, which was bearing down on her like a giant projectile, lay the Portuguese tanker, riding high in the water, her immense side less than a ship's length away. Death in a rust-flecked hull . . .

Inexorably the *Morroc Bay* plowed ahead.

And hit!

The noise was mind-destroying. Steel tore into steel as the bow of the *Morroc Bay* sliced into the metal bowels of her target. The *Morroc Bay* pitched and bucked and heaved as she rammed, until brought to a shuddering stop imbedded deep in her ruptured victim.

A shower of sparks shot into the air—to fall back into the foam blanket shrouding her bow.

The sudden, wrenching jolt pitched Harry and Leif to the deck. But one thought blazed in their minds.

There had been no explosion!

There would be none.

No tanker.

No bomb.

No trigger . . .

The watchdogs of Abaddon had been muzzled.

But . . .

For how long?

The ADL Bulletin   Spring, 1979

THE NEO-NAZI MENACE

NEW YORK, N.Y. . . . *We're Back Again!*—reads the legend below the black swastika on stickers that have begun to appear in West Germany. What the defiant claim really means is "We're in the open again," for the existence of groups of old and new Nazis in Germany, as elsewhere on the Continent, was never a secret to those who cared to know. Over the past nine months, however, their activities have changed in character, increased in frequency, become more public—and are causing concern. . . . Justice Minister Vogel says that ". . . the increase in neo-Nazi activities is being watched with anxiety," and according to former Interior Minister Maihofer, "the violent aspect of those groups and the widening circulation of neo-Nazi literature are developments of concern. . . . " These groups increasingly train with weapons. For the immediate future, the outlook is for an increase in violent acts by the Nazis—and intensification of ties among extreme rightists of not only the European countries but also with South Africa, South America and the United States. It is more than interesting to note that those *We're Back Again!* stickers originate in the U.S.

—Lawrence S. Leshnik, M.A., Ph.D.
Director, Department of European Affairs
Anti-Defamation League of B'nai B'rith

EPILOGUE

Los Angeles

21 April 1978

Los Angeles Times,   April 21, 1978

EGYPTIAN AUTHORITIES RELEASE TWO U.S. CITIZENS

PORT SAID, April 20 (AP) Two U.S. citizens, Harold Bendix, a retired Los Angeles police lieutenant, and his son, Lief Bendicks, a Beverly Hills psychiatrist, were released by Port Said police authorities today after being briefly detained for questioning. The Americans had become involuntarily involved in a scuffle between members of the crew on board the tanker S.S. *Morroc Bay* of Liberian registry, following a minor mooring accident. The Bendix father and son had boarded the tanker to inquire about possible passenger accommodations.

During the scuffle, according to witnesses, the First Assistant Engineer of the ship, Werner Heinrich, a German national who had recently joined the crew, fell from a catwalk. He was dead at the scene when reached by other crew members and the Bendicks father-and-son team.

In an apparently unrelated incident the Chief Engineer of the same vessel, Eigil Knudsen, a Danish subject, was arrested in an altercation with an Egyptian police inspector, Mustafa Hamid Osman, when both men were attempting to board a small private plane at Port Said airport. No details are available.

When questioned by reporters about their further travel plans, the elder Bendix stated that he and his son would return to Los Angeles. "We are cutting our trip short," he added. "We have had quite enough excitement."

Los Angeles Times,   August 28, 1978

GANNON-BENDICKS NUPTIALS
AT DANISH CHURCH

Miss Susan Gannon, daughter of Mr. & Mrs. Patrick Gannon of Washington, D.C., and Leif Bendicks, son of former Los Angeles police investigator Harald Bendicks and the late Mrs. Edith Bendicks, were married in the Emmanuel Danish Evangelical Lutheran Church in Los Angeles on August 27.

The bride is a graduate of Columbia University in New York and has served as a librarian at the National Archives in Washington, D.C.

The bridegroom, a graduate of UCLA, is a doctor of psychology.

Among the guests at the reception following the ceremony were Lt. Jack L. Stein and Inv. II Pete Hastings of the LAPD and Dr. Arthur Rosenberg, chief of the Modern Military Branch of the National Archives.

The couple will make their home in Los Angeles.

AUTHOR'S NOTE

HITLER'S CHILDREN

Toward the end of the war persuasive rumors and informed speculation that Adolf Hitler had fathered a child—or children— flourished in Europe. And the reports persist even today.

Some of the claims and more or less educated contentions that were put forward and believed by many high-ranking Nazis in Germany, as well as by prominent persons in other countries, can now be summarily dismissed. Others, more intriguing, warrent closer scrutiny.

USCHI

One rumor especially popular among Hitler's intimate entourage, who saw in it an explanation for the uncanny "hold" Reichsleiter Martin Bormann had over the Führer, concerns one of Bormann's children. According to this story, Bormann's eldest son, Martin, Jr., was in reality the offspring of a tryst between Adolf Hitler and a girl named Uschi. Nothing else is known about this girl. Hitler did, however, often show a great interest in certain young women, especially from the entertainment world, and *tête-à-têtes* with them were not unusual. Uschi may well have been one of them.

The boy resulting from this affair is supposed to have been adopted by Bormann and his wife, Gerda. This account was lent a certain plausibility by the fact that Gerda's child indeed was born "prematurely" and under somewhat mysterious circumstances. However, no concrete evidence to support this theory has ever surfaced.

EVA BRAUN

Another report states that Hitler's permanent mistress, Eva Braun, had given birth to two children during her long and intimate relationship with the Führer, which culminated in their marriage on the eve of their double suicide on April 30, 1945. Eva was born in Munich in 1912 and met Hitler when she worked for his official photographer, Heinrich Hoffmann.

On June 12, 1945, *The New York Times* printed the following dispatch:

TELLS OF HITLER'S CHILDREN
Swede Reports Hunt for Them

LONDON, June 11 (UP)—An unconfirmed Stockholm dispatch said today that two children were born to Adolf Hitler and Eva Braun during their long illegitimate love affair and were hunted by Allied troops.

Hitler's marriage to Eva just before Berlin fell was undertaken to legitimize the children, the dispatch said. The marriage first was reported by Marshal Gregory K. Zhukoff, conqueror of Berlin, Saturday.

And a second dispatch was quoted in the *New York Times* article:

PARIS, June 11 (AP)—Supreme Headquarters said today it had no comment on an unconfirmed report, published in London, that Allied officials in Germany were hunting two children said to be the offspring of Adolf Hitler and Eva Braun. The report said the children were a boy, 5, and a girl, 4.

The rumors about these children that circulated in Germany and elsewhere claimed that Hitler's son was born to Eva in San Remo, Italy, during the night of January 1, 1938. Great efforts were supposedly taken to keep the secret, and included the reported arrest of an official of the Reich Chancellery who unwisely proposed a toast to "Hitler's firstborn" on the boy's birthday in 1939!

Although there were reports that the children had been spirited to safety in the National Redoubt in Bavaria, and despite subsequent ambiguous statements by members of Eva Braun's family, including her father, who in response to direct questioning said: "The important thing is that Hitler shall not be without a successor," no trace of the children is known to have been discovered, and their existence has never been proved—nor disproved.

French intelligence sources at the time claimed that the two children had been flown to a Nazi naval station in Norway—and from there evacuated by U-boat to an unknown destination.

Another account of the whereabouts of the son states that the boy was given to Eva's sister, Gretl, who shortly thereafter married an SS general, SS Gruppenführer Hermann Fegelein, Himmler's liaison officer to Hitler's staff. The Führer trusted Gretl with the secret—but not Fegelein, who was somewhat of a shady character even for a Nazi. In the last days of the war Fegelein left the Führerbunker without Hitler's permission. He was hunted down, arrested, brought back and executed. Many high-ranking Nazis believed Hitler had him killed to safeguard the secret of his son.

According to this account, a wealthy relative of Gretl and his wife took the boy with them when they fled to Argentina via the ODESSA escape route at the end of the war.

ELEONORE BAUER

One of the more plausible stories concerns a woman named Eleonore Bauer.

Eleonore Bauer was a nun known as Sister Pia. She became so infatuated with Hitler that she left her religious order to follow her idol. She accompanied him on the ill-fated *Putsch* at the Feldherrenhalle in Munich in November 1923, where she even came under fire. The infatuation ultimately grew into an affair which resulted in the birth of a son.

This child was cared for and reared by the Nazi Party from a special, ultra-secret fund administered by Martin Bormann. The mother, Eleonore Bauer, continued to be closely associated with the Nazi movement and was given an editorial position with the NSDAP publication, *Völkischer Beobachter.* But the whereabouts of her son—if indeed he does exist—remains a mystery.

TILLY FLEISCHER

Then there is the story of Tilly Fleischer, the mother of the controversial Gisela Heuser, who claims to be the daughter of Adolf Hitler.

Tilly was an athlete whose forte was javelin-throwing. At the Olympic Games in Los Angeles in 1932 she won the Bronze Medal, losing to "Babe" Didrikson, and in Berlin in 1936 she captured the Gold Medal. Here she also caught the eye of Adolf Hitler and was photographed with the Führer in her hour of triumph. According to the story, an intimate relationship followed.

Hitler saw in Tilly the symbol of German womanhood, and showered her with gifts, including a Mercedes sports car. According to Gisela's story, her mother and "Uncle Adolf" had many intimate get-togethers.

One year after meeting Hitler, Tilly married Dr. Fritz Heuser, one of Hitler's dentists and an avid Nazi. Five months later Gisela was born.

Gisela Heuser contends that her mother gave birth to her on December 15, 1937, at a special Nazi clinic near Frankfurt. In attendance were one of Hitler's personal physicians, Professor von Hasselbach; a gynecologist, Professor Scholten; and SS Gruppenführer Otto Lutz acting as security officer to safeguard the secret. Gisela claims that certain classified *Reichssicherheitshauptamt* documents, now supposedly among the captured documents stored in the American Documents Center at Alexandria, Virginia, give incontrovertible proof of her claim to being the daughter of Adolf Hitler.

Gisela made her revelations and claims in a series of articles which appeared in 1965 in such periodicals as the Italian magazine

Oggi (issue #18, 1965), the French weekly *Ici Paris* and the German publication *Bunten.*

Issue #30, 1965, of *Oggi* carried an article including a lengthy letter from a lawyer acting on behalf of Gisela's mother and Dr. Heuser refuting Gisela's claims.

In 1967 further articles and this time detailed claims were published by Gisela in the Italian women's magazine *Annabella,* published in Milan (National Archives, Modern Military Branch, Washington, D.C.).

In an attempt to get first-hand information regarding Gisela's claim from the one source that would know the facts with absolute certainty, Gisela's mother, now Frau Tilly Fleischer-Grote, this author, on July 17, 1977, wrote Frau Fleischer-Grote inviting her comments. No answer was received, and consequently on January 20, 1978, a second letter was sent by registered mail (#868251). Again no answer was received, nor was the letter returned as undeliverable.

Gisela's story was this time left unchallenged.

CHARLOTTE LOBJOIE

The latest claim of finding a son of Adolf Hitler was made in October 1977 by the respected West German historian and Hitler biographer Werner Maser. Maser's story involves a young French girl named Charlotte Eudoxie Alida Lobjoie, born in 1898, whom Hitler met while he was stationed in the village of Wavrin during World War I.

Charlotte's son, Jean Marie Loret, born in March 1918 in the French village of Sebancourt, insists he is the son of Adolf Hitler —a claim which Werner Maser fully supports.

In 1920 Mlle. Lobjoie was married to a M. Loret, and the boy, then two years old, was given Loret's name. He was left with his grandparents when his mother and her husband moved to Paris and did not see his mother again until 1940. Not until 1948, three years before her death, did Charlotte Lobjoie reveal the identity of his father to her son.

Much circumstantial evidence surrounds the claim. In fact, Dr. Maser has stated that he has voluminous and conclusive proof of its veracity. Documentary evidence includes blood tests which apparently establish the fact that Jean Loret *could* be the son of Hitler; some artwork supposedly depicting Charlotte and her village painted by Hitler; and the fact that after the fall of France in 1940 Hitler had young Loret traced and made him a high-ranking French police official, who reportedly cooperated closely with the Gestapo.

In Wavrin the old residents still remember Charlotte Lobjoie, the German soldier and the birth of her son. Jean Loret now has nine children, six by his first marriage and three by his second.

Nine grandchildren of the Führer, Adolf Hitler?

In addition to these women, perhaps there are others who gave birth to children fathered by Adolf Hitler but who never made the history books.

In the closing days of the war many top Nazis were able to escape from the defeated Reich, some since ferreted out and caught after years of living in hiding: Barbie, Stangl, Eichmann. Others apparently disappeared forever: Mueller, Mengele, Bormann. The list is a long and sinister one.

Perhaps it also includes a true son of Adolf Hitler.

BIBLIOGRAPHY

In addition to the many news events quoted between chapters, numerous other current news stories in the world press and several foreign-language works, the following English-language books have furnished authentication and facts for *The Watchdogs of Abaddon.*

Bar-Zohar, Michael. *The Avengers: The Story of the Hunt for Nazi Criminals.* London: Arthur Barker.

———. *The Hunt for German Scientists.* New York: Hawthorn Books.

Blum, Howard. *Wanted! The Search for Nazis in America.* New York: Quadrangle.

Bullock, Alan. *Hitler: A Study in Tyranny.* New York: Harper & Row.

Delarue, Jacques. *The Gestapo: A History of Horror.* New York: William Morrow & Co.

Diamond, Sander A. *The Nazi Movement in the United States, 1924–1941.* Ithaca, N.Y.: Cornell University Press.

Dollinger, Hans. *The Decline and Fall of Nazi Germany and Imperial Japan.* New York: Bonanza Books.

Doramus, Max. *Hitler's Speeches and Proclamations.* Verlagsdruckerei Schmidt.

Downing, David. *The Devil's Virtuosos: German Generals at War, 1940–1945.* New York: St. Martin's Press.

Ebenstein, William. *The Nazi State.* New York: Octagon Books.

Editors of *Freedom. Confidential Interpol Dossier.* Freedom News Journal.

Erdstein, Erich, and Barbara Bean. *Inside the Fourth Reich: The Real Story of the Boys from Brazil.* New York: St. Martin's Press.

Farago, Ladislas. *Aftermath: Martin Bormann and the Fourth Reich.* New York: Simon & Schuster.

Fest, Joachim C. *Hitler.* New York: Harcourt Brace Jovanovich.

Forster, Arnold, and Benjamin R. Epstein. *The New Anti-Semitism.* New York: McGraw-Hill Book Company.

Gordon, Harold J., Jr. *Hitler and the Beer Hall Putsch.* Princeton, N.J.: Princeton University Press.

Gun, Nerin E. *Eva Braun: Hitler's Mistress.* Des Moines: Meredith Corporation.

Hanfstaengl, Max. *Hitler: The Missing Years.* London: Eyre & Spottiswoode.

Heiden, Konrad. *Der Führer: Hitler's Rise to Power.* New York: Howard Fertig.

Hitler, Adolf. *Mein Kampf.* Boston: Houghton Mifflin Company.

Koch, H. W. *The Hitler Youth.* New York: Stein & Day Publishers.

Langer, Walter C. *The Mind of Adolf Hitler: The Secret Wartime Report.* New York: Basic Books.

Manvell, Roger. *SS & Gestapo: Rule by Terror.* New York: Ballantine Books.

———— and Heinrich Fraenkel. *Himmler.* New York: G. P. Putnam's Sons.

Maser, Werner. *Hitler: Legend, Myth and Reality.* New York: Harper & Row.

Modern Military Branch. *The Hitler Source Book.* Washington, D.C.: National Archives.

Payne, Robert. *The Life and Death of Adolf Hitler.* New York: Praeger Publishers.

Pia, Jack. *Nazi Regalia.* New York: Ballantine Books.

Pridham, Geoffrey. *Hitler's Rise to Power: The Nazi Movement in Bavaria, 1923–33.* New York: Harper & Row.

Riess, Curt. *The Nazis Go Underground.* New York: Doubleday & Co.

Shirer, William L. *The Rise and Fall of the Third Reich.* New York: Simon & Schuster.

Smith, Bradley F. *Adolf Hitler.* Stanford, Calif.: Hoover Institution Press.

Speer, Albert. *Spandau.* New York: Macmillan Publishing Co.

Steiner, Jean-François. *Treblinka.* New York: Simon & Schuster.

Toland, John. *Adolf Hitler.* New York: Doubleday & Co.

Trevor-Roper, H. R. *The Last Days of Hitler.* New York: Macmillan Publishing Co.

Wiesenthal, Simon. *The Murderers Among Us.* New York: McGraw-Hill Book Company.